Also by Jennifer Hartmann

Adult Romance from Bloom
Still Beating
Lotus
June First
The Wrong Heart
Older

Young Adult Romance from Bloom
Catch the Sun
Dream On

PIECES
of the
NIGHT

JENNIFER HARTMANN

Bloom *books*

Copyright © 2026 by Jennifer Hartmann
Cover and internal design © 2026 by Sourcebooks
Cover design by Antoaneta Lisak/Sourcebooks
Cover images © Ernesto r. Ageitos/Getty Images, swkunst/Getty Images, Mark Fearon/Arcangel, Todd Ryburn Photography/Getty Images, Getty Images/Getty Images, Bykfa/Shutterstock
Internal image © Tetiana Komarytska/Getty Images
Internal illustration by Hanny Traugott (@hdtarts)

Sourcebooks, Bloom Books, and the colophon are registered trademarks of Sourcebooks.

All rights reserved. No part of this book may be reproduced in any form or by any electronic or mechanical means including information storage and retrieval systems—except in the case of brief quotations embodied in critical articles or reviews—without permission in writing from its publisher, Sourcebooks.

No part of this book may be used or reproduced in any manner for the purpose of training artificial intelligence technologies or systems.

The characters and events portrayed in this book are fictitious or are used fictitiously. Any similarity to real persons, living or dead, is purely coincidental and not intended by the author.

All brand names and product names used in this book are trademarks, registered trademarks, or trade names of their respective holders. Sourcebooks is not associated with any product or vendor in this book.

Published by Bloom Books, an imprint of Sourcebooks
1935 Brookdale RD, Naperville, IL 60563–2773
(630) 961-3900
sourcebooks.com

Cataloging-in-Publication data on file with the Library of Congress.

The authorized representative in the EEA is Dorling Kindersley Verlag GmbH. Arnulfstr. 124, 80636 Munich, Germany

Manufactured in the UK by Clays and distributed by
Dorling Kindersley Limited, London
001-360967-Apr/26
10 9 8 7 6 5 4 3 2 1

To anyone who's ever held themselves together with music, moonlight, and just enough hope to make it through the night.

Content Warning

This book contains references to and descriptions of an emotionally abusive relationship (not between the FMC and MMC). Please be advised.

Prologue

A crack. A jolt. A metallic tang in the air.
And then—
Pain.

Fire tears through my thigh, shockwaves splintering down my leg. Fluorescent lights smear into shelving units, and the whole room tilts.

A panicked voice cuts through the static. "No… Oh, no—*shit*…"

My gaze drops when something clatters at my feet.

Then it pans lower: a bloom of red, seeping through my jeans, dark and spreading.

Heat pulses down my leg. My body teeters, but adrenaline holds me upright. I glance over my shoulder through the glass door.

An engine hums. A getaway, waiting.
All the best mistakes have names.
This one?
Stupidity.

CHAPTER 1
Annalise

ONE HOUR EARLIER

"Phone. Now."

I pivot away, holding the cell phone just out of reach. "No way."

"Annalise, come on. You'll thank me in the morning."

Three Tequila Sunrises pump through my bloodstream as I turn my back to my brother and dance my thumbs across the keypad without a care in the world.

> **Me:** I think we should book a trip! A vacation somewhere warm. Fiji? Thailand? The Zen life is calling. There are monkeys in Phuket. 🐵

Leaning back against the edge of a pool table, I chew on my lip, waiting for a response. Outside the window, snow buckets down in slanted white sheets, obscuring the Christmas lights twinkling from the shopping mall across the street.

I imagine a stress-free getaway, sans the twenty-plus hour flight both ways with multiple layovers and a likely abundance of screaming babies. Alex doesn't like being confined for too long. He doesn't like babies either.

Perhaps a quick flight to Florida would sway him more.

I start to pivot.

Me: You might already be looking into flights, but just letting you know I'm flexible! Miami is nice. We have a ton of vacation time saved up. I think we really need this. A break.

Panic ripples down my spine.

Me: A break from life. Not each other. Obviously. I love you!

Still nothing.

I stare at the screen, my anxiety climbing.

Me: You love me, right? 🩶

The messages are finally opened.

Three minutes tick by as I suck down another cocktail, my heels tip-tapping against the floor, but he leaves me on read.

My eyes narrow at the screen.

I'm pondering which collection of emojis I can ambush him with when Kenna materializes on my left, a scarlet vision. Bold cherry lips, ruby nails, and a shocking red cocktail dress.

I adore her.

"I adore you!" I announce, throwing my arms around her neck, momentarily distracted. "Your hair is so lovely. You smell like a symphony of citrus. I think we should dance."

My best friend hugs me back, snickering into my loose waves of hair.

She knows I get like this every time I drink—touchy-feely and high on life, a cornucopia of eternal love bursting at the seams.

"It's after eleven," Kenna says, glancing at her Apple Watch. "We should probably head out."

"What?" I straighten to full height, which is at least five inches taller than her. "We still have a couple hours until last call."

"We both have an early shift tomorrow. Tag's here to drive you home."

My face sours. I glance over my shoulder at my brother, who is collapsed on a high-top table, looking miserable. "You texted him to pick me up, didn't you?"

"Perchance."

"Traitor."

"Alex will rage if you get home too late. I'm just looking out for you."

I'm instantly reminded of the text messages that went ignored. A wave of tension sweeps through me, triggering my thumbs again.

Me: Are you there? ☹

Finally, his bubbles dance to life, and I hold my breath.

Alex: Where are you?
Me: We're still at Sand Bar.
Alex: Unbelievable. You're on the clock tomorrow at 6:30.
Me: Good thing that's seven hours from now. You know I'm a night owl. Also, you didn't answer my question...

A few seconds pass.
A ping.

Alex: Drink some water.

Before I can register the response, a hand flies out and snatches my phone away. "Hey!"

Tag stuffs the device into his back pocket, spearing me with a look of immense aggravation. His dirty blond hair glimmers under the strobe lights, a stark contrast to mine, considering mine has been dyed every shade imaginable over the years. Bubblegum pink, electric blue, even an unfortunate attempt at swamp green.

Currently, it's what some people call "bronde," striped with lively purple streaks.

"Drunk texting never ends well," he says.

"I was in the middle of a conversation."

"With the douche of the century. Unless you're texting that you're dumping him, I can't stand by and watch you embarrass yourself." He shrugs. "For the best."

"But...monkeys."

Wrinkling my nose, I glance around the busy bar, jam-packed with flannel-clad lumberjack types, ski bunnies in designer puffers laughing at their own jokes, and weathered locals who look like they've been sitting on the same barstools since the early '90s.

The bartender, a brute with permanent scowl lines, slides a whiskey across the counter to a man who looks like he sharpens knives for a living.

Welcome to Vermont's finest: where every guy owns at least one axe and every girl has a story about hiking in the rain with a pair of boots she swears were waterproof.

But I love it here in Rutland. Our small town is located on the western edge of the Green Mountains, near some of the best skiing and winter sports in New England.

It's always been home.

My gaze shifts back to Kenna as she twirls a cocktail straw between her fingers. "Do you have a ride?" I ask. "Weather looks nasty."

"Yep. Irving is on the way, and you know he drives like my granny's great-grandmother."

"She's been dead for decades," I note.

Irving. Kenna's boyfriend of one month, who wears loafers with no socks, corrects people's grammar mid-conversation, and describes himself as an "old soul" when he really just hates fun.

Yet, according to everyone I know, he's still ten leagues above my boyfriend of seven years.

Sighing with defeat, I tuck my hair behind my ear as the room spins. But it's only a marginal spin. I'm fine. "Okay. One last dance?"

Kenna shoots my brother an apologetic look. He grumbles, waving us off toward the crowded dance floor.

I snag her by the wrist with a glowing grin and drag her away, shimmying us between sweaty bodies and a cloud of B.O. that's infused with traces of cheap perfume.

Ten minutes pass before Tag saunters toward us in his ratty blue jeans and a random band T-shirt.

"Are you good now?" he implores, stuffing his hands in his pockets as two girls bump into him after a miscalculated spin. "Weather is getting worse."

I glance toward the small stage that occasionally hosts open mic nights. "You should play here!" I blurt over the new-age pop music.

"Pass. I hate this bar."

"It's great exposure."

"She's right," Kenna adds. "This place is packed on weeknights."

I see the reluctant acquiesce brighten his face as opportunity sweeps through him.

He's been working so hard.

Five nights a week, he plays. Coffee shops, wine bars, the occasional pub. It's hard to recall a time when Tag didn't have a guitar strapped across his chest and a euphonic dream in his eyes. Music is a part of him. An invisible limb.

He rubs his fingers along his lightly stubbled jaw, nodding slowly. "Yeah, I guess. I'll think about it."

"Yay! Let me close out my tab." Scurrying over to the bar counter, I collect my bill and smile my thanks to a woman when she compliments the colorful highlights in my hair.

Warmed by the flattery, I tell the bartender to add her drinks to my tab.

Moments later, I'm this close to tears when I wrap Kenna up in a bone-crushing hug, as if I won't see her ever again, even though we share a shift in less than seven hours.

"Text me later, so I know you got home safe." She squeezes my hand, her mocha-brown eyes shimmering with affection.

Everyone knows that's code for *I love you*.

"You too. See you in the morning." I fetch my purse—minus a cell phone thanks to my meddling big brother—and make a tipsy trek out the main doors, trying not to do the splits in the newly fallen snow.

Tag tosses his keys in the air, catching them with his opposite hand as he stomps through several inches. "This blizzard is shit."

"I think it's pretty." A smile crests as my tequila-glazed eyes take in the wintery wonderland around us. "It wouldn't be Christmas without snow."

I think about that vacation again and how nice it would be to park myself on a secluded beach while drinking in the turquoise water and sea-salt air, a canopy of palm trees billowing on all sides.

Someday.

We pile into the red sedan, and I immediately collapse into a sleeping position in the back seat.

"Seat belt," Tag chides.

"Mm-hmm." Sluggishly, I reach to click the belt into place, my body still draped across the interior. "Can you turn on some music? You know what I like."

The engine hums to life. "Really? You're going to subject me to doo-wop after I've already been coerced into picking you up in a blizzard?"

He says it with love, then promptly turns on an oldies station, confirming that love.

I grin, my hands tucked underneath my cheek. "Runaround Sue" by Dion infiltrates the vehicle as the scent of hour-old fast food wafts under my nose.

"You're going to be famous one day, Tag," I murmur, already half asleep as we veer onto the main road, tires struggling against the ice-packed pavement. "I feel it. I know it."

Silence settles in for a few beats. "You sound so confident."

"I am. You deserve to have your dreams come true."

"Not sure how much longer I can keep doing this alone. I need a band. A group of other guys just as desperate and thirsty as I am."

I curl my knees up as far as they'll go. "It'll happen. Keep pushing, keep playing. You just have to outlast all the other people who think they won't make it either."

Tag doesn't answer right away. All I hear is the crackle of the song playing and the drone of rubber against the slick road. Just as I'm about to drift off completely, he says, "Thanks, sis. Means a lot, having you in my corner."

My eyes flutter closed. "It's the truth, dumbass. Don't forget it."

Some kind of wrapper is thrown over his shoulder, landing on my face. Smells like grease and chicken.

"Great. Now I'm hungry," I mumble, tossing the paper bag to the floor.

Tag curves onto a new road, and I nearly slide off the seat. "I'll make a stop at the gas station. Gotta take a piss anyway. What do you want?"

"Lobster bisque."

"Try again. We've got stale chips and expired beef jerky."

"Stale chips, please. Thanks, Tag."

I doze in and out of sleep as we pull into the nearest gas station. One eye flicks open, and I unlatch my seat belt, moving into a sitting position to glance around. I catch sight of a man covered in snow as he winds through the gas pumps and beelines for the main door.

Tag leaves the car running with the heat blasting as he parks in front of the building. "I'll just be a few minutes."

"You're the best," I say groggily, watching as he hops out, closes the door, and jogs over to the entrance. The other man, wearing nothing but a hoodie, holds the door open for my brother, and they exchange a friendly nod.

I plop back down to the seat.

The alcohol fog steals me away.

Vivid dreams flicker through my mind. I'm a kid again, chasing Tag with a water balloon. Laughter bounces off wet pavement as fireworks paint the sky on the Fourth of July. A balloon bursts in my hand with a muted pop as the sky flashes red and blue.

The sound jerks me awake for half a second before fading into black. It feels like I've been asleep for hours when the car finally revs back to life, jostling me. We accelerate. A new song plays, a retro lullaby that triggers another wave of sleepiness. My eyes remain closed as we careen out onto the main drag, going faster than I'd expect given the weather conditions.

The brakes tap. A sharp jolt forward causes us to fishtail. I spill across the seat, confusion racing through me.

Someone growls, "*Fuck*."

Eyes flying open, I lift up on my elbow, my vision glazed and unfocused.

Tires squeal. A hand smacks the steering wheel.

Another round of *fucks*.

I snap my head up as I launch into a sitting position, now fully alert.

My gaze flicks to the rearview mirror.

Two startled eyes stare back at me. Wide, panicked, and decidedly unfamiliar.

I blink.

Blink again.

And then I scream.

"What the—" The stranger loses control of the wheel, veering off the road and careening toward a ditch.

Holy shit.

I think I've just been kidnapped.

CHAPTER 2
Annalise

"Who the *shit* are you?" I scramble in place, grappling with the seat belt as the car skids in and out of the ditch before ungracefully finding its way back to the main road.

The vehicle jolts left and right, vying for stability, and I topple sideways, nearly face-planting on the floor.

"Fuck. My. Life." The driver slaps a flat palm against the wheel.

My eyes dart around as I try to gather my bearings: familiar gray upholstery, a stain on the back seat from the Blue Slushy Fiasco of 2019, and a little red guitar charm swinging from the rearview mirror.

I'm still in Tag's car.

But the driver is most certainly *not* Tag.

Instinct has me searching for my phone, but I already know that my brother has it.

An unfortunate consequence of drunk texting.

Shit.

I manage to prop myself upright, dragging the belt across my chest and locking myself in. "What the hell? Who are you? Where's my brother?" The evening's alcohol haze is gradually replaced with confusion and terror. "Let me out!"

I scream again, tugging on the door handle.

"Whoa!" The stranger cants his head over his shoulder, his face ashen, eyes wild. "Hey, hey, I'm not going to hurt you, okay?"

"Bullshit!" I gape out the window as starlight blurs with the occasional streetlamp and snow barrels down in angry white swirls. "Stop the car!"

"It's blizzarding!" he yells back, voice pitching. "There's nothing but snow and woods for three miles."

"Jesus, I'll take my chances!"

Oh my God.

This isn't happening.

My fingers curl around the door handle. The wind is howling outside, rattling against the car, promising a wintry mix of hypothermia and death.

I probably wouldn't survive ten minutes in this dress and these heels, even with the cropped faux-fur jacket I threw on for style over substance. But I refuse to let that be the reason I end up murdered.

This guy just kidnapped me.

A messy mop of light-brown hair swings back and forth as the man scrubs a hand from forehead to jaw. "Christ." His fingers tighten around the wheel, his knuckles pale from the force of his grip. "Look, I'm not dangerous. This was a mistake. I didn't know you were back there."

My hands are trembling, my nails biting into my bare thighs beneath my cocktail dress. "Where are we going?"

He exhales sharply, squeezing his eyes shut for half a second too long before focusing back on the road. "Jesus. I need to think."

"You need to explain yourself! Where the hell is my brother?" I bounce up and down in the seat, tears pricking my eyes, my pulse acting as the percussion in a marching band. "Did…did you hurt him?"

"No, God—I told you I'm not dangerous," he insists.

I cup a hand around my mouth, my stomach coiling with alcohol and anxiety.

One minute I'm gulping down cocktails, dancing the night away with Kenna, and the next I'm trapped in a stolen car with a frantic stranger and no way to call for help.

I glance outside at the precarious weather conditions, then at the emergency brake. I'm not sure if pulling it would increase or decrease my chances of dying.

My mind races with different scenarios: hydroplaning on the icy road and flipping over in a ditch with the car bursting into flames, or becoming the tragic main character in a true crime documentary.

Neither was on my bingo card tonight.

Swallowing the fear, I try to reason with him. "Listen, you don't want to do this. You're a good person, right? I'm sure you are. We can still chalk this up to a random, terrifying, extremely far-fetched accident and giggle about it later." Feigning a nervous laugh, I take in his reflection, and it looks like he's in pain. I'm rambling. And that's never been a great motivator for getting my way. "If you're not dangerous, then drop me off at the next gas station. Or just—" But the words die in my throat as my gaze dips, and the moonlight catches on something dark and wet.

His jeans are soaked through, the fabric clinging to his thigh.

"Wait, is that blood?" My voice raises an octave as I jerk forward in the seat to get a better look. "Are you bleeding? Oh my God."

He clutches his injured leg, blood seeping through his fingers. "Someone shot me."

"*Excuse* me?" My stomach does backflips. Surely, I misheard. "Someone shot you? Why? Are you in a gang?"

"Jesus, no," he says, wincing through the obvious distress. "Gas station clerk."

"Holy shit. Is Tag okay?"

"Who the hell is Tag?"

"My brother!" The car briefly swerves into a ditch again, and I slam against the side door, bonking my head on the glass. "Jeez, you're going to get us killed!"

The guy saws out a breath, struggling with the wheel, the movement making him hiss before he regains control. "Last I saw, your brother was fine," he finally says. "I was leaving with something I couldn't pay for. The clerk panicked and lost his mind."

"You were stealing?"

His jaw tics, but he doesn't deny it.

This horror-movie evening has just taken a sharp turn into full-on *Reservoir Dogs* territory. "And then you stole my brother's car?"

"I didn't have a lot of options, okay?" He cuts me a sharp,

poignant glance in the mirror. "I was bleeding all over the floor, and I didn't exactly have time to weigh my moral choices."

"Where's *your* car?"

"It died. I walked."

"And your phone?"

"In my car."

I let out a stunned sigh, my head spinning, temple throbbing. I don't know anything about this guy, except that he's committed multiple felonies.

I'm so screwed.

"Listen," he grits out. "I'm telling the truth. I just need to get home and deal with this. I wasn't thinking. I'm not a bad guy—"

"You're not a bad guy?" I interrupt, my voice cracking under the weight of everything. My pulse is a damn train wreck. "You're hemorrhaging all over the place, and you're driving me through a snowstorm. I don't know you. I don't know who the hell you are!"

"Chase," he answers quickly. "My name's Chase. Please, just let me get home, all right? I didn't mean to drag you into this."

"Home…" I gawk at him, my focus shifting from his face to his bloody leg. "You clearly need a hospital."

He lets out a humorless laugh. "You think I can walk in there with a gunshot wound, a kidnapped woman, and no story? Cops would surround me before I even sat down."

"Not my problem!" I shake my head, trying to make sense of the mess, the chaos, the fear pooling in my gut. "But if you pass out behind the wheel, that *is* my problem. You say you're not trying to hurt me, so prove it."

A moment of silence stretches.

His jeans are drenched with blood, his complexion ghostly white.

I'm locked in the back seat of my brother's car with this wounded stranger in control of my fate. And yet I'm not getting psychopath vibes—more like a person on the verge of a full-scale breakdown. I don't trust him, but he doesn't look like he knows what the hell he's doing either.

Tag always says that my inherent trust in human beings will be my downfall one day, and maybe he's right.

But I don't get the sense that this guy wants to hurt me. He's trying to survive.

And I suppose that's the only thing we have in common right now.

I rake a hand through my tangled hair, my heart rate still in shambles. I should be running. I should be demanding he stop the car, blizzard be damned. But there's something about the way he's slumped against the door, hand gripping the wheel like it's the only thing tethering him to this world.

I swallow the lump in my throat. "What were you stealing?"

The car swerves again, tipping me off-balance. Fear creeps up my windpipe, and I wonder if he's going to lose consciousness before we make it someplace safe.

He steadies the vehicle, flicking me a glance in the mirror. "Does it matter?"

"Yes, it matters. Did you pull a gun on the clerk? Were you robbing the register?"

"No," he forces out. "I don't have any weapons. It was just a can of dog food. Fucking stupid."

My gaze pans to a little tin can rolling around the floor of the passenger's side.

A can of dog food?

"What's your name?" he asks me, tone tentative.

I tap my feet in opposite time and wring my hands together in my lap. "You don't need to know my name."

He nods once. "Fair enough." His profile is illuminated by dashboard light, his expression tortured.

When I sweep my eyes over him, taking in the way he's gripping his thigh, trying to stop the bleeding, I spot the faint outline of ink etched into his forearm beneath his rolled-up sleeve.

A guitar tattoo.

The neck of the instrument is wrapped in flowy sheets of musical notes, the body a vibrant shade of violet.

My chest tightens.

Tag has a guitar tattoo. Different placement, different size, different design.

But I know what kind of guy gets that tattoo.

My brother got his when he was nineteen, the night he swore music was the only thing that would ever keep him alive. He's been scraping by ever since, working as a car detailer, playing gigs that barely cover anything outside of rent, and drowning in the same desperation I see in this man's eyes now.

I'm familiar with that kind of struggle. I know what it looks like when someone is losing.

And I can't help but think that in a different life, this could've been my brother.

"My name is Annalise," I say slowly.

Our eyes lock for a moment in the rearview mirror before he returns his attention to the road. And then he practically wheezes out a lung when he lifts up and reaches into his back pocket, pulling out a tattered wallet.

He tosses it in my direction.

The wallet lands on the seat beside me, smeared with blood. Gingerly, I open it, squinting at the name on his driver's license: Chase Rhodes.

"Why did you give me this?" I glance at the birthday and attempt to do math while still inebriated and going in and out of shock.

He's twenty-four. Hardly a year older than Tag.

"Just in case," he murmurs.

I blink up at him. "In case what?"

"That's my current address. My dog is there. Toaster."

I can't stop blinking, trying to process what he's saying.

"Look, if I don't make it…I don't have anybody else. I just need someone to make sure my dog is okay and finds a good home." He falters, turning onto another street. "A better home."

I'm horrified when my eyes start to mist.

My God. I've gone from petrified to pissed off to empathetic in a matter of five minutes.

And I have no idea how to respond to that.

I collapse back in the seat, watching blowing tree branches and snow whiz by. I've wanted a dog since I was four years old, but my mother is allergic. And Alex? He says a dog would be too much responsibility, given our hectic schedules at the restaurant. He's not wrong.

Chewing on my cheek, I cross my arms and look into the mirror. "You really don't have anybody?"

Chase's jaw flexes, his gaze fixed on the road. "No. Not anymore."

The words sit heavy in the space between us as a new song starts to play on the radio: "I Only Want To Be With You" by Dusty Springfield.

Something in my chest tugs, but I shove the feeling aside. I need to be smart about this. Strategic. My adrenaline's still pumping, my blood swimming with booze, my mind sorting through the havoc of the last few minutes. I'm not about to let my guard down just because he has sad eyes and a dog named Toaster.

I don't know anything about this man.

But I know what it's like to make a bad decision that changes the course of your entire life.

"I'll make sure your dog is okay." I look down at my magenta-tipped toes peeking out through my heels. "Just in case."

His head snaps toward me, bewilderment clouding his already wrecked expression. "You're helping me?"

I guess I am. Because if I were him—if I were bleeding out in the middle of a frozen highway with no one to call, no one to help me—I'd want someone to give a damn.

And maybe because I can't shake the memory of my brother last year, sitting on his couch at three in the morning, his hands in his hair: "I don't know how much longer I can do this, Annalise."

I wonder if Chase has ever said something like that too.

If anyone was listening.

I inhale a frazzled breath and reply, "You said there's no one else."

The upbeat song echoes through the car, and I study the man behind the wheel. He's fading. The hospital can't be far, but I'm not sure how much longer he has before he succumbs to his injury, and I'm almost positive we're heading in the opposite direction.

"You need a hospital, Chase." I crane my neck, glancing out the back window and watching as the storm swallows the highway in a harrowing white vortex. "Turn around."

"Can't."

I whip forward. "There's no other choice. You're losing too much blood."

"My house…" He blows out a shaky breath. "It's closer. Just another mile…"

My hand slaps against my forehead, fingers curling into my hairline as I watch his complexion turn a chalky shade of gray.

He's not going to pass out. No way.

Peering down at his driver's license again, I frown at the address: 112 Silverleaf Avenue. A sense of familiarity settles in.

Silverleaf.

I know that street. It's just a few blocks from my parents' old house. Tag and I used to cut through there all the time on our bikes, racing past the same handful of houses until the street curved toward the park.

Chase groans out a pained sound, his breathing shallow. "Think I might need you to…drive."

My spine straightens with a jolt of unease as flashbacks assault me.

Shit, shit, shit.

"I-I can't," I whisper with regret, the traumatic memories

tunneling through the fear. Truthfully, taking over the wheel sounds less hazardous than letting him bleed out in the driver's seat, but that doesn't change the fact that I can't do it. Not after what happened to—

No.

I squeeze my eyes shut, willing the past to stay buried.

The shattered glass. The flashing lights.

"Please," he rasps.

"I…I literally can't. I don't have a driver's license. I don't know how to drive."

A quick shake of his head, fused with disbelief. "Phone?"

"My brother has it." Unlatching my seat belt, I scoot forward, inching between the seats. "Listen, I'll try to help. Just stay focused. We're not far. I'll call for an ambulance when we get to safety."

He attempts a nod, his eyelids fluttering. "No police. No hospital."

Right. We'll deal with that later.

"Chase. Chase Rhodes?"

Another sluggish nod.

"That's a cool name. Sounds like a frontman in a band or something." This has to be the most bizarre moment of my life. I'm making small talk with my kidnapper while trying to keep him conscious, all while creeping down the snowy highway toward his house. "I noticed your tattoo. Do you play?"

"Yeah, I…build them." His eyes dance over to the guitar charm dangling from the mirror.

"You build guitars?"

Those eyes start to close, his head drooping.

"Hey! Chase, whoa, stay with me. Keep talking." Frantic, I shimmy my way onto the center console, squeezing between the seats until I clumsily plop into the passenger seat. "Shit. Please don't black out."

The car swerves, and I reach for the wheel.

"Keep your foot on the pedal."

Blinking, he frowns, moaning in agony.

"Come on. Say something. You're going to be fine. We're almost there."

"I'm…so sorry…"

My free hand flies to his leg, adding pressure to the wound. He's lost so much blood. "This is a great song. Do you know it?"

His throat bobs through a swallow.

I start singing along, trying to keep him present, awake, *alive*.

A groggy smile twitches on his mouth, his eyes half-lidded. "You're a good…singer."

Blood oozes onto my palm as I press harder against his thigh, my attention split between the windshield and his face. I look up as a suburban part of town comes into view, a few approaching headlights warped by snow. A stoplight takes shape through the blustery haze, glowing red. "We have to stop. Red light."

His head lolls to the side.

"Chase, red light!" My bloodied hand slaps against his cheek, jarring him back awake.

"Shit," he grunts, slamming on the brake.

My pulse jackhammers in my ears as residential homes loom ahead. I recognize the area. Silverleaf is just past this next intersection. "We're almost there, okay? I love your dog's name. What breed?"

"Stella…" he says, hardly audible.

"Is that your girlfriend?" The light turns green, and I tap his cheek, once, twice. "Green light."

He blinks several times, forcing himself to stay coherent. The car rolls forward, losing traction in the snow as I even out the wheel.

"Sheltie," he exhales, breaths stuttered, his limbs trembling as sweat dots his hairline.

"I love Shelties," I say. "Tell me about your tattoo. My brother has one that's similar." I purposely pivot the conversation again, attempting to keep his mind sharp.

"Mm," is all he mutters.

We're going slow enough that I could easily escape the car and run to the nearest gas station, restaurant, convenience store, anything.

But I don't.

Empathy pokes through my self-preservation, and I'm not sure how I feel about that. All I know is that I couldn't live with myself when the news broke that my brother's car was located on the side of the road, the driver DOA.

"We're almost there." I return my hand to his leg, the denim sticky and wet. "The street is on the right. I'll turn the wheel, you press on the gas."

He finds the strength to ease us onto the next side street, and I take control of the wheel, guiding us through two more turns until we're rolling down the familiar tree-lined road.

Chase's eyes roll up, his head slumping against the headrest. "Don't go…Stella…" His voice is barely a breath now, the fight slipping from his body.

A second later, his chin drops to his chest.

"Chase?" I shake his shoulder, but there's no response. "Shit... Chase!"

The car inches to the right, tires crunching through fresh snow. Panic spikes as I scramble into action, reaching for the gearshift with one hand while keeping the other on the wheel.

Alex's face flashes through my mind, his instructions, the way he screamed at me before everything—

Neutral.

I grasp the shifter and yank it into N, the engine whining as momentum carries us forward. My heart is a bass drum in my throat.

"Come on, come on." I lift off the seat and brace my knee against the center console. The car is still moving too fast, moments from coasting onto the curb. I throw myself sideways, half straddling his lap, my dress bunching around my thighs as I stretch for the brake.

My heel skids against the floor mat. "Dammit—" I yank it off, my toes barely grazing the pedal.

Old brick and vinyl houses materialize on both sides, address numbers bleeding into the whiteout.

206...202?

Some numbers are on mailboxes, others plastered to pillars and siding, too obscured for me to make out.

My attention shifts between maneuvering the car and locating the right house. There's no way I can drag this giant man through five inches of snow in my stilettos and too-tight dress.

I scan the homes, my vision muddled from snowfall and

streetlamps casting hazy light over the porches. The numbers flicker past, my pulse skidding along with the car.

There.

A small dark-blue house appears, the porch light glowing faintly. On the mailbox 112 is in big block letters.

The car bumps over a patch of uneven pavement, jolting Chase's body against mine. His head flops to the side, and a weak moan escapes his lips.

My palm slams against his chest for balance as I shift lower, pressing down on the brake with every ounce of strength I have. The tires groan, the car jerking as we finally lurch to a stop.

I don't breathe for a second.

Slamming the lever into Park, I lean over him and shove the door open.

"Somebody help us!"

CHAPTER 3
Annalise

The world swirls, spins.

Freezing air shocks my skin as I fly out of the car and turn toward Chase. My hair blows in front of my eyes, the life-and-death panic crashing into a dizzy blur of cheap alcohol and the unsteady relief of finally being on solid ground.

I shake his shoulders, trying to bring him back to life, while kicking off my other heel. "Chase, let's go. We're here. Can you stand?"

His eyes flutter open, and he tips sideways, spilling out the door and toppling onto the pavement. I react quickly, bending to catch his head before it smashes on the driveway.

"Dammit…come on, don't die on me." Using all my strength, I reach under his armpits to lift him, huffing and puffing as I prop him against the frame of the car, while mentally thanking those extra planks I did this afternoon.

His skin is even paler now, lips parted, eyes hardly open.

Desperation claws up my throat.

Chase teeters in place. Blood spreads in a horrifying pool around his entire leg.

My heart stutters, knees wobbling as the reality of the evening sinks in. "Chase, I swear to God, you better help me out here."

A groggy mumble meets my ears.

Not helpful.

I let out a grunt of frustration, adjusting my grip as I brace my feet, sliding his arm around my shoulders, then tugging him forward until I'm half dragging, half guiding him up the driveway. His boots slide against the snow as I stagger forward, his broad frame pressing into me.

My gaze zigzags from left to right, and I silently pray that Chase lives next to smokers who are willing to brave the storm for a quick nicotine rush on their front porch.

But there's no one around. Only a ghostly, mocking howl of wind.

"Why're you…helping me…" Partially limping, he leans in farther, his arm deadweight around me. "I don't…"

"Doesn't matter. We just need to get inside. Is the door locked?"

No response.

Guess I'll find out.

It's a short driveway, and a single step brings us to the front door. He trips on it, nearly toppling us both onto the frosty concrete. "Shit," I mutter, my body shaking from the weight as my hand flies out to grip the pillar for balance. My bare foot connects with the welcome mat, sliding it out of place, and a small silver key catches my eye, glinting beneath the porch light.

Steadying us both, I bend over, then pull the screen open and jab the key into the lock, twisting sharply.

The taupe door unbolts with a creak.

Instantly, a wet nose grazes my shin, followed by a mass of long, scraggly fur coiling around my ankles. Chase stumbles through the threshold, and I maintain my grip on him while we beeline toward the couch, and I deposit him with a grunt.

The living room is dark and cluttered, only the glow of streetlight filtering through the half-cracked blinds. Multiple guitars, in varying stages of completion, lean against the far wall. Jackets hang haphazardly by the door. A pair of shoes, a dog leash, a dripping faucet cutting through the silence.

I blink at the man sprawled out on the couch as my toes curl into the old carpeting, my feet wet and frozen.

Phone.

I need to call for help.

My eyes dart around the darkened space, looking for a landline. Do people have those anymore? I race forward as my hands claw at the walls in search of a light switch. A moment later, warm yellow light brightens the space. "Do you have another phone?" I call out.

I wind through the small kitchen, then double back to the living room, my gaze shooting left, right, forward, back. No phone in sight.

My focus pings back to Chase, who is now slumped sideways on the muddy-brown sofa. His dog is curled up beside him, both paws dangling over the couch as the animal stares at me, silently begging me to help.

I have no idea what I'm doing.

Emotion seizes my chest, and I rush forward, slapping Chase's cheek. "Hey. Are you still with me?" I place my ear against his ribs, registering the echo of subtle heartbeats and shallow breathing. "Do you have a first aid kit? We need to get this bleeding under control. And I need a goddamn phone."

The dog whimpers beside us, pawing at his owner's leg. The image breaks my heart.

I grip my hair with both hands, telling myself to focus, stay calm.

Surveying the room, I look around, desperate for something I can use. There's a metal toolbox shoved halfway under the coffee table, its lid slightly ajar. Lunging for it, I yank it open. Wrenches, screwdrivers, a roll of electrical tape.

I push it aside and jump to my feet.

Think, Annalise.

Where would a guy like this keep—

The bathroom.

"Stay with me, Chase."

Sprinting down the short hallway, I throw open the first door. Bingo. I rip open the cabinet beneath the sink. Cleaning supplies. Old shampoo bottles. Then, shoved toward the back, a battered first aid kit that looks like it was dug up from ancient catacombs.

My fingers close around it, my pulse thundering. I snatch a towel off the rack and rush back to the living room.

Chase hasn't moved.

Dropping to my knees, I shove the coffee table aside and tear open the kit. Gauze, alcohol wipes, bandages. Not nearly enough for a bullet wound, but it'll have to do.

"All right, rock star," I mutter, forcing steadiness into my voice as I press the towel to his leg. "You're not dying on me tonight."

His lids flutter, eyes barely opening.

Exhaling sharply, I peel the wrapper off a roll of gauze with my teeth. I wind it around his thigh, my hands shaking as I pull it tight. Chase groans, his head pressing back against the couch.

"I know," I whisper. "I know it hurts."

But I have to keep going, because if I don't get the bleeding under control, it won't matter how much it hurts.

The dog whines again, nosing Chase's limp hand. My chest clenches. I focus, knotting the gauze with quick, jerky movements. Blood still seeps through, but not as fast.

"Hey," he murmurs. His lips are dry, throat bobbing. A hand tentatively lifts, two fingers flicking my hair. "Thanks, Annie."

Annie.

Nobody calls me Annie.

I swallow. "Yeah. Sure."

Then he passes out cold.

Triple crap.

He begged me not to call the cops or bring him to a hospital, but I'm running out of options.

I glance over at Toaster, the dog's pointed nose resting on Chase's hip, two brown eyes aimed hopelessly at his owner. Tears well, melancholy stabbing at my heart like a hot skewer. But the feeling is quickly replaced by a sense of determination as I lift off the floor, reach for a ratty quilt, and drape it over this stranger who has spun my evening on its axis.

I bolt for the front door. There has to be someone. I just need a phone.

Frigid air and serpentine snow smack me in the face as I rush outside in my bare feet and bloodstained party dress. "Help!" I call out, pitching my voice over the hissing wind. "I need help!" Glancing left and right, I choose right, stomping toward the brick tri-level with dim lighting bleeding through the pulled curtains.

Catapulting myself up the three porch steps, I start banging on the screen. "Hey! I need a phone!" Demonic music and shrieking snares seep through, vibrating the walls. I press the doorbell fifty billion times, pounding both fists against the frame. "Please help me!"

Footsteps. I hear them shuffling toward the front of the house.

A pang of hope slices through the fear.

A moment later, a scruffy guy in a white T-shirt opens the door, looking high as a kite. "Who the fuck're you?"

I begin my rambling spiel, my words tripping over each other like a collapsing house of cards. "Please. I need to use your phone. The guy next door—Chase—he's hurt. Really hurt. I just need—"

"Whoa." He squints at me, frowning. "Your hair has…purple in it."

"Oh my God. Can I please use your phone?"

More squinting, frowning, blinking. Finally, he snaps back and fishes out a cell phone from the pocket of his sweatpants. "Yeah, yeah. Do your thing."

The phone slaps against my palm, and I move, racing back down the steps and hightailing it to the blue house on the left.

"Add your number in before you bring it back!" the guy yells after me.

My icy fingers stumble over the number keys, and in a

moment of conflict I press ten numbers instead of three. Alex's voice answers while I make a quick stop in the driveway, searching for the can of dog food in the car before running back to the house.

"Yeah?"

"Alex! Thank God. It's me."

A short pause. "Annalise? Where the hell are you? You were supposed to be home by now."

"Just listen," I rush out. "I need you. 112 Silverleaf Avenue. I'm only a mile from the condo. Please. Get here fast."

"The fuck?"

"I'll explain everything, I promise. I need your help. It's urgent."

He barks a laugh that's tinged with confusion. "Wait, are you in trouble?"

"Yes." I push through the open door, finding Chase and his dog right where I left them. "I mean, no. It's not me, it's…" *Shit*—how do I explain this? My brain stumbles over a story, a little white lie. "He's Tag's friend. He was shot in the leg, and he's bleeding out. I just need—"

"Call a goddamn ambulance. Jesus. It's like Armageddon outside."

"I'm calling *you*. Please, just get here."

"This is batshit. Where's Tag?"

"He's…not here." I rip the lid off the can of dog food. "Dammit, Alex, we're running out of time. Please."

"Fuck this." He growls out a series of curses, the jingle of car keys resonating through the speaker. "You better have a damn good explanation when I get there."

Click.

My cheeks burn, eyes stinging with more tears. Toaster's tail wags as he lifts off the couch, attention aimed at the can of food. Whimpers escape. The dog's. Mine.

"Here you go, buddy. Eat up." I place the can on the floor, watching as the animal hops down and devours the meal.

Next, I call my brother.

Deep breath.

Somehow I need to convince him not to press charges against the guy who just kidnapped me from a random gas station.

I punch in the number. It rings twice. And then—

"Please tell me this is my fucking sister."

My breath falls out in a plume of relief. "It's me, Tag."

"Jesus Christ, where are you?"

"That guy from the gas station. He was shot, then he took the car and was trying to—"

"Yeah, I know what happened. Caught the tail end of it as I was coming out of the bathroom." His long sigh filters through the speaker. "I'm at the police station. They brought me in for questioning as the only witness. It's a goddamn mess."

"Are you okay? Are you hurt?"

"No, but I've been freaked out of my mind, thinking that asshole tossed you in the woods and got the hell out of Dodge. Or worse."

"I'm fine. Just shaken up." I peer down at Chase, his chest inflating with thin, feeble breaths beneath the gray-blue quilt. "He didn't hurt me."

"He's a dead man."

"He might already be a dead man, with or without your help. He's in bad shape."

"Good. He's a fucking criminal, and if he did anything to hurt you—"

"He didn't," I interrupt. "I promise I'm okay."

"Where are you?"

"I'm…at his house."

"*What?*"

"Listen, this is going to sound borderline certifiable, but I need you to trust me. I don't think he's a bad guy. He was desperate. He'd just been shot." My stomach twists with indecision, but I go with my instincts. "Tell the cops I drove him willingly. Don't press charges."

"Hell. Fucking. No. Annalise, come on," he shoots back. "I watched him steal my car with my little sister sleeping in the back seat. I've been worried sick. There's a literal search party out there looking for you."

"Call them off."

"Are you out of your mind?"

"Maybe. Probably." I take a seat on the couch beside Chase, tugging the quilt up to his chin. "You trust me, right?"

He falters. "You know I do."

"Remember when you wrecked Dad's truck?"

Tag exhales sharply. "Not the same thing."

"It's close enough." I press the phone tighter to my ear. "You were nineteen, scared shitless, and you made a bad call. You left the scene, hoping you could fix it before anyone found out."

Silence.

"But someone did find out," I continue. "And you were lucky it was me. Because I covered for you. I told Dad I borrowed the truck, even though I didn't even know how to drive, and that I lost control. And you let me lie for you, because you knew if it came from you, he'd never forgive you for it." I glance at Chase, unconscious and barely breathing. "This is the same thing, Tag. He made a bad choice. But he's not a bad guy."

"How do you even know that?"

"I just do."

Another pause, longer this time. "Dammit," he mutters. "I hate when you do this."

"Do what?"

"Make me go against my better judgment." His voice is gruff, but there's a thread of reluctant understanding woven through it. "Do not make me regret this. If this guy touches a hair on your multicolored head, I'm burying him."

My eyes squeeze shut. "Deal."

"I'll come pick you up as soon as they let me go. Send me your location."

"I have a ride. Alex is on the way."

"That's comforting," he grumbles. "Call me from his phone as soon as you get home."

"Yeah." My lips purse, throat stinging. "I will."

The call disconnects, and I toss the phone on the skewed table across from me. An eerie silence drapes over the room. My eyes gradually shift from the messy space to the lanky, doe-eyed dog, then to the unconscious man barely breathing on my left. I take a moment to study him now that the adrenaline has tapered off and my safety is no longer in question.

By all standards, he's good-looking.

Not the kind of person I'd expect to find in a situation like this. He looks like someone who should be thriving, not scraping by. How does a guy like him have no friends, family, or even enough money to buy a can of dog food? No one should ever look this defeated, this alone. Like a solitary soldier left behind on the battlefield, too beaten down to fight.

All so his dog could have a meager meal.

I extend my hand, looping my fingers around his palm and drinking in his profile: strong jaw with week-old scruff, long, fanning lashes, and unkempt brown hair hanging over his brow.

I'm not sure how much time he has left, or if he'll even make it through the night. The notion is a missile to my ribcage.

Swallowing the burning lump of sadness, I part my lips. He said he liked my singing voice, and I feel like everyone should experience something joyful and sweet in their final moments. He's a music man. It's obvious, given the plethora of hand-carved guitars, the tattoo, the rock-band posters taped to his walls, their corners curling with age.

I close my eyes and start to sing that Dusty Springfield song.

My love for the 1960s started when I was nine years old and watched *Breakfast at Tiffany's* with my mother, the two of us huddled up on her favorite loveseat in the den. I'd become bewitched by Audrey Hepburn, to the point of mimicking her style. Pearls strung around my neck, oversize sunglasses slipping down my nose, my mom's old pleated dress dragging at my ankles. I'd parade around the house, humming "Moon River" under my breath as Tag shot me annoyed glances from his perch at the video game console.

But it wasn't just Holly Golightly's charm that captured me; it was everything. The music, the fashion, the effortless cool of an era that felt untouched by time and technology. It was the crackle of a needle dropping on a vinyl record, the poetic rebellion of Dylan's lyrics, and the cinematic magic of Technicolor dreams.

And now, years later, with a closet full of mod dresses and a heart that beats to the sound of a Fender Stratocaster, I still wonder if I'd been born in the wrong decade.

I don't think Chase is a "Swinging Sixties" kind of guy, but music is music.

Songs have lungs. They breathe.

So I do what I can to keep *him* breathing.

I make it through one more song—Carole King's masterpiece, "Will You Love Me Tomorrow"—before the front door barrels open and the peaceful moment is eclipsed by Alex stomping through the threshold with snow in his hair and murder in his eyes.

"I swear I'm going to kill you for this."

Literal murder, apparently.

I try not to take his threats to heart because I know he doesn't mean it. He's different now.

And that's *my* fault.

"Alex."

My long-term boyfriend, and best friend since we were kids, storms over to the couch and gawks at the barely breathing man beside me.

I jump to my feet, reaching for Alex's arm. "Thank God you came. I'm so sorry. I didn't know what else to do."

"Really? You didn't know how to dial 9-1-1? Jesus, Annalise, use your fucking brain." Alex shoots me a glare before approaching Chase with a frustrated growl and giving him a once-over. "This guy needs a surgeon. Possibly a coroner."

My pulse hitches. "Don't say that."

"What do you expect me to do here?"

"I-I don't know…help him, try to patch up the wound or something." My fingers curl around his fully tattooed forearm as I bounce on both feet. "Please, Alex. You were a Boy Scout. You've taken first aid classes. And you helped that dog that was hit by a car last year."

"Seriously? That dog had a broken leg, not a bullet wound and liters worth of blood loss. And I was a Boy Scout for five fucking seconds. Christ. What the hell even happened?" Minty colored eyes lock on mine as he rakes a hand through his tar-black hair. "Are you roping me into some seedy crime that'll land me behind bars as an accomplice? Fuck. No way. I'm out."

I gouge my nails into his skin, wrenching him back. "Alex! Wait. You haven't even looked at him yet."

"My vision is just fine. You asked for my opinion, and I'm giving it to you: he needs an ambulance or a body bag. Your choice."

"I—" The words die in my throat as I glance over my shoulder at Chase. Something tells me Alex is right. I can't worry about hospital debt or legal trouble. This is life-and-death. Nodding frantically, I reach for the phone on the coffee table. "Okay… okay, you're right."

"Of course I'm right," he snaps, something brittle in his voice. "You drag me out here, beg for my help, then you want to ignore my advice. Classic Annalise."

Turning away, I punch in the three numbers and try not to cry. The dispatcher answers on the second ring. "Hello? Hi," I say, my voice squeaky, shredded. "I need an ambulance. Someone's been shot."

Alex continues his tirade, pacing in circles beside me and kicking at loose clutter on the floor. "What the hell are you even doing with him? Alone, at that. In his house. Why have I never seen this guy before?"

I keep my back to him. Focus on the call.

I try to block out the noise.

This will pass.

"After everything I've done for you, and you don't even respect me enough to answer?"

I give the dispatcher the address, my voice tight.

Alex lets out a humorless laugh. "Are you screwing this dude?"

My eyes squeeze shut.

"You are, aren't you?"

The woman tells me to stay on the line, but I end the call, chuck the phone, and scramble away.

"Hey!" Alex's hand snags my wrist in a bruising clutch. "Fucking hell, woman. Answer me."

I whip back around, ready to erupt. "I'm not cheating on you! God! He's Tag's friend. I hardly know him." Fat, hot tears spill down my cheeks, a culmination of the night, the lingering tequila, and the misplaced words boomeranging at me. I can hardly catch my breath. "I was just trying to help him."

Toaster jumps off the couch and plops down on my bare toes. The warmth temporarily soothes me as the room goes quiet and Alex sighs, palming the back of his neck with both hands.

He stares at me, unblinking. "Fuck. I'm sorry."

"I know."

"I love you."

"I know," I repeat, the words ragged.

Alex pulls me to him, pressing a tender kiss to my forehead and circling his arms around my shoulders. "I'm sorry, baby. You're okay, right? You're not hurt?" He cups my jaw, angling my face from side to side, searching for signs of injury. "You're shaking."

"I'm fine. It's been a scary night."

"Tell me what happened." He kisses my nose.

"I will. I just…" Hesitation seizes me for a beat before I relax, surrendering to his hug. His heart is racing, his hold on me strengthening as I nuzzle against his chest.

Sirens blare in the distance, slicing through the snowy night. I peer out the window through the cheap vinyl blinds, watching flurries zigzag between power lines and tree branches.

Inching back, I find Alex's eyes. "One second. I need to grab something. I'll meet you by the door."

As the sirens grow closer, I jog into the kitchen, find a napkin and a pen, and jot down a few scribbled words. I place the note on the coffee table before giving Toaster a quick scratch between the ears and meeting Alex at the front of the house.

I spare one last look at Chase as the ambulance pulls up. He doesn't stir when the flashing lights streak through the frosted glass, painting him in red and blue. Toaster hops back on the couch and snuggles against Chase's thigh, the dog's ears perked to full attention.

For a guy who crashed into my world like a wrecking ball, Chase looks devastatingly fragile right now.

My hand clamps around Alex's palm. I pivot back around, watching the paramedics rush inside, their voices urgent, their movements practiced. Toaster doesn't budge, his small body curled protectively against Chase's side.

I should look away. Should let go.

But as they hover over him and check for a pulse, I find myself holding my breath, waiting, hoping, feeling like a listener clinging to the final note of a song…

Praying it doesn't end just yet.

CHAPTER 4
Chase

Images flicker behind my eyes. Dreams, memories, a tie-dye swirl.

Stella's voice trickles through me.

"My brave little Toaster..."

My brave little sister.

Water fills my lungs, and I choke on chlorine. My vision muddles, my feet skid against a wet surface, my voice howls with an inhuman sound. Everything is garbled, muddy, wrong.

I can't breathe.

Someone is singing. Not Stella.

A girl.

My hand extends, reaching. I see blood. It starts at my fingertips, seeps under my nails, travels up the length of my arm until it takes me over. A costume, a morbid disguise.

Pain shreds my leg.

A gunshot pierces the air, vibrating my skull. More blood, drenching my jeans, fusing fabric to skin. My knees buckle.

Ice-cold water pulls me under.

Then that voice returns.

Soft, urgent. The girl.

"*Stay with me.*"

The weight of her hand presses against my chest, grounding me. A different kind of drowning. A different kind of rescue.

My lungs strain, dragging in breath after breath. Chlorine. Gunpowder. Perfume. My sister's laugh curls around the edges of it all.

The past bleeds into the present.

Stella is gone.

But someone else is here.

And as my eyes crack open, one at a time, I realize—

So am I.

There is nothing quite as sobering as leaving the hospital after major surgery with no one on speed dial and no friends or family waiting with smiles and bouquets. No reunion hugs, no happy tears, no speakerphone group calls with relatives across the country squealing with profound relief at your recovery.

There is only silence.

I realize I've forgotten what real happiness is. Every day for years, I've woken up, and I'm just trying to survive.

Today is no different.

Snow blankets the ground in a patchwork of white, gray, and brown. Exhaust fumes, oil spills, piss, and mud. I stare at it for a long time as I wait on the hospital curb in my freshly washed clothes, courtesy of Nurse Janelle. Bloodstains are a bitch. The snow will melt into plush green grass and colorful flower buds, but there is no washing away the evidence of the second-worst night of my life.

"Beep, beep, motherfucker!" Solomon leans out the open window, his voice pitching over a gust of wind that whips my hood back. "Get in before you freeze your nuts off."

The only person I could call was my boss.

The same guy who helped get me into this mess.

I limp to the car on a pair of crutches, every step reminding me just how much my life has unraveled. Sol watches me approach, one hand on the wheel as he smacks a wad of gum between his teeth.

When I'm finally settled, he shifts the car into Drive and whistles under his breath. "Jesus, kid. You look like hell."

"Thanks." Better than looking dead, I suppose.

"Can't believe they set you free already. Damn. It's like a fuckin' drive-through these days." He shakes his head with dismay, pulling out onto the main road. "Hope they fed you, at least. Did you get a toy with your Happy Meal?"

My good leg bounces up and down, jarring my injured leg and making me wince. "Ate enough. No toy, but possibly a lifelong limp."

"Brutal."

The bullet missed my femoral artery, just barely. That's what the surgeon told me—some doctor with tired eyes and a voice that didn't match the gravity of what he was saying. Another inch, and I'd be gone. Instead, I got emergency surgery, a blood transfusion, multiple nights in the ICU, and a hospital bill I'm praying is all covered by state insurance.

A gunshot wound to the thigh isn't the kind of thing you just walk away from, no matter how much I want to. My future will be filled with a boatload of follow-up visits and months of rehab.

Sol spits his gum out the window, then rolls it back up. "Listen, man, I feel like shit for what happened. Can't help but feel responsible."

My stomach sinks at the reminder that I have nothing but loose change and lint in my pockets and an empty fridge waiting for me at home. "It was a team effort."

After all, I had options. I chose the path of most resistance, which involved theft and carjacking.

I press two fingers to my forehead, rubbing away the migraine as my mind flashes with visions of no heat, surviving on cans of beans and jellied cranberries leftover from Thanksgiving, and showering at the neighbor's house while Rock shreds two sets of drums—his kit and my ears—and rambles off conspiracy theories.

It's a horror movie reel I'm forced to watch, while Christmas lights glitter from pine trees and rooftops, whizzing by in a multicolored stream outside the window.

I haven't gotten a paycheck since before Halloween, thanks to the man on my left. My rent is long past due, my savings account is in the negative, and my phone is moments away from being shut off.

Tugging the hood over my head, I lean back and stare at

the snowfall carpeting the earth. Sparkling, weightless, free of burden. The opposite of this feeling that hollows out my chest.

"Yeah, well, you're due for a lucky break, my friend." Plucking a cigarette from the dashboard, Sol reaches for his lighter and flicks the little wheel, smoke pluming from the embers. "I made a call, pulled a few strings, and managed to get some cash together that covers your wages since your last paycheck. Plus that bonus I promised."

My eyes flare, a shot of cautious elation zipping through my chest. "Shit, really?"

"Pop the glove box."

I pull it open and spot a white envelope stuffed with bills. Sighing with the first breath of relief in months, I snatch it from the compartment and glance at what looks like a few thousand dollars. "You have no idea how much this helps."

I realize it's my own fault for agreeing to this under-the-table bullshit; I should have known better. But when I was laid off from my welding job last year due to the factory closing down, I was desperate. The woodworking ad on a local listing's post caught my eye.

It was supposed to be temporary while I got my custom guitar business off the ground. And I guess that's the thing about temporary plans. They have a way of stretching into permanence when you're flat broke. A false sense of security.

One month turned into three, then six, until a full year of late nights in freezing warehouses slipped by as I sanded down someone else's vision for cash that barely covered the rent.

"Get yourself a good lawyer and some new clothes." Sol

snickers, eyeing me up and down. "Can't have you showing up to work looking like you moonlight as Dexter."

I sift through the money before dropping the envelope on my lap. "It might be a bit before I'm back on the clock."

"I get that. I've got you covered for a few weeks. You have someone to look after you?"

My jaw tics through the lie. "Yeah, my neighbor. Rock."

"Good deal."

The truth is, my neighbor is usually too stoned to know which day it is, let alone if I'm still breathing. But I'll manage. I've lived through worse things. "My dog was doing okay when you checked on him?" I shift in my seat with a hiss, dropping my head against the headrest.

Given Sol's track record with breaking promises, he wasn't my first choice for keeping Toaster alive in my absence. Unfortunately, he was my only choice.

"Oh, yeah, the ragamuffin was happy as a clam at high tide. Your neighbor must've stopped by before I got there."

I frown. "What?"

"Someone was already at the house. The dog was eating like a king. Had multiple bowls filled with kibble, enough water to hydrate the Sahara, and a few chew toys that looked like they were put to good use."

My heart stutters.

There's no way Rock took the time to spoil my dog. He told me once that he didn't trust dogs, convinced they were plants by the government to condition us.

"Right." I clear my throat. "Thanks for going over there to check on him."

"Told you before, I got you. Better late than never, eh?"

I rub a hand over my chin, my mind reeling with possible good Samaritans.

Surely it wasn't her…

I close my eyes, and a pretty girl flickers across my memories: big blue eyes clouded with confusion and dread, pink cheeks dampened with tears, and dark hair threaded with violet streaks while wisps of pale blond framed her porcelain face.

She sang to me.

Everything about that night is a blur, but the sound of her voice—a soulful, throaty melody—somehow trickled through the haze and buried deep.

Annie?

Stella loved the movie *Annie*. The music, the bright, hopeful energy of it. She used to sing the songs around the house, her voice filling the empty spaces with a kind of innocence I can't get back. I'd catch her twirling in the living room, laughing at her own off-key rendition of "Tomorrow," a little girl lost in her own joy.

I swallow hard, trying to smash the foggy pieces together until they take shape.

Panic, screaming, chaos.

Softness, warm touches, sweet songs.

At some point, the girl I inadvertently kidnapped found an ounce of sympathy for me and kept me alive. I can't help but feel like she's responsible for keeping my dog alive too.

It doesn't make sense.

Anyone with an ounce of self-preservation would have jumped from the car at the first stoplight and left me to bleed out and rot on the side of the road.

But she didn't.

I squeeze my eyes tighter, willing the memories to brighten, to glow. She was talking to me, trying to keep me coherent. Asking questions. I think her name was Annie, but I can't be sure.

Annabelle, Annemarie, An—

"Saw that store clerk all over the news," Sol says, flicking the radio dial until the Police serenade us from the speaker. "Looks like he's in deep shit."

I blink away the fading images of the woman and stare down at my dirty boots. "It's my fault."

"Don't do that pity-party shit, man. Who in their right mind shoots at a guy who's just trying to feed his dog? That's a hell of an overreaction." He swerves onto a side road and barrels toward my part of town. "Deadly force isn't justified against a person who poses no imminent threat. According to Google, anyway."

I cringe.

I'm dreading the legal mess I've landed myself in. The cops came, asked their questions, and left. The clerk's story kept changing. First, he said I lunged at him. Then it was that I had something in my hand. Everything about that moment is a black-tar haze, but I know I didn't do anything to warrant getting shot.

Vermont's got strong self-defense laws, though none that cover putting a bullet in a man for pilfering a three-dollar can of dog food. They took the guy in on an aggravated assault charge after security footage confirmed I made no violent threats and had no weapons on me.

Maybe he'll go to prison, maybe he won't.

Either way, I'm the one left sitting here in this rusty Honda with my oddball boss, half numb from painkillers, staring out the window at the slushy pavement like it might have answers.

"He was panicked," I finally say. "People don't act rationally when they're scared." Clearly, I'm an expert on the subject.

"How'd you get away? Your car is still at the warehouse, deader than disco. Saw your phone in there too."

I drum my fingers on my knee, debating my answer. Interestingly enough, the cops never drilled me about a grand theft auto charge, nor about the woman in the back seat of the stolen car. I can't help but wonder if she covered for me. Still doesn't make any fucking sense. "There was a witness. She gave me a ride to the hospital."

But I don't think that's true.

Images glimmer to life—arms tightly wrapped around me, hauling me up my driveway, small hands winding bandages around my thigh, the ugly chandelier in my living room going in and out of focus while whispered words floated to my ears.

"All right, rock star. You're not dying on me tonight."

She brought me to my house like I begged her to. Tried to fix me herself.

"Lucky break," Sol muses, scratching at his beard. "Who knows if that dude would've taken you all the way out if you hadn't gotten away."

Something tells me he wouldn't have. I don't think he ever meant to shoot me in the first place.

Guilt tunnels through me, mingling with the residual pain. I glance out the window, up toward the sky that's finally clear and swimming with ethereal white clouds.

I recall standing in that empty parking lot after Solomon

broke the news that he didn't have my money. Again. I looked up at the star-freckled sky and swirling snow, waiting for a piano to get dropped on me after my car refused to start.

There was no piano. No cosmic punchline.

No miracle either.

But as I peer down at the wad of money on my lap, I decide this is as close to a miracle as I'm going to get.

Minutes later, Solomon pulls up to my faded blue gable-roof ranch. It's about the size of a shoebox and has as much charm as a gas station bathroom.

Too soon, my brain chides.

"Alrighty, my man." Sol pops the gearshift into Park and unlocks the door. "Keep me posted. If you need anything, you know my number."

And thank fuck for that. If I hadn't known his number, I likely would have found myself walking the twelve-mile commute home on a bum leg.

"Thanks again." I force a smile, holding up the envelope full of cash. "Appreciate everything."

"You still crankin' out custom guitars?" He nods at the house. "You should sell that shit. Maybe you can double those funds by the time you're back in the warehouse spinning oak and cedar into an upper-middle class mom's dream credenza."

"Yeah, I'm working on it. I'll have extra time to get things sorted."

"Do it. You've got talent, Chase."

I send him another smile, less forced this time. "Thanks. I'll keep in touch." It takes a grotesque amount of energy to push the door open, collect my crutches, and plant my feet on the snow-dusted curb. Close to ten inches have been barfed all over my front lawn, but at least a neighbor stopped by to clear the driveway for my invisible, nonworking car. "See you."

He offers a quick wave before peeling down the residential street, leaving me teetering in front of my house with an empty feeling in my gut.

Back to the grind.

I manage the trek up to my porch, locate the silver key from under the dirty welcome mat, and push inside. Toaster greets me right away, sailing from the couch and circling my legs with eager whimpers. "Hey, buddy. Missed you too." It takes too much effort to bend over, so I haul my ass over to the sofa and collapse, my dog jumping up beside me.

The emptiness is temporarily squashed by the feel of companionship and familiarity. Toaster sniffs my leg, almost as if he remembers the blood pooling around it last week.

I lean back with a sigh, my fingers tangled in slightly matted fur.

The house is mostly the same, aside from looking more organized than I remember. While I keep the space sanitized, the size is equivalent to a dorm room, so clutter is inevitable. But somehow it's tidier, like a mysterious housecleaner zipped through in my absence, picking up stray jackets off the floor, fluffing pillows, disposing of a few empty beer cans, and even folding two of Stella's old quilts into neat stacks on the adjacent loveseat.

Definitely not Rock.

Blowing out a breath, I glance at the four guitars lined up against the far wall, unfinished yet so close to completion I can almost taste it. The bodies are sanded smooth, the curves just right, but I still need to fine-tune the neck profiles, wire the electronics, and perfect the finish.

There's also the branding, logo, website, and the way I'll convince people that these aren't just guitars; they're something special. Something worth owning.

I may have a busted leg and legal hassles on the horizon, but my mind is sharp, my dreams are big, and my hands work just fine. It's fucking time.

Standing from the couch to let Toaster out for a potty break, I decide that my plan will be to sleep for the next twelve hours, then catch up on bills before I lose water and power.

Toaster follows me to the sliding door off the kitchen and disappears outside, swallowed by snow and winter air. I take a few minutes to eye my guitars, new ideas and technological advances brimming to life, before letting my dog in and retreating back to the living room.

I stall, staring down at the worn couch cushions.

More memories wash over me—a bleary picture of dark hair and crystalline eyes, the sensation of chilled fingers hooking around my hand, and songs I recognize but can't place. Pretty sure I passed out on this couch. Nearly died. But the blood has faded into the upholstery, almost like someone tried to scrub away the stains.

Huh.

Just as I go to sit down, my attention snags on my missing wallet resting on the coffee table, a little napkin beside it. Inching closer, I gaze at the black ink, squinting, trying to process the smeared words and unfamiliar handwriting.

A warm tickle travels through me and shocks my heart.

Every word is a defibrillator paddle, zapping electricity to my chest and giving me new life. Tiny waves of second chances.

Picking up the note, I read it again, again, again.

I read it every hour, on the hour, over the course of the next two days.

I read it until I start to believe it.

All the best songs have bridges
The strongest ones don't burn

CHAPTER 5
Annalise

"Everybody, stay calm!" Famous last words, of course. In fact, I'm apt to believe that phrase was intended to trigger the exact opposite reaction in people. "I've got it taken care of!"

I say this, knowing I certainly do not have it taken care of.

A spray of blood lands on my teased hair and patterned bow.

A woman ducks underneath a dining table, taking her plate of pancakes and homemade maple syrup with her.

Two little girls bounce in the cherry-red booth, one giggling and pointing, the other banshee-screaming into her chocolate milk with her hands over her eyes.

The goldfinch arches overhead, swerving left and right, another trickling of blood from her injured wing dappling the black-and-white checkered floor. Kenna hides in the corner, covertly recording the chaos for social media clout. She sends me a toothy grin and a thumbs-up as I lift my pleated skirt and hightail it over to where the bird has landed on an older gentleman's table while he casually sips his coffee and reads the newspaper.

"So sorry," I say, out of breath, inching toward the bird. "Can I just…?"

He nods, perusing the sports column. "Mind if I get a refill, darling?"

Blinking, I attempt to hold the smile as my attention shifts between the man and the bird. "Absolutely. It's on the house."

"You're a gem."

"Just give me…one…second—" My hands extend, successfully cupping around the tiny creature until she's nestled between my palms. "Got you!"

A few cheers echo throughout the restaurant.

I beam brightly, moving across the floor in my chunky heels. "Everyone's meal will be comped today! So sorry for the inconvenience."

Barreling toward the front door, I hold the bird close to my chest, grazing the pad of my thumb over her silken body. The sky is gray and colorless today, the air colder than our freezer-burned calamari. A gust of icy wind steals my breath as I land on the front stoop, the door slamming closed behind me. The bird startles, burrowing into my hands. "It's okay, little one. You're safe now."

I take a moment to inspect her wing. It's bent at an odd angle, and a thin line of blood stains the delicate feathers. Not a lot, but enough to make my stomach twist.

"You're tougher than you look, aren't you?" I murmur, shielding her from the wind. She trembles against my palms, her frail chest rising and falling in rapid, uneven beats.

I scan the street, but there's nowhere safe to take her. No vet nearby, no time to find a wildlife rescue. My options are limited, so I go with the best one I have.

I rip off my apron and create a makeshift nest, tucking her inside to keep her warm.

"I know this isn't ideal. But you're gonna have to trust me for a little while." Thinking quickly, I march over to Alex's car in the parking lot and place her on the floor of the passenger seat, hoping she'll hang on until my shift is up in an hour. Then I'll need a better plan.

A sweet, songful chirp sees me off, wrapping my heart in a tender hug.

As I jog back over to the restaurant, my brain conjures up poetic words, as it often does. It's always spinning with rhymes, haikus, and makeshift lyrics. I've never been great at math, but give me adjectives, adverbs, and alliteration, and I'll spin it into something meaningful.

I rush back through the diner, my eyes meeting with Kenna's as she refills the newspaper man's mug of coffee.

"What the hell?" she mouths to me, her box-dyed blond hair reflecting off the ceiling lights, a contrast to her warm, golden skin.

I stretch a strained smile and wave her off, my anxiety spiking as I approach the kitchen. Alex is going to be pissed.

The double-swing door pushes open, and sure enough—

"Annalise, what the fuck? Where've you been?" Alex is tenser than a coiled spring as he looms over the industrial stove, sweating bullets, his hair pulled back into a small bun at the nape of his neck. "All these orders are backing up and getting cold. You're pissing me the fuck off."

"One minute!" I reach for a square napkin and scribble down the new words brewing in my mind before they leave me. Fetching a fresh apron, I tuck the scrap of paper into my front pocket, eager to add it to my growing mountain of random napkin poems.

> *Bleak skies and shattered wings*
> *And still she sings*
> *Hope shines brightest in fragile things*

"Sorry," I call out, returning to the expo window that's already filled with orders waiting to be expedited. "We had a situation."

"What situation?" He hollers over at Maurice tending to the deep fryer. "I need that fried chicken five minutes ago. Jesus."

"On it, Chef!"

I read through the tickets, my chest constricting, knowing how behind we are after the ten-plus minute bird fiasco. "There was a bird bleeding all over the dining room. I took care of it."

"Took care of it? Why didn't you ask the maintenance guy, whatever-the-fuck his name is?"

"Bradley." My lips purse. "I was already there. I panicked."

He grumbles under his breath. "All American, table seven."

Another order of hot food slides onto the metal shelf. Panic grips me for a beat as I stare at the array of plates and drinks, feeling overwhelmed, too clogged up to get back on track.

I'm twenty-one years old, and this isn't how I envisioned my life: pulling double shifts at my boyfriend's restaurant, getting screamed at on the daily, going home with sore feet, greasy skin, a bruised ego, and a dying sense of self-worth.

I just want to write. Breathe music, words, and experiences.

Live.

A spatula clatters to the countertop, making me flinch.

"What the actual fuck?" Alex shoots me a death glare from the kitchen, his back rippling, shoulders drawn tight. "Why are you just standing there? Move!"

Hot tears lance my eyes as I scramble to catch up. "Sorry. I'm moving."

Plastering on a fake smile, I grab a tray and pivot back to the dining area.

There is frustrated, mean Alex, and there is kind, attentive Alex.

As the days press on and the hours at the restaurant grow longer and more tiresome, the man I love with all my heart—since the day we played in the sand together at the neighborhood park—becomes a man I don't even know anymore.

The good and bad days bleed together, the bad outshining the sweeter moments, eclipsing the late-night cuddle fests and long talks over cheap Moscato, and erasing all the glorious, defining moments along the way.

I'm in a constant state of grieving, and grief on its own is hard enough. But when grief masquerades as guilt, there is no telling the damage it will do.

That's why I stay.

That's why I'll always stay.

Alex is on break behind the restaurant, puffing on a cigarette as he leans back against the timeworn, ruddy brick. When he spots me, he lets out a long sigh and flicks ashes to the cement. "Hey."

"Hey," I reply, zipping up my puffer coat. "Are you okay?"

"Another day, another dollar." He blows out a smoky breath. "Sorry I lost my shit on you. It's been a morning."

"I understand."

"You good?"

Nodding, I cross my arms to counter the chill in the air. "Yeah. My shift is up. I'll be back for tonight's dinner service."

"Need a ride?"

"Uber is on the way."

"Cool." Alex studies me under the overcast sky, his pale-green irises gleaming with suppressed emotion. Then he swallows, glances down at his gray performance sneakers. "You did good today. Caught back up like a champ."

My lips pucker as I peer up at the overhead signage: *Charlie Barker's*. The name is a nod to his old family dog, a lanky labrador retriever who lived till he was sixteen years old. Alex always had big dreams of owning a restaurant—one he took over from his father after his parents moved out of the country—but now I don't think he loves it like he used to. The culmination of stress, debt, and dwindling free time is swallowing his already fractured soul, adding enormous strain to our relationship. It's a burden. A headache with no relief in sight. And when dreams become a curse, they lose their luster, turning into something he's stuck with rather than something honorable he's worked for.

"Thanks," I murmur, gnawing on my lip. "Maybe we can start that new show after we close up tonight. The thriller one."

"Yeah, sounds good. The freezer is stocked with your favorite ice cream."

"It's a date." I smile a little sadly. "Well, I'm taking off. I'll see you later."

"Are you headed home?"

"In a bit. I'm pet-sitting for one of my old neighbors." Not technically a lie. "I'll probably get a nap in before I circle back here at four."

His eyes narrow with a trace of suspicion before he shakes it off. "All right. Have fun."

I pivot to leave, but his voice pulls me back.

"Annalise."

Pausing, I tilt my head over my shoulder, glancing at him. "Yeah?"

"Remember when you ate that entire carton of Amaretto cherry ice cream because you didn't want the night to end? You figured if you just kept eating it, we'd have no choice but to stay up, fighting sleep, talking about pointless bullshit, laughing until we couldn't breathe." The corner of his mouth ticks up, and a tired laugh slips free. "I miss that."

I spin all the way around, gripping the handle of my purse, staring at him like I haven't seen his face in years. "I puked in your lap," I choke out, nostalgia glittering in my eyes.

He inhales deeply and lifts his chin, drinking in the muddy sky. "Worth it."

My heart squeezes. A thorny fist around the tattered valves.

"Thailand, huh?" he says.

Warmth slithers through my chest, knowing he remembers my ridiculous text-a-thon that night. "Oh…yeah. Sorry, I was a little drunk. But it would be fun, right?"

"Yeah. It would be." He tosses the half-smoked cigarette to the concrete and kicks at a loose rock. "We'll talk. I gotta get back to work. I love you."

"Love you too." Our eyes meet for a fleeting moment before I turn away, stride to Alex's car to fetch the bird, and wait for the Uber to pull up.

It's a quick drive to Silverleaf.

As the sedan winds through the neighborhood, I glance at the tiny creature nestled in my coffee-stained apron. The heater is on full blast, blowing warm air against her frame.

"What should I name you?" My hands hold her steady on my lap, my attention panning from the bird to the blue house approaching on the right.

Names and titles are the hardest for me. I could probably write a dissertation on everything under the sun, but force me to give it a name, and I'll freeze up.

They are permanent. Forever.

But one name coasts across my mind like it's meant to be. "Haiku," I murmur.

The driver puts the car in Park. "This the place?"

Haiku lets out a sharp chirp, pulling a twitch from my lips. I don't know how long I'll get to keep her.

But first there's another living being who needs me.

"Yep. Thanks so much for making a pit stop. I'll only be a few minutes." I take a calming breath, setting the little bundle on the floor. "Can you, um…keep an eye on my bird?"

"Yeah, sure." The twenty-something guy shrugs and starts playing on his phone.

After hopping out of the car, I wander up the now-familiar driveway, pluck the house key from the stoop, and step inside.

The lingering scent of coffee wafts around me, wrinkling my nose. Someone must have been by recently.

A neighbor?

"Hello?" I call out, just in case. The lights are off, the house in similar condition to how it was forty-eight hours ago. I wasn't sure if I could make it over here yesterday, so I left out a giant pot of water, extra food, and pee pads strewn across the kitchen floor.

No one answers me, but a sable-and-white ball of fur on four legs races out from the primary bedroom, tail wagging, ears jutted toward the ceiling.

A giant smile spreads across my face as I bend down, allowing the dog to crash into me and topple me backward. I laugh, my hands roaming over Toaster's body, my fingers scratching, massaging. "You look like you're plumping up already. Must be all those Frosty Paws."

His wet tongue bathes my hands and arms in kisses.

Rising to my feet, I march into the kitchen, my heels clicking against the tile. I survey the small space for the plastic container of kibble, but someone must have moved it.

Hmm.

I think about Chase. Where he is, how he's doing, and if he had friends and family after all. Surely there's someone.

Maybe he's self-isolated to the point of thinking he's alone in the world, when in reality, somebody is out there, just waiting for him to let them in again.

The police haven't reached out since Tag swore it was all a mistake, that I willingly drove the gunshot victim. And even if they knew anything, why would they tell me? I'm nobody to him. Just a stranger on the periphery, waiting for news that won't come.

A chill burrows in my bones. I haven't discussed getting a dog with Alex, but I've already made up my mind: if Chase doesn't come home, Toaster will be mine.

I promised.

"Okay, let's see where someone put your—" When I twist back to face the living room, I let out a terrified shriek. "Holy shit!"

Chase.

He's standing at the edge of the hallway in a pair of pajama shorts, his hair sticking up in all directions, and his eyes wide with shock.

I cup a hand around my mouth and breathe out, "Oh my God. You're alive."

CHAPTER 6
Chase

The girl.

She's in my house.

Frozen with confusion, I trail my gaze over her, from her poof of teased hair, to her amethyst lips, to her bulky black heels clicking against my kitchen floor as she fidgets in place. My throat constricts when I meet her eyes again. "Annie, right?"

She hesitates, slowly dropping her arm to her side as she assesses me. Her focus lingers on my bare chest for a second longer than she seems comfortable with before panning down to the gnarly wound taking over my upper thigh, wrapped in gauze and bandages. "Um, yeah..." she says, a shell-shocked whisper. "That's right."

I nod, rolling my tongue against my cheek.

I'm at a loss. I should say something, apologize, thank her. But

I can't help but wonder if she's here to turn me in. The notion ices my blood, though I wouldn't blame her if she decided to call the cops. I'd go willingly.

My lips part to speak, but whatever word vomit might spill free is eclipsed by her voice.

"I smell like a deep fryer," she blurts. "I'm so sorry."

This takes me off guard. Toaster's overgrown nails clack against the faux-wood planks as he paces around the dining table, hunting down month-old muffin crumbs. "You're…apologizing." A frown creases, and I stare at her, stunned. "To me."

She wrings her hands together, nails tipped with robin's-egg blue. "I guess. I broke into your house, reeking of hash browns and breakfast burritos."

I drag a hand over my jaw, scratching at the grown-out stubble, stalling.

Annie's cheeks redden by the second, her eyes betraying her as they flick downward—once, twice—before she snaps out of it. She pivots sharply, tucking her hair behind her ears with blatant aggression, like she's trying to reset herself.

"Uh, sorry…" Glancing over my shoulder, I do a double take at the wall hook, falter, then lumber over to the front door to snag a zip-up hoodie off the coat knob. I shove my arms into the sleeve holes and clear my throat. "Wasn't expecting company."

"Right. Of course you weren't. I just…" Her voice trails off, a tangible awkwardness filling the space between us.

She doesn't know me, and I don't know her. But here she is, standing in my house, trembling in her chunky heels, and staring at me with glazed blue eyes. Meanwhile, I'm half naked, looking like I just clawed my way out of a coma. I sort of did.

"I was taking care of your dog while you were in the hospital. I didn't realize they'd let you out, or if you even…"

Survived.

She starts chewing on her thumbnail.

I study her, rake a hand through my hair, though it does nothing to tame the mess. "Shit," I mutter.

"Yeah. I should go—"

"No, wait." Taking a sharp step forward, I nearly hiss through my teeth as I tip against the wall and remove pressure off my battered leg. "I…owe you an apology. Of epic proportions," I say. "Seriously. I don't even know where to start, but that night was like a fucked-up fever dream, and I'm really sorry I dragged you into it. I honestly wondered if I made you up."

That dream fizzes beneath the surface of my memories.

Stella's voice. Annie's voice. Faraway songs.

Crystal-blue water morphing into the same colored eyes boring into mine.

She continues to shuffle in place. "Well, surprise. I'm real." It looks like she's about to do a little twirl to showcase her existence, but she stops herself.

Annie stares at me like I'm an otherworldly being. An alien, or a divine deity, or one of those sickishly pale Victorian-era children that show up in your dreams to warn you about impending doom.

I shake my head, dislodging the haze. "I don't know how to thank you. For everything."

"You don't have to thank me."

"You literally saved my life. And took care of my dog. And…" I glance around the tidy space. "Cleaned my house?"

She rubs her lips together and shrugs. "I did what any decent human being would do."

"I kidnapped you. Stole your car. Probably gave you lifelong PTSD." The puzzled frown deepens. "I don't think most human beings would be so forgiving."

"I mean, I can't speak for the majority of the population, but I can speak for myself. I couldn't *not* do those things. It's not in my nature to stand by idly and watch someone drown. Self-inflicted or not," she says softly, glancing away. "So, you're welcome. Every one of us hits rock bottom at some point, and all we can do is hope someone is there to help pull us out. You just happened to steal the right car."

Jesus.

I'm starting to question if she's real again. A metallic buzzing whirrs between my ears, causing my temples to pound.

I don't respond; I don't know how to.

As the silence stretches, I watch as she peers over at the wall I'm leaning against, her attention skimming the four guitars propped up against it. Guitars I've built. She blinks at them, taking in the hand-carved bodies and colorful lacquers. "Do you play? Or just build them?" she wonders.

I stuff my hands into the pockets of my hoodie. "I play. It's just a hobby."

"My brother plays too. He's good. Really good." She snags her lip between her teeth, chewing on it. "Tag. I think you met him briefly that night."

"Yeah."

The doo-wop guy. Old-school music seeped from the car when he hopped out of the driver's seat and joined me at the entrance. He looked more like a grungy rocker than someone with a sixties playlist, but I'm not one to judge.

"It's his dream to start a band one day and tour the world. He does a few solo gigs around town. Breweries, coffee shops. Mostly covers."

I analyze her, wondering where she's going with that.

"You should come watch him play sometime."

"Um…" I send her a quick headshake, the offer seeping in like half-set grout.

She laughs lightly, embarrassed. "Sorry. That was weird."

"A little. Mostly because I suspect your brother wants me dead."

"Maybe, but that's fixable."

My head tilts to the side as I try to read her pale-sky eyes shimmering with uncertainty. Or maybe it's certainty. It's like she truly believes fate intervened that night and we were meant to cross paths. And now she wants to summon me into her social circle. Her life.

"I'm not much of a people person these days," I admit, lifting from the wall. I half limp over to the couch and collapse with a pained exhale. "And you realize I'm kind of a felon, right?"

Her nose scrunches. "Are you, though? In the eyes of the law? We never reported the car stolen. I convinced my brother to tell the cops I drove you willingly."

"Still struggling to understand that."

"You don't need to understand. It is what it is. You had enough on your plate, death being at the forefront."

"I'm also still wondering if I'm hallucinating."

It's as if she can't help herself—she does the twirl. "Still real."

One side of my mouth quirks up with the barest smile before it fades. "Listen, Annie…I'm not really in a good place right now, as you've noticed. I'm not sure it's a good idea to pal around with the people I've victimized. But I appreciate the invitation."

She takes a small step forward as Toaster flies past her and joins me on the couch. "Yeah, of course. It was a dumb idea."

"It wasn't. I just—"

"I get it." She looks around the room one more time, her shoulders deflating. "Anyway, my ride is waiting, so I'll get out of your hair. I'm glad you're okay."

Moving to the front door, looking dejected, she stops short when I call out to her one more time.

"Hey."

Annie blinks down at the dingy carpet in my living room before turning to glance at me.

"You left that note, didn't you?" I ask.

Her cheeks pinken again as she clears her throat with a nod. "Yeah. I do that sometimes."

"Leave strangers little words of encouragement after they abduct and traumatize you?"

"Write," she corrects, smiling faintly. "Lyrics, poems. You know, whenever the muse strikes."

I lean back against the cushions, burying my hand in Toaster's fur. "Well, it meant a lot. What you said."

My chest spasms at the memory of the words she left behind, scribbled on a wrinkled napkin leftover from a food-delivery order. I wasn't expecting it. I'm not used to acts of kindness.

Undeserved, at that.

"Good. I'm happy to hear that," she replies.

"You were kind to me," I continue, inching forward, catching her eyes before she disappears for good. If this is the last time I ever see her, she needs to know it mattered. That someone like her looked at someone like me and didn't turn the other way. "Why?"

Annie doesn't miss a beat. Her lips curl up with a flash of teeth. "Because kindness is a testament to our own character. It's not about external factors. If it ever feels difficult to be kind, we need to look within."

My eyes glaze over as I stare at her, processing. Warm tendrils of light journey through me, curling around each rib. I don't say anything with words, but hers have infiltrated. Punctured tiny pinholes in my armor.

Before turning away, she leaves me with a final thought, almost like a lifeline. Just in case. "Tag plays at that café off Devlin Street every Thursday night at seven. You know…if you're ever bored."

Then she walks away, swallowed by the afternoon light, her violet-striped hair bouncing at her back.

If I were anyone else, I'd call after her. Tell her I'll be there, that I'm always bored, eternally looking for a telltale spark.

But I don't.

I just sit there, holding on to her words like a matchstick in the dark.

Two weeks pass me by, filled with restless nights, stiff muscles, and the persistent, nagging ache in my thigh that no amount of ignoring can shake. The first few days were the worst, every movement a reminder that I took a bullet and that my body isn't bouncing back the way I want it to. That I'm not invincible.

The follow-up appointments are tedious. The doctor pokes at the wound, asks about my pain levels, and reminds me to "take it easy"—as if I have any say in the matter. Stitches out, more bandages. More rules about what I can and can't do.

At home, I go through the motions, begrudgingly following my physical therapist's instructions. Push too hard, and my leg reminds me that I'm fucked. Laze around, and my brain tells me I'm useless. It's a constant battle, one I keep losing.

Somewhere in the clusterfuck of it all, I pick up a guitar again. My fingers move easier than my legs do, and for a few minutes at a time, I forget that I'm stuck in this body that refuses to cooperate. I can sink into something that still feels like mine.

But the music always stops, and reality sets back in.

I'm still partially behind on rent, using the cash from Solomon to catch up on utilities, stock the fridge and freezer, and fix my car. Thankfully, my landlord is a little old lady who was definitely a saint in a past life.

I'm not allowed to drive for another two weeks, so some of the money is going to rideshares to take me to and from my appointments.

But today I've landed somewhere else.

Somewhere I probably shouldn't be.

The familiar jingle bell greets me like a bone-deep trigger. My skin starts to sweat as I use my crutches to drag my weight through the entrance, my attention landing on a middle-aged woman behind the counter, her dark hair threaded with glints of silver. There's another woman beside her with similar features. Mid-twenties, maybe.

Mother and daughter.

Together they sift through the register, talking among themselves, glancing up with smiles as I struggle to keep myself upright.

"Good afternoon," the younger woman calls out.

I hesitate, my heart pounding in my chest.

Invisible voices scream at me to turn the other way, to book it before they realize who I am. The damage I've caused. But guilt is a fucking parasite, and I need to do whatever I can to relieve myself of its weight. To set it free.

"Um, hey." Slowly, I inch toward the checkout station, leaning my crutches against the counter topped with an assortment of panic-buys. Fishing through my pockets, I pull out a handful of change.

Three dollars and twenty-seven cents.

I place it on the counter and meet the daughter's eyes.

Her smile falters. "Are you…buying something?"

"Yeah. Sort of. I'm…" Flashbacks trickle through me. Fluorescent lights streak across my vision, disorienting me. Gun smoke. Clipped, garbled words. Fiery pain sheathed in a crimson haze. "I was here a few weeks ago. I owe you for a can of dog food."

The older woman lets out a squeak. A strangled, choking sound.

"I'm sorry," I whisper. "For everything."

The daughter's face shifts in an instant, smile gone. Her whole body tightens like a bowstring as she rounds the counter.

"Get out," she snaps, standing right in front of me, her voice low but shaking. "You need to leave."

"I'm so sorry—"

"You ruined our lives. Do you realize that? My father is under investigation. We're drowning in legal fees."

I force a swallow. "I'm not pressing charges."

"That's not the point," she grits out. "He never meant to hurt anyone. We've been robbed three times this year, and he's been working double shifts just to pay off my medical school loans. This store is all we have. Now we could lose everything."

"Parvati…" The older woman rushes over, placing a palm on her daughter's shoulder.

"I'm going to rectify that," I say, extending a hand like a peace offering. I can hardly stay upright, partly from my pulsing leg, but mostly from the devastation I feel soaking into every pocket of this gas station, trying to pull me under. "I will, I promise. It was an accident."

"Stealing is not an accident." She steps two inches closer. "Do you know how terrified he was going to work every day for the past few months? He didn't have a choice. But you did."

"I didn't mean—"

"I can't believe you had the nerve to show your face here."

"I'm—"

"Leave. Right now."

The mother says nothing, just stares at me with tightly drawn lips and wide, glossy eyes. I glance between them. I see their pain, feel it as if it were my own.

There's nothing more I can say.

I send them a dejected nod, reach for my crutches, and haul myself out the door.

But I'll make this right. Someday.

When my guitar business takes off. When the money starts

rolling in. When the full debt has been paid and they stop hating me.

Or maybe when I stop hating myself.

Whichever comes first.

CHAPTER 7
Annalise

THREE MONTHS LATER

The mid-April breeze catches my hair as I approach the entrance to the café, Kenna right behind me. I flatten the skirt of my lavender top-waist swing dress, then fiddle with the multistrand gold necklaces draped around my neck.

Kenna takes a final drag from her iridescent rainbow vape pen, blowing out a cloud of something fruity, before hiding it away in her purse. "I live for Thursday nights, you know. Coffee and bangers with my bestie. So wholesome."

I yank open the main door, and we shuffle inside. "It's definitely my favorite night."

Tag is setting up on the small, one-person platform, a

microphone situated in front of him as his guitar case lies sprawled open near his feet. A proud smile blooms on my face.

"Damn. Your brother looks positively giddy up there." Kenna moves to the counter to order her usual cinnamon cortado.

I peer across the room at Tag again—no smile, no twinkle in his eyes. Giddy is not the adjective I'd choose. He's the poster child for brooding musician.

"It's a shame my vocal contributions didn't work out," she continues, swiping her card through the reader. "We could've made a good team."

"I love you, but your singing voice is akin to a dying giraffe."

Kenna frowns. "Do giraffes make noise?"

"Probably when they're dying."

Nodding, she discards the receipt and moves aside so I can place my order. A few wayward strings pluck from the front of the café as my brother drops to the stool, doing a quick tuning.

"How come you don't sing with him?" Kenna asks.

I glance at my best friend while ordering a vanilla latte with no foam. "You know I hardly have time for these outings, let alone vocal practice. I just sing for fun."

"You're so good at it. If I had your voice, I'd have a Spotify profile, a YouTube channel, and a website with merch, a mailing list, and a fan club up and running."

My brain shuts down at the mere thought. "At least I'll know who to hire if anything changes."

She takes a big sip of her coffee, wincing when it burns her tongue. "I feel like you're wasting your potential at the restaurant. Respectfully."

"You work there too."

"That's because I'm only good at two things: shmoozing the late-seventies retirees with a penchant for competitive bird-watching, and rocking those cute retro aprons." She pauses, taking another hesitant sip. "I can also throw tennis balls with my toes. They're prehensile. But I don't foresee any beneficial uses for that."

"I can tie a cherry stem with my tongue." I collect my coffee, and we saunter through the café, looking for an empty table. "One hundred percent success rate."

"There are many beneficial uses for that."

As we locate a table closest to the makeshift stage, I send a cheerful wave to my brother. He spots me, offers me a nod, and pops a pick between his teeth. He's in the zone.

I set my purse down on the two-person high-top table, assessing the crowd. Families are scattered about, toddler-age children glued to electronic devices while their sleep-deprived parents suck down espresso and attempt to partake in a rare moment of socializing.

My eyes scan the room.

A few college girls, musician types eager to take notes on Tag's performance, an elderly couple bonding over matcha, and—

I blink. Do a double take.

My jaw drops.

No way.

Shock slices me from chest to toes as I zero in on the familiar man at the back of the room. His attention is fixed on his cell phone, one leg bobbing up and down under the table.

A black hoodie, dark-wash jeans, dirt-smudged boots.

Messy waves of caramel hair and golden-brown eyes to match. Those eyes lift, flicking in my direction.

Our gazes lock.

I waste no time snatching Kenna by the wrist and hauling her over to the man I never thought I'd see again. Especially not here.

"Whoa, whoa, these heels are not made for marathons," Kenna huffs out, scampering behind me, trying to keep up. "Are you kidnapping me?"

"No, but he might." A grin stretches as we near the table.

"Wait, what?"

Chase straightens in place, setting his phone down and skimming a hand through his hair. A silver thumb ring glints beneath the kitschy pendant light.

He looks everywhere but at me, but I can tell by the way his shoulders square, his biceps twitch, and his jaw tightens—he recognizes me.

"Oh my God. You came." We land at the edge of his table, and I watch as his gaze gradually shifts in my direction, eyes panning up the length of my dress until they settle on my stunned expression.

He swallows, leaning back in his chair, the front legs elevating. "Annie. Hey."

Kenna makes a face, and we share a look.

She kicks my shin. "Annalise. Are you going to introduce me?"

"Annalise," Chase repeats, squinting as he reads the room. "No one calls you Annie, do they?"

"You do." My smile beams brighter; I can't believe he came. "I didn't think I'd see you here."

The chair legs descend back down to the tile. "I was bored."

My eyes taper as I recall my final words to him that day before I walked out of his house. Then I clear my throat and turn to my friend. "Um, this is Chase. I told you about him."

She blinks at me, peers over at Chase. Her gaze dips to his denim-clad thigh, hidden underneath the table, before awareness splashes across her face. "Holy shit. You're the guy who kidnapped her."

The elderly couple twist around in their seats, sending us a sanctimonious look.

I finger my assortment of necklaces. "Accidental kidnapping, if we're getting technical."

"Dreamy," Kenna sighs.

Chase frowns. "Every girl's fantasy."

"You'd be surprised." My friend takes a seat across from him and extends a hand. "I'm Kenna. Annalise's best friend, coworker, and future one-woman PR firm."

Tentatively, he takes her hand, focus still aimed at me. "Chase."

Pulling back, she smooths her fingers over her wavy, bleachy blond topknot and dark roots. "She filled me in. Exciting stuff. How's your dog doing?"

"Fine."

"Kenna, can you give us a second?" I tap my foot against the earth-toned ceramic tile. "Maybe go save our seats. I'll be over in a sec."

"Yeah. Sure." With a quick turn, she sends me a look that says I need to tell her everything, immediately, no details left out.

When she floats away, I hesitate before taking a seat in her abandoned chair. I rub my lips together. Chase doesn't say anything, appearing decidedly out of place, out of his element, and out of words. Can't say I blame him; it was brave of him to show.

Curiosity spurs my tongue. "Are you here to watch Tag play?"

He looks down and swipes invisible crumbs off the tabletop, tapping his thumb ring against the surface. "Yeah. Figured it was time to venture out into the world."

"Adulting is hard, I know." I prop my chin in my palm with a sincere smile. "How's your leg? Back to normal?"

"Questionable. Still hurts, but I'm over the worst of it." He glances at me, and our eyes hold for several heartbeats before his brows lower. "Actually, I don't know why I came."

My breath catches, and my smile slips. I drop my forearms on the table and start drumming my fingernails. "Well, I bewitched you with the prospect of good music. You're a music guy. The math checks out."

"Right," he says. "The music."

There's an inquisitive look in his eyes that I can't quite decipher. Like he's weighing something, turning it over in his mind.

Anxiety clogs my throat when I realize it's possible he didn't come for the music.

He may have come for me.

I should tell him I have a boyfriend, but the words stick like taffy, wadded up and lodged in my throat. That feels awkward and presumptuous.

"Tag is talented," I tell him, my voice growing smaller. "You'll see."

"What about you?"

"Me?"

"I remember you singing to me that night. You were good."

My cheeks heat at the memory. "Oh, thanks. I guess I can carry a tune. But I work a lot of hours. Double shifts and such. My free time is limited."

"Where do you work?"

"Charlie Barker's. It's that diner off Fifth Street with the dog mascot on the sign."

He nods, processing the information. Then he glances around the room with an audible sigh, scratching at his jawline. "I should probably go."

Surprised, I inch back in the seat. "Why?"

"Once your brother knows I'm here, he's going to call the cops and have me arrested. I probably deserve that, but—"

"No. He won't."

"What makes you so sure? I doubt he's going to be as chill as your friend." Wary eyes sweep over to where Tag tests the microphone and strums the opening chords to a City and Colour song.

"Because he's my brother and we're a team. I told him not to. It's done."

Our eyes meet.

And then words tumble through me like snowflakes at dusk, delicate and pure.

It's instant. Effortless.

Honeycomb eyes
Music in the air
Broken strings hum
A song of despair

"Hold that thought." I leap from the chair and race to the counter where a pile of napkins rests beside flavored syrups and plastic straws. An associate hands me the pen I request, and I head back to the table to scribble down the disjointed poem.

"What are you doing?" Chase stares at my moving hand.

I scoop up the napkin and stuff it in my skirt pocket, hiding it away. "Inspiration strikes unexpectedly sometimes. I have a treasure trove of these things at home. It drives—"

Alex nuts.

But my words clip off prematurely.

"Anyway, ignore me," I continue, eager to change the subject. "Do you sing?"

He hesitates. "Not really. I mean, I can, I guess…but I don't."

"That's unfortunate."

The look he sends me tells me he agrees.

Tag continues to play, his raspy voice filling the room as people watch, talking among themselves and sipping overpriced lattes. I glance over at Kenna, who gawks at us from twenty feet away, looking impatient as she pulses her eyebrows at me.

I pivot back to Chase. "Did you want to come sit with us?"

"Uh…"

Jumping off the seat again, I signal him to follow. "Come on. I'll grab another chair."

He moves in behind me, and I get a whiff of something smoky and earthy, like leather and burnt sandalwood, fused with a touch of citrus.

When he rolls up the sleeves of his hoodie, I sneak a peek at his guitar tattoo, a warm, kismet feeling coiling in my chest.

"We're moving closer to the person who wants me dead," he notes, his posture stiff as he shoves his hands into his pockets and follows me toward the table near the platform.

"Kenna would never. She's a lover, not a fighter." I shoot him a teasing grin. "Actually, she's both. But something tells me you're safe."

I nearly get a smirk out of him.

Maybe I'll get a real smile one of these days.

Dragging a third chair to the table, I peer over at Tag, who furrows his brow and shakes his head through the chorus, silently asking me who the hell the guy is.

I spin away and reach for my lukewarm coffee as Chase settles into his seat, his head bowed.

"So, Chase, tell me about yourself. Are you a musician too?" Kenna's vape pen materializes out of nowhere, and she points it in his direction like a mini microphone.

"Put that away," I scold, shoving her arm back. "You're not allowed to have that in here."

"We're a table of rebels. It's fine." She tosses the vape back into her purse.

Chase folds his hands on the table, pursing his lips. "I build guitars. Just sold my first one on Reverb."

"No shit?" I hop onto the seat and swivel to face him. "That's impressive."

"It's something. Still a long way to go."

"You and Tag should start a band together." Kenna's espresso-tinged eyes light up. "That would be something, wouldn't it?"

We both stare at her, waiting for the third arm to appear.

"I mean, I didn't say it was a good idea. Just that it was something."

Chase scratches the back of his head. "Right."

I clear my throat. "I'm not sure if that's—" I'm cut off when my phone starts vibrating from my purse. "Sorry. One sec."

Fishing it out, I glance at the screen.

Alex: Hi my love. I cooked your favorite dinner. Spicy salmon and Brussel sprouts.

My chest tightens, my thumbs swiping across the keyboard.

Me: You're so sweet! But it's Thursday, and you know I'll be home late tonight… ☹
Alex: So you're not eating with me?
Me: Kenna and I usually grab food here at the café, remember? But I can skip that tonight and head out early. Maybe keep it warm for me? Just give me an hour. Muah!

The anxiety flourishes as I watch his bubbles come to life, pause, then start dancing again.

Finally:

Alex: Forget it. I'll toss it. Have fun.

My eyes burn.
Dammit.

Blowing out a breath, I glance between Kenna and Chase as my friend fills him in on her extensive collection of rare succulents, her soft Spanish lilt quieting the unease barreling through me.

Chase pretends to act invested as he nods at random intervals, but I can tell he's not paying attention. He's focused on the music. His eyes close, long lashes fluttering as if the acoustic strings are cutting through the sound of Kenna's voice and resonating deep inside him. A hand taps against his uninjured thigh. His leg bobs in perfect time, body swaying slightly to the beat.

For a moment, Alex fades away. The text messages dissolve, and my anxiety peters out like smoke curling from a snuffed out candle.

He's moved by it.

He's moved in the same way Tag is moved.

The same way I'm moved.

It's clear he didn't come tonight because of me—he came for the music.

Heaving in a breath, I finally turn back to my phone.

Me: I'll leave now. Thank you for cooking and I'll see you soon. 🩵🩵

Alex opens the message but doesn't respond.

Swallowing the bone-dry lump in my throat, I glance up and pocket my phone. "Hey, listen, I need to head out early. I know I suck. I'm sorry."

Kenna jolts from her seat. "I got you."

"No, please stay. Enjoy the show. Tell Tag I'll catch him next time."

"I drove you here. I'm not making you pay for an Uber back." Collecting her purse, Kenna does some sort of hand gesture to Tag to alert him of our departure.

She knows why I need to go.

She always knows—we just don't talk about it anymore.

Chase studies Kenna for a beat before his gaze shifts to me, searching. "Everything okay?"

"Yeah. Yes, of course. Something came up." I muster a small smile, though my heart wilts like a sad, sunless petal. The truth is, I don't want to leave. Chase finally showed up, and I'm walking out before my brother's even finished his second song.

I don't know if he'll show up next week.

Once again, I wonder if this is the last time I'll ever see him.

His eyes flicker with something. Curiosity, concern. "You sure?"

"I'm sure. Thank you for coming tonight. I'm sorry to cut it short."

"You never have to apologize to me."

I hesitate. "I just feel like…" My sentence trails off. For once, I can't catch any words.

As Kenna moves toward the exit, I snatch up my purse, loathing the hot pressure that swells behind my eyes.

Before I retreat, I pause, placing my hand on Chase's shoulder, feeling his muscles tighten and strain. "Come back next week."

He meets my eyes and holds before looking away and palming the nape of his neck. "Yeah, I don't know. I think—"

"Please."

Another glance. Another hold.

Finally, he relents with a single nod.

Relief spirals through me, golden and warm. I shouldn't want to see him again, not after everything that happened between us. But I think he needs this. This music, this outlet.

He needs it like my brother needs it.

And I've always been a sucker for a person in need.

I look over my shoulder as I waltz away, smiling a mournful goodbye to Tag and watching as Chase stands from the table, preparing to leave.

Then I stick my hand inside the pocket of my skirt and head outside, my fingers curling around the napkin.

CHAPTER 8
Chase

A week rolls by.

It's Thursday.

Toaster sits beside me, a chew bone clasped between his paws, as I tighten the final tuning peg. The scent of sawdust and lacquer sticks to the air, mingling with the faint burn of solder from earlier. The body—a pale, arctic blue with a mahogany neck and a rosewood fingerboard—gleams under the makeshift clip-on lamp attached to a floating wall shelf.

I run a hand over the polished wood, checking for imperfections.

Satisfied, I reach for the pick resting on the table and strum a slow, resonant chord. The sound is clean, rich, carrying through the quiet room like a hymn.

Toaster abandons his bone to sniff the guitar, tail wagging.

Progress.

I'm getting closer to finishing my second guitar.

My eyes lock onto the time glowing on my wristwatch: 6:32 p.m.

I'm getting closer to a lot of things.

The busy café bustles around me as I order a vanilla latte with no foam and a hot Americano, then carry the drinks to an empty table in the back. Annie's brother traipses around the small wooden platform, a pick clasped between his teeth, a dark beanie on his head. There's a look in his eyes—determined, haunted—and I recognize the weight in them. The weight of dreams, of struggle, churning and foaming with no place to go.

Taking a seat, I collapse into a tall chair and lean back, fingering the rim of my coffee cup. Only a few minutes whiz by before the front door opens and familiar laughter fills the space.

Annie strolls inside with a smile, her friend by her side, and her hair piled up in a crown of braids, a plum-hued flower woven into the ringlets.

My stupid heart starts to race; she's fucking beautiful.

And I don't know if my coming here is because of the music, our shared connection, or because of the girl who emanates passion like a flame in the dark.

Vivid, untamed, and impossible to ignore.

It's probably all of the above. But when she finds me across the room, her smile widening, her eyes locking onto mine with a glimmer of surprise, I know which one weighs heaviest.

Fuck.

I'm out of my league.

My heart is racing, and she's still smiling.

"Chase." She's nearly out of breath as she floats away from Kenna and approaches my table. "Once again, you manage to surprise me."

"Odd, given our initial introduction."

Her eyes flash, but it's not with residual trauma or scorn. It's playful, teasing.

"Touché," she says. "I wasn't sure if you'd actually show."

"I grabbed you a coffee." I slide the latte over to her.

Last week, I heard her order as I tried to remain invisible near the register, partially hoping she wouldn't recognize me. It was difficult enough dragging my ass over here, and I wasn't sure I was ready for another face-to-face meeting with the woman I terrorized. But she spotted me instantly. And there was no anger, no resentment—only smiles and chitchat, as if we hadn't crossed paths under the most fucked-up, harrowing circumstances.

As if she'd been waiting for me to show.

Annie hesitates, eyeballing the steaming paper cup. She blinks at it like she's never seen a cup of coffee before. "Oh…thank you. That was sweet."

"No problem."

Kenna hangs back to place an order, eyeing me with interest from the counter.

Reaching for the latte and taking a sip, Annie waves her hand at the stage. "I want to introduce you to my brother."

Record scratch.

My stomach sinks.

Part of me was hoping I'd dip in and slip out before ever having to come in contact with her brother, who undoubtedly despises me.

"Don't worry," she says before I can protest, linking her small hand around my forearm and tugging me off the seat. "I talked to him. I said you might show up again and to play nice."

I'm not convinced her version of "play nice" is the same as his, but I reluctantly follow, the scent of watermelon and something flowery guiding me forward.

Tag looks up, pulling the guitar strap off his torso, his tawny, shoulder-length hair catching on the overhead light fixture as it spills from his beanie. He falters, stuffing his hands into the pockets of his jeans and sending his sister a scowl before turning his attention to me: the felonious stranger she's just thrust into his orbit.

He says nothing. Just glares at me.

The imaginary sound of a needle against vinyl morphs into a symphony of crickets.

I scrub my mop of hair, trying to summon words that will get this introduction over with. "Tag, right?"

"Yeah."

"That short for something?" I've never been much of a conversationalist, which works for me, considering I live alone, have few friends, and voluntarily cut off contact with all remaining family members.

Therefore, this is fucking painful.

A sigh leaves him as he hops off the platform and crosses his arms.

"It's short for Montague," Annie explains, acting like this

moment isn't akin to being strapped to a chair and forced to watch paint dry. Except the paint is judging me, and the chair might spontaneously combust. "Mom has this weird infatuation with Shakespeare."

"Romeo and Juliet?" I wonder, remembering how my sister used to watch the nineties adaptation all the time.

"Yes. He still hasn't forgiven her."

"Understandable." I look away, my eyes settling on absolutely nothing.

Tag clicks his tongue, addressing his sister. "You were almost Beatrice. Instead, you were named after some dead relative, while Mom had her heart set on tragic and theatrical."

Annie hums. "Sounds like I should be haunting an old middle-England mansion or something. Still pretty tragic."

"Better than being named after a guy who gets stabbed over a miscommunication."

My attention ping-pongs between them.

Tag glowers at me, his stare so sharp it might as well be the knife that took out his namesake.

Clearing my throat, I conjure up more words. "Heard you play a bit last week. You were good."

"I'm decent."

"This your full-time gig?"

"This and car detailing. Still trying to get your blood out of my upholstery."

Ouch.

I'm starting to learn how he plays nice.

Annie mimics a cough, not-so-covertly kicking his leg. "Chase is a musician too."

"We have so much in common."

I glance at his guitar, now perched on the platform. "Is that a Fylde Orsino? Don't see many of those outside of the UK."

Tag blinks, frowns, then peers down at the instrument before swinging his attention back to me. He pushes his tongue against his cheek. "It is. Good eye."

"Must've cost a pretty penny."

"Parents gifted it to me for my eighteenth."

"Chase also builds guitars," Annie adds, a levity in her voice.

I clear my throat. "I build a bunch of things. Furniture, mostly. If you ever need—"

"Great. I'll keep that in mind." Tag drops his arms at his sides and bends to retrieve the guitar. "Gotta get started. Are you sticking around this time?" His eyes are fixed on his sister now, ablaze with things unsaid.

She smooths back her hair and inches away. Her energy changes, shifting into a noticeable tension that strips her of her smile. "That's the plan."

A short nod.

Tag steps back and situates himself behind the mic, gearing up to perform.

Moments later, we're seated while Kenna fills me in on her newest succulent, as if I've been waiting all week for an update.

I look over at Annie, and she looks at me. Her lip stain is the same color as the streaks in her hair and the flower petals buried in her braids. I watch as her eyes trail down my bare arm that is sans hoodie today. They linger on the tattoo, a violet outline of a guitar roped with wisteria vines and musical notes.

My forearm flexes. I fiddle with my thumb ring.

She swallows, looks away.

Tag plays. I zone out Kenna's chatter, lost in the music, wishing it were me up there, spinning melodies into magic. But I can't. I can't because it's impossible to find the courage to bare my soul in that way.

Not without her.

Annie laughs at something Kenna says, nudging me with her shoulder, as if I'm one of them, a new friend in the making. The weather has warmed, winter finally melting into spring. Her outfit matches the season—a daisy dress with a flared skirt. She smells like a flower garden.

Straightening, she spins her coffee cup between her hands, and I swear her chair moves closer to mine.

"So, how weird is this?" she asks, half grinning, half cringing. "These coffee dates. Hanging out. Be honest."

A smile itches to break free, but I squash it before it has the chance to bloom. "On a scale of one to committing-felony-level-petty-theft-followed-by-an-impromptu-kidnapping? Solid six."

Kenna gets distracted when a cherry-haired girl approaches the table, pulling her into an animated conversation.

"Not too bad." Annie bites back a grin. "All memorable stories have messy beginnings."

"Pretty sure that's just a lie we tell ourselves to make things feel better than they are."

"What's your story?"

The question takes me off guard, has me itching to pull away and put distance between us. "The messy kind, from beginning to end," I say and take a sip of coffee, hiding my darkness behind my cup of Americano.

"Presumptuous of you to assume the ending." She studies me, full of questions, curiosity clouding her eyes. "Bad breakup?"

"Not the kind you're thinking."

Those big blue eyes continue to poke and prod. "Maybe you can tell me one day."

"Yeah, maybe."

"Does that mean yes?"

"Maybe means maybe."

"It sounded like a yes."

"Maybe it did." Our eyes catch, and I wonder if she sees the twinkle I know is there.

She snorts into her coffee, looking away. "You're confusing me."

Feeling is mutual, but I don't say it.

She's affecting me, plaguing me with questions I don't have the nerve to ask, unraveling something knotted deep in my chest, and threading herself through thoughts I have no business entertaining. It's in the tilt of her head, the curve of her mouth, the kindness that seeps from her touch. I don't even think she realizes it; it's just who she is.

It's in my best interest to pivot. "The stuff you write…does it translate into songs?"

Ambient lighting shimmers in her eyes like a silent secret. "Not really." Her voice dips with a touch of regret. "They're just pieces. Random thoughts about random things. There's no harmony in them."

"Write me something."

She blinks. "Right now?"

I nod.

"I don't know…"

"She's amazing," Kenna interrupts, the mysterious redhead disappearing from the table. "All she has to do is look at something and haikus pour out of her like an oil spill. But prettier."

Annie's gaze flicks to mine, and warmth unfurls in my chest. I watch the spill take shape.

She grabs a napkin, pulls a pen from her purse, and starts writing. But she hesitates; whether from doubt, the fear of judgment, or something else, I can't tell.

The napkin crinkles in her palm. A fleeting, uncertain glance is sent my way.

Then she hands it over.

> *Quiet like the moon*
> *His gaze holds a thousand storms*
> *Words trapped in the dark*

Throat thickening and pulse revving, I read it once, twice, ten more times. "You can sing. Write. Why are you pulling double shifts at a diner?"

She slinks back in the chair, like she's questioning her life choices. "It's just the way the cards fell."

"Cards are meant to be played. It's different when you don't have any cards at all. Then you're just sitting at the table, watching everyone else reshuffle."

She blinks back up with a frown. "Are you implying you don't have cards?"

Kenna jumps in. "She's incredible, right? I've been saying for years she should learn guitar and start performing. Or team up with Tag. They'd be electric together." A beat of silence stretches before she leans forward, eyes gleaming. "Or, hey, maybe the three of you should start something. I can totally see it."

I almost spit out my coffee.

This is the second time Kenna has mentioned me joining forces with Annie's brother, even though the guy would rather shit in his hands and clap than make music with me.

Annie brushes off the suggestion, her knee grazing mine when she shifts in her seat. She draws out the contact for several seconds before pulling away.

The show wraps up two hours later.

Annie texts furiously on her phone between songs, her cheeks pink, expression strained, and I can't help but flash back to her sudden departure last week. I wonder who she was talking to, who had the power to pull her away from something she obviously loves and looks forward to.

But I don't ask; it's not my place.

As Tag packs up his guitar, and patrons filter over to the tip jar, padding it with tens and twenties, Annie tucks her phone into her purse, takes a steadying breath, and turns to me. "We should hang out again sometime, outside of here. You know, maybe work on music and write some songs. I love my brother, but he doesn't have a poetic bone in his body." She breathes out a small laugh. "Unless that's weird."

I freeze, unprepared for the invitation.

Her eyes flare. "Shit. It's totally weird."

"No, no—not weird. Unexpected."

"Do you write at all?"

"A few songs back in the day, but it's been a while."

"But you play. Guitar, I mean."

"I do."

"Okay. Well, think about it. I've been meaning to make more time for myself, for the things that matter. I work so much, and everything is just…" She trails off, the light in her eyes sinking beneath the surface like the sun dipping below the waterline, leaving twilight in its wake.

I try to get a read on her, unsure of her motives and whether it's just a friendly invitation sparked by shared interests, or if something deeper lingers, veiled by the quiet innocence in her gaze.

"Will you be back next week?" she asks me.

Shaking away the seesawing thoughts, I drag my tongue over my teeth, letting a smile tease at the corners of my mouth. "Maybe."

Something flickers in her eyes. A renewed torch. A flush creeps into her cheeks, turning them rosier. "Sounds like a yes."

Rising from her chair, she steps closer, the faintest lean drawing me into her scent.

My breath catches.

I hold still, waiting.

"Everyone has cards, Chase," she murmurs, her fingers curling around my shoulder. "Even the worst hands can still be played."

CHAPTER 9
Chase

The restaurant buzzes with an early lunch crowd, the smell of deep-fried food and sautéing burger patties assaulting my senses. The space boasts a 1960s flair with checkered tiles, red vinyl booths, and chrome-trimmed barstools lined up against a long counter. A jukebox hums in the corner, crackling as it cycles through old rock and roll hits.

It's definitely a vibe.

But I'm not here for the vibe; I'm here for the girl.

I slide into an empty booth, eyeing the servers in retro-style aprons, searching for the one with purple streaks in her hair.

That's when I spot Kenna.

She brightens when she sees me, gifting me with a flash of teeth. "Be right with you!" she calls out, balancing a tray of loaded fries and milkshakes, her voice nearly drowned out by the steady drone of conversation and clinking silverware.

When she approaches my table, she pulls a notepad and pen from her apron pocket. "Can I get you something to drink?" Her accent carries a distinct inflection, the kind you might hear along the Puerto Rican coast.

I set my plastic menu down. "Is Annie working today?"

She wrinkles her nose. "I'll never get used to that. But yep, she's in the kitchen. I'll grab her. Did you want anything?"

"Coffee is good."

"Coming right up." She pops the *P* and saunters away, disappearing through the double doors.

What the hell am I doing?

Scratching at my overgrown hair, I slump back in the booth with a weary sigh. Every week since the beginning of April, I've showed up at that café. First out of curiosity, then out of habit, and now because something in me feels off-kilter when I don't. With every new week, a piece of me feels a little less lost and a little more connected to the outside world.

Somehow, our coffee meetups have rewired my brain, flooding me with this unexpected sense of drive. An undercurrent of possibility I can't ignore.

I wouldn't call it fate, but it feels like something. A cracked door, a thread to pull, a spark waiting for the inevitable matchstick to strike.

A moment later, Annie traipses out from the kitchen with Kenna tight on her heels. I straighten in my seat, watching as they both veer in my direction, Annie fluffing her hair and adjusting her apron as she plasters on a glowing smile and finds my eyes across the diner.

As she nears the table, I'm hit with the scent of sweet maple syrup. A nametag sits crooked on her chest, a tiny mole dots the skin above her upper lip, and stray crumbs cling to her chest-length waves of kaleidoscopic hair. But with those big, pale-blue eyes, long legs, paper-white skin, and watermelon lips, she's about as pretty as they come.

I'd categorize her as stupidly pretty.

"Hey."

She studies me with a hint of surprise, reaching into her pocket for a notepad. "What can I get for you?"

Kenna is ushered away to assist another customer, leaving me second-guessing why I came here as I mull over words. "I was thinking about your offer."

She writes something down, then steals a glance over her shoulder that's aimed at the kitchen. "Good choice. Highly recommend."

"To hang out. Write some music together. If you still want to."

"Mm-hmm." More scribbling.

"Um." I follow her gaze toward the kitchen, catching a man's face peering through the window hole. He vanishes as quickly as he appears. "Listen, if it's a bad time—"

"Not at all. Kenna said you wanted coffee?" She blinks down at me.

"I feel like we're having two separate conversations here."

She traps her bottom lip between her teeth before leaning in slightly, voice dropping just enough to make me stretch my ear. "We are."

"Okay. Care to loop me in?"

"Order something."

I peer down at the menu, not actually reading it. "Pancakes?"

"We do have the best." She jots it down on the paper pad and caps the pen before leveling me with a softer look. "What are you doing at midnight?"

Midnight?

"Uh, sleeping?"

"Bummer." She shrugs. "I'm kind of a night owl."

"I can probably rearrange some things."

"Great."

I hesitate, but before I can ask her to elaborate, a busser calls out to her.

"Hey, Adams! Chef is looking for you."

Adams. Must be her last name.

The kitchen doors pop open, and the man from the window hole walks out, wiping his hands on a dish towel. His gaze locks onto me, narrowing, his jaw tightening with something that feels dangerously close to hostility.

Annie takes a step back, tossing a playful wink in his direction. "Coffee and pancakes. I'll be back in a jiffy."

She strolls away without a backward glance, leaving me wondering what the fuck just happened. But I get my answer soon enough.

The man with inky hair and volatile eyes snags her by the wrist before she can retreat through the double-swing doors. He pulls her close, wrapping his arms around her waist in a smothering embrace. A firm kiss is pressed to her hairline as he continues to watch me from across the room, a storm brewing underneath the surface.

A chill courses through me. Gnawing, nibbling. It hits me like a slap to the face.

He's marking his territory.

She's taken.

Of course she is.

Here I was thinking I had a goddamn chance with her. She invited me to hang out, alone. But wrapped up in his arms, she looks like she belongs there. Like she's always belonged there.

Pathetic waves of disappointment run rampant through my blood.

Coffee is eventually set in front of me, followed by a plate of pancakes, oozing with syrup and melted butter. Annie floats through the restaurant, from table to table, chatting with customers as if she's known them for years. "It's The Same Old Song" by the Four Tops pours from the jukebox, pulling her into a series of silly dance moves with Kenna. She rotates her hips, lets her hair take flight, throws her head back with a laugh. It's almost enough to yank me into her bubble of joy as I stab my fork into the sugary stack with nearly enough force to crack the plate.

The smile never leaves her face.

Winded, she skips over to me, refilling my coffee mug.

I don't say anything. Don't smile back.

A receipt is slapped beside my plate a half hour later, and she sees me off with a warm expression. "I'm glad you stopped by, Chase. Give Toaster a kiss for me."

Annie dashes off, linking arms with Kenna as they scurry back into the kitchen, leaving me stewing in my fifty-billionth round of unfortunate luck.

The metaphorical piano crashes through the ceiling and lands on my head as I skim over the receipt. But I do a double take when I spot an arrow drawn in sparkly purple ink scrawled beside the dollar amount.

Flipping over the scrap of paper, I read the message she left behind.

> 23 Acorn Street
> Midnight
> Bring your guitar

I glance up, the doors still swinging on their hinges.
All the best mistakes have names.
Something tells me this one goes by the name of Annalise Adams.

CHAPTER 10
Annalise

"Are you out of your mind?" Tag paces around the coffee table in the finished basement, one hand curled around his hip, the other palming his nape. "Alex is going to lose his shit."

"Why?" I prop my feet up on the hand-me-down ottoman and cross them at the ankles. "He knows I'm here. Midnight is my thing."

"With me. It's *our* thing."

"Who cares if we bring someone else into the fold?"

My brother stops short, pivots to face me. "Christ, Annalise. This is next-level absurdity. Are you hearing yourself?"

My defenses activate. "It's not a big deal. We're just going to work on music together. He could be talented."

"Yeah, he's wildly skilled at committing felonies and terrorizing unsuspecting drunk girls."

"He didn't intend to terrorize me. We've been over this."

"Intention is irrelevant. The fallout is what matters."

I sigh with exasperation, sinking deeper into the muted beige couch cushions. "Something tells me he's been through a lot. I just want to help."

"Not everyone has a tragic backstory. Some people just have every intention of fucking up their life left and right, digging themselves deeper, until some poor sucker swoops in to temporarily save the day. It never lasts." He pauses for effect. "Spoiler alert: you're the sucker."

"Fascinating how you seem to know his entire biography." I reach for the bag of puffy Cheetos and make myself more comfortable. "Besides, I thought intention was irrelevant."

This earns me a glare. "I'm just saying, it's not your responsibility to fix everything. Like that sad little bird you tried to smuggle."

He gestures to the corner of the room where a thin-wire cage sits perched on a side table, now empty. Sadly, I was forced to relinquish Haiku over to the vet. Apparently, keeping a wild bird without a license violates about seven wildlife regulations.

I miss her.

Broken bird buckles
Moonlight catches trembling wings
Stars mourn in silence

"She looked at me like I was her last hope," I say. "What was I supposed to do?"

"Maybe not adopt every broken thing you come across?"

I pop a cheesy puff into my mouth. "I guess it worked out. Alex doesn't like birds. Says their twitchy heads are creepy."

"That's called projection." He flicks me a look. "Also, Mom and Dad said they texted you. They want to come out and visit next month."

My heart twists. "Oh. Yeah. I've been meaning to text them back," I murmur. "Alex says it'll be too hectic at the restaurant. Springtime is our busiest season."

"Seriously? Jesus, he—"

The doorbell chimes from above.

My stomach does a gymnast vault into my ribcage.

Tag stares at me, annoyance glittering in his dark-blue eyes like a dusky, pissed-off sky. He rubs his forehead with two fingers. "Are you going to get that?"

I leap from the couch, tucking my floral-print shirt blouse into the waistline of my lavender capris. "On it."

"Let it be known, this is by far the most ridiculous idea you've ever had, and I assure you, that list is twenty-one years long. Kudos on the accomplishment."

Ignoring him, I bound up the carpeted steps and wind toward the front door. The silhouette of a guitar case greets me through the vertical glass panels, zapping a tickle in my chest. My throat closes, a bundle of nerves catching in my windpipe.

Maybe Tag is right—I'm being ridiculous.

But I've always trusted my instincts, and right now they're telling me that Chase is supposed to be here. We were meant to meet that night.

When I open the door, I'm met with two honey-colored eyes,

a blank stare, and tangible waves of apprehension rolling off the brick wall of a man standing on my brother's front stoop.

So, I do what I always do in awkward situations: I overcompensate.

"So glad you made it!" My voice bleeds exclamation points, my arms extending at my sides with gusto. "I mean, yay. I wasn't expecting you to show."

The blank stare continues for a few beats before he tears his eyes away, glancing down at the guitar case clutched in a tight grip. "Uh, yeah. Yay."

"Sorry this is super unconventional. At the very least, it'll make a good story one day. Maybe even a song." I realize I'm babbling while failing to invite him into the house. "Oh, sorry. Come in. We usually hang out in the basement, so we can convene down there."

I don't know why I said *convene*. I sound like I'm about to lead a board meeting. Maybe I'll offer him a PowerPoint presentation on why this whole thing isn't the worst idea ever.

"Thanks." Chase shuffles inside, scuffing his boots on the welcome mat. Tugging off his beanie until a mop of dark-caramel hair emerges, he runs his fingers through the mess and glances around. "Your boyfriend is cool with this?"

My heart teeters. "What?"

"The guy from the restaurant. He's okay with you spending time with me? Alone?"

"Um...sure. Why wouldn't he be okay with it?"

His eyebrows crawl up to his hairline. "Just a hunch."

Heat skates its way down my neck, dappling my collarbone.

Despite our issues, Alex and I have always been loyal to each other. There's nothing sneaky or unsavory going on. But I can see it in Chase's eyes—he's not convinced.

My mind races back to when Alex made a theatrical show of possession after he overheard Kenna summoning me out to the dining area for a customer. For a man.

He wasn't subtle about it.

And I guess that's why I never told him about this get-together, knowing he'd jump to conclusions, fly off the handle, and assume the worst. It wasn't worth the ensuing damage control when I know this is nothing more than an outlet for me.

A tentative friendship, at most.

"It's fine." Lies. "Alex isn't like that." More lies. "He's always encouraging me to make new friends and pursue my passions." A tangled web of all the lies.

I chomp down on my tongue, forcing it to stop spewing fabrications before they weave themselves into a rope that promptly strangles me.

Chase squints at me. "Right."

Footsteps thunk up the staircase, amplifying my jitters.

Tag appears behind us.

He wedges his shoulder against the wall and just stands there. Stares. A statue made of scorn.

Chase peers across the room before wheeling his gaze to me. "Your brother is here."

"Oh. Yep. This is actually his house."

I must have forgotten to mention that.

His grip tightens on the guitar case, like he's about to double back through the front door and evaporate into the night.

A disgruntled sigh leaves my brother as he saunters into the kitchen, and I hear the telltale sound of a beer can popping open.

"Don't worry about him," I say, waving Chase toward the basement opening before Tag returns with a pointy weapon. "He'll get over it."

"Something tells me the permanent bloodstains in his car will be an eternal reminder."

Tag reappears with two more beers clasped inside his inhumanly large hand, catching us before we disappear down the stairs. "I'll supervise." He hands me the grapefruit-flavored beer.

"You say it like you're my babysitter."

"Think of me more like a correctional officer here to make sure you don't commit any more crimes against sound judgment."

"That is not comforting, or funny, or even remotely necessary."

"My house. My rules." Tag offers Chase the remaining beer. "Thirsty?"

Chase glances between us, taking in the dynamic, this strange new predicament I've yanked him into. "I'm good. Thanks."

I tromp down the staircase as Chase white-knuckles the guitar case and follows suit. Tag trails behind, his footsteps heavy. A warden making his rounds.

Plopping down on the couch, I abandon the fruity beer and reach for my spiral-bound notebook filled with a torrent of lyrics, notes, and poems. A pen is plunked between my teeth as I flip through pages, landing on one of the remaining blank ones.

"How long have you been playing?" Chase asks my brother, lingering in the center of the room, still prepared to bolt. After several uncertain seconds tick by, he finally sets his guitar beside the coffee table.

Tag collapses in the loveseat, draping an arm over the back. "Forever. Since I knew what music was."

"I came out of the womb to the sound of a toddler xylophone," I provide.

"You're older, then?" He glances at Tag.

"Twenty-three."

A moment of silence hums between us. I force a smile, bending over to unlatch Chase's faded guitar case. Inside rests a stunning piece of art, its body painted in a striking black burst with hints of midnight blue gleaming from the gradient. It looks like a dazzling night sky.

I pluck the pen from my mouth, jaw dropping. "Holy crap. Did you build this?"

"My first prototype." Chase takes a tentative seat beside me, spreading his legs, right knee bouncing up and down. "Built it from a kit I bought off the internet."

"Is this the one you play on?"

"Yeah. I had a few others, once upon a time. A PRS. I also had a Parker I scored for a good price. Unfortunately, I had to sell them, so this is the only usable one at the moment."

Tag studies the electric guitar, rubbing his fingers and thumb over his lightly stubbled jaw. He won't admit it, but he's impressed.

"And you're building more?" My eyes are wide and starstruck, transfixed on the instrument as I skim my fingers over the surface.

Chase removes the guitar from the case, angling it just right so the ceiling light catches on the iridescent finish, making it come alive. "That's the plan. I have a few more in the works, but they're not ready yet. It's a process." He sends me a glance. "But I needed something to shake me up. Get my ass in gear."

"Nothing like a casual carjacking and kidnapping to help rouse the muse."

If that was my brother's idea of a joke, it falls flatter than a wet noodle hitting the floor.

"He's kidding," I interject, feigning a laugh while shooting Tag an icy glare.

Chase sets the guitar on his lap and scrubs a hand down his face. "Yeah. That was a catastrophic misfire. I'm sorry. That night was a domino effect of shit luck and bad choices. And I just…" He trails off, looking wrecked, embarrassed. "The details don't matter. There's no excuse."

Tag sips from his beer, studying Chase with equal parts curiosity and distrust. "Can't say it was all bad luck."

I stare straight ahead and slouch back, hoping I'm at least partially invisible. A subtle hologram.

"How's that?" Chase wonders.

"You happened to steal the one car that had my sister in it."

Another wash of silence blankets the room, making me feel itchy.

I know what my brother is implying; I'm an empath, a forgiver, a believer in human beings and the inherent goodness in them. He knows anyone else would have done things differently. Chase would likely be behind bars right now. Possibly dead.

I think Chase knows that too.

"So," Tag exhales, straightening like he's bracing for impact. "Since I've been roped into this weird-ass kumbaya session, let's see if you can actually play."

"I can play." Chase's gaze flicks to me.

Our eyes tangle, charged with something unspoken. A quiet

understanding, a shared pulse of possibility. There's something in him I recognize. A flame, left dormant for too long.

I twist around, snatching up one of Tag's acoustic guitars from where it rests against the wall. A Martin—his pride and joy, the one he scraped and saved for.

Without hesitation, I hand it to Chase.

"Seriously?" Tag bristles. "That's my baby."

"Your baby will be fine."

Chase palms the neck and takes the rusty orange pick I hand him. "What's that?" He nods at the notebook smooshed between my knees.

"It's my book of midnights."

He studies me for a long beat, his bangs fallen into his eyes. "What's with the midnight theme?"

"Taylor has her midnights. So do I."

"Taylor? Is that a guitar reference?"

I gawk at him like he's been living in a hermitage for several centuries. "Taylor Swift. I'm always working during the day, so this is my time for hobbies and stuff that feeds the soul. My late-night musings. Tag and I started the tradition a few years back when we both realized we didn't sleep normal human hours."

"When do you sleep?"

"A little here and there. Lots of naps. I function well on little sleep."

He hums under his breath. "And you want to be a lyricist?"

I pull my feet up on the couch until I'm cross-legged. "That would be cool. Right now it's just an ununified jumbling of random words. There's no real connection or underlying story to any of it. A lot of haikus. More poetry than anything."

Despite my brush off, I see the light in Chase's eyes flicker to life, his interest piqued.

"It's nothing, really." My skin flushes. "Everyone has their thing."

He holds my stare, then blinks a few times, squeezing his eyes shut as he rubs at his forehead.

"You okay?"

"Yeah, just a headache. Still on a few pain meds. They've been messing with me." He blows out a breath, clears his throat. "What do you want me to play?"

"What do you know?" Tag chugs down the rest of his IPA and leans forward. "Anything but '60s doo-wop, for the love of God."

"That's offensive," I grumble.

"I know a lot. '90s rock, '80s hair metal, some new-age folky stuff. Pearl Jam, CCR, Fleetwood Mac, the Beatles—"

"Beatles. 'I Am the Walrus' is gold." Perking up, I curl my fingers around the wrinkled notebook and stretch a smile. "It's kind of like if I pieced all my gibberish together and made a song out of it."

"While tripping on LSD," Tag adds.

Chase's lips twitch—a semi-smile.

He goes quiet for several seconds, plucking at the strings, his features softening with focus, earnestness.

Then he starts to play.

I recognize the song after a few indicative chords: "While My Guitar Gently Weeps."

Long fingers move with a gentle precision, his gaze engrossed in the strings, lost in the music. The melody winds through the room like blue smoke, haunting in its simplicity. My brother hums a verse under his breath, jumping in, strumming along on his backup guitar—a cheap model handed down to him from our late grandfather. The catalyst for his dreams.

These are the moments I wish I could play.

I've never bothered to learn guitar. My favorite instrument is my voice.

Inhaling a breath, I let the song flow through me, melancholy lyrics spilling free when the guys reach the first bridge.

Chase lifts his head, pulling his attention off the guitar and slowly panning his gaze toward me. He watches me sing. Neither of us misses a beat as our eyes hold, the room dissolving around us, only plinking strings and moody notes piercing the heavy air.

The three of us move on to a new song. Tag's voice grows louder, fusing with mine. His isn't as clean. It's raspy and flawed, a contrasting balance. Our harmonies blend in imperfect unison as Chase continues to weave chords into a spell.

We run through one more classic, a poignant feeling in my gut, swirling and spinning.

When the guitars grow quiet and last notes fade, I can't stop the giddy grin from spreading across my face. "Hello, magic."

My brother refuses to acknowledge it. He looks over at Chase, his eyes less wary but still dubious. "Do you sing?"

Chase finally pulls his focus off me, a slow-motion withdrawal. "I mostly just play."

"Why don't you sing?" I inch forward on the couch until our knees touch. "I'd love to hear you."

"Maybe another time."

I study him, the way his body tenses, his leg bobbing again. Something tells me it's more than nerves. "Okay. I get it."

"Gonna make some food," Tag says, standing from the couch and discarding his guitar. "Want anything?"

He addresses me only; I decline.

As the sound of footsteps taper off, I swivel toward Chase, the energy in the room still palpable, frenetic. His gaze glows with renewed passion, a luster I haven't seen yet. He's always looked so jaded and locked away. The metal bars over his eyes begin to disintegrate.

"What are you even doing?" I murmur, my voice barely reaching a whisper. His puzzled expression makes me realize I've given him no context. I shake my head. "I mean, with your life. With everything. You have so much talent…the way you play, the guitars you've built. If you can sing even half as well as you—"

"I can't."

"I don't believe you."

He shifts, uneasy. Not because of me, but because of what I'm saying. Because of everything he's not reaching for. If it were me, I'd chase it until my legs gave out. Run like I was on fire and never stop, not until I burned. Burned alive or burned bright. Either way, it would be worth it.

Chase presses his elbows to his thighs and looks down at the floor. "And you?"

"What about me?"

He reaches for the notebook resting between us and starts thumbing through the pages. Settling on a page featuring a recent poem, I watch his eyes scan the smudged ink, the random doodles, the little pieces of my heart wrapped up in em dashes, dotted *i*'s, and metaphors.

I'm no good with numbers, but I can measure
the weight of empty pages
I can count the beats between heartache and
hope
One, two, three
The bridge between what is and what could be

His eyes lift, embers igniting among the golden flecks. "If we're on the topic of untapped potential, I have a few thoughts I can add."

I scoff, snatching the notebook from his grip. "That's different. I can carry a tune and write haikus. Not exactly a recipe for a lifelong career."

"Says who? You?" His eyes are heavy. "Who are you to stand in the way of your own dreams?"

His words rattle me.

I blink at him, tongue-tied, my chest inflating with a volley of responses I can't seem to expel.

A frown creases his brow, and he ducks his chin. "Sorry. That wasn't my place."

"No, it's fine. I hear you."

I do hear him. The hypocrisy echoes loud and clear. The double standard of it all.

But this is different; Chase's dreams are within reach, career-worthy and life-changing. Mine are buried in overtime and back-to-back shifts, where the clatter of dishes and the endless call for orders stifle any room for ambition. My dreams don't fit between refilling water glasses and balancing trays. They aren't bright enough to outshine Alex's impossible standards and short fuse as he stands over the line, splotchy-faced and sharp-tongued.

Anything worth fighting for feels smothered by the exhaustion clinging to my bones.

My cheeks grow warm, my eyes scratchy.

I dig my palms into the spiral coils of my notebook, leaving red marks behind. "My boyfriend…he's not overly supportive. Says I need to grow up, that my head is in the clouds. He's been running a restaurant since most people were still figuring out what they wanted to be, while I'm pouring myself into things that don't pay the bills. These moments, these midnights, they're all I have right now. All I can afford."

This seems to fire him up again. "Your boyfriend doesn't support you?"

"No, he does." I try to backpedal, my pulse running away from me. "He does, in all the ways that count. We've been together for years, been friends since we were kids. He's always been with me. It's just…this…" I hold up the notebook. "There isn't room for *this* in our lives right now. Not in the capacity you're talking about."

His gaze is hooded as he stares at me, unblinking. "That's tragic, Annie."

Pressure throbs behind my eyes, and my heart feels like a ninety-pound dumbbell floating in my chest. With a sharp breath, I release the notebook and swipe my hands down my thighs. "It is what it is. I'm okay with where I'm at." We're getting off track, edging toward the deep end, and I'm not ready to drown him with my complicated relationship history. Biting my lip, I glance up. "Are you?"

He doesn't hesitate. "No."

We stare at each other in charged silence. Something trembles inside me. A fault line cracking.

Before I can reply, Chase rises from the couch, setting aside the guitar. "I'm going to head out," he says.

"Right. Yeah, it's late." Standing with him, I fiddle with the sleeves of my blouse, wishing the session wasn't over so soon. We didn't get to write or compare notes. We compared ghosts instead. "Um…you should stop by the café next week. The first Thursday of the month is open mic night. Anyone is invited to take the stage."

He pauses, case in hand. "Are you going to sing?"

"Yeah," I murmur. "I might."

"I'll see you there."

I watch as he hauls his guitar forward and trudges up the staircase, favoring his left leg, and disappears without another word. I'm still zoned out, marveling at the stairwell, when Tag returns with a plate of bubbly pizza rolls. He stuffs one into his mouth and promptly curses when it scalds the crap out of his tongue.

He spits it back out. "The felon has left the building?"

I snap out of the daze and gift him with another glare. "You were an ass."

"Better than being a felon. I should've pressed charges."

"That's a lie, and you know it. I saw the way you watched him play. You heard what I heard."

"Mm." Tag narrows his eyes at the piping hot rolls as a cloud of steam billows from the plate. Then he peers over at me, an earnestness filling his gaze, curling with shadows. "You're playing with fire, Annalise."

I swallow hard. Don't respond.

My eyes track my brother as he takes a seat on the couch and reaches for his Martin, strumming the strings with calloused fingertips.

He's wrong.

The only fire I'm playing with is the one inside me.

CHAPTER 11
Annalise

A heavy arm is draped around me as daylight tickles my eyelids. I blink myself awake, my gaze trained on the half-open blinds as the sun crests over a line of lush green treetops. Birdsong floats into my ears, chasing away the dreams, and I release a slow breath, snuggling closer to the man pressed against my back.

"Morning," I say, voice cracking with sleep.

Alex stirs, squeezing me tighter. "Does it have to be?"

"The birds have spoken." Kicking my feet, I shove the blankets away and roll onto my back, my white tank top inching up my stomach as I stretch through a yawn.

Alex mimics my position, his hair mussed, bare chest inflating with drowsy breaths. He props both arms over his head and stares up at the ceiling. "You were out late last night."

"Oh, sorry. Did I wake you?"

"Little bit."

I cant my head, blinking at him through the dimly lit room. "Tag and I were in the zone. I lost track of time."

He purses his lips, then changes the subject. "I was looking into flights. Thailand is a haul."

My eyes round as warmth fizzes in my chest, my belly. "You're serious about taking a vacation?"

"You want to, right? We have the time. I'll have Maurice take over for me while we're gone. And I'm sure Kenna won't mind a few extra shifts. Jess too."

"Oh my God. Yes. That would be incredible."

"Still need to work out the finances. Airfare isn't cheap."

"We can do it. We've been saving."

"Yeah." Sighing, he shifts slightly, turning to glance at me. "Maybe we can go over an itinerary tonight."

The familiar coil of anxiety invades me, slithering around my heart. "It's Thursday," I remind him. "I'll be at the café. You know that."

His jaw tenses, face going hard. "You can't cancel one night?"

"I…I guess I can. But it's open mic night, and I was planning on singing. I've been practicing a few covers. Oldies. What about tomorrow? I only have a morning shift, and we can—"

"Sure. Whatever." Alex tosses off the blankets and swings his legs over the side of the bed. "I'm gonna take a shower."

I sit up straight, pulse spiking. "No, wait, it's not a problem. I'll reschedule."

"I said it's whatever. We'll do it tomorrow."

"Alex, don't—"

"Jesus, calm down, will you?"

All the air sticks in my throat. "I am calm."

"No, you're freaking the hell out." He stands abruptly, veering toward the dresser and swiping a clean shirt from the drawer. "It's too early for this."

I scramble out of bed, my bare feet sinking into the plush carpet. "Alex. Hey."

He leans forward on his palms, gripping the edge of the dresser. His shoulder blades flex. "It's not a big deal."

"I don't want you to be upset." I step closer, inching along the tightrope I'm constantly walking. "This vacation is important. The café isn't going anywhere."

"You're just…always gone." Long, tense fingers twitch against the wood. "At that damn coffee shop, out all hours of the night doing God-knows-what. Bar hopping with Kenna. I hardly see you anymore."

"I only went to the bar that one time." When he swivels around to face me, eyes dark and unreadable, I reach for him, pulling him into a tight hug. I feel his heartbeat pounding between us, both a weapon and a comfort. My head dips, my temple resting on his shoulder. "I'm sorry. You're so tired after work, and that's when I get a second wind. But you're right. I'll make more time for us. We can wake up earlier and go for a run, or have a breakfast picnic, or—"

"Yeah," he murmurs into my hair. "Sure."

But I can tell he's only half listening. His body is still rigid, his mind elsewhere.

I loosen my hold, giving him space. He untangles himself from me and slaps the T-shirt over his shoulder, pivoting toward the en suite bathroom.

He gets halfway before he falters. Teeters in place.

I hold my breath.

Not a second passes before he spins back around, grabs my wrist, and tugs me to him, crashing our mouths together. The shirt tumbles to the floor. The air is yanked from my lungs.

I cup his face with both hands, sinking into the kiss. His stubble tickles my chin, fingers dig into my cheeks. Our tongues dance and twine, his teeth nicking my bottom lip. Then he pulls away, skin flushed and eyes glazed.

His grip on me tightens, just for a second, before he lets out a sharp exhale and eases up. "I don't want to fight."

"Me neither." I press my lips to his jaw, to the tip of his nose, swallowing down the weight of memories clawing up my throat. The screech of tires, the shatter of glass, the shrieking horn.

The blood.

His hands slip to my hips, grounding himself. Or maybe grounding me. "I'll make you breakfast when I'm out."

"Okay."

Alex's arm lifts, his thumb grazing my cheekbone and lingering. "I love you."

"Love you too."

When he disappears into the bathroom, I touch my fingertips to my puffy lips, still tingling from his kiss.

It wasn't a lie.

I hope it never will be.

It's the first Thursday of May, and the weather is a refreshing balm to my frazzled mind. The sun sits low in the sky, painting the remaining blue in a canvas of color, like a melted rainbow Popsicle. A light breeze dances across my skin, filling me with new life, the second wind I crave after a long day of taking orders, entertaining customers, and blocking out Alex's endless tirade of pressure-infused wrath.

I love open mic nights at the café. Anyone with an instrument and a voice is invited to take the stage, to fill the room with lyrics and harmonies. It's often an assortment of wannabe musicians, college girls looking for karaoke, and some newbies eager to get a taste of the spotlight.

It's just me and Tag tonight, since Kenna is holed up in her apartment with the flu.

Entering the café, I stroll past what looks to be a father-daughter duo. A teenage girl is perched in a wheelchair, her coffee-dark hair framing a rosy-cheeked face. I send her a smile as I pass, and she returns it twofold.

But as I move closer to the familiar table in the back of the room and spot Chase, I notice there's something different about him. He looks rattled, on edge. Like he's just seen a ghost.

"Hey," I greet him, his back to the table I just walked by. "Everything okay?"

He rubs a hand over his face. "Yeah. Can't stay long, but I said I'd drop by."

"Do you have plans?"

Glancing over his shoulder, he starts tapping his feet in opposite time, scratches at his scruff, heaves in a shaky breath. "Something like that."

"Fill me in?" I plop down beside him and scoot the chair closer. "You don't look so good."

"I'm fine."

My instincts prickle with worry. "Does this have to do with the no-context breakup you mentioned?" With ten years of being Kenna's friend under my belt, I've basically taken a masterclass in post-breakup pep talks. Irving was the last one; now she's already talking to a new guy.

"What? There was no breakup…" Frowning, he shakes his head, my words registering like cakey mud. "No, nothing like that. I just have somewhere to be."

"Sure. Of course." I look up as Tag mumbles something offensive under his breath and purposely finds a separate table across the room.

My eyes swing back to Chase, then dip to the tabletop.

No coffee today.

Over the last few weeks, Chase has always been waiting with a vanilla late, no foam.

Tossing my hair over my shoulder, I lean back in the chair. "You should sing something."

A blank stare. "Zero chance."

"It's not so bad," I say through a smile. "I've witnessed a lot of questionable talent over the years, and I doubt you'll even come close to that."

"Sorry, Annalise."

"Um…yeah. No worries." I curl a strand of hair around my finger. "Did you want me to move? I know I can be too much sometimes. If you want space, I'll just—"

"No." His response is sharp, immediate, startling me into stillness. He finally looks at me, and his eyes fill with a sadness that makes my chest ache. "You're not too much. Never. Not at all."

Those words shouldn't hurt.

They shouldn't wash over me like a storm-charged tidal wave and steal the breath from my lungs. But they do. Because I've spent so long believing the opposite, being told the opposite, that hearing him say it like it's the most obvious thing in the world feels foreign.

I don't know how to respond, so I don't.

As the first person takes the platform—a mid-thirties dad looking to impress his preschool-age twins with a lively rendition of *Frozen's* "Let It Go"—I stand from my seat and approach the counter, ordering three drinks: a latte for me, an Americano for Chase, and a decaf Frappuccino with extra chocolate syrup and a gazillion cherries for Tag.

After depositing two of the drinks on my table, I breeze over to my brother and slap the cup in front of him with a napkin note that reads, *"Something sweet to awaken your dead soul."*

"Hilarious." He pushes it aside as if it might come to life, levitate off the table, and force its way down his throat. "Are you singing next?"

"Eventually. Chase seems distracted, so I'm going to keep him company for a bit."

"He's probably just busy plotting out his next crime."

"You're literally dreadful." My eyes wheel to the front of the room, where the suspender-clad father belts out the iconic chorus. "Hey, you should take notes."

"Hey, what does your boyfriend think of these secret meetings with your abductor?"

My eyes slant with scorn. "He's unaware."

"Clearly."

"It's not a big deal. But it would be to him. You know how he gets."

"As do you. Which begs the question: What the fuck is a sensible, intelligent woman such as yourself still doing with that asshole?"

Anger crawls its way under my skin, making me flush. "I'm taking this back." With a kill-on-the-spot look, I snatch up the faux coffee and whip around, hightailing it back to the less-caustic table. Chase sits there, fidgeting in place, glancing around the room like something might jump out and bite him.

I take my seat as the man onstage finishes his animated performance, and everyone claps. Out of my periphery, I notice the wheelchair-bound girl inching her way toward the front of the room. She peeks over her shoulder at her father, her eyes wide and terrified, her knuckles locked around the wheels with an iron grip. Nerves have her trembling, rooted to the spot.

Chase watches with cautious interest, slinking down in his seat. He taps his ring against the tabletop. Reaches for the cup of coffee. Twirls it in circles, but doesn't take a sip.

Clearing his throat, he looks over at me. "Thanks for this. You didn't have to buy me coffee."

"Just returning the favor." I grin widely, hoping my optimism will brighten his spirits.

It doesn't.

The young girl makes it to the platform, and a kind stranger helps her up the ramp. She settles in front of the microphone, hands folded, fingers tightly locked. The café quiets, a hush of anticipation filling the space as she stares down at the floor.

Her lips part, but no sound comes out.

A beat passes. Then another.

She clears her throat, tries again. A small, fragile note escapes before her voice frays at the edges. She winces like she's been kicked, her body curling inward.

Poor thing.

She's petrified.

Tears mist my eyes as I watch, silently offering support with the biggest smile I can muster.

The silence stretches into a cloud of unease. Her father leans forward in his chair, his expression caught between encouragement and helplessness.

Chase exhales sharply through his nose.

Falters.

Then he mutters "fuck me" under his breath and pushes his chair back, the legs scraping against the floor with a grating echo.

I gape at him. "Chase, what—"

But he's already moving.

He stands, adjusting the hem of his faded leather jacket, and saunters toward the platform.

The girl looks up with alarm as he steps in beside her with his hands buried in the pockets of his coat. Her fingers grip the arms of her wheelchair, knuckles pale, while Chase hovers to her left, completely still, visibly second-guessing his decision.

My eyes pan back and forth. I clutch my coffee cup so hard the cap snaps off and liquid dribbles over the rim.

Oh my God. He's going to sing.

I skate my attention over to Tag, catching the way his eyes move, assessing the scene.

Chase doesn't touch the mic, doesn't address the audience. He just crouches slightly, so he's at eye level with the girl. "What's your name?"

She blinks hard. "Clara." Her voice is thin, reverberating through the microphone.

Everyone watches, eager, expectant.

Chase nods.

For a second, I think he's going to walk away. But instead, he leans in again, muttering something too low for me to catch.

Clara's expression wavers.

Whatever he said softens her nerves.

An unreadable look flickers across her face. Then, after a long, heavy pause, her shoulders deflate and she murmurs something else over her shoulder.

A rough voice crackles through the mic. "Yeah, I know it."

The café holds its breath as she turns back to the audience. Her voice shakes through the opening notes, barely a whisper, and for a second, I wonder if she might stop altogether.

But Chase joins in.

Not loud, not stealing focus. His steady vibrato threads through hers like an anchor, until, gradually, Clara's grip on the chair's arms loosens. Her voice stabilizes, growing stronger with every songful word.

"Have You Ever Seen the Rain?" by Creedence Clearwater Revival.

It's a cappella. Just their voices weaving through the crowded space.

Clara is too focused to look at him.

But I do.

As warm coffee trickles down my fingers, I stare, mesmerized and transfixed, watching, listening, branding the rich sound of his voice into my marrow.

Songs have lungs. They breathe.

And right now, this one is alive.

Haunting lyrics roll through the café like a tide, swelling and receding. The quiet hum of chatter fades, replaced by the raw, unfiltered harmony of their voices.

Chase sings like the words mean something. Like they cost him something. His eyes close, his fingers twitch against his jeans. There's something unspoken, something that lingers like smoke from a long-dead fire. I nearly choke on it. Cinders in my lungs, ashes at my feet.

Clara's voice strengthens.

She starts off hesitant, a delicate rose waiting for the moment she'll collapse under the storm. But Chase keeps her steady, and by the second verse, her nerves dissolve.

She sings.

Her talent shines.

And Chase…

God, he's perfection. I knew he would be.

Pivoting in my seat, I look across the room at my brother. He feels me staring, waiting, knowing. Our eyes lock. Mine are blanketed in tears. Emotion bubbles to the surface, a deluge, pressing against my ribs as hot tears streak down my cheeks.

Because I hear it.

I hear everything Chase isn't saying.

It's in the way his voice dips and rises, how he eases into the song like he belongs there, like music is stitched into his bones.

My brother pulls away, rubbing a hand down his face.

He knows it too.

Knows that Chase was made for this.

Even after the last note fades, it clings like the scent of fresh rain. For a moment, everything is still. The calm before the downpour.

A round of applause crashes over us.

A boom of thunder.

Clara's lips part slightly, stunned, as if she forgot they weren't alone, didn't realize the entire room had been hanging on her every note.

Chase steps back and ducks his head. Lets the rain fall where it belongs.

I swallow hard, gripping my coffee cup, my fingers sticky from the spill.

If there was any shred of doubt before…there isn't now.

Chase *belongs* in the storm.

Finally, Clara looks up at him, and a slow-blooming smile crests on her mouth. She brightens, thanks him. Sending her a terse nod, Chase shuffles off the platform, palming his neck, avoiding everyone's bewitched gazes.

He stops at my table, just briefly, offering a quick goodbye. "I gotta go. Take care."

"Wait—"

He's already speed walking toward the exit.

Bolting from my chair, I follow, swiping tears off my cheekbones, trying to catch up. "Chase, wait. Just a minute."

He pushes through the door, falters, then pauses on the walkway. Spinning around, he releases a frazzled breath as he faces me. "Listen, I have somewhere to be, so I—"

"Do you believe in fate?"

He blinks twice. "What?"

"Fate. You know, divine intervention. Coincidences that feel too profound to be random." I gesture at the leather sleeves of his coat, the fabric glued to lean, muscular arms. "Your tattoo. Tag has one that's similar on his wrist. Music is his whole life."

Chase shakes his head, confusion scrawled across his face.

"He's been trying to start a band for years," I continue. "It's his dream, but nothing's ever panned out. No one has that same drive, that hunger, that raw talent."

The air shifts between us. Realization seems to dawn.

Hesitating, he breathes out a soundless laugh. "Are you implying you want me to start a band with your brother?"

An awkward chuckle slips free, but I don't confirm nor deny.

"That's not…" He exhales, rubbing the back of his neck. "Annalise, that's not going to happen."

"Why not?"

His brows shoot skyward. "I can write it out for you. Bullet points, columns, a few brief essays."

"Perfect. My notebook is in Tag's car."

Cocking his head to the side, he gawks at me, dumbfounded. "You're actually serious."

Am I?

I hear myself talking, but the words don't make sense. Maybe I froze a few brain cells on that blizzardy night. Or maybe Kenna's commentary wormed its way deeper than I thought.

Whatever the reason, my eyeballs have the audacity to water again. "The way you just sang up there, Chase, I… God, I wasn't expecting it."

Something tells me he wasn't either.

Moonlight bathes him in a muted glow, a faint spotlight. His expression changes, shoulders loosening as he tilts his face skyward like he's waiting for something to appear. To materialize among the sea of stars and cannonball to earth.

Then, softly, "That was the first time I've ever sung in public."

"Impossible."

"It's not. I only went up there because…" His voice trails off, gaze drifting back to the concrete.

"You felt for her," I deduce. "Did you know her?"

Chase remains silent for several beats before murmuring, "She reminded me of someone. Someone I lost. She looked… just like her."

He doesn't elaborate.

I want to know more. I want to know everything.

But more than that, I want to take the reins of this delicate beginning and charge forward, turning potential into certainty, promise into something real.

For Tag. For Chase.

For me.

I dig a pen out of my purse and reach for his hand, flipping it palm-side up, before scribbling down my phone number. "That's my cell. Just think about it, okay?"

He angles his hand left and right, studying the inky blue numbers that gleam beneath the starry canvas. "Would you be involved?" he wonders. Then he shakes his head, as if shooing away the question. "Never mind. You said you don't have the time."

I falter. "I have my midnights."

"Those are just fragments. Scattered pieces of a much bigger picture," he counters, closing his eyes, curling his fingers into his palm. "It's not enough."

"I disagree. When you truly want something, you make it enough. Pieces are still pieces. You collect them, maneuver them, and you don't stop until the puzzle becomes whole."

I'm finally realizing that.

I've been stagnant, stunted, marinating in lost potential and broken dreams. It's my own fault. I can always do more, be more, try harder. Sometimes all we need is a catalyst.

A spark.

Our gazes cling for another beat before Chase breaks contact and inches back into the parking lot. "Yeah," he says, pushing his tongue against his cheek. "I'll think about it."

He spins around to leave.

I watch as he treks toward his vehicle and slips inside, revving the engine, reversing, then veering out of the parking lot and onto the main road. He drives away, the taillights evaporating. Swallowed by the night.

My feet remain glued to the pavement.

The air has chilled, nipping at my skin, but it's not enough to snuff out the fire blazing through me. It burns, smolders, turning all remaining doubt into ash.

Stars glimmer from above, milky and glowing, and I glance up, smiling wider than the moon.

Fate isn't always logical.

But it is, in fact, inevitable.

CHAPTER 12
Chase

"I don't feel good. I don't want to go."

Stella flops back on her bed, curling into the fetal position. Sweat shimmers on her hairline. Groaning with misery, she tugs an ashy blue quilt up to her chin.

Mom sighs with exhaustion, clinging to her last rope, as she yanks the blanket off my sister. "The scouts are going to be there. You don't have a choice."

"Mom, please. My head is absolutely killing me."

"Take some Tylenol. It's just a headache, Stella." A firm hand presses to her shoulder, squeezing. "This is your dream, everything you've worked so hard for. You're a Rhodes, honey. We see our dreams through."

I watch from the hallway, leaning back against the wall, my arms folded. She's so pale. Trembling, in pain. Her eyes find me through the threshold, begging for me to intervene.

But there's nothing I can do.
The backdrop shifts into a carousel of noise, color, motion.
Water splashes at my feet.
Two weary eyes find me from the edge of the Olympic-size pool. Light, light brown.
No light at all.
She sends me the barest smile, then jumps in, making her laps.
Minutes tick by. People scatter, distracted.
My father cracks a joke, nudging my shoulder with his fist as he guffaws. I turn to face him. We share a smile, a few words. A few minutes.
I don't remember the joke, but I remember the moment after.
The screaming. Commotion.
A blur of frantic movement, pitching voices, bodies scrambling in and out of the water.
And there—
My sister.
Floating.
My feet move. My brain shuts down. My voice splinters with agony.
I dive.
But there's nothing I can do.

By day, I shape the unshaped.

In a hollow warehouse that reeks of sawdust and varnish, I skim my hands over coarse slabs of wood, studying their imperfections. I carve, sand, and stain, coaxing each piece into something valuable.

Tables that will hold family dinners. Bookshelves for cradling stories. Beds where people will dream.

It's honest work. The kind where effort equals outcome with every pass of the chisel, every stroke of the brush.

By night, I build something else entirely.

I trade in sanders for soldering irons, chisels for circuits. My living room workbench becomes a different kind of warehouse, scattered with wires, pickups, and polished wood waiting to be transformed.

I mold guitars that don't just play music. They breathe it. Instruments with bodies carved from exotic woods, necks reinforced with carbon fiber, touch-responsive LED fretboards that glow beneath my fingertips. Sound that doesn't just echo but bends, warps, evolves.

Each one is a puzzle. Pieces of a dream that becomes more whole as the weeks sail by.

By day, I build for others.

By night, I build for me.

And on a lonely Saturday evening in early June, I finally build for something bigger.

I text her.

Me: Hey. It's Chase.
Me: I think I might be in.

Ten minutes later, I hear my phone ping as I'm mopping up a puddle near Toaster's water bowl. My head pounds, chest squeezes, and my nerves multiply.

Toaster races past me, leaps onto the couch.

Watches.

I reach for my phone, swiping open the message.

Annie: See you at midnight. 😊

CHAPTER 13
Chase

Therapy.

That's what she feels like.

Early June melts away into late June, painting the world in hues of Siberian irises and butterfly-blue scabiosa, as peonies blossom like coral sunsets in garden beds. But while nature is fast asleep, I have never felt more awake.

These midnight meetings we indulge in three times a week have become the driving force behind my dreams. My goals.

Ultimately, my healing.

I'll never tell her that.

Annie is the type of person who internalizes everything, always wanting to help, reach, dig deeper, until she's stretched too thin and buried among a graveyard of everyone else's skeletons. I refuse to be another bag of bones she feels responsible for bringing back to life.

Instead, I take each moment as it comes. Maintain a reasonable distance. Keep my guard up. We write, play, sing, and muse, directing that fire into music, while she remains oblivious to the light she's reigniting inside me.

I pull up to the familiar cape-style house with a wraparound porch, the siding an off-putting color of peach. Annie paces in tight circles beneath the awning, wearing leggings and an oversize sweater, a cigarette trembling between her fingers.

She doesn't smoke.

Smudged kohl rims her eyes, lining her cheeks in inky smears. Porch light sets her ablaze, illuminating all the burdens she carries but refuses to resent.

She's a wick burning at both ends.

She's also a Scorpio—pain is passion, and passion is purpose. I'm not sure who or what has caused the sudden bout of chain-smoking, the trembling limbs, or the slow-drying tears, but it doesn't take much to break her open.

That I do know.

I park along the street and hop out, tossing my leather coat inside the car as a balmy midnight breeze clings to my skin and the lingering scent of afternoon rain drifts under my nose. Rolling up my sleeves, I step forward, careful not to spook her. "Annalise."

She stops pacing. Snaps her head up.

I watch her exhale a plume of smoke she doesn't even want, as if trying to purge something deeper from her lungs.

"Oh, hey. Chase." A smile appears, just like that. A well-trained disguise. She flicks the half-smoked cigarette to the stoop, crushing it beneath the toe of her Mary Janes. "I didn't even notice you drive up."

"Everything okay?"

"Of course. Definitely." She waves away the cloud of smoke and feigns a small laugh. "Sorry. Jeez. I'm not even a smoker, but Tag had an old pack lying around, and I just—"

"You were crying." I saunter up the walkway, hands shoved into the pockets of my jeans. "Did your brother say something offensive?"

I know it wasn't her brother. Despite our ongoing tension, the guy adores her.

Another laugh breaks free. She sniffs, frantically swiping at her cheeks. "A fair deduction, but no. I was just getting in the zone. Preparing for that heartbreaking hit we're inevitably going to write tonight." Her nose scrunches in a way that's gravely adorable. "I'm harnessing my inner method writer."

"Ah."

"Don't worry about me. I'm good now."

Swinging her arms back and forth, she keeps the smile firmly in place.

Impressive. Typical.

"Anyway," she says, twisting around. "Let's go out back. It's such a pretty night."

Annie shuffles into the house, composing herself, skimming her salmon-tipped fingers through a tangle of purple, brown, and blond.

I follow behind, glancing at the couch where Tag sits as he practices a song on his Martin.

He hardly pays me a glance. "Hey, asshole."

"Hey," I manage.

Annie harrumphs.

Collaborating with Tag has been an experience, to say the least. He seems inclined to despise me until his deathbed, or until I become the missing piece to his music-fueled dreams.

At this rate, I'm not sure which will happen first.

"We're going to collab out on the deck." Annie collects her notebook and a small clutch filled with an assortment of multicolored pens, then continues forward. "Want to join?"

"Nope." The response is muffled through the pick between his teeth. "Have fun."

She halts in place. "You know, in order to start a band, you need to eventually interact with your fellow band members. It's not rocket science."

"Noted. Thanks for the revelation."

"I'm serious, Tag. You're being stubborn."

"I'm being more than reasonable." He plucks the pick from his mouth and leans back, the picture of casual disdain. "I've already surrendered to your misguided vision. He's standing in my living room. Pretty sure that counts as my contribution."

She shakes her head, frustration radiating off her. "You're only holding yourself back."

"I'll take my chances. Enjoy your little rendezvous." With that, Tag scoops up his guitar and sweeps past us, disappearing into the basement.

I rub my forehead, a dull headache simmering behind my eyes.

Annie slumps, defeat creeping into her expression as she

fiddles with the baggy sleeves of her tea-rose sweater. "Sorry. I promise, one of these days—"

"It's fine. I get it." I push my bangs aside. "He has every reason to hate me."

"He's being irrational. He's seen you play, sing, write. You belong here."

"I put his little sister in a compromising position. Could have gotten her killed," I remind her, as if she needs reminding. She doesn't. She just forgives too easily. "That's not irrational. That's love."

Her eyes flare.

But it's only a brief pause before she shakes off whatever trace of understanding seeped through, clenches her jaw, and continues to the deck. "I already grabbed an acoustic for you. I was thinking we could work on new material tonight. I made some notes."

"Sounds good."

I still don't have my own acoustic.

Every last cent has been put toward keeping myself afloat, caring for Toaster, and investing in the tools needed to bring my guitar business to life. I sold another one last week: a sleek, midnight-black custom build with an asymmetrical body, gold hardware, and a fretboard inlaid with mother-of-pearl constellations. It sold for just under fifteen hundred dollars, which was double what the last one went for.

Similar comps tell me it undersold, but I don't have the name to back up those prices yet. No credentials, no reputation. Just an obscene amount of drive and a craft I'm sharpening every day.

Annie collapses onto a wicker rocking chair while I take the seat beside her.

She looks at me.

A few steady beats pass, and I don't know how to unravel that look. What it means, what it says. We've become closer over the last few weeks. While I never cross any lines, never let my thoughts drift too far, sometimes I wonder if she does.

Her lips part like she might say something, but she only exhales a slow, quiet breath that barely stirs the air between us.

I should look away, put space between us. But I don't.

Finally, she tucks a loose strand of hair behind her ear, blinking hard like she's dislodging something. "Here," she murmurs, reaching for the guitar. "If you want to warm up."

I take it, grateful for the out. Because no matter how close we may become, no matter how many nights we spend lost in music, there are lines that can't be blurred.

It's for the best; I prefer hard lines and sharp edges.

The fallout always hides inside the blur.

My fingers settle on the strings, my thumb ring glinting off a rope of bulb lights draped around the deck. The scent of summer wraps around me—rain-soaked mud, damp wood, and wild honeysuckle. I'm not sure if the latter belongs to nature or the shampoo in her hair.

"Sing an oldie for me."

I lift my chin and find Annie staring at me again. "Yeah?"

"I need something cheery and familiar. It's been a day." She pulls her legs up crisscross-applesauce style and settles back in the seat. "If you don't mind?"

Sixties tunes aren't exactly my jam, but I know a few. One in particular.

Sometimes that song bleeds into my nightmares, drowning out the ghostly howls of my mother's screams.

I locate a pick on the little garden table between us and strum a few chords along the strings.

G-C-D minor.

Annie's eyes brighten with recognition.

I clear my throat. Tear my gaze away from hers before I lock up.

Then my voice pours out like a raspy, controlled lullaby as I sing the first verse to "I Only Want To Be With You" by Dusty Springfield.

I move into the chorus. Forget some of the lyrics to the second verse and shift into the bridge.

Chorus again.

Outro.

The last note hangs on, clinging to the midnight air like sticky adhesive. When my focus floats back to Annie, I blink through the haze, watching her watch me. She's curled up in a ball on the wicker chair, legs tucked to her chest, fresh tears coating her eyes.

Not pain this time. Just passion.

She looks spellbound.

The sentiment has me fidgeting as my left knee bounces, skin itches, hairline sweats. She shouldn't be looking at me like that.

Too fucking dangerous.

"God, you're so good," she breathes out, a choked-up whisper. "I can't believe you just started singing in front of people."

"Yeah." I swallow. "Singing is…vulnerable."

"It is, but it's also so raw. Like tearing your chest wide open and hoping someone hears what's inside."

Her words have me swallowing again, smoke and grit lodging in my throat. Nearly six long years of clogged grief.

I glance down at the weathered planks of knotty pine. "It's not something I ever planned to do. Not alone, anyway."

"Were you planning to start a band?"

"Not a band, no. But my sister…she wanted to start something with me someday. It didn't pan out. And I never felt right about doing it without her."

"What happened?" she asks, still breathless, soaking up every word.

Annie's hair looks electric beneath the accent lights. A pop of color in a monochrome world. The blue in her eyes does everything it can to melt away my steel.

But I don't know how to answer that. Not without letting my guard all the way down and dragging her into my army of demons. They don't play nice. They'd eat her alive.

"It didn't pan out," I echo, leaving it at that. For now. "You mentioned new material?"

She blinks, the deviation catching her off guard. Slowly, she unfurls her legs until they're draped over the edge of the chair. When she sits up, the tightness in her posture returns, coiling back into place.

Nodding, she flips open the notebook and pulls a pen from her silvery blue pouch. "I, um…had a few thoughts at work. I scribbled some lyrics on a napkin, then pieced them together the best I could when I got home. It's not much, but it could become something?" Her lip disappears between her teeth, fingers curling around the spirals. "Or maybe not. I don't know."

"Show me."

"It's not finished yet. Not even close." Two shimmery eyes scan the first verse. Once, twice, five times over. Her breathing becomes more labored, and her bottom lip slides out from the hook of her teeth, now puffy and quivering.

She stares blankly at the page, no longer reading.

I stare at her, reading everything.

"Or we can run through some more covers," I pivot, sensing her uncertainty.

"Sure. Yeah, I…" The skin between her eyes pinches as she blows out a shaky breath, then tosses the notebook on the deck. Annie pops up from the chair and starts to pace. "What am I even doing? I can't write songs."

The honey-tinged moon bathes her in a soft glow, highlighting her misery.

Black mascara still veins her cheekbones. Her limbs tremble with trapped emotion. A hint of cigarette smoke wafts from her clothing.

I rest the guitar on my thighs and lean forward, tracking her disjointed movements. "Want to talk about it?"

"No. I don't know."

Her shift in energy is like a sudden stormfront. Jarring, unexpected. The pain returns tenfold.

But I'm no good at this.

A year of therapy was hardly enough to instill me with pearls of wisdom powerful enough to impact this broken, passionate, beautiful girl.

And that's the downside of these late-night meetings—it's

impossible not to feel something when I'm with her, which is a level-ten mistake. She has a boyfriend. A serious, long-term boyfriend. The kind that leads to wedding bells and baby swaddles.

I shouldn't be looking at her like I want to be the guy to wipe the tears off her face, hold her until the trembling ebbs, and be that soothing alternative to a stick of nicotine.

That's fucked. Catastrophe in the making.

But she's hurting.

And he's not here.

Releasing a sigh, I set down the guitar and lean it against the side table. I stand from the chair. Take two steps forward.

Annie's eyes lift, widening, welling with a new dusting of tears. "I'm fine, Chase." She swipes at her face, erasing the evidence. "I'm okay. I'm calm."

"I never said you weren't." I squint, drinking in her micro expressions, her cues. She's always making offhanded comments that belittle her worth. Thinking she's too much. Worried she's not enough. Apologizing for everything. "What happened?"

"Nothing. It doesn't matter."

"You look like you just had your heart ripped out."

She shakes her head, glancing at the patio door like she's waiting for someone to barrel through it. "I don't know what I'm doing."

"With what? Music?"

"Everything. My whole life." She's rattled, shaking from head to toe. "I'm exhausted. Wasting my days sweating over hot stoves and forcing smiles for customers. This is the only part of the day I look forward to. And that's sad, Chase. It's pathetic. And then he's always…" Her gaze drops, voice fading. Both arms fall to her sides as she deflates. "He doesn't understand it."

I frown, stepping closer. "Who? Your boyfriend?"

Alex.

The guy Tag seems to loathe and Annie seems to love.

I can't shake the memory of him at the restaurant. Of him, with her.

Hard. Overbearing. Emanating control.

She doesn't talk about him much, but she's often on her phone, texting, looking stressed. Can't imagine he appreciates her late-night getaways.

The thought has me taking a step back.

"Yeah," she whispers, the word wrung out with defeat. "He thinks this is a waste of time. The music, the writing." Her attention flits to the notebook discarded on the deck. "He says I should focus on what actually matters."

"And what actually matters?"

"Paying bills, work, thinking about the future. Growing up." A small laugh scrapes past her throat, but there's no humor in it. "He doesn't mean it like that. Not really. He just…worries, I guess. About stability. About us. And I get it, I do. I can't live off late-night jam sessions on my brother's deck."

"No," I agree. "But you shouldn't have to pick one or the other."

She glances up.

"Work and stability matter, but so does having something that makes you feel alive. It's not about choosing. It's about balance."

Her hands ball at her sides. "He doesn't see it that way."

"But do you?"

She presses her lips together, jaw shifting like she wants to say something but isn't sure she should.

I watch her for a moment before exhaling through my nose. "Look, all I'm saying is your life isn't just what happens in the daylight, or in the nine-to-five grind. It's this too. The things that make you *want* to keep going. You showed me that. Hell, it's why I'm here."

Her eyes flutter closed, chest inflating, deflating.

Then her face completely crumples. A brittle crack in the sunny façade she always wears.

It catches me off guard, stilling me for a beat. But instinct overrides hesitation, and I step forward, bridging the space between us.

My arms lift—slow, unsure—before I carefully pull her in.

She doesn't think twice. Just folds into me like it's second nature.

We've never hugged before. Hardly even touched.

I still remember the last time I comforted someone with a hug. *Stella*.

The day before she died, she shuffled down the stairs with a warm compress and collapsed beside me on the couch. Her temple fell to my shoulder, the heat pack plopped atop her head.

I wrapped an arm around her, drawing her in, unknowingly giving her the last moment of comfort she'd ever have.

The memory tightens my grip on Annie, my arms looping around her back, tugging her closer. My chin brushes her wisps of hair as she trembles with a devastation I can't fully grasp.

All I know is that it's because of him. The man who's supposed to love her.

And in that moment, I want to strangle him.

My heart kicks harder when she nuzzles into my chest, her breath topsy-turvy, her sniffling muffled against the fabric of my dark Henley. Warm tears seep through, dampening my skin.

A telltale buzz fizzes in my blood. It's been years since I've been this close to a woman. No sex, no fleeting intimacy, no vanilla musk clinging to my sheets.

I thought I was broken. Dead inside. Immune to the need for physical connection.

But I'm not.

And this is the wrong damn time and the wrong fucking girl to start figuring that out with.

"I'm sorry," Annie mumbles, her lips hovering just above my galloping heart. "I don't mean to fall apart like this. I don't know what's wrong with me."

"There's nothing wrong with you."

"I just…I want to pursue my dreams. Live large and free. I want to travel the world, experience bright lights and sweeping cities. But I also want to settle down one day, live simply, savor the little moments." She inches back slightly, her eyes rimmed with red. "Alex says I can't have both."

"You can have both," I say, releasing her, putting a much-needed distance between us. Then, without thinking it through, I add, "Maybe just not with him."

Shit.

That was a massive overstep.

Number one rule of friendship: never give unsolicited relationship advice, especially when you're the outside party with borderline selfish intentions.

Not my place. Not even fucking close.

Annie's eyes widen to glistening spheres, burning under the string lights and the moon.

Panic surges through me.

I can't tell if she's about to slap me, storm inside, or if she's having an ah-ha moment.

My muscles lock as I stand there, staring, trying to conjure up some sort of backpedaling, apologetic spiel.

The words don't come.

An owl hoots from a faraway tree as branches shift and sway against the breeze. The air is heavy, thick, suffocating.

A dish crashes in the kitchen.

Annie nearly leaps out of her Mary Janes. She looks toward the house, eyes darting to the small, dusty window, where her brother stands at the sink, his face an unreadable mask.

But he saw.

The hug. The forbidden contact. The cloud of tension so tangible it might as well have a pulse and a mouthful of teeth.

She smooths out her sweater, her hands vanishing inside the sleeves. Her gaze draws back to me, just for a millisecond, before she swivels around and disappears inside the house. The sliding door claps shut, snapping me back to reality.

I grit my teeth. "Fuck."

With a low growl, I press my palms to my temples before dragging them down my face.

What the hell was I thinking?

Through the window, I catch a glimpse of Annie's silhouette evaporating down the hallway, her shoulders drawn tight, arms curled around herself. She'll probably spend the rest of the night convincing herself I didn't mean it the way it sounded. That I wasn't implying anything. That I was just being supportive.

Or maybe she won't.

Maybe she'll let it fester until it picks apart the foundation she's been teetering on for years.

I shake my head, sinking into the chair she abandoned and gripping the arms like a flimsy anchor. My attention pans downward, looking for a distraction, anything to pull me out of my messy, scrambled thoughts.

That's when I see it.

Her notebook, half open, forgotten on the floor of the deck. A few crumpled napkins are stuffed inside, scrawled with ink.

Scribbles in the margins. Crossed-out lines. Colorful doodles.

And at the center of the page, a partially written song.

Unfinished and raw.

[Verse 1]

I used to chase the sun
A ~~beacon~~ fire, bold and bright
But now I'm ~~choking on the fumes~~ standing in
the ashes of a hollow, wasted fight
Every promise turned to smoke
A matchstick in the sky
~~Flickering out~~ (??), a smothered flame
Our pieces drifting by

[Pre-Chorus?]

But you, you never faded
Even when

The words stop there.
Like she lost the nerve, or the hope, to write the rest.
But in my head, the song keeps going.

CHAPTER 14
Annalise

I'm a walking zombie the next day.

Dishes clatter from the stifling, hectic kitchen as voices compete for dominance. Oldies croon from the vintage jukebox. Alex barks orders to everyone within earshot, while patrons laugh, converse, tell stories.

But the only voice I truly hear is my own.

It's whispering to me. Singing unfamiliar songs.

Maybe just not with him.

The day sails by in an anthem of eerie chords and ominous prose.

Not with him.

When I trudge through the front door that evening and close the door on the sunset-kissed sky, I drink in the aroma of sizzling salmon and savory greens.

Alex glances over his shoulder from the kitchen. Candlesticks flicker from the dining room table, adorning the ivory cloth, as smoke curls toward the ceiling.

He sends me a smile.

Not. Him.

I stare at the smoke, in a daze, slipping out of my heels and securing my purse on the hanger. I blink, and I'm in the kitchen. I don't remember moving.

"Hope you're hungry." Alex flips the salmon in the saucepan and drizzles it with lemon butter and sprigs of fresh dill.

The smell is rich and warm, an invitation that feels too good to be true. I grip the edge of the counter, my fingers pressing into the cool stone.

I should say something. A thank-you. But all that comes out is a breath.

"Sit. I'll bring you a plate."

Another blink, and I'm seated at the table with a fork clutched inside my sweaty palm. Alex's chair squeaks against the tile as he yanks it back and plops down.

He starts talking. Rehashing his day.

A laugh, a scowl, a rant.

There's a death-metal orchestra banging cymbals in my chest.

Th-thump. Th-thump.

My eyes lift toward the ceiling. Tendrils of smoke curve toward the light, twisting and vanishing before they reach it.

"So maybe I'll just—"

"I think we need a break."

I inhale sharply. The crescendo abruptly stops.

My voice cuts through his like a blade, severing his words at the quick.

Alex freezes, fork hovering midair. A slow, cautious smile flickers. "What?"

My mouth snaps shut. Panic slithers through my chest, plunking in my stomach like lead.

He chews his bite of salmon, slow and deliberate. "I'm working on Thailand, don't worry. I reached out to a travel agent to help us score the best deal. I was thinking fall, after the summer rush. We can—"

"No, I mean…a *break*. For us." The words barely make it past my clogged throat. Meek and pathetic. "Something temporary. I don't know. I just…"

Regret sets in the second his smile fades.

"What the hell are you talking about?"

My eyes sting. "I just feel…sad."

"Sad?" His brows shoot up. "What are you sad about?"

"I don't know."

He scoffs. "You don't know." The fork clatters against the plate. "Hire a therapist. We have insurance."

"Maybe, but it's more than—"

"What more do you want from me?" He leans back in his chair, arms crossing as his expression hardens to gravel. "What's your plan? Huh? You work at my restaurant. Sleep under my roof. I cook, pay the bills, indulge your half-assed ideas about writing. What else can I do?"

I hate that his words ring true.

I've become so…codependent. Some days, I don't know where he ends and I begin.

And that terrifies me.

I twist my napkin between my hands, trembling through my next words. "I feel lost. I'm twenty-one, and I have no idea what I'm doing with my life. I don't want to spend the next decade pulling double shifts at a diner."

"Unbelievable." He pushes back from the table so hard his chair nearly tips. Running both hands through his hair, he paces, exhaling sharp, ragged breaths. "Do you even hear yourself? Do you realize how selfish you sound? It's always been me and you. I take care of you. I love you. I want to fucking marry you."

"I know, I just…" I stand with him, my lips trembling, sluiced in salty tears. "I'm sorry. I don't know what to do. I feel like we're headed toward a dead end, and I can't see a way out."

"So your solution is to break up with me?"

"I said temporary. Just some space to clear our heads, think about what we really want—"

"What *you* really want."

I swallow. "I guess."

"Fuck." He kicks the chair, launching it halfway across the room.

I flinch back. "Alex, please—"

"Please what?" He whirls around, his face flushed and splotchy. "I. Do. Everything. For. You." Each word is a hot knife, punctuated by the quick jab of his finger. "I've built my life around you. Where are you going to work? Where are you going to sleep?"

"I can stay with Tag for a few days."

"Tag," he repeats, his tongue pressing against his cheek. "Your brother, the aimless dreamer who thinks strumming his guitar and singing pretty songs will pay the bills. Must be genetic."

Heat trails up my chest, my neck, my ears. "That's not fair."

"Fair?" He lets out a bitter laugh. "You're the one blindsiding me with this."

"I'm trying. I am. I'm trying to figure out what's best for both of us."

"Don't play the martyr."

"I'm not. I'm—"

"*Christ.*"

My voice cracks. "Alex, you—"

"Just calm down, my God."

"Stop saying that!" The words wrench from my throat, splitting at the seams. "I am calm. I'm *always* calm."

I'm not.

Not even close.

This is the most uncalm I've ever felt.

He stares at me, chest heaving, jaw tight. The veins in his arms distend as he clenches his fists at his sides.

I take a shaky step back. Then another.

Alex doesn't move to stop me. He just watches, his expression dark and unreadable.

The air feels smothering. Every breath tastes like lemon butter and doubt.

I grab my purse off the hook, my fingers fumbling with the strap. My body screams at me to say something, to fix this before it spirals further. But I don't know how to fix it. All I can do is replay Chase's words like a scratchy old record.

You can have both. Maybe just not with him.

"Where are you going?" he demands, low and controlled.

"I told you. I need space."

"Space. Right." He paces a few steps before snapping his head toward me. "You don't get to tell me you're leaving like it's some casual fucking announcement over dinner."

"I don't want to fight."

"Then don't start one!" He gestures wildly between us. "Jesus, I've given you everything. And you're seriously walking out? Like that's going to suddenly give you direction, bring all your bright-eyed dreams to fruition?"

I squeeze my eyes shut. "I don't know what else to do."

"Bullshit. You know exactly what you're doing. You're bailing." His nostrils flare. "That's what you do when things get hard."

"Stop."

"I wake up every damn day, working my ass off, making sure we have a life, a home, a future. I stuck by you when you had nothing. And now, because you're *sad*, you want to run."

"I'm not running!" My pulse hammers, the room narrowing on all sides. "I've stayed. Longer than most people would have."

His face hardens like I just struck him.

Silence stretches between us, thick and fragile.

I reach for the handle.

"Annalise."

I freeze, fingers curled around the doorknob.

His tone softens, barely above a whisper. "You'll come back."

It's not a question. It's a promise, a warning, a hook lodged under my skin, tugging me back toward him.

But I close my eyes. Breathe. Swallow down the remorse, the indecision, the seesaw of conflicting emotions climbing up my throat.

Then I twist the knob and step outside.

Calling him was stupid. I know that.

But Tag didn't pick up, Kenna's stuck on the closing shift, and my parents are busy chasing their live-off-the-land fantasy in Georgia, turning their retirement into a micro-farm experiment.

I didn't know who else to call.

And that realization is another dagger to my chest.

Have I really become this isolated?

This alone?

I slam the passenger door shut, sealing myself inside the car.

Chase hesitates, his fingers looped around the steering wheel. "You okay?"

"No." I slump back in the seat, fold my arms, and stare out the window. "Do you mind dropping me off at Tag's? I'm going to crash there for the night."

I have nothing to my name. Not even an overnight bag. Just my purse, my cell phone, a threadbare heart, and today's work clothes that are dappled in stains.

"Yeah. Sure." He glances at me in my periphery before the engine purrs to life and we accelerate out of the café parking lot that I power-walked to.

I careen into the past, to the last time I was stuck in a car with Chase Rhodes. Somehow this feels worse. Scarier. This gnawing sense of limbo, this existential crisis.

More tears lance my eyes as I whip my head toward him. "Why did you say that to me?"

He frowns, taking his eyes off the road for a beat to catch my gaze. "What?"

"'Not with him,'" I echo, feeling torn, divided, confused. "You said I can have both, but not with him. Why?"

"Annie—"

"I'm trying to understand it. Because I've been with Alex my whole life, and I've never truly considered that. I've never pictured a future without him. And now I'm having these awful thoughts, these combative feelings, this pang of *doubt*—" I slap a flat palm to my chest, to the bleeding source of my inner conflict. "You don't know me. Why would you say that?"

"I shouldn't have said it."

I blink at him, fresh tears slipping free. "But you did."

We ease up to a stoplight, and Chase turns to look at me, his gaze piercing, apologetic. "Look, it wasn't my place, and I realize that. I regretted it the second I said it." His hands tighten on the wheel before he glances away, out the windshield. "I just…I know what it looks like when someone is drowning. And I know what it looks like when they don't even realize it. So it just slipped out. And I'm sorry if I made it worse."

The breath leaves my lungs in a shaky whoosh.

Locking my jaw, I turn away, pressing my forehead against the cool pane of glass. Streetlights blur past when the light turns green, striping the dusky sky in gold and shadow.

I've heard it before.

Tag, in his blunt, no-bullshit way. My parents, in softer moments, their words carefully chosen but still laced with concern. Even Kenna, who swore she'd never meddle, let it slip between sips of wine on her couch: *"Don't you think you deserve better?"*

And every time, I brushed it off. Called it worry. Misunderstanding. I told myself they didn't see the whole picture.

That they didn't know Alex like I did, didn't grasp the guilt I've carried, all the little weights that have turned into an anvil and kept me rooted by his side.

But Chase?

We only just met.

He has no reason to care, no reason to say something just to soothe me, or push me, or convince me that this life I've chosen might not be the right path.

Yet he saw it. Just like everyone else. And for the first time, the thought didn't bounce off the armor I've built around this relationship.

His words reached me. Stuck.

Lingered.

And now they're hollowing me out.

I close my eyes, swallowing the sticky knot in my throat.

Minutes whisk by while I'm lost to my battling thoughts. The car smells like a bamboo diffuser and the faint trace of woodsy cologne. I don't look at Chase; I can't. All I do is stare out the dust-streaked window until we pull into my brother's driveway and I launch myself out of the vehicle.

"Annalise."

He follows me. My work heels slow me down, his gait doubling mine. I whip around to face him, panicked, teetering on the edge of a nervous breakdown. "What did I just do?" I croak out, shaking my head back and forth. "God. I can't believe I—"

"Hey. It's okay. Whatever it is, it's fixable."

My chest feels like it's crumbling, the falling debris making my stomach churn. I almost double over. "Oh God…"

"Annie, listen." Chase takes both of my hands in his, squeezing softly, centering me. "It's okay. I promise. Fuck what I said last night. It was stupid, presumptuous, and clearly counterproductive. You were right. I don't know you, and you never asked for my advice."

His hands are calloused and cool, but his touch warms me. Defrosts my frozen bits. And I don't understand it. We're essentially strangers, yet I feel comfortable with him.

Safe.

The thought only heightens my nerves again.

It jumbles my thoughts until I blurt out the unexpected: "I almost killed him."

His grip on me tightens, just for a breath, and then he lets me go. "What?"

I take a step back, nearly tripping over the first porch step. "Five years ago. Alex. He was teaching me how to drive, and we got into this argument, and I…" My eyes slam shut, memories pervading, intruding. "I lost control. Hit a tree. And he…he almost died."

Chase studies me beneath the awning, his whiskey-brown eyes digging. "Shit," he whispers. "I'm sorry."

I cross my arms, nails biting into my skin. "I walked away with a few scratches, while he suffered a TBI. He was never the same. A lot of the time, things are good. He's loving, attentive, spoils me. But when he's under pressure, frustrated…he's like a different person. Mean, angry, volatile." The words feel polluted on my tongue, like admitting it makes it more real. More damning. I wrap my arms tighter around myself, trying to hold in the ache. "But I can't blame him for that. I did this to him. I broke him."

Chase exhales, raking a hand through his hair.

"I know what you're thinking. That I should've left him a long time ago. That I'm making excuses."

He doesn't answer right away. Just watches me, his expression hard to read, until finally, he says, "I think you're carrying something too heavy for one person to bear."

I swallow, pressing my fingers against my temples. "There's only me. I'm all he has. His parents moved to Rome, and they're hardly in the picture. They just abandoned him—left him with a restaurant and all this trauma. He's an only child, has no friends, no relationships. What kind of person walks away?" My breath is shaky, riddled with despair. "What kind of person just gives up on someone like that?"

Chase shifts his weight, his hands flexing at his sides like he wants to reach for me again but doesn't. "I don't have any answers for you," he says. "But I don't think you're asking the right questions."

The words settle between us, heavy and unmovable.

My throat tightens. I dig my fingertips into my temples, trying to force some clarity into the dust storm inside my head. Chase doesn't push, doesn't fill the silence with empty reassurances or platitudes. He just stands there, watching me with an intensity that makes my skin prickle.

I blow out a breath and step back, sinking onto the porch steps. The wooden slats creak as I drape my arms over my knees, staring down at the cracks in the pavement. "I don't even know why I'm telling you this," I admit.

Chase hesitates before lowering himself beside me. He stretches his legs out, hands clasped loosely between his knees.

"Sometimes it's easier that way. Talking to someone who doesn't have a stake in it."

I nod, grinding the heel of my stiletto into a weed-laden groove. "No judgment. No expectations."

"No history," he adds.

The mood shifts, less strained now, something more delicate settling into place. The porch light flickers above, moths flitting toward the glow, chasing the elusive warmth.

"You were sixteen?"

I glance at Chase, rolling my lips between my teeth.

"When you had the accident," he clarifies.

"Yeah." Sighing, I look up at the navy canvas dotted with tiny stars. "I was sixteen."

"That's how old my sister was when she died."

My heart clenches, muscles locking. I peer over at him again, studying his profile, the tight lines of his jaw and the tick in his cheek. "I'm so sorry."

"She drowned." He bows his head, hands dangling between his thighs. "She was a swimmer. As professional as you can get at sixteen. It was a big day—scouts were going to be there, college coaches watching. She was practicing before everyone arrived. And then, while I was talking to my parents…" His jaw flexes. "She was floating facedown in the pool."

A sharp, uneasy weight settles in my chest. "Oh my God… that's…"

"I was right there. Right fucking there. I jumped in, tried to pull her out, but she was already gone." His voice is raw, scraped clean of anything but grief. "She was a strong swimmer. The strongest. She trained every day, pushed herself harder than anyone. But she was exhausted. Dehydrated. They said she passed out in the water and...that was it."

A breeze drifts through the porch, but I barely feel it.

Chase stares past me, lost in something I can't see. "It kills me," he says after a minute. "It kills me because she didn't want to go that day. Said she had a headache, didn't feel good. But our parents made her go. I could have intervened, could have said something, could have prevented it...but I didn't. And I have to live with that every day."

His words strike a chord deep in my chest.

I think of Alex, of the accident, of all the ways I've twisted myself into barbed-wire knots trying to make sense of what happened.

What I did. What I didn't do. What I owe him because of it.

"God, Chase..." A tear trickles from the corner of my eye, carving a pathway down my cheek. "I understand."

Chase notices the wayward tear but doesn't call attention to it. Maybe he understands too, that sometimes acknowledging grief out loud only makes it worse. More cumbersome.

He pulls away and leans against the porch beam, tilting his head toward the sky. I follow his gaze, my breath hitching at the sight of the moon, bright and full, hanging low over the trees. It shimmers like it's been dipped in liquid gold.

"The moon," I murmur, squinting at the warm, ambrosia globe. "Looks like a floating ball of honey."

Chase stares at it, a smile flickering as the silence stretches for a handful of seconds. Then he says, "We're in our honeymoon phase."

I look at him.

He looks at me.

I blink. Blink again.

And then a burst of laughter escapes. A snort. An unbidden explosion of joy. "Our honeymoon phase," I echo, barely containing another wave of giggles. "I like that."

Our smiles linger, scaring away the shadows for a little while. We sit side by side, staring up at the honey moon as the remnants of our losses drift further out of reach, beyond the night sky.

We both shared a piece of ourselves tonight. The most broken piece. The dirtiest piece.

And I guess that should make me feel worse somehow.

Sadder. More burdened.

But all I feel is less alone.

CHAPTER 15
Chase

"It won't last, you know."

The voice drags me away from the song. I fumble a chord, the sound dying out as Tag's lumbering footsteps clomp across the deck. He hands me a beer.

My eyes dip to the sweating can like it might be laced with a pinch of cyanide.

A smirk flickers on his lips, the strap of his Martin fastened around his torso. "It's just a beer. Hardly the riskiest thing I know you're considering."

Leaning back in the wicker chair, I take the Blue Moon and pop the tab, my gaze wary. "Did you want something? Can't imagine I'm the most interesting part of your night."

"Really?" He swivels the chair beside me, then takes a seat. "There's a criminal sitting on my deck at two in the morning, playing songs on my guitar. Most people would find that awfully interesting."

"Mm."

"But the breakup won't last," he repeats. "If that's why you're here."

I glance left, through the narrow window above the sink, watching as Annalise washes a dinner plate with a yellow sponge, her fingers drenched in suds, her face pinched in concentration. A dark twist of hair is piled on her head, the pale-blond strands bobbing in front of her eyes as she scrubs at crusty streaks of marinara sauce.

She looks tired. Fucking exhausted.

My face must do something that gives me away because Tag lets out a knowing sigh.

"That's what I thought," he mutters.

I jerk away from the window and bring the beer to my lips. "I'm here for the music."

"A poetic way of saying you're trying to get into my sister's pants."

A headache pulses between my eyes. I can't tell if he sounds bitter, indifferent, or low-key supportive. Tag Adams is impossible to read.

Either way, this conversation is a slow, torturous death.

But that could be the cyanide.

Discarding my can, I prop the guitar back up and situate it across my lap, leaning forward, plucking at wayward strings. Tag watches for a minute. My form, my silence, my avoidance.

He spins his IPA between his hands while dishes and tumblers clatter from the kitchen. "For the record, I said it *won't* last. Not that I didn't want it to."

My eyes lift. A few more chords breach the air, new and unfamiliar. Annie's unfinished song, a work in progress. "I'm sensing you're not a fan of Alex."

"Fucking hate the prick."

I nod slowly, deciding that this guy must be a real piece of work, given the fact that Tag is sharing a beer with me out on his deck—the criminal who nearly killed his only sibling.

My throat sticks as the words sink deeper.

There's a buzzing under my skin. Hot, festering. A shiver races down my spine.

"Does he hurt her?" I ask, the question tumbling out almost like a prayer.

I've wondered. Worried.

I haven't noticed any bruises, but those can be hidden. Makeup, baggy clothes, strategic placement. The notion seizes my heart, and the few sips of beer turn to cement in my stomach.

Tag sighs, propping his ankle on his opposite knee as he inches the guitar up his body. "Depends on how you define it. Does it get physical? I haven't sensed that. But does he hurt her? Yeah. Definitely."

My gut tightens, my gaze panning back to Annie through the window. She swipes a piece of hair out of her bloodshot eyes, scrubbing faster. "What are you going to do about it?"

"Me? Nothing. Annalise is a grown-ass woman, and I'm her meddling big brother." He flicks a hand in the air. "Goes in one ear and out the other. Has for years."

"But she walked."

"She didn't walk. She waffled." He chugs down the rest of his beer, crushes the can, then tosses it on the table between us.

"Listen, as much as I wish someone could step into her life and make her see the light with midnight musings and napkin songs, it's a losing battle. A dead end. That shit runs too deep."

A frown creases.

My eyes draw back to the window as I mull over the past forty-eight hours since I answered her text message.

Annie: Hi. Sorry to bother you, but can you pick me up from the café? Please. Thank you.
Annie: So sorry.

Annie asked me to bring Toaster over tonight, and I did.

While he's been thrilled by the new scenery, his real joy is Annie. He shadows her every step, settles at her feet, curls up against her hip. Soaks up every belly scratch and butt rub like they're the highlights of his life.

Seems to be her highlight too.

She told me these midnight meetings were the only part of her day she looks forward to, and I'm not sure if that's a shot of hope to my blood or the saddest thing I've ever heard.

Tag watches me reflect, and the steady, potent look in his eyes makes me feel itchy and out of place. I clear my throat. "Is that supposed to be encouragement or a warning?"

"Take it how you want."

I reach for my drink, needing the distraction, the liquid burn. "Told you," I say, avoiding eye contact. "I'm here for the music."

A dismissive huff. "Just because I don't participate in your la-la-land adventures doesn't mean I don't see it. I know my sister. She likes you."

The can pauses before it reaches my lips.

Those words shouldn't affect me, shouldn't have my hand curling around the aluminum like a vise around my heart. But they do. Because he's not wrong.

There's something unspoken thrumming between us with every look, every pen to page, every guilty glow that washes over her eyes when my voice pitches with falsetto or rumbles with vibrato. She'll never admit it. I don't think she even understands it.

But I feel it. This foreign thing taking root.

The knowing look on Tag's face lingers, though he doesn't press the matter. He just nods at the guitar in my lap and changes the subject. "New song?"

His question pulls me from my cluttered mind. "Uh, yeah. Something Annalise was working on."

"Let me hear."

"It's not finished. She only wrote a verse, and I added a little to the pre-chorus, but—"

"Play it."

Sighing, I glance at the window again as Annie presses forward on the sink, the water still running, her eyes trained on the steady stream. She doesn't move. Doesn't blink.

"All right." I straighten in the chair and press the pick to the strings.

The first chord hums a low, drawn-out note. My fingers find their place, the melody unraveling, unpolished. Annie's words come first, the ones she scribbled onto a dirty napkin like they weren't ripping her open. I keep my voice controlled, but it's impossible not to feel the weight, the muted heartache tangled in every syllable.

Through the window, she hasn't budged. Just stands there, gaze locked on the running faucet, lost in something I wholly understand.

The pre-chorus fades into nothingness. A premature ending.

Tag doesn't say anything for a while, just plucks a few strings as he tunes the neck. "It's good," he finally murmurs. "I question my sister's instincts on the daily, but she's not wrong about you. You can fucking sing."

"Thanks." The compliment hits different, coming from him. From this guy who has little to compliment me about.

"You've got that…thing." He waves his hand around, cool and casual, like he recognizes something he doesn't want to name. "Whatever you want to call it."

Interesting.

I'm debating a response when the patio door slides open.

Toaster darts out first, while Annie slowly shuffles behind, her bare feet smacking against the wood planks. She pauses beside my chair, a big smile bringing light to her face. "Are you two finally bonding out here?"

Tag grumbles, jumping from the chair. "Suddenly have somewhere to be."

"Nothing to be ashamed of," she says as he sweeps past her like something set his ass on fire. "I don't judge."

"No, but you poke." He jabs a finger into her upper arm, tipping her off-balance. "Like a damn woodpecker."

"I can't help it. I live to harass you."

"Harass me tomorrow. I'm going to bed." Tag disappears inside the house, waving a disparaging hand over his shoulder.

Annie turns back to me, the smile still there. Still beaming.

But her eyes…

So fucking tired.

"Surprised you're still awake." I place the guitar beside me. "It's late."

The beam dwindles, losing its fight. "I can't sleep. Honestly, I haven't slept alone in years. It's an adjustment, I guess."

"How are you holding up?"

"Managing. Coasting."

I nod. "Better than standing still."

"Yeah. For sure."

She doesn't believe that. I see the ambivalence painted all across her face. It's then I know that Tag was right…

It won't last.

Something in my chest tugs. Aches. But not for me.

For her.

Because I can see she's not happy.

I fidget with my thumb ring, tracing the silver band in slow circles. "We can talk about it."

"Nah." She shrugs, scrunches her nose. "I'm only going to rain on your parade."

"Good. Never liked parades, but I love the rain."

Her eyes flare, just a fraction. Then she lets out a quiet laugh, drops her chin, curling her bare toes against the weathered pine. "How do you know when you're making the right decision?" She lifts her gaze, hesitant, searching.

I take my time with this one. "When you know you deserve better than what you're settling for."

"You think I'm settling?"

"Only you know the answer to that. If you are, then you'll know."

Something in her deflates, but I can't tell if it's frustration or defeat. She collapses into the chair Tag was sitting in and snatches the notebook she abandoned on the table an hour ago. Hunching over, she drags her fingers through her hair, the swell of her breasts spilling out over the low-cut neckline of her tank top.

My eyes linger.

Perfect porcelain skin. Full, pillowy lips pressed together in thought. The delicate slope of her neck as she tilts her head, lost in whatever storm is brewing there.

A little mole freckles the skin below her ear, matching the one above her lip. I wonder what it would feel like, brushing my thumb over it. Just a graze.

Her fingers drum against the page, then smooth over the worn edges, absently tugging at a loose thread on the binding. I should look away, but I can't stop staring at her, drinking in her soft curves like she's the world's most compelling prose.

Because right now, she looks like something I could ruin myself for.

When she sits back up, she hands me the notebook, her attention aimed at Toaster as he licks his paw from the middle of the deck. "I wrote some more. Part of the chorus."

I exhale through my nose, head swimming like I've been drugged, and slow-blink at the offering. "Does it have a title?"

"Not yet. I'm terrible at titles." Her face sours. "But I'm terrible at writing songs too."

"Who told you that?"

"My inner voice. She's kind of a dick."

Reaching over, I take the notebook as she picks invisible

lint off her tank top, shifting in place, a ball of nerves and insecurity.

My eyes dip to the page, scanning the chorus.

> *Do you hear the echoes?*
> *Do they haunt you in the night?*
> *All the words we left unspoken*
> *Longing for the light*
> *If I fall, will you still catch me?*
> *If I run, will you let go?*

> *Blah, blah, blah*

I glance back up, a smile twitching. "My inner voice says it's good. We can work with this."

"It's crap." She scowls.

"It's not crap."

"Fine. It's a heaping pile of shit left to rot under the sun."

Jesus.

I scrub a hand over my face, then press forward on my forearms. "Do you honestly believe that? Because I don't think you do."

"If you're implying I'm fishing for compliments, I'm not." Annie curls into herself, wrapping her arms around her body as she rocks back and forth. Like she wants to disappear.

"Not compliments," I say, gazing at her, wishing she'd look at me. "But you're searching for something. For proof. For someone to believe in you."

She stops rocking.

Slowly, her head turns, those big blue eyes locking on mine. My smile fully forms. "I do."

A swallow hooks in the curve of her throat. Pain, passion—it's all the same. "You hardly know me."

"Don't I?" She's said that before. Two days ago, in the front seat of my car. But time is irrelevant. You can go a lifetime knowing someone without truly *knowing* them. And then someone walks into your life and you see them clear as day. Like they were always there. "I do know you," I tell her, tapping the notebook in my lap.

She shakes her head, eyes glazing with trapped tears. "No. You know that I like '60s music, write random poetry, think your dog is the cutest thing I've ever seen, and have enough relationship baggage to fill a cargo hold. That's nothing. You don't know—"

"Annie," I cut her off, watching as her eyes grow twice their size. "I know the only thing that matters."

She swallows again. Holds her breath and waits.

I hold up the notebook. The evidence. The undeniable truth. "I know what moves you."

The air shifts between us, thickening in my lungs. In my mind, those words didn't sound so heavy. But they poured out like a storm. Black rain and broken thunder.

There's lightning in my veins and dew drops in her eyes.

A tear slips down her cheek. She swipes at it, frantically, wanting to erase whatever cracked open inside her.

I reach for my beer. But the moment I move to take a sip, my dog barrels toward me and leaps into my lap.

"Shit—" The beer jostles, tips, spilling nearly a full can of liquid wheat down the front of my T-shirt. Some of it lands on Toaster, and he shakes his fur, spraying the rest of it all over me.

Awesome.

I'm drenched in Blue Moon and regret.

Annie hops off the chair, still wiping at her face. "Oh, jeez. You're soaked."

"I'm fine." Toaster plants himself on my thighs, tail wagging with delight. I pull the wet fabric off my chest, but it bounces back with a squelch. "I should head out anyway."

"I'll grab you a clean T-shirt. Tag has plenty."

"No, it's—"

But she's already dashing away.

With a sigh, I flop back against the chair, running my hand through Toaster's long, damp mane. He releases a contented sigh, pressing his chin to my knee.

> *If I fall, will you still catch me?*
> *If I run, will you let go?*

Annie escapes into the house.

And as I watch her retreat, I finish the chorus in my mind.

> *I've been lost inside this winter*
> *Tracing footsteps in the snow*

CHAPTER 16
Annalise

I scour the upstairs laundry room, searching for a clean T-shirt. They're all too small. Chase is broader, more muscular, while my brother is slim and lean.

An array of colorful fabrics are scattered around. Blues, greens, rusts, burgundies. Bath towels, boxers, dresses, and bras.

My mind races. My eyes burn.

The last forty-eight hours come to a churning boil in the hub of my chest, a dammed river. I am bound to break. Splinters and flood.

But I keep sifting through the laundry basket until my fingers curl around a cream-colored band shirt featuring Young the Giant.

Mind over matter, it reads.

Good enough.

I spring to my feet and spin around, rushing into the darkened hallway.

Then I halt abruptly. "Oh!" I squeak in surprise, taking a startled step back.

Chase stands at the top of the staircase, a towering silhouette framed by the soft glow of the living room light below. His wet shirt is bunched up in his hand.

In his hand.

Not on his body.

My gaze snaps up, locking with his chest—exposed, glistening with remnants of spilled beer. He's all muscle. Sculpted with defined pecs that taper down to a tight, chiseled abdomen. Shoulders that fill out his frame like they were built for hard work. Thick arms, tanned skin, and a tattoo that snakes around to his upper back.

I trace the faint trail of dark hair that leads from his stomach, disappearing into the low-slung waistband of his jeans.

Everything inside of me locks up: thoughts, oxygen, words, balance. My vision blurs, mouth going dry. Cotton balls and tumbleweeds.

What the hell?

A strange feeling unfurls, a physical tug. It begins in the deepest part of my stomach—a tempest, dark and swirling. Then it cannonballs up my body, corkscrewing around my throat, siphoning my air. My cheeks burn, flushing with color. With horror.

No.

Oh no.

"Is that for me?"

His voice drags me from the undertow, and I shake myself out of the haze. My eyes ping up to his. He's draped in shadow, only inches away. "What?" I croak out.

He nods at the T-shirt crumpled in my fist. "The shirt."

"Oh, yeah, I…" My fingers slowly unclench as the air returns to my lungs. "Yes. Sorry. It might be a little small."

"All good." He reaches out, takes it, our fingers grazing. "Thanks."

Chase studies me for a moment, a wrinkle between his brows. Humidity clings to my skin; it's too hot in here. He must have left the back door open.

He turns away, tugging the shirt over his head.

Before he's fully covered, I catch the outline of his tattoo dancing along his shoulder blades and the planks of his back as his arms slide through the sleeves.

A canvas of motion, the water tattoo stretches from shoulder to shoulder, waves rolling and crashing in inky, fluid lines. The design moves with him, rippling as his muscles flex, swirls of deep blue and black curling along his spine.

There's a single word etched into the seafoam: *"Hallelujah."*

It knocks the air out of me, the same breath I just fought to catch. "Your tattoo," I say, my eyes scanning, skimming. "Is it religious?"

He glances at me over his shoulder, tugging the shirt down until it just touches his waistband, then turns to face me. "Not really," he says. "Not to me, anyway. It's a song. My sister and I used to sing it together all the time."

I know it. Of course I know it.

That song is a masterpiece.

My gaze drags up in a lazy slide, finding his eyes. "It's one of my favorites."

"Mine too." His expression softens as he stares at me, allowing the moment to marinate, stretch. Then he pulls in a shaky breath and murmurs, "Tomorrow?"

I clench my hands. "Yeah."

"Midnight," he confirms.

"Midnight."

No smile, no nod. Just a final piercing look before he pivots away and heads downstairs, collecting his shoes and Toaster's leash.

Meanwhile, I collect what's left of myself.

My composure. The pieces of my disjointed mind.

The fragments of my shame.

An hour later, I crawl into bed.

Not the stiff, lumpy bed in Tag's guest room—my bed.

It's cool and familiar, the silken gray sheets welcoming me home. Alex sprawls out on the right side of the mattress, his designated side. Moonglow highlights his bronzed skin and coal-black hair. He stirs beside me, one knee lifting beneath the covers.

And then he reaches.

An arm loops around my waist, tucking me to his chest. "Knew you'd come back."

My eyes water as I nestle closer. "You never returned my texts."

"Didn't need to," he mumbles, voice rough with sleep. "You know where you belong."

Alex presses a kiss to the top of my head.

Soon his grip slackens, his breathing shallows, and he drifts back to sleep.

The loneliness dissipates, but I can't tell what replaces it. Something still feels hollow. There's an empty cavity in my chest aching to be filled. Maybe I expected more. A celebration, an emotional reunion. Confetti and violins. But all I hear are the swift beats of my heart and the whir of the ceiling fan from above.

I close my eyes.

This is where I'm supposed to be.

That sudden pull toward Chase was just a test. A crack in the glass, not proof it should shatter. Love isn't about butterflies or stolen glances. It's about staying when things get heavy.

It's about loyalty.

Chase is a distraction, a temptation that tricks you into thinking it's salvation. But I don't need saving. I need to be strong, to prove to myself that I don't give up when it's hard.

I'm not settling.

I'm embracing what is meant for me.

CHAPTER 17
Annalise

"I'm not sure if this is the best or worst idea you've ever had." Kenna takes a final drag from her vape pen, then stuffs it in her purse. "Kind of like when you cut your own bangs. Or when you signed us up for that underground poker tournament because, and I quote, 'How hard can it be?'"

I cringe, fluffing the skirt of my pleated baby-blue dress. "Both fall under the worst category."

"The lines are blurry. That's my point." She yanks open the door to the karaoke bar and hauls me inside. "Your track record is impressive."

"You said 'concerning' wrong."

"Again, blurry."

Alex saunters up behind us, clamping a firm hand around the nape of my neck. He squeezes. "How long are we staying?" His voice rumbles with irritation. "If this dude is anything like your brother, I'll either be here until closing because I'm too drunk to stand, or I give it five minutes."

Alex still doesn't know the truth about Chase. He thinks he's Tag's friend.

The lie gnaws at me, heating my skin.

I melt into him as his arm wraps around me, and he plays with the shoulder tie of my dress. "Um, he's great. He and Kenna really hit it off." I'm not sure if that part is a lie or not, but I guess we'll find out.

Kenna primps her hair in a kitschy mirror off the entrance, smacking her glossy lips together. "Yep. Sparks were flying like bullets."

I ram my elbow into her ribs, the heat morphing into a brushfire down my neck.

She sends me a sly wink.

"You're sure you're over Irving?" I pivot.

She feigns a tear. "Irving is a part of my past, Annalise. We are go-getters. Future setters."

Swallowing hard, I glance toward the karaoke stage where a DJ is setting up. The place is jam-packed, filled with sticky floors, neon beer signs buzzing against wood-paneled walls, and a low ceiling that traps the heat and noise. This is the absolute last place Alex would choose to be, but he can't complain about not spending enough time together while brushing off my attempts.

Besides, it was starting to feel like that brushfire was a wind gust away from multiplying into a blaze beyond my control. All these late-night get-togethers. All this time spent collaborating, making music. I needed to introduce them. Quickly.

Double date to the rescue.

I scan the rest of the room, looking for a familiar tousle of earthy brown hair and broad shoulders. Chase is nowhere to be found. Taking the lead, I guide Alex and Kenna over to an empty four-person table.

I wonder if he'll even show. Reluctance shimmered in his gaze when I broached the subject. More like absolute dread. Chase is far from an extrovert, so convincing him to join me at a karaoke bar after a long shift at work, while playing matchmaker to my best friend, while also introducing him to my boyfriend, was a herculean task. Yet…somehow, he agreed.

I definitely owe him a drink.

Alex collapses into a chair, looking downright miserable. His leg bounces with unease, his stony eyes casing the room. "Looks like he bailed. Let's grab food."

"He didn't bail," Kenna says, plopping down across from him and discarding her purse. "He's eager for a frontrow seat to my karaoke debut. Britney. Obviously."

"You can't sing." Alex glares at her, pursing his lips. "At all."

"That's subjective," she snips back.

Alex doesn't like Kenna. Says she's a "bad influence," whatever that means. But all she's ever done is love me unconditionally since we were seated next to each other in the third grade.

We share a smile.

I wring my hands together, sliding in next to Alex. My cheeks puff with a trapped breath. Kenna drives the conversation—because she *is* an extrovert—while I watch the entrance like an unwavering hawk. Only a few minutes pass before Chase shuffles through.

That feeling swells in my gut again. Strange, instinctual. A warning.

I veer my attention toward the bar, hoping to summon a double-shot of tequila with only mind voodoo.

Kenna twists around in the seat, following my stare. Then she lifts her hand with an animated wave, snagging Chase's attention. There's a slight limp to his gait. There always is. He moves to the table, catching my eye for a beat, before panning over to Kenna, then Alex. A muscle in his cheek ticks.

He peels off his leather coat as he approaches, draping it over the back of the empty chair. "Hey," he says, tone unreadable.

"Hey!" Of course I overcompensate. "You made it!"

"Yeah." A beat of hesitation, and then he sits down, falling silent again.

Nobody knows what to say, what to do. I told Kenna to act natural, but now I'm concerned. Her version of natural is the same as my version, which is never natural.

And the only thing we hate more than tofu is awkward silences.

She hooks her arm through his and beams with the glow of an army of suns. "Chase! So glad we're finally doing this. The will-they-won't-they stage was getting tiring."

Her eyes swerve to mine as she sends me a full-fledged grimace.

I shake my head, a silent plea to tone it down.

Chase clears his throat, stiffens to a board. "Good to see you, Kenna." He glances warily at the man beside me. "Alex, right?"

"Yup."

"Chase." He extends a big hand across the table. "Annalise talks about you all the time."

"All the time?" Alex scowls at Chase's hand before accepting it. Brief, reluctant. Bordering on the epitome of pain and suffering.

I go still.

"Um, yeah…when we met," Chase backpedals. "That one time."

"When you were bleeding to death on your couch?"

"After. Second time, I guess." Chase scratches his mop of hair, looking like he'd rather be cast as the corpse in a low-budget horror film than sitting here. "At the restaurant."

Oof. This web of lies is tangling into terrible knots.

My poor friends.

"Drinks!" I blurt, catapulting off the chair. "First round is on me. Any requests?"

"I'll help you carry them." Chase stands, then immediately storms over to the bar.

Alex is halfway out of his chair when I press a hand to his shoulder. "It's fine. Maybe help me choose a song to sing?" I hand him the giant booklet of karaoke songs beside the table.

He grabs my wrist before I retreat, and we lock eyes. "I don't want to stay long," he says.

I force a smile, my fingers curling into my palm. "Yeah. No problem."

Kenna sends me a soft look as I pull away and wind around the table to join Chase at the bar. He's a stone wall of tension, but when I slide up beside him, our arms brushing, he relaxes a bit. "I'm sorry," I murmur, my voice barely carrying over the chatter and music. "This is so awkward. I feel bad."

A whiskey neat is set in front of him. "Little bit. But it's fine. I have nowhere else to be."

"I really appreciate you covering for me. It's ridiculous, I know. I just—"

"I get it," he interjects, spinning his glass. "I don't want to cause any more problems."

Nodding, I bite down on my lip before ordering a Jack and Coke for Alex and two mai tais for Kenna and me.

"How have things been?" He takes a small sip, eyes lowering to me.

"Good. It's been a long week of reconciling, but I think we're making progress."

That's an exaggeration. The truth is, things haven't changed all that much. Alex is still Alex, and I'm still…

I don't know.

But I'm trying. I'm working hard to fix what's broken, while trying to find where I fit amid the scattered rubble.

Chase studies me, his glass hovering below his chin. "I know this isn't the place for a heart to heart, but you can text me whenever. If you need an outlet. To vent or talk."

He says it casually, but the words dig, pry, and twist. They mean something. More than I should allow them to. And I can't tell if it feels like a noble invitation or an omen. "Thank you."

Nodding once, he looks away.

As I reach for the set of glasses placed on the bar counter, the tipsy woman on my left stumbles, crashing into me. One of the drinks sloshes all over my hand as I bump into Chase.

"Oops! Sorry!" she apologizes, smacking her friend's arm.

A warm palm presses to the small of my back, steadying me.

Gentle, a whisper of a touch.

The contact steals my breath.

It's hardly anything, just a graze. But I'm so used to angry fingers curling around my wrist, hard hugs, kisses that bruise, and looks that burn holes through me. I've grown familiar with it.

"You okay?" he asks, his hand lingering.

No.

I inch away slightly, feeling his palm splay, warm fingers intimately coasting over my bare skin through the opening of my dress.

He doesn't know how much I've craved this. Needed this. Something so simple.

He couldn't.

I don't think I knew.

My skin flushes warm, and I scratch at the back of my hand for no other reason than to remove the tickle racing through me. "Yeah. Sorry." When my breathing evens out, I gesture toward the bartender. "Can I get some extra cherries?"

The man nods, filling a small bowl with a heap of maraschino cherries.

"Cherries?" Chase eyes the glossy fruit.

"I'm addicted. I could eat a whole jar in one sitting." Popping one into my mouth, I grab the bowl and the mai tais and trek back to the table.

Alex watches me approach, gaze simmering with ominous things. Instinct has me picking up the pace, adding distance between me and Chase as he trails behind with the remaining drinks. The moment I sit, an arm envelops my shoulders, a sharp tug pulling me right. I barely manage to discard my hoard, ungracefully depositing the glasses and cherries on the table.

Nuzzling his nose against my neck, Alex whispers, "You look

fucking sexy tonight." He nips my earlobe. "Tell me when I can get you out of this dress."

My throat tightens through a swallow, and I place my hand on Alex's knee, giving it a small squeeze. Chase watches us as he takes his seat, grip firm around his whiskey glass. "Um, I just want to sing a song or two first." I reach for the Jack and Coke and slide it over. "Have a drink. Enjoy yourself."

"I'd be enjoying myself more if you were riding me." He flicks his tongue against the mole below my ear. "Tell me I can have you tonight."

Embarrassment prickles my skin. He's not being subtle or quiet. The bar lights blaze from above, sluicing me in sweat. "Of course," I whisper.

We haven't had sex in over a month. I realize I'm to blame for that. My libido thrives on intimacy and emotional connection, and things with Alex have been so tense. A disjointed black hole. But I can't help but wonder if that's only adding to the disconnect, the chaos. Maybe I just need to block out the noise and suck it up. After all, men are wired differently. I can't say Alex isn't trying when I'm not putting in one hundred percent either.

I clear my throat, glancing across the table to where Kenna is doing her best to distract Chase from the aggressive PDA.

"Are you a plant daddy?" she asks him, stealing one of my cherries.

Alex scoffs, disentangling himself from me. "What the fuck is a plant daddy?"

"A man who appreciates the quiet dignity of houseplants," Kenna snipes, low-key offended.

Chase takes a sip of his drink, masking the flickering smile. "I do have a rubber tree."

"No shit?" She twirls back around to face him, eyes alight with enchantment. "Rubber trees represent resilience. I love that for you."

I prop my chin in my hand, watching my friend ramble on about the history and symbolism of a rubber tree. I watch Chase too. He's polite but uninterested. His attention sweeps to me every few beats, like we're having our own silent conversation on the sidelines. I wonder if he's writing poems and lyrics in his mind like I am. My fingers itch for a napkin and a pen.

Instead, I reach for a cherry. It's sweet and distracting as it pops between my teeth, and I use my tongue to twist the stem into an easy, practiced knot. Chase does a double take, his gaze dropping to my mouth the moment before I pluck it out and set it on the table.

A perfect little bow.

His eyes lift to mine. No longer uninterested.

A text pings.

Flustered, I look away and fish my phone out of my purse, noticing Kenna's name glowing on the screen.

Sneaky.

I go to read the text, and on autopilot, swipe down with two fingers, triggering the Speak Screen function that I left on after using it on the treadmill earlier.

A robotic voice erupts from the phone: "I would ride him like a stolen bike down a steep hill with no brakes."

All three heads snap in my direction.

Kenna chokes on her drink.

Mortified, I fumble to mute my phone, but the voice keeps going.

"Again. And again. Fire emoji. Eggplant emoji. Sweat—"

Why is my volume all the way up?

I slap the screen like it vehemently assaulted me, then chuck the phone under the table. I'm tempted to crush it beneath my shoe, but the voice finally goes silent, along with everyone else.

Chase rubs a hand over his face, scratching at his stubble.

Alex shakes his head, downing his drink in one go.

My cheeks are every shade of red as I grab the karaoke booklet and start flipping through pages. "Well, we could sing now. Any suggestions?"

Kenna—inherently shameless—smirks around her straw as she slurps up the rum. "'Bicycle Race' by Queen," she suggests. "Or 'Save a Horse (Ride a Cowboy)?' That song slaps."

"Mm," I hum, the titles blurring into the pages.

"Hey, you two should sing a duet." Kenna glances tentatively between me and Chase. "That would amp things up. It's rare to find actual talent in this place."

"You sing?" Alex eyes Chase, body stiffening.

He strokes his chin, glancing at the book of songs. "Not really."

"But you—" Stopping herself short, Kenna appears to recalibrate. "I mean, you sang that one time. To me. NSYNC."

"That never happened."

"Maybe it was One Direction."

"I don't mind a duet," I say, more to remove ourselves from this smothering furnace. This was a terrible idea. The worst I've ever had, bar none. "We can put in an oldie. Something up-tempo."

Chase considers it, his eyes narrowing, hand combing through his hair. "Yeah. Sure."

Alex looks at me, then at Chase. There's a recognition there that breathes cold air along the back of my neck.

I'm on my feet before Alex can intervene, the motion automatic as I head toward the DJ booth, the weight of Alex's gaze heavy on my back.

The DJ gives me a distracted look as I lean in and ask him to cue up "Good Vibrations" by the Beach Boys.

This will be fun. Easy. A much-needed break in the tension.

We're geared up to sing next, and as I move onto the stage with a chest full of lead, something stops me. Chase ambles up on my right, hands in his pockets, a look of dread in his eyes.

"Wait." I turn to Chase as he grabs one of the two microphones. "Do you want to sing 'Hallelujah'?"

The suggestion slips out unbidden. Twists my stomach into a cherry stem.

I should have stuck with the oldie—upbeat, free of deeper weights. His tattoo flickers across my mind, an ode to his late sister.

This is too much.

But Chase swallows. Falters. Then nods once.

Mind spinning, I traipse over to the DJ and ask him to change the song. It takes a minute before the haunting opening chords of "Hallelujah" reach the air. As I return to the stage and move in beside Chase, my arm brushes his as I take the second mic. For a moment, all I hear is the rush of my heartbeat, a thundercloud of nerves and doubt.

I can do this.

This is what I've been working toward. A pinnacle of all my midnights.

I open my mouth and sing the first verse solo, grasping for that secret chord. A hush washes over the room, the voices dying out, the echo of glassware fading into raw poetry.

Surely nobody expected this song, a melancholy hymn thrown into a divey pub filled with pop songs and overplayed classics. But I think this is what people search for. A voice that moves when they least expect it. A song that connects. Stands out.

Maybe that's the secret chord.

I don't look at Alex, but I know he's watching. Studying our dynamic like he's waiting for the right moment to pull the strings tighter, just enough to remind me of where I belong. But I already know where I belong.

Alex is my home, even when it hurts.

And yet, standing on this stage next to Chase, I've never felt more grounded. More indelible. More like myself.

Chase enters at the chorus, his voice intertwining with mine, the harmony both fragile and euphoric. Our voices rise with the words, with the lyrical poetry, pure and profound. A threaded tale of faith and purpose and tragic love.

He takes the second verse, and I grip the mic harder, my palms slick. I stare straight ahead, faces blurred and color muted. My eyes close. I drink in the sound of his voice like sustenance. This feels too natural, too kismet. His voice doesn't waver, steady in its sorrow.

Suddenly, it doesn't feel like a song anymore. It's a story.

His grief. My burdens. Losses that linger like smoke-steeped air, each note a confession.

My throat burns, the tears gathering before I even realize they've ambushed me. I blink rapidly, try to eviscerate them, but they bloom and swell, stinging the backs of my eyes.

I sing with him. Dips and crescendos. Brokenness and hope.

I can't tell if it's an exorcism or a possession.

Maybe both.

And it hits me like a rogue wave, how deeply I've been avoiding my own feelings. Shunned them like trespassers. My purpose, my dreams, everything that makes me...*me*.

It all breaks free.

The sobs I've been holding back for so long burst like a brittle dam cracking. Hot tears pour out, one after another, and I can't stop them.

Embarrassment and despair bleed together.

Clarity too.

I'm drowning. Lost at sea.

Chase stops singing, leaving the final verse unfinished. He turns to face me, stares like he doesn't know what to do. What to say. How to help.

Not with an audience. Not with Alex storming over to the stage.

I cup a hand around my mouth, my arm dropping to my side with defeat.

I'm not sure what hurts more...

The pain I see in Chase's eyes, or the fact that I've spent so much time running from my own pain.

CHAPTER 18
Chase

Just like that, she falls apart.

Frays at the seams.

I stand there frozen as the room tilts around her collapse. The audience murmurs. The song cuts off prematurely. Snickers echo from one corner, a slow-clap from another.

Everything in me screams to reach for her, to pull her close and hold her together. She's breaking. Crumbling in plain view.

I set the mic back on the stand as Annie drops to a crouch, covering her face with her hand. The other goes slack, the microphone slipping from her grip and rolling across the stage. Her sobs slice through the static of the bar.

I hesitate. I'm not the guy who should be comforting her.

But I can't just watch her break like a useless bystander.

Lowering beside her, I stroke a hand down her back, soft and gentle, as if she's a frightened animal ready to scratch or bolt.

Once, twice.

But that's as far as I get.

Alex charges onto the stage with murder in his eyes. "I got it." His voice is all bite as he hauls her upright and into his arms with reckless force.

I rise to my feet. The outlier once again.

Kenna hovers near the steps, eyes wide and tearful, ushering me toward her. I move on autopilot, watching out of my periphery as Alex drags Annie toward the bathrooms, his grip too hard. Possessive.

Annie's panicked voice floats into my ears. "Don't. Please. I'm fine. I'll be fine."

A headache flares behind my left temple.

I press my fingers to it as I reach the table for my leather jacket. Noise floods back in. Chatter, laughter, the DJ apologizing, a grungy '90s song cutting through the speakers.

I jab the heel of my palm against my head.

"She will be, you know." Kenna's voice penetrates, pulling my gaze to her.

Her face blurs. I teeter in place, the migraine stabbing deeper. "She'll be what?"

A small smile. "Fine."

Tension coils around me.

Fine.

That's not good enough. It never has been.

But who am I to say otherwise? To challenge it with wisdom, experience, or hollow hope? I've been coasting on *fine* for years.

My job? Fine.

My house? Fine.

My music? Fine.

I'd only be a hypocrite. A hypocrite with no claim to her, no right to want more.

"Yeah," I manage, shoving my arms into my jacket sleeves. "Take care, Kenna."

The headache hammers in time with my pulse. I need air. Space. A second to breathe without feeling like my ribs are a noose.

I push toward the door.

But a figure steps into my path.

Alex.

His smile is all teeth, a lazy stretch that doesn't reach his eyes. "Heading out?"

My muscles lock. "Yeah. Tell Annie I said goodbye."

"Annie?" His dark brows lift, a crude laugh slipping out. "That's interesting. Yeah, I'll tell her."

I turn to leave.

But he moves with me, blocking the way. His cologne clings to the stagnant air, his presence a wall I'll have to scale just to get the fuck out of here.

My eyes cut down to his. I've got five inches on him, but he doesn't seem fazed. "Did you want something?" I ask, tone flat.

His mouth twitches. "Just curious why you picked that song. Felt a little out of place, you know?"

"It was just a song."

"Right." His lips press into a thin line. "That all it was for you?"

The headache claws deeper, turning the bar lights into razor wire.

I roll my shoulders, forcing my muscles to loosen. "I don't

know what you want me to say."

His gaze flicks to the bathroom door, to where Annie hides inside. "I mean, there was just this…" He gestures vaguely. "What do they call it?"

I blink. Waiting.

"Harmony."

I exhale sharply, shaking my head. "Glad it resonated. Have a good night."

As I move to step around him, a solid arm slams into my chest, shoving me back against the wall.

The smarmy smile is gone. In its place, something colder.

Alex leans in, voice a low snarl. "Stay. The fuck away. From my girlfriend."

Our eyes lock.

My blood simmers.

The headache explodes behind my eyes.

Then a door creaks open, and Annie steps out.

Quickly, Alex backs away, slapping a too-friendly hand to my shoulder. "Good chat," he says. "Enjoy the rest of your evening."

Swallowing, I glance over at Annie in her retro blue dress, her eyes red and swollen, complexion ashen. A frown creases. She looks between us, searching for the context. The missing pieces.

But I have nothing to give her.

I drag my eyes away, pull up from the wall, and make a swift exit out the front door.

You don't bring your heart to a battleground and expect it not to bleed in the same way you don't bring a stick to a swordfight.

It only ends one way.

You lose.

CHAPTER 19
Alex

The front door snaps shut behind us.

Annie.

A roar fills my head, waves surging through an angry sea.

Far away, a voice fights to be heard.

Don't lash out. Act rationally. Stay fucking calm.

But the waves are louder. A stormfront edging closer. I can't stop it, can't keep it at bay. One man against a storm is nothing but a piece of driftwood.

Dead in the water, doomed before it ever reaches the shore.

My hands curl into fists.

Fury surges through my veins, my only friend.

I whip around, locking on her tearstained face as she sags against the door. "What. The. Fuck."

She cowers, a frightened hermit crab who lost her shell. "I just…had a moment."

"A moment?" I stiffen and vibrate all at once, my words weapons. Thunderclaps. "Yeah, I'm aware of your fucking *moment*. You paraded it onstage for an audience. Dangled it in front of me like a carrot on a stick. Were you trying to make me jealous?"

Her eyes lift, confused. Like she's realizing we're talking about two different moments. "Chase?"

"Don't say his fucking name." Holy hell, I sound demonic.

"That was nothing. That was just—"

"Now you're gaslighting me. Beautiful." I drag my hands through my hair, spin, then pivot back, inching closer. "Do you think I'm an idiot? What aren't you saying?"

"There's nothing to be said." She swipes a piece of hair out of her eyes and moves away from the door, her chin glued to her chest.

Avoiding eye contact.

Because she's lying.

I follow, tight on her heels. "We're not done here."

"I'm tired, Alex. I just had a breakdown at a karaoke bar, for God's sake."

"Could be the guilt."

She whirls around, teeth clenched tight. "There's nothing to feel guilty about. He's just my brother's friend."

"He called you *Annie*," I seethe. "A pet name. Do you realize how fucked that is?"

She falters for a beat, the statement registering, taking her off guard. "You have no idea what you're talking about."

"No? I saw the way he was looking at you. I was watching him all night."

"I have no control over the way someone *looks* at me. If I did, I'd be a hell of a lot happier in this relationship."

Her words hit hard. Stop me in my tracks. "You're not happy?"

Some people might say that should be obvious based on her forty-eight hour departure last week. Her request for a "break." But that was just a bump in the road. It's always been us, Alex and Annalise, best friends from day one. High school sweethearts.

Soulmates.

I was there when she fell off her bike in second grade, scraping her knee so bad she swore she'd never ride again. I sat beside her on the sidewalk, pressing my Captain America Band-Aid over the cut and promising I'd hold on to the seat until she felt confident again.

She was back on her bike by the next afternoon.

I was there in seventh grade when she got braces and refused to smile for an entire month. I made it my mission to change that, cracking the dumbest jokes I could think of until she finally caved. The first time she really smiled, she smacked my arm and called me an idiot.

But she kept smiling after that.

I was there the night of our junior prom, when her dress zipper broke ten minutes before we were supposed to leave. She was near tears, convinced the night was ruined, but I found a safety pin in my mom's office and fixed it. I told her she was the most beautiful girl I'd ever seen. She laughed and called me a liar.

I wasn't.

I was also there when she needed driving lessons. When she

stalled at that stop sign and I lost it. I screamed until she cried, and she jerked the wheel and sent us spinning into a tree. She shattered the fender. I cracked my head. Blood everywhere. She begged me not to hate her, and I didn't. I forgave her. I stayed. Unlike my shitty parents, who ditched me to sip wine on some sun-drenched piazza in Rome and never looked back.

When everything else in my life fell apart, I stayed. If that couldn't break us, nothing will. I can't lose her now.

Her eyes shimmer with frustration, with pain. "Alex…"

I shake my head. "You can't mean that." My voice is quieter, almost desperate. "Not after everything."

This is just a phase. A temporary snag in the long-term plan.

What do they call it? The "Seven Year Itch"? That's all this is. It's fucking psychology. We're literally in our seventh year of dating.

"Annalise, come on. We'll get through this. We always do."

"I just…I don't know if love is supposed to feel like this," she says, breath shuddering.

The room skews, my stomach hollowing out. "Like what?"

Her gaze flicks to the floor. "Like drowning."

The waves roll back in.

There's a sharp snap in my brain, like an electrical current. I can't stop it. Can't fight it. The beast inside me claws its way up, hungry, restless, desperate to prove something.

Heart pounding, I advance on her. My eyes skim down her body, her full breasts, curvy hips, long, toned legs. She's a work of art.

She's *my* work of art.

My arms fly out and yank her to me by the hips. A breath

leaves her in a sudden whoosh when our chests collide. I grip her cheeks, pressing our foreheads together. "You said I could have you tonight."

Annalise tenses in my arms. "That was before."

"Before the karaoke foreplay with another guy?" I roughly tug her head back by the hair until her eyes meet with mine. "If you want to play dirty, I'm all in."

She presses her hands to my chest, not a shove, but far from intimate. "Alex, please. I don't want it like this."

"You don't seem to want it at all." I pull her closer. "How long has it been? A month? Two?"

"Things have been messy between us."

"That'll only make it hotter."

"Alex—"

I scoop her up, hauling her into my arms. Her legs curl around my waist, arms looping behind my neck. Carrying her into the bedroom, I toss her on the mattress and crawl over her until she's splayed out beneath me. Heart to heart. Breath to breath.

Colorful hair fans out across the pillow, her skin milky-white like whipped cream. Plump cherry lips quiver with emotion.

Her eyes squeeze shut. Cheeks flush with color. A whimper escapes her throat.

She doesn't want you.

She's repulsed by you.

She fucking hates you.

That goddamn voice.

It only makes me angrier. More determined to prove it wrong.

"Look at me." I grip her wrists, pinning them to the pillow. "Look at me, Annalise."

Her lids flutter open.

And I'm sickened by what I see.

Emptiness. Hopeless resignation.

Proof.

The voice laughs with spite.

I kiss her.

Our mouths crash together in a desperate, frenzied clash of teeth and tongues. My hands move with menace, shoving her dress up her thighs, fingers fumbling with her underwear. Tears spill down her temples, but she doesn't fight me.

She just deflates.

"Tell me you want this."

Her legs fall open like surrender. A small nod.

"Say it," I demand.

Another nod. "I do. I want you."

I tug off her underwear, shove down my zipper, grip her wrists harder. Bruising, needy, begging for something. A spark. A reckoning. Anything.

Look at me.

Look at me.

Look at me.

She does.

And as I sink inside her, watching her face, the sadness in her eyes, I feel it.

She doesn't want you.

She's repulsed by you.

She fucking hates you.

The voice is still there. Still mocking me.

This time, I don't think it's lying.

CHAPTER 20
Annalise

I roll over, searching for my phone on the nightstand, and glance at the time.

12:22 a.m.

I should be at Tag's right now, penning songs beneath the moon.

My gaze drifts to the open window as a summer breeze filters inside. The moon isn't full—a waning crescent—but it still glimmers like honey among the stars.

The imagery has my throat squeezing, heart kicking up speed.

Wide awake, I collect my phone and slide out of bed. Alex doesn't stir as he lies facedown on the mattress, head turned away as his arms cradle the pillow, a small comfort. He looks peaceful like this. Free of turmoil and inner demons.

My breath hitches as I turn away, quietly padding from the

room. There are two cigarettes buried in my purse, calling to me. I need something to quell the chaotic butterflies in my stomach, my own small comfort.

I carry the cigarette and a lighter out to the tiny balcony off the living room, closing the door all the way so the smoke doesn't carry over to Alex. He'd hate that I'm smoking.

The air is still and fragrant as I take a seat on the metal chair. Crickets hum in the tall grass, and the trees stand dark and unmoving against a sky dusted with stars. A firefly gleams once before vanishing into the black, here and gone in a blink.

I flick the lighter, watching as the night sky distorts around the edges of the flame. My thoughts are parchment paper. Thin, brittle, and ready to burn.

I did it. I gave in.

I'm not sure how I feel now. Alex cherished me in the aftermath, kissing away my tears, apologizing, holding me until I dozed off. But something was missing.

And I think that something was me.

As I light the cigarette and inhale a lungful, my eyes dart to the phone sitting on my lap. Two missed text messages illuminate the face.

Kenna: Call me when you get a minute. I love you.
Chase: Just making sure you got home okay. LMK.

My thumb hovers over the texts, idling between the two. I want to text Kenna, let her know I'm okay, that the moment onstage tonight was just a glitch. Nothing to be worried about.

But I open Chase's message instead.

Anxiety swims through me, mingling with adrenaline. I should respond with something short and sweet, nothing more.

I'm fine.

I'm home.

Thanks for checking.

Against my better judgment, different words materialize on the screen.

I press send.

Me: Are you awake?

The feeling expands in my gut, both a warning and a buzz. I take another long drag on the cigarette, my hands trembling as my gaze fuses to the blue text bubble.

Don't be awake.

Please be awake.

The message shows Read. A moment later, his three dots dance to life.

Chase: I'm here.

I let out a breath that feels like relief.

I wonder what he's doing.

Lying in bed. Carving wood into instruments. Writing music. Staring at the sickle-shaped moon.

My eyes snap shut, tamping down the visuals that don't matter.

Me: I'm sorry about earlier.

The text goes through with a swoosh.

Chase: I already told you, you never need to apologize to me.

A smile twitches on my lips.

Me: Because you lost that privilege when you kidnapped me?

It takes a few minutes before he starts typing again.

Chase: Yeah. But also because you don't owe anyone an apology for feeling what you feel. For being vulnerable or scared. What happened tonight was a human moment. That's nothing to be sorry about.

My throat stings at the unexpected response. It was deeper than I was anticipating.
The floodgates crack open.

Me: Can I ask you something?
Chase: Go ahead.

I exhale a plume of smoke through my nose, watching as it evaporates into the moon.

Me: I know you've been through a lot. With your

sister. My problems seem insignificant compared to that, but... How do we separate who we are from all we've experienced?

His reply is quick. Like he knows exactly what to say.

Chase: We don't.
Chase: But our experiences aren't all we are.

I read over his words a dozen times. Two dozen times. They seep inside me, battling with every misguided, baseless belief I've fed myself. Lies that don't serve me.
Holding my breath, I keep typing.

Me: I guess I just feel lost lately. Like a side character in my own book. That sounds really pathetic, but I'm trying to figure out what I want, what's right and what's wrong.

I pause.
This part...
It feels too raw. But it's there, poking at me. So I add it.

Me: And something tells me you're supposed to be a part of that.

He goes quiet.
Two minutes drag by as I puff on the cigarette, second-guessing my own intentions. I don't know what I'm searching for here.

A text flashes on the screen.

Chase: How does that make you feel?

Conflicting emotions bubble to the surface.
But mostly I feel—

Me: Scared. Guilty.
Chase: Why?
Me: Because you're not my boyfriend. You're not the guy I should be texting in the middle of the night, or the guy I wish I was with right now, writing music beneath the stars. It feels wrong.

I swallow hard.
It feels wrong because it is.
Tag said I was playing with fire, but it feels more complex than that.
Fire is straightforward. Honest.
This is something else. Muddy, blurry, and snarled.

Chase: This probably won't make you feel any better...
Chase: But I wouldn't say no if you wanted to meet up somewhere and write.

My breath locks up. Temptation seizes me.
He wants to meet up, right now, at almost one in the morning.
Alone.

It's not like we haven't spent alone time together, but something feels different. Ever since that night in the hallway.

I wonder if Chase feels the shift, this strange new dynamic, or if it's all in my head. Intrusive thoughts infiltrate, twisting pure intentions into something that feels scary.

Scary enough to trigger my rational mind.

Me: I can't. I'm sorry.

Oops.

Me: Oops.
Me: Sorry for being sorry.

He shoots back a smiley face.
And then…

Chase: Was everything okay when you got home?

I frown at the screen, peeling back the context.

Me: What do you mean?
Chase: With Alex. He was coming on a little strong at the table and you looked uncomfortable. Just making sure you're good.

My cheeks burn. This could easily delve into TMI territory. But my walls are down, and I feel safe with Chase.

Me: Yes, thank you. Honestly, I don't always feel present with him. Like sometimes I just kind of slip out of my own head when it comes to intimacy. (Which sounds way more dramatic than I mean it to, promise, LOL)

I scrunch my nose, wondering if that was a massive overshare.

Chase: But nothing happened? Nothing bad I mean?
Me: Nothing bad. Just the usual. I'm fine.
Chase: It shouldn't have to feel like that. Checking out, going someplace else.
Me: Eh, long-term relationships. You know how it is sometimes.

Chase's bubbles start to move again, but I'm not sure I want to see his reply.
Time to pivot.

Me: Well, thank you for singing with me tonight. And for being there when I fell apart.

His response falters. Then he starts typing again.

Chase: I would have done more.
Me: But? Feels like there should be a but...
Chase: You know the but.

I hesitate, my emotions getting the better of me again.

My thumbs glide over the keyboard, having a mind of their own.

Me: What would you have done?

God.
I need to shut up. Chuck my phone over the balcony.
He leaves me hanging for several beats.

Chase: Doesn't feel safe to answer that.

I tap my feet, fidget in place, choking on the smoke-tinged air.

Me: I can be your safe space. You feel like mine.
Chase: I know. That's why it doesn't feel safe.

Tension wraps around me. Sinks deep.

My heart is beating a mile a minute, my limbs putty, thoughts askew.

It's time to say good night.

Me: I should get to bed. If you're near a window, look at the moon. It's a floating sliver of honey.
Chase: I'm out on the patio. I see it.
Me: Honeymoon phase. ☺
Chase: Here for it.

Embers singe my fingers, and I flick the charred stub to the ground, watching the orange glow disappear, leaving only the faint smell of burnt tobacco.

I glance back at the phone.

Me: Good night, Chase.

A final text pings.

Chase: Good night.

I set the phone on my lap, staring at the cinder's ghost curling into the night. The air is thick with summer, warm and quiet, but my skin prickles like I've walked into something dangerous.

I shouldn't have texted him. Shouldn't have let the conversation drift into uncharted territory. But I wanted the weight of his words, wanted to feel something other than this restless ache in my chest.

I drag my hands down my face, exhaling hard.

Pushing up from the chair, I step inside, detouring to the kitchen for a napkin, a pen, and a few aimless lines I'll probably trash by morning.

Ticking clocks don't sing
They warn
Darling, do you hear the horn?

It's time to run
To break, to bend
Or sit and mourn the bitter end

Back in my room, I delete the text string and climb into bed.

CHAPTER 21
Chase

"Need a favor."

I glance up from Tag's couch, half focused on the song I'm playing and half watching Toaster sniff around the room for stray crumbs. "A favor?"

Tag looks like he'd rather ask a favor from the IRS after accidentally claiming his ex as a business expense than ask me. "Don't get too excited. It's a one-off thing."

"The excitement is dizzying," I say with a straight face. "Please elaborate."

"My friend is getting married in two weeks, and the band he hired for the reception bailed."

"Good thing there are about fifty DJs within a thirty-mile radius."

"He doesn't want that overproduced bubblegum-pop bullshit. Jesus." He scowls. "Fuck Bruno Mars."

My lips twitch. "Understood."

"It's a low-key reception. You know, that backyard, DIY type of shit. Burlap, mason jars, fairy lights. Pinterest board nonsense."

I stare at him, waiting for the punchline.

"Anyway, he asked me if I could fill in last minute. Bands are booked up. It's prime wedding season."

"You seem to know an awful lot about weddings."

A glare. "I've only got my acoustics. His fiancée wants a whole-ass band."

"Okay."

Tag glances at my guitar case, then blinks over at me. "You gonna make me say it?"

"Yes."

"Fuck off. I'll ask my buddy Zach."

I sigh, placing the guitar beside me on the couch. "You can borrow my custom, if that's what you're getting at."

"Yeah, well, I was actually getting at something else." He looks extra pale, like he might puke up his four pieces of bacon pizza. "Thinking you could join me. Annalise too."

I freeze, my head snapping up. "Wait, what?"

"Never mind. Terrible idea."

"You want me to play the wedding with you?"

Pivoting away, Tag swipes a hand through his shoulder-length hair, his posture tense. He releases a defeated breath. "It kills me to say it, but you're a better singer. You both are. One of my coworkers is in a band—plays drums—and he offered to bring his bassist along, so I just thought…" A shrug. "It's three thousand bucks, split five ways. Figured there are worse ways to earn a paycheck."

"I'll do it."

Jabbing his tongue against his cheek, he swivels to face me. "It's just a one-off."

"You mentioned that."

"I don't want my sister getting any wild ideas. She loves to poke."

As if summoned, Annie traipses down the staircase in a pair of cotton shorts and a heather-gray tank top, hair damp from her shower. Toaster darts straight to her, pawing at her bare legs.

"What about poking?" she asks, distracted, crouching to scratch between his ears.

My skin buzzes at the sight of her, a physical reaction. Instinctual, inherent.

Fucking catastrophic.

Wet strands of hair fall over her shoulders, curtaining her face. Remnants of her citrusy shampoo fill the room, overpowering the scent of cheap delivery pizza. I swallow, shifting in place and picking the guitar back up.

I'm sensing Tag hasn't filled Annie in on his plan yet.

"It's nothing. Just had a bad idea," he mumbles, collapsing into a reclining chair and reaching for a triangular slice of pizza, now cold and crusty.

She makes a humming sound. "Groundbreaking."

I stare down at the taut wire strings. "Your brother wants us to play a wedding with him."

An involuntary laugh slips out. But when a wash of silence answers, she lifts her head, attention flicking from Tag to me, then back to Tag.

Slowly, she rises to her feet. "Wait, what?"

"That's what I said." I keep my head bowed, watching her from beneath my lashes as she floats across the room, staring at her brother like he just dropped the bomb that "Blinded by the Light" does not, in fact, say *douche*.

"Tag." Her voice pitches higher. "Explain."

He fills her in, avoiding eye contact, barely decipherable between giant bites of pizza.

Annie blinks at him. Turns to face me. "Are you doing it?" she asks, close to breathless.

I nod. "Yeah."

It's a no-brainer. Who am I to pass on six hundred bucks, doing something I love?

"Oh my God." A smile lights up her face, one that's been absent lately. Suppressed by broken dreams and no-way-outs. "We need to start practicing. There are so many good covers. They need to be upbeat, songs about love. I can research. A mix of classics and modern. Maybe…"

Her voice fades out. She's still talking, alive and soul-stirred, practically singing the words. But all I do is watch her, drinking in the new bounce to her step, the animated way her hands move, the grin that doesn't falter. No tears, no sorrow, no ghosts.

Just joy.

Ten minutes later, we're out on the deck.

Tag called it a night, but 1:00 a.m. is prime time for us. Annie is still buzzing, a fireball of energy, pacing back and forth with a cigarette between her fingers. Her eyes are wide, gleaming in the low light. "God, this is going to be incredible. I can't believe we only have two weeks to put together a setlist." She takes another puff. "Think we can do it?"

My mind is somewhere else. "Maybe."

"Maybe, as in, yes?" A grin flickers. Another pull, another cloud. "Sounds like a yes."

My gaze pans to the half-burned cigarette as she flicks ashes to the ground. "You've been smoking more."

She stops pacing and glances at me, the smile slipping. "Yeah, I know. It's becoming a habit." Her arm drops to her side, tiny live coals scattering. "Guess I'm in my rebel era. Did you ever have one of those?"

I've had plenty. But one stands out. "Told my parents to fuck off, packed a box of essentials, and moved across the country with my dog and no plan." I pop a shoulder. "That count?"

"Yeah," she murmurs, a small frown forming. "That counts."

She takes another drag, lips glossy, parted. A plume of smoke slips through.

Her chest rises and falls beneath the thin fabric of her top, the breeze bringing her nipples to a tight peak. My gaze dips for a beat too long before I force it back up.

What I don't say is that I'm one wrong look away from diving headfirst into another rebel era. All I've got keeping me grounded is a shred of integrity and a few threads of willpower, frayed like old guitar strings.

One bad pull, and I'm snapping.

I step toward her.

She watches me approach, still as the night, save for the slow rise and fall of her breath. The cigarette dangles between her fingers, delicate kindling against the dark.

I reach for it, my hand brushing hers, our gazes still tangled.

The energy shifts.

A jolt of electricity.

Her eyes flare. She waits for me to crush the cigarette beneath my boot, to kill the moment before it becomes something else.

Instead, I lift it to my lips and inhale deep. Heat curls through my chest. The paper tastes like whatever watermelon lip balm is smeared across her mouth.

I want to taste more. Fucking all of it.

Her throat bobs, gaze flicking to my lips wrapped around the cigarette.

My dick jumps.

Fuck me.

Just like that, we're both reminded.

I see the memories come alive in the blue swirl of her eyes.

Our texts.

I didn't say anything outright damning, but the context was there. And she's not an idiot.

I exhale slowly, smoke winding between us like a dark secret.

Annie looks away, breaking the spell. Moonlight spills across her face as she stares at the inky horizon. "Why did you move?" Her voice cracks on the last syllable.

I hesitate. Not just because it still hurts, but because I'm afraid of what might come out.

Taking another drag, I hand the cigarette back to her and blow a thin stream of smoke toward the sky. "I couldn't look at them anymore," I admit. "Or maybe because when I looked at them, I saw my own sins reflecting back at me."

She spares me a timid glance. "Your sister?"

Turning, I lean against the side of the house. "Sometimes we run from something. Sometimes we run from ourselves."

"Sounds like a losing race," she whispers.

I nod. "Maybe that's the point."

Something shifts in her expression. Pain, understanding.

She drops her cigarette to the wood planks, grinding it out beneath the toe of her shoe before settling next to me, mirroring my stance. "I don't think you're a sinner, Chase. You're a good person."

We're too close. Feels like nothing but a flimsy sheet of lace between us. Everything seeps through.

My jaw clenches as I look at her. "We're all sinners, aren't we?" I wait for her to find my eyes before adding, "Some of us just hide it better."

Annie's lashes flutter, fanning out in thick, dark wisps.

I think she's about to reply. Counter the pain in my voice with enlightenment or wisdom.

But she surprises me.

Her hand reaches out, clasping with mine.

I nearly buckle. Her touch is warm, intoxicating. More soothing than the midsummer breeze, more healing than any carefully sanded fretboard beneath my fingers. She holds on to me like she wants to put me back together, piece by piece. A song taking shape, the melody uncertain but the rhythm undeniable.

I consider pulling away, putting distance between us…

But I surprise myself too.

My palm opens, and I thread our fingers together.

The contact slams into me, raw emotion locking in my throat. I tip my head back against the siding and close my eyes. I can't look at her. My heart is fucking dynamite in my chest, a match strike away from detonating. It's been years since someone has touched me like this.

Like they meant it. Like I mattered.

My mind races, telling me to run.

New city. New life. Different girl.

That's what I do.

I run.

But she squeezes my hand, her thumb brushing against my skin.

As if she hears me howling.

"I hate that you lost someone so important to you," she breathes out. "Something irreplaceable. It's not fair."

Her thumb keeps moving with careful, gentle strokes.

Is this how it's going to be?

Every night, a new line crossed. A glance, a song, a hug.

This.

With every waning midnight, tragedy looms closer. She'd fucking hate herself if something happened. It would ruin her. And I think that's the only thing keeping me from pulling her to me and kissing the watermelon balm off her lips.

Our hands are still loosely entwined as her words sink in. I'm not sure what to say. A few nights ago, I was the one holding her together, talking her through it. Now she's the anchor.

"Yeah," I finally answer, my ring dusting along the side of her knuckle. "It's staggering what stays with you. Shapes you. You lose something, and you think the memories will fade, but they don't. They just latch on tighter, like a song on repeat, getting louder every time you play it."

"Songs are kind of like people," she muses, staring at our joined hands, looking dazed. Conflicted and settled, all at once. "Some people you just notice. You see their smile, hear their voice, but they don't leave a lasting impression. And then you come across the kind of people who burrow deep. They become more than smiles and eyes, more than just another voice in the crowd. They become ingrained. Even when the songs are over and those people leave, you still feel them. They just…stick."

My chest hammers as I stare into the dark abyss, the stars blurring into streaks. "That's when you know it's a good song."

She hums thoughtfully. "That's when you know it's love."

I blink. Look back down at her.

Our eyes meet beneath the string lights, and something stirs. A quiet moment, soft and unseen, but so tangible it reaches inside and whittles me down to bare bones.

I feel it. I feel that *she* feels it. This attraction. This insidious draw, armed with teeth and wings and a pounding pulse. It's not one-sided.

It's mutual.

And fuck how I wish it wasn't.

"No matter what," she says, her attention drifting to the snuffed out cigarette on the deck. "At least we still have music."

I let go of her hand. But I don't reply.

I can't.

Because something inside of me knows…

She's the music.

And that's one thing I'll never have.

CHAPTER 22
Annalise

"Hey. Check this out."

I'm sitting cross-legged on the living room floor when Alex appears from the bedroom with a few pages of printed paper. Shirtless and shower-damp, he strolls over to me smelling like sandalwood and tea tree. There's a lightness about him, a weight lifted.

It makes me smile.

Gone is the man from hours ago, overworked and stressed out, hollering for refires while the ticket rail overflowed. The kitchen was a war zone. Grills hissing, fryers spitting, the scent of charred meat and melty cheese clogging the air. By midafternoon, his shirt was stuck to his back, his fingers raw from heat, his patience running on fumes.

But he's my Alex again.

As if the day's grind was all a hazy dream.

He stops just short of my chaotic mess: notebooks, pens, sheets of music, and a taupe mug filled with round three of milk-diluted coffee.

"Are you working on some sort of thesis?" Both arms cross over his bare chest, the papers dangling from his hand.

My smile falters. I need to tell him about the wedding gig. Tonight.

Right now.

Unlinking my legs, I lean back on one hand. "I have some news."

He nods, biting his lip. "Me too."

"Really?" I eye the loose sheets of paper again, curiosity eclipsing my nerves. "You go first."

Alex takes a seat beside me, moving the half-filled mug out of the way, and plops the stack on top of my notebook. "I did it. It's booked."

Eyes rounding, I stare at him for a beat before dragging my gaze to the printout in front of me.

It's an itinerary. For Thailand.

A flight out of Boston the night before Thanksgiving, touching down in Bangkok just as the city wakes up. Two nights in Chiang Mai, tucked inside the walled Old City, wandering temples and lantern-lit alleyways. Then south to the islands. Blue-green water and white sand, a bungalow right on the beach where the ocean would be the first thing we saw every morning.

There's even a monkey excursion.

I can almost feel the humid air clinging to my skin, taste the mango sticky rice, hear the hum of motorboats drifting toward limestone cliffs.

Alex watches me, expression alight with anticipation. "We'll get lost in the night markets, eat everything we can't pronounce, take a longtail boat to the Phi Phi Islands…" He nudges me gently with his knee. "Just escape for a while, you know? No stress, no work. Just us."

Just us.

Words lodge in my throat. Because he planned all this for me. Because he knows how much I've wanted this.

Hot pressure burns behind my eyes. "Alex…this is incredible."

"I know." He smiles.

"Are you sure we can leave the restaurant for that long? Over a holiday?"

"It's already covered. Don't worry about the job."

I swipe at the warm rivers streaking down my cheeks. Then I leap into his lap, wrapping my arms around his neck. "Thank you."

"We deserve it," he murmurs into my hair.

My eyes slam shut, more tears leaking through. A debilitating wave of guilt crashes over me. Guilt for the time spent with Chase. For keeping that information from my boyfriend. For my shameful thoughts, the chain-smoking, the secretive texts.

Three nights ago, I was holding another man's hand, all while Alex was creating this romantic getaway for us.

I'm horrible.

A cracked sob breaks free, and I squeeze him tighter. Try to bury the anguish before it kills the moment.

He pulls back, a small frown furling between his eyes. "What's wrong? You look upset."

I shake my head. "Just emotional. Happy."

Swallowing, he nods, but there's a wary glaze over his eyes. "What did you want to tell me?"

"Oh, um…" I tuck a tear-drenched strand of hair behind my ear. My thoughts go crooked, my heart on a teeter-totter. I have no idea how Alex is going to react to this. "Well, there's this opportunity. It feels big. Important."

"Okay." The frown deepens. Alex scoots back, his gaze shifting to the scattered mess on all sides of me. "You're working on music?"

"Yeah. Yes." I clear my throat. "Tag was asked to fill in for a live band at his friend's wedding. Declan. And his fiancée, Lillian."

He blinks at me.

"They go way back. From high school. You probably met him once when—"

"The point, Annalise."

"Right." My voice hitches. "Anyway, he said yes, of course. And he asked me to join him. To sing. You know, cover songs. It's in less than two weeks…"

His eyes narrow. "What else?"

"I'll, um…need that Saturday night off work. If that's okay. Kenna already said she'd cover my shift."

"What else?"

There's a ringing in my ears.

My chest nearly caves in, taking my air with it. It's like he already knows there's more. Something worse hiding in the things unsaid.

Closing my eyes, I wring my hands together and blurt it out. "Chase is performing too."

Silence.

I can't open my eyes, too terrified of what I'll see.

The timing is terrible. Alex just presented me with a weeklong vacation to Thailand, and I'm ambushing him with news of singing live music with a man he actively hates.

He witnessed our dynamic firsthand. Felt the tension. Saw the way Chase was looking at me, the way we sang together like we were the only two people in the room.

I inhale a shaky breath, bracing for the fallout.

My eyes flutter back open.

He doesn't say anything at first. Just studies me, jaw tight, lips pressed into a rigid line. That eager, travel-high glow in his eyes dims, as if I've stolen something from him.

"Got it," he says, nodding to himself.

My stomach twists. "Alex—"

"I mean, it makes sense. It's music. Your big dream." A laugh-like breath. "Perfectly reasonable."

"It's just one night," I argue. "One set. Tag asked us to do it. It's not like I went looking for this."

He shakes his head, staring at the itinerary. "But you didn't say no either."

"Because I want to do it. So much. This is an outlet for me—"

"*This* is your outlet." He jabs a finger at the stack of papers, then stabs at his chest. "Me. Not him."

"It's not about him," I say, a whispery appeal.

But that's not entirely true. Chase is a large part of that outlet. The way we connect over lyrics and chords, guitar strings and songs.

He gets it. He gets me.

And I can't tell if that's a blessing or a curse.

"Try to understand," I plead. "I've been working double shifts at the restaurant for over *four years*. I sacrifice sleep just for a taste of something that matters to me. And now I have an opportunity to taste more. Spread my wings. See if music is where I belong."

"And where does that leave me?"

"Nothing has to change between us. You should be proud of me. Supportive."

"I support the things that benefit us. Our relationship. I don't support you singing love songs onstage with a guy who clearly wants to fuck you."

"He doesn't—"

"No. Don't *fucking* do that." His voice drops, lethal. "Don't insult me by acting like I'm seeing shit that isn't there."

Alex jumps to his feet, starts pacing in anxious circles, scrubbing a hand down his jaw. Then he stops. Pauses as something coasts across his face.

Dread.

When he turns to me again, he looks as close to petrified as I've ever seen him.

"How much time have you been spending with him?"

I choke. The question is too direct. Too damning. There's no room for lies.

Color drains from my face. "He's…at Tag's sometimes. Working on music."

A heavy beat.

Awareness. Pain.

"Your midnights," he says.

All I do is nod.

I've seen Alex angry. I've seen him volatile, frustrated, confident, and passionate.

But never scared.

Not even when he woke up in a hospital bed after the accident, attached to needles and wires, head bandaged and bleeding, doctors warning him about possible long-term effects. I held his hand and sobbed against his chest. But he wasn't afraid.

He had me.

I push to my feet, my legs unsteady. We stand there, staring at each other as a car alarm wails outside. The ceiling fan whirs overhead. Cicadas sing from the cracked balcony door.

Alex swallows. "Do the gig."

I frown, confused. "What?"

"Do the fucking gig, Annalise. It's clearly what you want."

It *is* what I want.

But I want something else too.

I want his support. His respect. I want him to see that my dreams are worth pursuing, not something he throws back at me like an accusation.

"Alex—"

He turns away, storms into the bedroom.

The door slams so hard, the walls rattle, and I flinch.

My eyes pan down to the papers strewn across the carpet.

Music. Thailand.

Two different worlds. Two different lives. Pulling, calling, reaching. Filling separate pieces of my heart.

Both could be the death of me.

I just don't know which death will hurt more.

A text comes through the next day, somewhere between refilling water glasses and mopping up a syrup spill.

Chase: Working on the setlist. Thoughts?

I scan the list. There are enough songs to fill three hours.
"Can I get another coffee, darling?" a man asks as I linger near the jukebox.
I force a smile. Nod.
Then I send a short reply.

Me: Looks good.

Two minutes later, another text.

Chase: You okay?

A knot tightens in my chest, heat pooling behind my ribs.

Me: Yup. See you tonight.

I slip into the break room and shove my phone into my purse.
It pings again.
I don't check.

The guys seem to be well on their way to bonding, which is a weight off my shoulders.

I purposely take a seat in the recliner, giving Chase and Tag the couch.

"The key is too high," Tag grouses, his voice fracturing as he tries to sing the ultra-high notes. "No way I can sing this song."

"Annalise and I can take the lead," Chase says. "We'll lower the key."

My nose wrinkles as Tag makes a second attempt to sing "I Believe in a Thing Called Love" by The Darkness.

Growling his frustration, my brother slumps back against the cushions. "My range is shit." He glances at me. "You try, sis."

I peer down at my lap, where a gazillion printed-out lyrics sit in a messy pile. I flip through, searching for the song in question. Ink bleeds together. Titles, lyrics, notes.

This is the worst time to get cold feet.

"Something wrong?" Tag plucks at a few strings. "You look wiped."

"Long day," I murmur, my mind floating in la-la land. I feel Chase's eyes on me, probing, digging. "Maybe we can start with something easier. 'Shut Up and Dance' by Walk the Moon?"

"Yeah. Sure." Tag tunes his guitar, clearing his throat.

Chase jumps in, and I join at the chorus. We blend seamlessly.

An hour rolls by in a blur.

Sighing, I toss the stack of papers onto the coffee table. "I think I'm going to head out early. I don't know why I'm so tired tonight."

"Probably because you sleep two hours a day, max. You look morgue-bound." Tag makes a face. "But is this the best time to suddenly catch up on your beauty sleep? Our practice window is bleak."

"I know. I'm sorry." Avoiding all eye contact, I jump from the recliner and pull out my phone to order an Uber. "You guys stay and practice. Promise I'll be one with the living tomorrow."

Running from the inevitable interrogation, I escape from the basement and haul myself up the stairs, beelining for my shoes and purse. The moment I'm out the door, waiting for my ride and itching for a cigarette, I hear the screen snap closed behind me.

My body tenses; I already know who it is.

"Hey," Chase calls out, joining me at the edge of the driveway.

Squaring my shoulders, I stare out at the empty street lined with dark houses. Doors locked, blinds drawn shut. Just like me.

"What's wrong?" He settles in beside me, our fingers brushing.

"Nothing's wrong." I fold my arms, tucking my hands underneath my armpits. "I'm just tired."

"You haven't said a word to me all night. Hardly looked at me."

"It's not intentional."

False. It's next-level intentional.

But it's not because of Chase. It's because of me.

A sigh escapes as he pivots into my sightline, forcing me to look at him. His expression is weary, pained. "What did I do?" he wonders softly.

My heart pangs.

All I want to do is close my eyes and wash him away. Evict this horrible feeling from my blood, this destructive squatter.

This is a test, Annalise. You can do this. Be strong.

I brave his stare, soften my stance. "You didn't do anything."

"Feels like I did."

"It's just…I think maybe we should keep our distance. After

the wedding is over." It hurts to say it. I don't want to give up these nights. These sessions. But I don't know what else to do.

Chase studies me, the hidden meaning seeping to the surface. "Alex," he deduces, hands slipping into his pockets.

I nod. Swallow.

He rocks back on his heels, gaze dropping. "Yeah. That makes sense."

"It's nothing personal. I like spending time with you. You feel like…an escape." My throat chafes like a fresh roll of sandpaper. "But it's weighing on me. A lot."

"I understand."

I can see that he does. And while neither of us voice the context aloud, we both know why. Something shifted. An abrupt modulation, minor to major, just like that. Now we have to find the rhythm again. Simple, safe, and easy to play.

He looks up, over my shoulder, a soft smile on his lips. "The show," he says. "It'll be good."

"Yeah, I think so too." I'm grateful for the change in subject. The reprieve. "Tag seems like he's warming up to you."

"Was only a matter of time." He finds my eyes, the smile lingering. "Thanks for bringing me into all this. The music."

"Of course. You're talented, Chase."

Tires crunch in the distance as headlights flood the dark neighborhood street, inching closer.

I drink in a shaky breath. "I wrote another verse to that song I was working on. You can finish it if you want. Maybe something will take off, and you'll have another song in your arsenal."

His gaze flicks from the headlights to me, brows knitting. "What do you mean?"

I shrug. "You never know. You and my brother work well together. I can see it going somewhere."

"But it's your song."

"Yes…but I don't know if I'm cut out for this. Alex is right. My dreams are too big, and the sacrifices are too heavy. I need to focus on what I have, not on what could be."

A frown bends. "But when you sacrifice what could be, you'll never know what you're giving up. What you're capable of."

The response settles in the crux of my chest, triggering a rush of tears. I'm getting vulnerable again. With Chase as my witness.

And that's a mistake.

But I can't stop the words from pouring out. "I think I just expect too much," I admit, my voice quiet. "Out of life. Out of people. Out of myself. And when it all crumbles—when I realize I'm not enough—I don't know how to deal with the fallout. The failure. It's easier to wade in the shallow end sometimes. Less disappointment."

Chase stares at me, silent.

The car rolls up in front of the house. My ride.

I blink at the black sedan, grinding my teeth. "Anyway… that's me," I say, gripping my purse strap. "I'll see you tomorrow."

"Yeah." He swallows. "See you."

I break away, heading for the car. My fingers curl around the door handle when his voice cuts through the night.

"Annie."

I hesitate, turning back.

His eyes hold mine, steady. "You'd be shocked to know how incredibly enough you are, just the way you are."

I freeze.

All the air leaves my lungs.

A whoosh. A gasp. A hurricane.

He sends me a faint smile before turning away. "Good night."

I watch him stalk back to the house and disappear inside, my chest stretched thin. A flimsy rubber band, ready to snap.

"You coming?"

The driver's voice startles me, just as a tear slips loose. "Yes," I breathe out, pulling the door open and collapsing inside.

The man makes chitchat while we roll away, but I'm not listening.

I feel paralyzed.

Fishing my phone out of my purse, I unlock the screen and scroll through my contacts, landing on Chase's name.

My eyes burn, hot and wet. Through the blur, I copy a chunk of text from my Notes app and paste it into the message box.

I press send.

Then I delete his number from my phone.

[Verse 2]

We used to dance in time with thunder
Never feared the lightning strike
But now the storm's gone silent
Lost its will to fight
And so we dance on broken glass
To notes we left unsung
A song that never started
Ashes on my tongue

CHAPTER 23
Annalise

"Annalise! Thank you so much for doing this." The bride hobbles over to me in her strappy heels, dodging pockets of lumpy grass. "Declan told me Tag put a whole band together just for our special night. It means the world to me. To both of us."

Stepping off the makeshift stage in the center of their lush backyard, I greet Declan's new wife with a warm hug.

I've only met Lillian a handful of times. House parties, barbecues, a triple date two years ago when Tag was seeing a law student named Marissa. But Lillian is the kind of person you don't forget, with a permanent sun-kissed smile and shiny blond hair to match.

She wraps her arms around me, smelling like she walked out of a Bath and Body Works ad. When she inches back, she smooths her hands down a layered boho wedding dress, the delicate lace drenched in pink-and-gold hues from the setting sun.

I twist a spiral of freshly curled hair around my finger, smiling wide. "We're so honored to be here. Thank you for trusting us with this."

"Are you kidding? Your brother is an amazing performer. If you can sing even half as well as he can…" She splays her palms near her head with a sharp flick, signaling *mind blown*.

I blush through the grin.

Behind me, the guys finish tuning their instruments, the hum of Chase's electric guitar fusing with the tap of drumsticks against the snare. Tag adjusts the mic stand, giving me a quick nod, as the glow of string lights paint the polished wood in a dreamy haze.

A low strum echoes through the speakers as Declan jogs over, draping an arm around Lillian's shoulders. "Ready to party, Mrs. Sanders?" He presses a kiss to her temple.

Her eyes shimmer as she pops her hip, hands curling around her waist. "More than ready."

I turn back to the band, inhaling deep as Tag gives the downbeat. The night is ours. Time to shine, or drown in the mortification of my failure for decades to come.

Gulping, I retreat to the stage. "See you two on the flip side," I say, harnessing my smile. "Enjoy the show!"

"No doubt." Declan lifts his beer in cheers.

They sound so confident. As if they hadn't panic-plucked five random people off the streets to play a three-hour set on the most important night of their lives, two of those people having never performed live in this capacity before. Even Tag hasn't done anything this big, this brave.

Heart in my throat, I clomp back up to the platform in my brand-new white sneakers. The shoes were a deliberate choice—comfort over glam. The last thing I need is to trip over a pair of sky-high heels in front of a hundred wedding guests and a petite chihuahua wearing a bowtie.

The beady-eyed creature stares me down, as if waiting for my shoelaces to magically unravel and tie my ankles into a knot.

Focus, Annalise.

As I traipse across the stage and find my spot, Chase rakes his eyes over me before peering down at his guitar.

My dress is a powder-blue shift with a high neckline and a scalloped lace overlay, straight out of the sixties. The fabric flutters as I move, airy and effortless, like something Twiggy might've worn in a sun-doused Polaroid.

I gulp again.

A swarm of butterflies escape their cocoons and skitter up to my throat. The crowd beneath us gathers with champagne flutes and dessert plates topped with cake and buttercream. The weather is stunning, the backdrop romantic and picturesque, and all I can do is pray that our grueling, all-night practice sessions have paid off. Luckily, the bassist and drummer—Dan and Aaron—are seasoned pros. I know they'll steer us around the curves.

Tag leans over to whisper in my ear. "You good, sis?"

My eyes flare wide. "Don't ask me that. You're reminding me that I'm not even close to good."

"Well, you look like you're about to vomit."

"That's the impending catatonia."

He sighs, his expression softening as he props his foot up on the amp. "You got this, all right? Just picture everyone naked or some shit."

Instinctively, my gaze veers over to Chase. "Not helpful," I croak.

Feeling my stare, Chase turns to look at me in his gunmetal-gray vest and matching slacks, the stark white of his rolled-up sleeves highlighting the lean muscle in his forearms. With his guitar slung low and a few strands of warm brown hair falling over his brow, he looks like he belongs on a stage, under the lights, the whole world as his audience.

He smiles. Soft, confident, reassuring.

Then he cups a hand over the mic speaker and tilts back. "You ready?"

Tag gives my shoulder a squeeze as I attempt to conjure words. "Ready."

Stepping up to the microphone stand, I inhale a centering breath. I feel bare and exposed with no instrument. Just a mic clasped between my hands, slick from sweat. My eyes close as chatter from the guests fades out and music filters to my ears.

Tag gives a countdown, and the beginning chords of "September" by Earth, Wind & Fire take shape.

Dan's bass line thrums through the humid air, a heady pulse that stabilizes my heartbeat. To my left, Chase's fingers dance over the strings, his body swaying in time with the beat. He's loose, natural, lost in the rhythm, while I'm locked in place, white-knuckling the mic stand like it might float away if I let go.

But then he looks at me again.

Just a flick of his gaze, steady and knowing, because he feels what's churning inside me. His fingers pick a playful riff, an improvisation that isn't in the song but fits like it was meant to be.

A reminder to have fun. To just go with it.

The corner of his mouth quirks. "You can do this, Annie." The words are low enough so only I can hear them. "You were born to do this."

Something clicks into place.

The nerves don't flee, but they morph into something bigger. Soul-spun electricity. The energy in the air is contagious, winding through me in glimmering tendrils and settling in my chest. I loosen my grip on the mic stand.

Then I start to sing.

The first verse rolls off my tongue, tentative but building, each note zigzagging through the crowd. People start moving. The bride twirls in her lacy gown, her husband spinning her under his arm. Champagne sloshes. Heads tip back with untamed joy, the kind only music can bring. That unparalleled elixir of life.

Chase's voice finds mine in the chorus, a flawless harmony that sends a jolt down my back. Our eyes meet again, bold and energizing. There's this unspoken thrill of creating magic, of bringing something to life. His smile deepens as he leans into the mic, long fingers gliding over the guitar, coaxing out a solo that makes the crowd go wild.

Tag picks up the groove, throwing in a deep, rolling rhythm. Aaron matches him beat for beat on the drum kit, driving the song forward like a runaway train.

And then the real magic happens.

Another song rolls out. Then another.

I step away from the mic stand.

My sneakers scuff against the wooden platform as I dance, my body giving in to the music. The feeling. A wave of confidence unfurls, scaling my limbs, my voice, my whole damn heart. I extend my hand toward the crowd as the chorus to "Don't Stop Believin'" swells.

Guests whoop and holler, sing along, raise their drinks in the air. The joy is infectious, a wildfire spreading through the backyard.

Through me.

I laugh, breathless and free, and Chase catches it, watching me with something unreadable in his eyes. Like he's seeing me for the first time.

No…

Like he's seeing *me* see *me* for the first time.

I'm more than a voice. More than an overworked waitress. More than a girl too scared to chase what she really wants.

I have a place on this stage.

We slow it down with "Fade Into You" by Mazzy Star, a personal selection by me. I take the lead, the haunting, moody lyrics stripping me bare. And then we move into another song. Something so familiar it claws at my heart.

"I Only Want To Be With You."

Chase and Tag ditch the electric guitars for a raw, acoustic rendition.

As Chase strums the opening chords, the moment stretches, fragile and aching. My breath locks up. The music is softer, more intimate, wrapping around us like the stifling heat of late July. The lyrics are light and playful, but the words dig deep.

Chase sings with me, his voice threading through the chords like melted butter. His harmony wraps around mine, lifting it, blending it, creating richness.

My chest tightens. I feel him in every note, every inflection. We step closer together, hardly a foot between us.

When the chorus hits, we lean in at the same time, sharing a microphone, our faces inches apart. The air crackles. He watches my mouth as I sing.

For a fleeting second, it feels like we aren't at a wedding. Like it's just us, playing in some dimly lit bar, lost in the music. The moment. And God, I wish I could freeze it. Hold on to the way he's looking at me right now, like *I'm* something worth holding on to.

As the last note fades out, Chase lets out a breath, eyes on mine, his lips parting like he's about to say something.

But the applause surges, swallowing the moment whole.

It's a drug. Both a sedative and a high.

Just under three hours roll by in a fairy-tale fog. I'm on the outside looking in, the night too good to be true. But it is true. It's real, and it's happening.

We finish the set.

Chase slings his guitar aside and grabs me without hesitation. Suddenly, I'm weightless—lifted, spun, my legs kicking back as he whirls me in dizzying circles, like we've just sprinted across the finish line of a never-ending marathon. Sweat clings to my skin. My hair whips around me. I'm laughing so hard it hurts, my arms tightening around his neck, anchoring me.

We did it.

When he sets me down, I don't have time to recover as Tag rushes over and pulls me into a bone-crushing hug. He inches me backward, grips me by the shoulders, bending to meet my eyes, his face the proudest I've ever seen it. "You killed it, sis. You absolutely fucking *killed* it."

I'm crying. I'm laughing. I'm free.

The guys hug while hands clap together, hair is ruffled, and backs are smacked.

Everything is glorious.

We're ambushed the second we step off the stage, champagne glasses pressed into our hands. Lillian and Declan make the rounds, engulfing us with praise. Tears stream down Lillian's cheeks, the pinnacle of the night and too much bubbly making her weep.

I've hardly caught my breath when a mid-thirties man waltzes over to us in a crisp suit, his hair a mess of dirty-blond curls.

"Name's Crowley," he introduces. "Second cousin to the bride."

He shakes our hands. Chase hovers to my right, Tag on my left.

"I own a music venue out in New York called The Soundproof," he continues, straightening out his tie. "Bit of a hike, I know. But if you can swing the drive, I'd love to get you guys on the schedule sometime."

I blanch.

New York.

That's *huge*.

It's less than a five-hour commute. Hardly anything given the enormous opportunity dangling in front of us.

Tag's eyes bulge. "The Soundproof." He nearly chokes. "Shit. That place is iconic."

"It's been a labor of love, no doubt."

"That's where Misfire got their big break. Arlo Knox became an overnight legend."

Crowley chuckles, bows his head. "Arlo is something else. Quite the presence."

I hold my breath, my eyes ping-ponging between the two men on either side of me.

My smile wilts.

There's just one problem.

"We, um…don't really have a full band yet." I bite my lip, disappointment rolling through me. "Dan and Aaron were just filling in for us as a favor. They already have a band."

"Mm, I see." Crowley's face falls. "Well, if anything changes, take my card. Give me a call."

I take the business card he hands me. Light and weightless, yet brimming with serendipity.

Crowley looks directly at Chase. "Having been in this business for over a decade, I have a keen eye for talent. The raw, gritty stuff you can't manufacture. The Arlos of the world," he drawls, expression turning earnest. "I see a lot of up-and-comers breeze through my doors, but only one percent of them stick. And that's probably a generous estimate."

I study Chase, the way he swallows, stiffens, his eyes glazing over.

"Take what you want from that," the man adds, a smile cresting. He smacks Chase on the shoulder, then sends me and Tag a quick glance. "Congrats on the show."

He saunters away, leaving me speechless.

My brother swipes both hands down his face, spinning around, then pivoting right back. "Jesus. Did you hear that?"

I down my champagne. "Mm-hmm."

"Shit. Holy shit."

Chase scratches his jaw, eyeing the business card tucked inside my hand. "We need a drummer and a bassist."

Tag nods, eyes still bugged out of his head. "I have connections. I'll ask around."

"I might know a drummer," Chase adds, his gaze faraway, wheels spinning. Then he looks at me. "Is this something you want?"

Both men watch me, waiting.

The sparkling wine fizzes in my throat.

Of course it is. On the surface, it's everything I want. Music, writing, creating, living.

Yes.

But Chase isn't just asking a question. He's telling me to think. To peel back the layers, examine each piece, and see it for what it really is. This isn't a spur-of-the-moment decision. This is a crossroads. A life upheaval. A domino effect of shifting dreams, abandoned safety nets, and terrifying decisions.

This is another test.

My job will take a back seat.

My relationship will be pushed to its limits.

My conviction will be analyzed and picked apart, leaving me in pulpy pieces.

Life, as I know it, will change.

This is more than music. I'm signing up for everything that comes with it. And at the center of that conundrum is Chase: the one person I swore to avoid after tonight.

Our eyes meet through the dusky night, his burning into mine.

I swallow hard.

Around him, I don't trust myself.

And yet…

Every road seems to lead back to him.

CHAPTER 24
Chase

"What do you think of this lyric?"

Stella sings one of the lines to "Hallelujah." The part about love being compared to shooting someone who outdrew you. She leans back on her hands as we stare out at the wind-churned lake, her bare toes coated in ruby polish and clumps of sand.

I shrug, pulling my knees to my chest. The late-summer afternoon is hotter than a space heater in hell, but the breeze is sharp, adding a much-needed balm. "Never thought about it before."

She gapes at me. "Really? Lyrics make the song."

"I tend to focus on the musical progression. The structure, movement, melody."

"Typical guitarist."

"I guess." I glance at her, the humidity curling the baby hairs around her forehead. "Why? What do you think?"

"I don't know. That line has always stumped me," she muses, wiggling her toes.

"You're not supposed to take it literally. It's poetry."

"But it doesn't make sense." Her nose scrunches.

Before I can reply, a beach ball smacks me in the back of the head. Stella bursts out laughing, collapsing in the sand as a little girl races over to us, apologizing.

Grinning, I toss the beach ball back to her. She scampers away in her Strawberry Shortcake swimsuit and pink bucket hat.

Stella's coffee-brown hair fans out over the lake-stolen sandcastles and glittering pebbles. There's music in her eyes. While my sister was born a fish—and our parents have always steered her toward competitive swimming—I know that with every year that passes, her dreams blur. She's almost sixteen. Old enough to know that dreams aren't always linear.

"Do you ever think about quitting?" I ask, nodding at the water.

I watch her trace circles in the sand with her toe. She doesn't respond right away. Just stares at the lake like it might answer for her.

"Every time I dive in," she finally says. *"The water feels like home. But music feels like me."*

And there it is. The silent tug-of-war between expectation and identity. Between what we've always done and what we might become.

"You've got time."

"Yeah." She sighs. *"Maybe if I become a lyrical genius like Leonard Cohen before college gets here, the path will become clearer."* A beat. *"Even though I still don't get that line."*

A smile tugs. *"Doesn't matter what it means. Just what it means to you."*

"So…someone he loved hurt him first, and he had to learn how to hurt them right back?"

"Could be."

"Okay, but how do you shoot someone who outdrew you?" She looks up at me, her hazel eyes narrowing in the midday sun. "You'd already be dead."

"Maybe that's the point," I murmur. "Love is a losing battle."

I press back on my hands, breaking away to look out at the water.

Baby waves ripple across the surface. White egrets flock overhead. The air stills.

I glance down at Stella. "No one gets out alive."

My knuckles rap against the red door.

Nerves flick down my spine; I have no idea what I'm doing. But options are low, and given the way my neighbor is tearing it up on that kit—clean fills, steady timing, no overplaying—I'd be stupid not to ask.

I ring the bell. Once, twice.

The drumming cuts off mid-roll. A second later, the door swings open.

Rock appears in a pair of ratty jeans and a wrinkled T-shirt, twin drumsticks in his hand. "Yo. If you're here to complain about the noise—"

"I'm not. Kind of the opposite." I wedge a shoulder against the age-old pillar and stuff my hands in my pockets. "I was wondering if you'd help me make it."

He blinks half a dozen times. Slow. Processing. "Pretty sure I'm too high to get the context."

"I'm putting a band together," I say, my gaze swinging to the sticks. "And I need a drummer."

"A band?" He glances around me, as if waiting for Kurt Cobain's ghost to pop out of the bushes. "I don't know, man. I'm kinda over the startup-band grind. They're all busted strings and sheer luck these days."

Can't say I disagree. But maybe I can improve the luck.

"Listen, we're sort of scrambling. And I can tell that you're good, thanks to the 3:00 a.m. jam sessions rattling my walls."

He sends me a salute.

"We're still on the hunt for a bassist, but the rest of us were asked to perform at The Soundproof," I continue. "It's a music venue out in New York—"

"No fucking shit."

"Yeah. It's a big deal."

His eyes widen as much as they can. "Whoa. Hell yeah. Shit yeah."

"We practice a few miles away at my buddy's house. It's just been covers up till now, but we have some new stuff we're piecing together. If you're interested—"

"Sign me the fuck up."

"Really?"

"I'm in. I don't have shit-else to do."

"Cool. Give me your number and I'll send you the details. We usually practice around midnight, but I realize that's not normal. We can figure something else out."

"Nah. I'm a night owl." He stares at me, eyes narrowing. "Hey, what about that girl you're friends with? Borrowed my phone a few months back. She's got blueish hair. Kind of pink."

I blink at him. "Purple?"

He jabs a finger in my face, nodding. "That's fucking it. Purple. She in the band too?" A drowsy smile stretches. "She was cute as hell."

"Uh, yeah. She is." My hands curl inside my pockets. "Annalise."

"Nice, nice."

"Her brother plays rhythm guitar and sings backup vocals. Tag. If you're free tonight, I'll introduce you."

"Freer than a mall Santa in January."

My left eye twitches. "All right. Sounds good." I add his number into my phone, my gaze lifting. "Is Rock your real name?"

"Nickname. Last name's Rockwell."

"And your first name?"

"Norman."

My head snaps all the way up. I stare at him, scratching my cheek. "Norman Rockwell."

"Yeah, man. Don't make a big deal about it. The folks didn't realize it was already taken."

"Got it." One more question simmers. "So, is the nickname because you were already into music, or did the nickname trigger your love for music?"

Rock's pupils dilate to giant inkblots. He breathes out a low whistle, shaking his head. "Dude. That's deep. I'll get back to you on that one."

I hold back the laugh. "I'll text you later."

Twirling the drumsticks in the air, he catches them with ease, then points them in my direction. "Let's fuckin' go."

When he shuts the door, I head back to my house. Toaster greets me at the threshold with a dental stick, tail wagging.

My eyes pan over to the wall of guitars, most of them nearly finished, except for one: my big work in progress. There's still a lot more to do. Right now I'm figuring out how to ditch the traditional pickups and build something revolutionary by integrating MIDI sensors into the fretboard. When you strum, the guitar sends a signal, not just to an amp, but to external gear that can manipulate sound and trigger lights.

Like a plasma ball.

The lights flicker, sound bends, the neck reacts, and it's all tied together by the MIDI system, controlling both sound and visuals.

It'd be the closest you could get to holding lightning in your hands.

The problem I'm running into is the weight. Plasma effects inside a guitar neck would require specialized materials like quartz glass, making it too heavy to take off. Any musician worth their salt would scoff at the notion of carrying this beast through multiple grueling sets.

But it's something. A start.

I pull my phone out of my pocket, reminded of the other fresh start taking shape.

Swallowing, I shoot Annie a quick text.

Me: Think we have a drummer.

An hour slips by. Then two more.

By midnight, I'm hauling my new amp, two guitars, and some solid news over to Tag's place, ready to light up the basement with ideas and hours of brainstorming.

But when I hit the bottom step and glance around, it hits me—

Annie never replied.

And she's not here.

CHAPTER 25
Annalise

"You've officially lost your mind." Kenna sends me a suspicious side-eye.

My face sours as I lick my cherry-chip ice cream cone, the sugar curdling into spoiled milk. "It wasn't official before?"

"You were like ninety-nine percent there. This puts you over the edge."

"Yay." An icy droplet dribbles down my hand as we browse the outdoor shops in downtown Rutland. "You can't pretend to know what you'd do in my situation."

"Yes, I absolutely can," she counters. "I'd go all in, Annalise. Fifty million percent. Balls to the wall."

"Your balls are bigger than mine."

"Fact." Humming under her breath, she peers over to one of

the quaint stores. "Oh! You need to start manifesting. It's a new moon. I'll get you a candle and some stones."

"I don't know anything about moon magic," I grouse.

"So? You can learn." She licks her half-eaten cone, grabs mine, then tosses them both in a trash can. Her fingers curl around my wrist as she drags me toward the entrance. "One time, I manifested front-row tickets to see Sleep Token. Then they just showed up."

I blink at her. "That's not manifesting. That was Rick Doherty trying to get you naked."

"All I'm saying is it worked." The doorbell jingles as we enter, and a dark-haired young woman welcomes us with a smile. "Let's get you properly aligned."

My shoulders slump as I glance around the shop that smells like lavender and patchouli. Every surface is filled with velvet-draped tables stacked with jars of loose herbs, shelves lined with multicolored crystals, and hanging displays of pendulums that glint under the amber light.

Kenna beelines for a shelf cluttered with gems, waving her fingers like she's scanning for the right vibe. "Okay, first you need clear quartz for clarity and amplification. Then rose quartz, because your heart chakra is a disaster. No offense."

"None taken."

"And this one"—she grabs a small handful of smoky black stones—"black tourmaline. For protection from bad vibes. And from guys who look like Tom Sandoval."

"Offense taken." My eyes narrow at the jab at Alex. "He's not as bad as you think he is. We're both putting in the effort."

This snags Kenna's attention. She whips around in her bright turquoise maxi dress, her expression softening. Her faux-yellow hair contrasts inky grown-out roots and tan skin, making her look like a sun-drenched punk mermaid.

"Annalise," she says, tone low and sober. "Your effort is in trying to fix what's broken. His effort is in keeping things broken, so you're forced to stay and fix it. Healthy effort is in the progress. The teamwork."

Her words make me itch. "That's not what's happening."

"You want to be in the band, right? That's where your heart is. Music, creating. Singing your soul to anyone who will listen." Stepping closer, she presses a hand to my upper arm. "Alex isn't listening. He's only making you feel bad and bringing you down. He doesn't hear you."

My cheeks flame. With anger or awareness, I can't tell. "I want to be with him."

"Do you? Be honest with yourself. Do you really want to spend the rest of your life with him, or is that just guilt and the fear of change whispering in your ear?"

I shake my head, slithering out of her grip. "You don't understand. We've built a life together. Everything I have is because of him."

"That's not true. You have me. Tag. Your parents, even though they're living it up with the chickens in Alabama."

"Georgia."

"I'm just saying, you have them. They're only a phone call away, and we both know they'd jump on the first flight out if you needed them." Her eyes mist, shimmering in the low light. "You also have a way out if you're brave enough to take it."

My eyes close.

She doesn't get it. It's not about being brave; it's about being smart. Quitting my job, leaving my boyfriend, and becoming a homeless, struggling musician isn't smart. It's reckless.

Kenna sighs, sensing my barriers. My hopes and dreams wrapped in steel. "What about Chase?"

My heart fumbles. I haven't confided in Kenna about Chase. Not entirely. Not about my dark thoughts, my seesawing emotions. The growing connection between us. "What about him?" I wonder, voice shaking.

"He's a lot like you. Works long hours, struggles to get by, uses music as an outlet. The difference is he sees opportunity as a tangible thing. Something within reach. For you, it's still this far-off dream." Her smile saddens. "Unattainable."

I look away. Fold my arms.

Keep those barriers sky-high.

Shoulders drooping, Kenna turns away and scans the shelves, plopping stones into mesh baggies. "Well, I can see my invaluable advice is going in one ear and out the other. And that's okay. But maybe some deep reflection and moonstone can help. It brings dreams and new beginnings into focus." She reaches for a chunk of moonstone, adding it to her haul.

We leave the store a few minutes later with magic stones, bamboo and jade, and a deep-blue pillar candle, supposedly good for initiating change and helping with healing and inspiration.

When Kenna drops me off in front of my condo, she shoves the bags at me. "I can send over more plants if you want."

"Thanks." I chuckle. "But I'm good for now."

"Listen, this stuff takes time. It doesn't happen overnight," she says. "Be patient. Open-minded. And most importantly, focus on what you really want. Listen to that voice inside your head. She's always been there, and she won't steer you wrong." She reaches over and wraps me in a warm hug. "I love you, girlie. And I'm here."

I squeeze her back, emotion sticking in my throat. "I love you too. Thank you for everything."

Collecting my bags, I hop out of the car and wave goodbye.

I'm left with a fissure in my chest.

Afternoon bleeds into evening, and the little chasm cracks wider with every passing hour. Alex gets home from work around seven. He cooks; I clean.

We hardly speak.

The voice inside my head—the one Kenna begged me to listen to—howls at me. I've never really researched manifestation before, passing most of it off as overpriced candles, glittery jewels, and good marketing, all wrapped in moon phases and cliché quotes.

But I'm ready. I'm ready to try anything.

Come midnight, Alex is asleep in the bedroom, and I'm on the balcony, cross-legged in an old hoodie, a cup of tea growing cold beside me. A crackle of thunder rumbles in the distance.

Kenna's starter kit is strewn across the wrought iron table like spilled thoughts: a rose quartz heart, moonstone, black tourmaline, and an indigo candle that smells like cinnamon and courage.

I light it with trembling hands.

My mother used to tell me that writing poems and singing songs weren't a phase or a hobby. They weren't something I needed to shelve when real life showed up. But I've let other voices get louder. The ones that tell me to be responsible and quiet. And somewhere in all that static, I convinced myself that my dreams had an expiration date.

Now, the big question looms in the back of my mind.

What are my dreams? Those burning, heart-bursting dreams?

What do you want, Annalise?

What. Do. I. Want.

My eyes water as I tip my face to the sky, and a few raindrops sprinkle down to earth.

"I want to stop being afraid," I whisper as the slim crescent moon glows faintly through the cloud cover. I feel stupid. I feel scared. I feel free. "I want to stop apologizing for the things that set my soul on fire."

I inhale a deep breath, pressing a hand to my heart.

Tiny raindrops dapple the stones. I don't even know what half of them are supposed to do, but I don't move them. I just stare.

At them. At the candle. At the sliver of honey moon floating in the sky.

I focus on the voice I've spent years turning the volume down on like a haunting old song.

But she's not whispering tonight.

She's roaring.

And her voice doesn't sound like some mystical thing—it sounds like me. My truest self. The girl who used to write lyrics on math worksheets and stayed up until 3:00 a.m. watching bootleg concert videos. The girl who used to believe that if she worked hard enough, poured enough of herself into a poem or a chorus, the world might listen.

And God, I miss her.

The answers don't hit me like a thunderbolt. They seep inside like a chord progression, a melody that's been humming in my bones since I was a pigtailed grade-schooler.

I want the music. I want the mess and the noise and the risk of it all. I want to be in the room where songs are born and mistakes are made and something real happens.

I don't want to keep living this muted version of my life just because it's safe.

I want that secret chord.

Blowing out the candle, I watch the smoke rise in a twisting trail.

Kenna was right; these things take time.

But the truth is, I already knew what I wanted. I just needed to listen.

"I want this," I say, my voice louder, laced with years-worth of buried conviction. "I want this so much."

Tears rush to my eyes.

And then I'm on my feet, racing out of the condo, forgoing an umbrella. The rain grows heavier with every step, pummeling down in unyielding sheets.

The sky applauds me. The night smiles. My heartbeat ricochets.

I run fast, down the street, past honking cars and rain-glazed porch lights. My sneakers slap against wet pavement, socks soaked through in seconds. I run for miles, my breathing ragged, my tears mingling with rainfall. I run until I reach Tag's house, nearly buckling in the grass.

Chase is there. Stepping out of his car with a guitar in hand.

He does a double take, watching as I hunch over, hands to my knees, my drenched hair smacking me in the face.

"Annie?"

I hear him call out to me moments before thunder strikes and lightning zips through the sky in white-hot veins.

Winded, I glance up, my lungs on fire, my heart beating a hundred miles a minute. "Chase."

He lets go of the guitar case. Tosses it into the grass.

I race over to him, and we meet in the center of the lawn. No hesitation, no falter. I leap, winding my arms around his neck and burying my sobbing face against his shoulder.

"Jesus," he whispers, his hug quieter, less sure. He holds me loosely, two soft palms splaying across my back. "What happened?"

A dizzying wave of laughter breaks through the tears. I inch back until we're face-to-face. "Honey Moons."

He stares at me, blinking. "What?"

"The band name," I say, laughing again, practically singing. "Honey Moons."

A twinkle lights his gaze. Brightens the hazel of his eyes to golden torches.

Everything clicks.

And just like that, he smiles. "You're in?"

I nod frantically as another downpour escapes the sky. "I'm in. I'm so fucking in."

His smile grows wings.

This time he reaches for me, scooping me into his arms, his face sinking to the arch of my neck, breath warm against my cold, wet skin.

I shiver. Close my eyes.

Just be.

"I'm done being scared." I cling to him, holding on to him like a tether, a lifeline. His arms grip me tighter, keeping me together. It's the final note I need to make the song complete. A coda. "No more half measures."

CHAPTER 26
Annalise

Crowley gets Honey Moons on the schedule for a show in mid-October.

It's late-August now, the muggy heat creeping into the practice space and baking us all alive. Three oscillating fans are the only source of airflow, now that Tag has turned his two-car garage into our new studio. Rock's drum kit was too massive to be crammed in the partial basement along with five musicians, amps, furniture, and a dozen bookcases stuffed with old vinyls.

Drenched in sweat, I plop down in front of one of the fans, sighing with contentment every time the draft swivels toward me. "We need AC," I declare, pressing back on my hands as I sit cross-legged on the hand-me-down rug.

Tag tunes his guitar beside me on a stool. "Currently accepting donations."

"How much can it be?"

"More than what I make detailing cars and playing coffee shops." A note dings sharply out of key, making Tag wince. "Besides, it'll be blizzarding before we know it."

I close my eyes and imagine myself naked in an ice bath in the dead of winter.

Meanwhile, Chase sits sprawled out on the shabby couch we hauled up from the basement last week. The bruise on my shin is a nasty shade of green, having bloomed sometime between step five and me cursing the existence of whoever designed Tag's staircase. Sadly, girl power does not equate to muscle mass in the face of a three-hundred-pound three-seater sofa.

Chase nods at our newest band member, Zach, who also happens to be Tag's old friend from high school. "Sounding good," he says.

I tip my head back, reveling in the breeze coasting across my neck as I glance at Zach, who is hunched over his five-string bass, locked into a groove so deep it practically carves a canyon.

After a slew of so-so bassist auditions, Zach walked in and nailed it. He's got the quiet confidence of someone who knows exactly what he's doing and reminds me of the lead singer of Sevendust, with warm, deep-toned skin and a head full of lush locs. He's more low-key than the rest of us, but every bit as sharp.

We've upped our practice time to 8:00 p.m. since Zach sleeps like a normal human and the ultra-late nights were starting to wear us all down. Breaking the news to Alex was harrowing. It's cut into our personal time, giving us only a small window to have dinner together after work, and making date nights less frequent.

Even talks of Thailand have been put on hold.

I've had to endure the frequent mood swings, passive-aggressive comments, and cold shoulder, but in the end, I was doing this whether he approved or not.

I'm not sure if that makes me selfish or driven.

My gaze swings back to Chase in his black jeans with unintentional rips, smudged sneakers, and lack of a T-shirt. All the guys are half naked. The air smells like a combination of body odor, Rock's weed collection, and an assortment of lavender-scented candles courtesy of Kenna. "You make my napkin lyrics sound good," I call out to him.

He flicks me a smile.

I can tell he's only half present, lost in a solo. He's buckling down hard, showing up an hour before practice every night and being the last to leave.

I don't blame him.

We're opening for a well-known band called Unbidden, a progressive rock group with flashy guitar riffs and heavy metal undertones. We're not quite as hard, less growl and more heart. But where they shred, we swell. Where they erupt, we simmer.

We're the slow burn, our sound akin to open windows during a summer storm.

Rivers of sweat trickle down my neck as I puff my cheeks with an exhausted breath. Zoned out from heatstroke, I stare at Chase's tattoo rippling across his skin like ocean waves as he focuses on the rhythm. It's cathartic, watching him play, listening to my lyrics become tangible. We have three new songs under our belt, the fourth one currently in production.

It's something I whipped up between diner shifts last week,

huffing and puffing, needing a quick escape from kitchen chaos and demanding customers.

Resilience folds like paper
Conviction frays like floss
We draw lines in the sand
Just before we cross

Chase looks up, catching me staring. He doesn't pull away, and neither do I. These are the only moments I allow. Tender glances tucked beneath the chords of whatever song we're playing. Though small and fleeting, I hold his gaze like it means something.

It feels better to know that we tried
We tried
But everyone knows
That's just another way to lie

"There's no topping Walter White. You can't change my mind." Rock's voice cuts in as he spins his drumsticks with a showy flick of his wrist.

Tag scoffs. "Saul was better. The character development was a masterclass."

"Snooze."

"You're a fucking snooze."

I look away as Rock busts out a quick drum solo. "Team Tag," I chime in. "That show was basically a tragic love story dressed up in legal briefs and cartel blood. Total brilliance."

"Team Tag," Rock parrots, a frown pulling. "Team Tag…Tag Team." His eyes glaze. "Whoa. Missed band name opportunity?"

Chuckling, I pull to a stand and take a seat beside Chase on the couch as Zach remains lost in his bass. "Thoughts on this debate?"

Chase's eyes dip to my soaked-through tank stuck to my skin before jerking away. "I've only seen *Breaking Bad*."

"Gasp?" My hands crisscross over my heart. "And here I thought I knew you."

He peers down at his instrument, effortlessly plucking a series of strings. "Guess I'll need to change that. Somewhere between daily practices, getting my guitar business off the ground, and sanding down rustic benches."

"I believe in you."

A smile ticks. "Sing for me. I'm trying to get this melody worked out."

The request makes my stomach flip-flop. While performance nerves have scattered for the most part, it still feels strangely vulnerable singing for Chase. Like my heart is a shoddily built dam, a storm away from splitting into pieces.

"Okay," I breathe, my eyes panning to the half-open garage door.

Chase leans back and spreads his legs wider, the rough denim of his jeans grazing my bare thigh. Ignoring the contact, I clear my throat, better my posture, and start to sing. With every note, Chase follows along, his gaze bouncing between my moving lips and his strings.

His fingers slowly glide across the fretboard, like he's more focused on the sound coming from me than the guitar.

His knee nudges mine. I feel him watching me, his breathing deepening as mine falters. But I keep singing, because if I stop, I'm afraid I'll forget how to breathe altogether.

This heat isn't helping.

I'm trapped in a furnace, body and mind, with no way out.

My voice tapers on the last word. I wring my hands together, short on air, dripping sweat, wanting nothing more than to peel my clothes off and launch myself into the neighbor's pool.

I brave a glance at Chase as his eyes track a bead of moisture running down the arc of my throat. I feel it there, itchy and distracting, but I leave it, a treacherous side of me addicted to the way he stares at it.

With a drowsy blink, he blows out a breath and looks at me like I'm a long-lost treasure. "Damn," he says softly.

That one word sends a swarm of buzzing bees racing south. Every piece of me is warm and gooey like a hive of honey.

The enchantment in his tone soothes me.

The look in his eyes scares me.

And then Tag's voice enters the chat.

"I'm fuckin' roasting like a burnt-ass turkey under a heat lamp at a deli." He swipes his discarded T-shirt down his face. "I need a break. Maybe John will let us borrow his pool."

My brother sets his guitar aside and disappears out of the garage, the door squeaking on its hinges as he lifts it all the way up. Rock and Zach follow. Chase hesitates now that we're alone, as if he's contemplating if it's a blessing or a tragedy in motion.

I lift off the couch. "A late-night dip doesn't sound so bad. You in?"

He clears his throat, pulls his guitar closer to his chest. "Nah. Gonna keep practicing."

I nod, even though he's not looking at me anymore, halfway buried in the strings like they're some kind of shield.

Outside, the air is churning with humidity. Tag is already across the yard, shouting something to the neighbor, John, who waves us over with a beer in hand like it's just another Tuesday. By the time I kick off my sandals and sit at the edge of the pool, removing my phone from my waistband and placing it beside me, the guys are diving in.

The water is cool against my legs. Abandoned pairs of jeans are tossed onto lawn chairs, the three men stripped down to boxers, cannonballing and roughhousing like they're fifteen again.

I slip in slow, letting the water take me piece by piece, until my cotton shorts and tank are soaked through. Laughter spills across the yard, and for a while, I let myself disappear into it.

Until the air shifts.

A shadow flickers in the corner of my eye.

Chase stands off to the side in the grass, barefoot, jeans clinging to his hips. He looks lost, a far cry from the lead singer with a mic in hand and the world as his stage.

"Hey." I offer a small smile, turning to drape my arms over the pool's ledge, my hair fanning across the surface like ink in water. "FOMO?" I tease.

His throat rolls, gaze flicking to the blue-green pool, tension tightening his features.

I frown. "Everything okay?"

A clipped headshake.

Propping my chin on my hands, I watch him carefully. His

eyes stay locked on the pool like it might come alive. Like it remembers something.

"I haven't been in one of these since…" He swallows hard, dragging a hand through his hair.

My body stills in the water, the words hitting soft but heavy. I don't need the rest of the sentence. "Chase…"

He doesn't speak, doesn't move. Just digs his thumbs into his palms, as if trying to ground himself in a pain he can control.

"You don't have to get in. Not for me. Not for them." I glance toward the far end of the pool where the guys are cracking jokes, oblivious. "It's okay. I promise."

I can tell he's not really here. He's somewhere else, some sunlit day gone wrong. The sound of a splash, a scream, and too much silence after.

My mind races with ways to help. To lessen his burdens, to scare away his ghosts. "You know…I used to think that if I revisited the worst moment of my life, it would swallow me whole," I say, my voice quieting. "But it's not a monster, Chase. It's just a memory. It can't drag you under unless you let it."

The air feels denser, more polluted.

God—I should take my own advice.

I squeeze my eyes shut, memories careening to the surface like a fire-licked buoy. The squeal of tires, the crunch of metal. The airbag spattered in a mist of blood.

Alex's blood. Red on white.

I still can't bring myself to drive a car.

So I get it; I do.

And maybe that's all he needs.

Expelling the flashbacks, I push off the ledge and inch

backward, until I'm facing him, chest-deep in the water. "Chase," I murmur. "Look at me."

He hesitates, his face ashen, as if he took a wrong turn and ended up in a memory he's spent years trying to outrun.

A hard swallow. Then a slow dip of his eyes.

Our gazes lock.

"I'm not going to pretend this water doesn't feel like grief." I send him a sad smile, studying him beneath the moon as I watch that grief paint bitter lines across his face. "If you're not ready, you're not ready. There's nothing to prove here."

"Sorry." He blinks through the daze with a flustered sigh. "Fuck…I didn't think it would hit me this hard."

"Don't be sorry. It's not nothing." Water swishes against my hair as I shake my head. "You don't have to act like it is."

He cups a hand over his jaw, the pain in his eyes baring its teeth.

A long silence stretches. The others are farther down, yelling and laughing, all light and movement. This part of the pool feels like a different world.

Stark. Quiet. Waiting.

Chase takes a small step forward. "I used to think that if I talked about it, she'd feel farther away. Like saying it out loud made it more real. Made her more…gone."

I shift closer, letting the water carry me a few feet. "I think people stay quiet about their pain because they're afraid no one will know what to do with it."

A muscle in his cheek jumps. "It's fucking lonely."

"Yeah," I breathe. "But loneliness isn't always about being alone. Sometimes it's about forgetting how to reach out."

He stares at me in silence, running a hand up and down his face. Then he glances at the glimmering water like it's daring him.

I don't move. Don't push. Don't reach for him.

I let him choose.

In one smooth motion, he steps forward, all the way to the edge.

Crouching, he dips his feet in.

His jaw clenches at the first cold shock. Both legs follow, his jeans clinging to him, heavy and soaked. For a second, I think that's all he'll give. Just his legs in the water.

But then he holds his breath, sinks lower, and slides all the way in, body rigid and eyes closed. When he's waist-deep, he finally looks at me.

Emotion surges, full of grief, pain, and harrowing relief. It feels like I'm witnessing something private, something fragile.

Chase's breathing turns labored, and his eyes glaze over. Not with tears, but with something older. More jaded and worn.

I move toward him, wanting to help, wanting to—

"Gonna grab some beers and towels." Tag's voice bursts through our bubble.

I flinch.

All three guys climb out of the pool, dripping wet, half running toward the house. John is gone. Television static seeps through the cracked patio door. Cicadas hum from tall grass.

Slowly, my attention returns to Chase. He's closer now, a few inches away. The water feels warmer, lapping at my waist.

Another step. Another closed gap.

His hand lifts, reaching for mine.

I don't think.

I reach back.

CHAPTER 27
Chase

Our fingers link together.

At the contact, a softness comes over me. A weight releasing. She feels like comfort and silent strength, leaving me in a trance-heady state.

My shoulders relax, muscles unlocking.

Annie's eyes glow like frosted blue moons dipped in pearls. Underwater lights reflect off her wet skin, the beads of chlorine sparkling. Hypnotizing. It's enough to banish the intrusive thoughts, the memories pulling me into a tailspin.

She glances down at our joined hands. Her eyes linger on the guitar inked along my forearm, then drift to the ring circled around my thumb. With her free hand, she reaches out—tentative, featherlight—fingertips brushing across the worn sterling silver. "You always wear this," she murmurs, tone curious. "Why?"

I give her hand a squeeze. "When we were kids, my sister's favorite movie was *The Brave Little Toaster*."

She frowns, confused by the pivot, as if that answered her question.

I rub my thumb over the ring, letting the memory settle. "The ring belonged to our grandfather until it was passed down to my sister after he died. He got it in a pawnshop right after the war. Had nothing but pocket lint and a half-healed bullet wound in his leg."

Her gaze blinks up to me, eyes rounding.

"Yeah. The irony." I falter, smiling softly, gazing at the smooth band. "Gramps said it cost him a week's worth of meals, but he bought it anyway. For our grandmother. She turned him down three times before she agreed, but he wore this ring for a year, as if it already meant something. Like he was betting on a future that hadn't said yes yet."

Her eyes soften, tracing the ring again. "That's beautiful."

"Stella loved that story," I continue, emotion lodging in my chest and journeying up my throat. "She said it reminded her of that movie and that Gramps was like the toaster—scratched up, stubborn, always burning breakfast, but brave where it counted. Loyal till the end."

I swallow down the raw lump, watching Annie's eyes glaze with awareness, with empathy.

"She gave me the ring on my seventeenth birthday, telling me I'd inherited the stubborn, break-yourself-for-love gene. And if I was going to keep throwing myself into things heart-first, I should have something to hold on to when life got too heavy. A reminder to breathe."

My eyes shutter for a beat.

Then I untwine our fingers long enough to slide the ring off.

Etched into the underside, glinting under the muted starlight: *Brave Little Toaster.*

"I had it engraved after she died. I've worn it every day since."

Lips parting, Annie zeros in on the band, entranced, moved, caught in the web of pain-laced memory just like me. She watches as I return the ring to my thumb, then blinks up to my face.

We stare at each other, time softening its wheels.

A feeling flourishes in my chest. I can't pinpoint it, can't name it. But it's there, growing with every sluggish second.

With no warning, I tug her to me.

My arms wrap around her waist until she's flush against my chest and I can feel the erratic beats of her heart. Water sloshes around us. A gasp leaves her.

But she doesn't pull away.

Everything goes still. The sound of my bandmates laughing inside the house is muffled as the water rides the edge of the pool, and all that exists is the space between us. This delicate, dangerous stretch where everything feels too much and not enough at the same time.

I tighten my arms around her waist, holding her in a vise as her warmth quiets my demons' roars. Pressure blooms behind my eyes, a tension headache creeping to the surface.

"Chase," she whispers, her face pressed to the planes of my chest as a tonic of chlorine, summertime, and watermelon tickles my nose. "You're allowed to let this moment be new. It's just me. It's just us."

Just her. Just us.

The thunder settles, not gone, but not as loud.

My mouth hovers near her ear, breath warm and ragged. "I'm sorry."

"No." She shakes her head. "You're not. You shouldn't be."

My fingers tangle in her waterlogged hair.

What I shouldn't be doing is touching her like this.

Like she's mine. Like she's here to stay.

My eyelids flutter, smoldering embers racing through my blood. I scrunch my hands behind her back as her lips paint whispers on my skin.

"Do you feel better?" she asks on a tremoring breath.

A beat, a smile. "Maybe."

The weight of her forehead burns a hole through my chest, and I glance down, drinking in the minimal gap between us. Every inch of us touches. Water swirls, and my legs shake.

"Sounds like a yes," she says.

My grip strengthens, fingers catching on her threads of hair as I skim them down the length of her back. "I should let go of you."

The words are low, rough, no intention behind them, and the air simmers, bubbling like seafoam.

It's a lie wrapped in a truth we're both avoiding.

She nods against me. "Yes."

But she sinks deeper. Clutches me harder.

With a mind of its own, my hand glides up the center of her back then down again. Up, down, up, down. Calloused fingertips tease the edge of her tank, dipping underneath the fabric.

The moment has a mind of its own too.

A power. A pull. A pulse.

She shivers, and a little squeak breaks free. Needy, breathless.

Damning.

The air shifts, thrumming with electricity.

I coast my palm along her bare back, dragging it up her spine, until I clamp the nape of her neck beneath the top, inhaling so deep I wonder if she feels it in her lungs. The tank rides up her stomach, revealing a sliver of wet skin, and my other hand drifts down her body, splaying over her abdomen. A broken groan escapes me as I nuzzle my jaw against her cheek, rough stubble over satin. I'm sinking, drowning, teetering on the edge of absolute disaster.

"Chase…" Her body bows, seeking more contact. She's trembling. Torn in two. Caught between right and wrong, standing still and no turning back.

My heart charges forward, good intentions snakebit by this need to get closer.

I fist a handful of hair and tip her head back until we're eye to eye, lips impossibly close. "Annie—"

A cell phone starts ringing.

The theme song to *Stranger Things*.

I'm ripped from the fog as I glance across the pool and catch her boyfriend's name lighting up the face.

A breath.

A clogged, cursed beat.

And then she unravels herself from my arms, as if struck by a fifty-ton weight. Smacked with guilt. Dismantled, toes to top.

Shit.

I stumble back, chest heaving, the water turning viscous around my limbs.

I don't look at her. I can't. I refuse.

The ringtone stops, but the silence it leaves behind is deafening. I see the phone still glowing along the side of the pool, Alex's name lingering like a slap.

My throat chafes. I want to say something, but the words tangle on my tongue and choke me instead.

I'm sorry. So sorry.

I think a part of her hates him.

I think a bigger part of her hates me more.

But mostly…I think the biggest part of her hates herself.

Not a moment later, she bolts from the pool.

CHAPTER 28
Annalise

No, no, no.

I push through the water and launch myself out of the pool, feet slipping once on the concrete surface before I'm running barefoot across the yard. I don't care that my tank clings to every inch of me, that my shorts are drenched, that I probably look like a winding billboard for guilt.

Yanking open Tag's back door, I rush inside, water trailing behind me, my heartbeat hammering in my ears. A second later, I'm in the kitchen, tearing through the cabinets.

Looking for something. Anything. A distraction.

I pull out a tumbler and fill it with sink water, shivering now that I'm doused in air conditioning. Hands shaking around the glass, I bring it to my lips, the liquid sliding down my throat, a cold balm to the inferno ripping through my blood.

My skin tingles from where his hands were.

Everywhere he touched feels raw and tender.

I slam my eyes shut, and guilt sears like acid through cotton, impossible to patch.

I'm a monster.

A traitor.

Alex may have his flaws, but I am far from innocent.

I'm staring at a chip in the plaster wall when Tag sneaks up beside me, causing me to fly out of my skin. "Jesus." I slam the glass on the counter. "You're a walking jump scare."

"And you're a slow-motion car crash."

I blink, caught off guard. "What?"

"You heard me."

He's not joking. Not smirking. Just watching me with that quiet storm look that only ever comes out when he's really, truly worried.

"What's that supposed to mean?" I ask, defenses spiking.

"You know exactly what it means."

"No, Tag. I don't. Please enlighten me."

My brother leans against the counter, arms crossed, not taking his eyes off me. "Months ago I said you were playing with fire. Now the fire is a fucking blaze, and you're not just playing with it, you're dancing in it."

I scoff, untucking wet hair from behind my ears to veil the flush on my cheeks. "Don't—"

"Leave. Your. Boyfriend." Tag swivels around and presses in until we're face-to-face, eye to eye. "I saw you out there. With him. And I know that look on your face, Annalise."

My eyes well with tears, hot and stinging. "What look?"

"The one you get when you're standing on the edge of something you can't come back from."

I stare at him, gut twisting. The guilt sits heavy in my chest, waiting for someone else to say it out loud.

"Alex is all wrong for you. A piece of shit if I'm being honest," he continues, shaking his head. "I'm worried about you. I love you to death, and I know whatever game you're playing is going to destroy you."

"It's not a game." A tear falls as my breath strangles on trapped air. His words reach inside me, fist my ribs, clench my heart, and coil my vital pieces into abstract art. "Nothing's happened," I whisper, my defenses shutting down, regret soaring to the surface. "I swear."

"Not yet. But you're halfway there. And if you don't kick that asshole to the curb, you're going to hate yourself for what comes next." He swallows. "Leave him, sis. He's not your person anymore, he's your prison. Start over. Clean slate."

"I…I can't."

"Why the fuck not? Spell it out for me. Help me understand, because I—"

"Because I almost killed him!" I shoot back, breaking under the truth. "I broke him, Tag. The accident. He's never been the same. And that's my fault."

He gapes at me, frowning. "No. No way. Don't do that. Don't rewrite history just to make him easier to forgive." His voice is low but cutting. "He was always angry. Always controlling. That didn't start with the accident."

"You don't understand what he was like before—"

"Of course I do. You think I didn't notice how he isolated

you?" His jaw clenches. "Tell me how many friends you have. Tell me how many he's driven away. Kenna is only still here because she refused to leave you. And look at Mom and Dad. Think about all the times they've tried to visit, but Alex always has plans. Funny how that happens."

I flinch, my head swinging back and forth with denial. "No…"

"You used to light up a room. Then he got inside your head and flipped the breaker," Tag goes on, voice tight. "He didn't change. You just stopped pretending it didn't scare you."

His words rattle me to the bone.

But Tag is wrong.

He has to be, or else everything I ever told myself starts to unravel.

It was just a bad day.
He didn't mean it.
It's my fault.
He's hurting too.

And if it unravels, what's left?

Just me, holding a thread I don't know how to let go of.

I look away, down at the floor. "I have it under control."

Tag blows out a breath, pinches the bridge of his nose.

We both know it's a lie.

My control is out the window, gone with the stuffy, oppressive wind. If Chase had kissed me tonight, I would have let him.

And my brother is right.

It would have destroyed me.

He sighs long and hard, the temper melting away. In its place, only brotherly love. "Listen. Please know that I want you in this band more than fucking anything. But if playing with us—if playing with *him*—is going to steal a piece of your soul, it's not worth it. Not at all."

My bottom lip quivers. I chomp down on it, Tag's image blurring through the tears. "I want this," I force out, emotion bending my words. "So much."

"I know you do." He pivots, leaning back on the counter and staring down at the crud-stained grout. "But what's your endgame here?"

"Wherever this leads."

"Are you sure?" He sends me another sidelong glance. "Because we both know where it's headed."

"Tag…" The tears fall harder, evidence of my shame. Then, like a glass heart underfoot, I break. "I…I don't know what to do."

His face falls as I crumble. Tag lifts off the counter and pulls me into a hug, his chin dropping to the top of my head as I sag against him, my fists balled at his chest.

He doesn't answer.

Just lets me cry.

Chase has awakened something in me, a part that has grown cold over the years, a slow-dying flame. Soon I'll be torn in half, pieces of me forever entangled with the little boy I fell in love with before I even knew what love was.

And these new pieces, dusted off and polished, brought back to life.

By him.

I just don't know which piece fits best.

CHAPTER 29
Alex

She crawls into bed beside me. The mattress shifts with the added weight, the covers moving with her as I face the opposite wall.

She thinks I'm asleep.

But I'm wide awake, simmering in anger and violence and loneliness. The loneliness hurts most. The anger gives it control.

"You didn't answer my calls."

A beat of silence.

I hear her breathing, and those wispy little breaths sound like shame.

They speak to the violence.

Rolling over, I watch her chest rise and fall through the dancing shadows. A shred of moonlight seeps through the pinstripe curtains, highlighting wet splotches on her cheekbones.

My hands curl.

Shame it is.

"Anything you want to tell me?" My voice is low and dark, teetering the brink of mass destruction. "Clearly, you've been crying."

She swipes at her face. "It was a tough practice."

That mocking voice throws its head back with a laugh.

I catapult over to her side of the bed like a rabid dog breaking from its leash until I'm spitting right in her face. "Bull. Fucking. Shit."

"Jesus!" The mattress squeaks as she jerks into a sitting position and scrambles against the headboard, our noses a lethal inch apart. "Alex, you're scaring me."

"Why are you wet?" I flick a strand of damp hair. "A late-night swim?"

"Yes. It was stifling in the garage."

"Naturally."

Her expression pinches with barely contained emotion. "Why are you acting like this?"

"Why did you ignore my calls all night?" I shoot back with venom. "You know I fucking *hate* this music shit. These practices. You spend more time with other men than me. I have a right to know where you are, what you're doing." I stab a finger to my chest. "You're *my* goddamn girlfriend."

She flinches at my words, though I haven't shouted.

It's the quiet rage that gets her. Always has.

Her arms fold over her stomach like a safeguard, as if I'm the blow she's bracing for.

I'm not that guy—*I'm not*.

But maybe I'm not far off.

She opens her mouth, closes it. I watch her throat work through the silence, her eyes glassy.

"I didn't mean to ignore you," she finally says. "It wasn't on purpose."

That should cool me.

It doesn't.

I run my tongue along the inside of my cheek, shaking my head.

"I was helping Chase through something. It wasn't—"

"Chase." I spit his name like a mouthful of blood. "Of course it was fucking Chase."

Fuck him.

Fuck her.

Fuck this.

I can *feel* the way he looks at her. Like she's a lifeline. And I can feel the way she softens when he's around, like he's someone worth saving.

But I'm the one who needs saving.

Me.

"Do you even see me?" she whispers brokenly.

I open my mouth, ready to snap back.

Nothing comes out.

Because I don't.

Because I do.

Because I can't tell the fucking difference anymore.

My shoulders sag, the weight of it all cracking through the surface. "You shut me out. You used to tell me everything."

She blinks, and the edge in her gaze softens, just a notch. "You used to listen."

A bitter laugh punches from my chest. "So this is on me?"

"It's on both of us. You and me. But you don't get to demand anything when you only show up with suspicion and control."

For a moment, I just stare at her. She's flushed, shaking, wearing pain like armor, and somehow she still looks like everything I want and everything I hate about myself.

My jaw ticks. I reach out to touch her cheek, but she flinches back. That tiny recoil cuts deeper than any of her words.

"Fuck, baby. I just…" I swallow hard, the anger starting to rot into something more sinister. Something uglier. "I don't know how to be okay without you."

It slips out before I can stop it. A confession dressed as an accusation.

And still, somehow, a plea.

She doesn't respond. Just exhales shakily and inches down beside me, tugging the covers up to her chin. Quiet tears break free.

She's not touching me, not holding me. Not close enough.

But she's not gone either.

As I lie there, fists clenched around nothing, trying to forget the way her hair smells like chlorine, I hear two little words wrench through her sobs, tainting the air:

"I'm sorry."

My mind reels. My chest fractures.

Then it hits me—there's only one thing left to do.

By noon the next day, I'm perched at the edge of the bed.

A thorn in my heart.

A prayer on my lips.

And tucked between my hands, a final shot in the dark.

CHAPTER 30
Chase

Somehow, it's the last thing I expect to hear.

"Happy birthday!"

Confusion washes over me as I stand at the opening of the garage, looking like a bewildered puppy. Rock busts out a zippy drum solo while Annie blows on one of those neon-red party horns, then tosses a clump of something at me. I blink down at my boots.

Confetti.

"We're going out. Hope you're well-caffeinated and fully hydrated." She does a hair flip, her heels clicking as she fetches her purse off one of the stools.

Tag smacks me on the back. "Congrats, old man. Another year around the sun."

I forgot it was my fucking birthday.

But Annie remembered. I mentioned it once, some late night when Kenna crashed our practice and dove into one of her astrology speeches. Said Virgos were perfectionists with a martyr complex—artistic, analytical, and too observant for their own good.

Annie had smiled then. Not in a teasing way, but like she was putting the pieces together. Like she understood why I overthink everything. Why I care too much and say too little.

When she sends me that same smile from across the garage, I know I haven't said enough.

Leave him.

Pick me.

I know you feel it too.

But I keep my mouth shut.

Because, martyr complex.

Zach downs his beer, his braids curtaining his face as he crunches the can. "Who's D.D.?"

Annie clears her throat. "Alex."

"Alex is coming?" My blood runs cold.

"Yeah." She won't look at me. "He has an SUV."

Tag grumbles under his breath, packing his guitar back up. "Yippee. Can't wait to be on the receiving end of death stares and backhanded insults all night."

"He'll behave," Annie insists.

"Whatever. But if you invite him to my birthday party, I'm cutting all familial ties."

I blow out a breath.

Part of me can't comprehend why she'd invite him to my birthday outing.

Then again, part of me understands completely.

A black SUV rolls up ten minutes later in the form of a hulking Kia Sorento with tinted windows. The horn blares.

Annie whooshes past me, gripping her purse strap, practically hugging the edge of the garage as she moves, putting as much distance between us as possible. A warm breeze steals her hair, wrapping multicolored ribbons around her face as she hightails it over to the vehicle.

She slips inside the passenger seat as the guys and I climb into the back.

Alex smirks, taking her hand in a firm grasp and smacking a kiss to her knuckles before planting it on his knee. "Hey, baby."

Her head bows. "Hey."

The car reeks of familiar cologne. Something cheap but meant to smell overpriced and provocative. I slink lower in the seat and latch my buckle.

"Comfortable back there, birthday boy?" Alex's eyes snag mine in the rearview mirror.

"Yeah. Thanks for the ride."

"Absolutely. It's nice to finally be included in these after-hours get-togethers." He shoots Annie a look, pops the lever into Drive, then slams on the accelerator.

It's a torturous fifteen-minute drive to Sand Bar.

Nobody speaks.

Nineties jams spin on rotation from the Bluetooth, "If You Could Only See" by Tonic a scoffing soundtrack to my discomfort. I watch Annie fidget in her seat, plucking invisible threads from her ruby-sequined cocktail dress. Her hand hasn't left his knee, and his finger hasn't stopped tracing little designs across her knuckles. He has her on a goddamn leash.

She peeks back at me every now and then, her chest inflating with stiff breaths, her floral perfume the only antidote to the spicy cologne plugging the air.

Closing my eyes, I tip my head against the headrest and zone out until we curve into the parking lot.

"I'll find parking," Alex says, dropping us off at the entrance. "Save me a seat."

I leap from the SUV as if my legs grew wings. Fresh air rushes into my lungs, doing what it can to filter out the stubborn cloud of lingering disappointment.

Annie calls my name, though I'm already charging ahead, toward the bar lights. The reprieve.

This is fine. Preferable, even.

I'll have a few drinks, socialize, and maybe meet a woman who isn't borderline betrothed.

Unfortunately, she's determined to follow like an all-consuming shadow, darkening my plans. And now she's right behind me, hot on my dirty, black boots, refusing to let me chase the light I fucking crave.

"Hey. Wait up, will you?"

The rest of the guys shuffle around us, entering through the main door. Tag sends an ambiguous look over his shoulder that I decide not to read into. "What's up?" My hands slide into my pockets, fingers curling.

"I, um…I'm sorry about the extra addition."

"Why are you sorry? He's your boyfriend."

"I know, but—"

"But nothing. He has a right to be here."

Edginess gnaws at me, gravel coating my tongue.

I don't know if it's the lack of sleep, the reminder that I'm another year older and Stella is another year gone, or the way Annie beams in her dress, gift-wrapped and glowing. The sewn-on sequins twinkle beneath the moon like bloodred stars, the fabric making love to her curves.

She blinks up at me, frowning slightly. "Okay. I just…I realize it's your birthday, and he's not someone you'd choose to celebrate with."

I shrug. "To be honest, I forgot it was my birthday. I haven't celebrated in years."

Her lips shape into an O. "Oh."

"So, I appreciate the effort. Extra addition or not." It's not a bold-faced lie. I appreciate the effort as much as I loathe it. Effort means she cares, and as long as she cares, hope dwells.

The hope is what I loathe.

Nodding, she draws her bottom lip between her teeth.

I can see she's about to say something. But I also see that Alex is storming around the corner with lightning under his white leather sneakers.

Whipping around, I push inside the bar, leaving her just outside the entrance.

Strobe lights paint the floor in watercolor lights. A live band plays from the stage while patrons dance below, a swirl of hair, limbs, sweat, and capsizing glasses.

That godforsaken pressure grows, pulsing between my temples.

Goddammit.

These migraines are shit.

I wind over to the bar, squeezing between two women in summery citrus dresses. Lemon rakes her eyes over me on my right. Orange sends me a smile to my left. An order is placed, a whiskey neat sliding across the counter through a puddle of melted ice. It goes down smooth, a quick, cheap remedy to the hole in my heart and the boulder in my brain.

Before pivoting away, I pause, glancing at Lemon. She's the opposite of Annie with sheaves of golden blond hair, cocoa-brown eyes, and a rail-thin frame. Pretty by all standards.

Yet the sight of her does nothing for me.

And that's fucked.

I'm twenty-five years old, have been celibate for longer than I care to admit, and have no ties to anyone, no loyalty in question, and no good fucking reason to not introduce myself. See where it goes. Open my eyes to someone other than Annalise Adams, who is currently arm in arm with her long-term boyfriend, a sun-kissed smile on her scarlet lips.

Pressing two fingers to the center of my forehead, I turn back around and slump against the bar. Another whiskey is placed in front of me several seconds later.

I down that one too, then order a third.

"You okay?"

A mousy voice registers on my right. Lemon.

I stare straight ahead, my liquor glass hiding the smile I'm not wearing. "Yeah. I'm good."

The truth is, I drink beer when I'm good. I drink straight whiskey when I want to forget that I'm not.

"I'm Jaclyn."

I finally spare her a glance, watching as she teases a plump cherry between her teeth.

To my detriment, all I can think about is the way Annie braided cherry stems into perfect little bows with only her tongue.

"You're too good-looking to look so sad," Lemon-slash-Jaclyn continues, inciting conversation.

My face sours. It's an odd thing to say, but it's nothing I haven't heard over the last few years. "I wasn't aware those two attributes were correlated," I reply.

The cherry disappears inside her mouth. "Good-looking people have a duty to uphold."

"Elaborate."

"It's nothing concrete, of course, but I feel like it's the tradeoff for being gifted with physical perfection. You have a responsibility to make the less fortunate around you feel beautiful too."

"Perfection," I echo.

I'm not sure why I'm humoring her, but the guys are huddled at the opposite end of the bar chugging Jägerbombs, Alex is grinding on Annie amid a mass of people, and I'm not sure what else to do but guzzle whiskey until I black out.

"Did I say that?" Another cherry finds its way to her mouth, lingering between her lips for a beat before sliding inside. "Tell me what you do for a living."

The migraine grows teeth, chewing through my skull. "I'm a woodworker. Also play in a band."

Her eyes gleam. "You're a musician?"

"We're just starting out. We have a gig in two months at The Soundproof."

"Where's that?"

"New York."

Pillowy pink lips curve up with a smile. "Wow, that's big-time stuff. What's the date?" She turns to fully face me. "I'll come see you."

My gaze flicks over Jaclyn's head, catching with Annie's. Her movements slow, her eyes meeting mine across the dance floor. She glances at the blond, then back at me. Notable tension creeps across her face, as if she doesn't like what she sees.

That's fucked too. Almost as much as the empty feeling churning in my gut while this pretty girl flirts with me.

Swallowing half my whiskey, I exhale a long breath. "October fourteenth."

"On my calendar." She pulls out her phone and pops in the date.

I'm all out of conversation.

Seconds slug by as I finish my drink and toss the glass on the counter, avoiding Jaclyn's throat clears and jittery limbs as she thinks of new ways to earn my attention.

But my attention is earned when Annie pushes her way between me and Orange. My body stiffens, skin starts to sweat. It's instinct. A physical reaction to her arm brushing mine.

"Hey. Sorry, I didn't mean to ditch you on your birthday." Annie orders a fruity cocktail and sends me a penitent smile. Then her voice dips to a hush. "I'm also here to save you."

I tell the bartender to put her drink on my tab. "Save me?"

"Yep. You looked uncomfortable." A sly look is sent to Jaclyn, who is now enmeshed in conversation with a woman on her right. "I know it's hard putting yourself out there. The dating scene is vicious, according to Kenna."

"I wasn't—"

"Not everyone rescues injured goldfinches and names them Haiku. Some people have body parts in their fridge named after their favorite serial killers."

Straightaway, my anxiety shakes loose and a smile teases. "You think Jaclyn's a closet sociopath?"

"Jaclyn, huh?" A pink cocktail with extra cherries and a coral umbrella is placed in front of her. She sips from the straw, her red-wine nails tapping the glass. "I mean, probably not. She looks like the type of person who doesn't even let her ground beef go a day past the expiration date."

A sharp laugh escapes, and I order a beer. "Guess we'll never know. Maybe she is a serial killer, and I just dodged a literal bullet."

"Maybe." Annie grins around her straw, then plucks a cherry from the endless slew of ice cubes. "Behind the ground beef is a collection of body parts. Elbows and clavicles because she's different and quirky."

"Heads and hearts are too predictable."

"And I bet she does name them after serial killers, but in an offbeat way." Her blue eyes glimmer under the indigo lights. "Bed Tundy."

"Jesus." I reach for my beer, veiling the toothy grin I can't tamp down. "Well, thanks for saving me then. I've managed to avoid becoming a shinbone named Jack the Stripper in Jaclyn's produce drawer."

"Here to help." She clinks her glass with mine. "Happy birthday, Chase."

The humor tapers off as I stare transfixed at the cherry between her lips. She scoops it into her mouth with her tongue, and a moment later, removes the perfectly knotted stem.

Silence settles.

The energy changes.

Then the whiskey turns on me. "Do you really love him?"

She chokes on her drink.

Her eyes widen like she can't believe I just asked her that.

Gulping hard, Annie peers down at the floor, jaw working, lashes fluttering. The glistening cherry bow tumbles from her fingers, landing beside my boot.

I exhale sharply. "Sorry." Taking a hard swig of my beer, I shake my head and slam the bottle on the counter, turning to face her. "No. I'm not sorry."

"Chase—"

"I'm fucking crazy about you."

Slowly, her eyes pan upward. Shock glitters in her ambushed gaze, stealing her breath.

Moisture pools as her mouth fumbles for a response.

Regret gnaws, and my head pounds. But my heart pounds harder. This need to lay it all out there before it's too late chomps through logic and morality.

Grit rolls up my throat as my voice lowers to a whisper. Sincerity bleeds through, honesty threaded with desperation. "I'm crazy about you, Annie."

Sound shrinks on all sides, the lights dimming until all I see is her. Standing there, mouth ajar, looking at me like I just ripped a rug out from under her. The gems on her dress sparkle and blur. Her cheeks redden to match. Two teary pearls breach the corners of her eyes.

This isn't fair.

I'm not being fair.

And still I wait, hoping, yearning, hemorrhaging at her feet. Silently pleading with her to see me.

Not him. Just me.

Annie makes a sound, a little squeak of despair. "I—"

"There you are."

A dark shadow trudges over, blackening the moment. Pilfering all the hope and wretched expectation from the room. Sound returns, the lights blaze brighter and hotter, and the whiskey sits like a concrete block in the pit of my stomach.

Whatever she was going to say is snuffed out as Alex wraps a possessive arm around her and she deflates. "Hey," she forces out. "I was just grabbing a drink."

"Loosening those inhibitions. I'm here for it." Alex nuzzles her neck, nibbling the soft skin.

Her eyes drift to mine.

She looks fucking broken.

"Come on. You like this song," he says, his big hand clamping around her wrist as he yanks her from the counter. Toward the dance floor. Oceans away from me.

Her heels skid across the linoleum as she attempts to find her balance, shuffling behind him while sending me a painful look of apology as she retreats.

My hand grips the beer so hard I nearly crack the bottle. I

shove it at my lips, swallowing the whole thing, the alcohol fizzing in my chest like a short-circuiting grenade.

I push away from the counter.

"It was nice meeting you—" Jaclyn's voice fades out.

Needing a better distraction, I join my bandmates as they form a loose circle around the corner, talking music, the sound of the live band filling the room with staticky noise.

"Yo," Rock greets me, shaggy dark hair covering his eyes. "Didn't want to pry you away from Goldilocks. Tell me you got her Snap."

"Yeah," I lie.

Tag studies me, his attention split between his sister and whatever dead thing is lingering in my eyes. I know he sees it. They're probably shaped like two sad broken-heart emojis.

"I warned her, you know," he mutters, low enough so only I can hear him. He folds his arms and nods at the dance floor. "Told her this wouldn't end well."

"Alex?"

"You. All of it."

My pulse runs away from me. "It doesn't matter. It'll end how it's supposed to."

"Yeah." He huffs. "With everybody ruined."

Muscles drawn tight, I watch Annie from a few feet away. The smile is gone, and her eyes are rimmed red. If Alex notices, he doesn't care. She's in his arms. Pressed against his chest.

Wholly his.

"I never meant to cause problems," I say. "And I know you don't like me, so—"

A gruff laugh cuts me off. "That's what's so fucked about this. I *do* like you. Doesn't make any fuckin' sense, but if I could rewrite the story, it would be you over there dancing with her, putting the smile back on her face. Because that's what you do. You make her smile. And it's not that fake-ass bullshit she whips out when she wants us to think she's doing just fine. It's real. Something I haven't seen in a long time."

His words sink in slowly, knocking the wind out of me.

"Annalise has always been good at pretending," Tag adds, sipping his beer. "But not with you. And if I can see that, I know he can see it too."

My eyes glaze, the bar spinning in and out of focus.

As if summoned, Alex looks up at me.

We stare at each other, two enemies at war, and I watch as his lips draw into a sneer as if he knows something I don't. Like he has some dirty little secret up his sleeve.

Whiskey taints my blood with vitriol.

The way he holds her is too severe, his arm a wrench around her shoulders, fingers white-knuckling her biceps. She has no choice but to sink into him. Submit. The image has my teeth scraping together, hot tension simmering beneath my skin.

The hopelessness curdles into anger.

Anger that after all these years, I'm still not happy. No matter how much I run or how deeply I try to disappear, nothing ever changes.

People leave. Love turns sour.

And now, the one person I do have was never really mine to begin with.

Fuck.

I need to go.

Just as I'm about to storm out of the bar and take an Uber home, I freeze, doing a double take.

Because the unthinkable happens.

Alex drops to one knee. Pulls out black velvet box.

Right in the middle of the dance floor.

The music cuts off like it was planned. A spotlight shimmies around the room, landing on my worst nightmare. Annie's hand shoots to her mouth as she stands there, paralyzed, looking just as blindsided as I feel.

Tag watches the scene unfold, his expression shell-shocked. "Holy fuck."

Words catch in my throat. "Did you…?"

"Not a damn clue."

My hairline dampens, and my skin crawls. I can't hear what he's saying; I don't want to.

But I hear her.

One word.

A soft, hesitant, "Yes."

My vision distorts, everything streaking around me in a monochrome blur. Hugging, kissing, people cheering from every corner. Tag and I just stand there while Rock and Zach applaud through congratulatory whistles, oblivious.

The world tilts.

My world crumbles.

And I should've fucking seen it coming—*seven years*. The guy has seven years on me. A life built, memories made, a future within reach.

And me?

I'm just the guy who stole the wrong car.

CHAPTER 31
Chase

Ten seconds later, I'm plowing through the bathroom door with a handful of painkillers chucked at the back of my throat. I cup my palm under the running faucet, gulping greedily from my hand as I tip my head back, savoring the bitter residue left behind. The overhead light flickers and drones, sounding like a hornet caught in my ear.

Fuck me.

I lean back against the pedestal sink and look around.

Graffiti lines the dated mauve walls. Sharpie-drawn love notes and Gen Z slang blur at the edges of my vision. Someone wrote "Maddie is a cunt" and added a smiley face to the *U*.

I stare at it for a long time as shrapnel scrapes behind my eyes and rocket fire shreds my temples.

She said *yes*.

The woman I've unintentionally fallen for is now engaged.

I don't give the meds time to fix my headache and attempt to bolt from the bathroom—

But the door whips open instead.

A vision of red sweeps inside. Annie hurriedly shuts the door behind her and clicks the lock, chest heaving as her eyes trail to mine across the locker-size bathroom.

What the hell is she doing in here?

Her boyfriend just proposed to her in front of a live audience. He's probably tearing the place apart looking for her. "What are you doing?"

"Chase." Her voice splinters with a sharp crack. "I'm so sorry."

She's sorry.

She's always sorry.

And now, more than anything, she has no reason to be.

I droop against the chipped heliotrope-toned sink, pretending it doesn't match the colored streaks in her hair. "Congratulations, Annie."

Devastation washes over her face, and it's not a look I'd expect from a newly engaged woman. She glances down at the diamond ring glittering on her finger, twirling it in anxious circles like she's trying to spin doubt into certainty. "The timing is terrible. I was on the spot and panicked. I-I didn't know he was going to—"

"It's okay." I force my eyes up, force a smile, force this pathetic wave of dejection to dissipate. "It's okay. I'm happy for you."

Her head shakes slightly. "What you said before…"

"Doesn't matter. I had too much whiskey."

"But…" She swallows, lacing her fingers together, shifting from heel to heel. "Did you mean it?"

"Would it change anything if I did? You already said yes." Alcohol courses through my blood as I inch up from the sink, taking a step toward her. The light fixture buzzes, sputtering in and out. "Unless that was a maybe."

She goes still, blinking up at me as the statement registers. "This is so hard."

"It shouldn't be hard. Not if you love him."

A tear zigzags down her cheek, dangling at her jaw. "It's not that simple."

My heart is a moving target. I should walk away, charge out the front door, and disappear into the crestfallen night. But I take another step closer. "Why?"

"Because it hurts." Her face crumples. "I hurt you, and I never wanted to hurt you."

I stop in front of her as my shoulders sag. "Annie—"

"I just…I've built a life with him, Chase," she says, licking away a salty tear, trying to find an ounce of rationale to cling to. "We've been through a lot together. He's not perfect, but neither am I, and I feel like I need to see this through, stay committed till the end, because—"

"You feel like? Or you want to?" My hand lifts, and I swipe away another tear, my thumb dusting across her skin. Her gaze shutters, jaw tilting into my touch. "There's a difference."

Pain coasts across her face. Guilt, sadness, and all the things she shouldn't be feeling right now with a ring on her finger. "I know we've gotten close," she says softly. "And that's my fault. I dragged you into this when I should have let you be, and I allowed this connection to grow into something bigger, and that's…that's not fair. It's not fair to you."

My hand falls away. "Life has never been fair to me. Not your fault."

"I've been so selfish." Her breath stutters, pupils dilating. Everything surges to the surface, and she starts to shake, wrapping her arms around her body to hold it all in.

The last thing I should do is touch her.

But I pull her in anyway.

She flops against me, fragile and breaking, her arms winding around my torso. Tears soak through my T-shirt. I hold her tighter than I should, every nerve in my body screaming at me to let go.

"You should go, Annie," I whisper into her hair, though my heart doesn't agree.

She glances up, tear-glazed and trembling. "Why?"

"Because I'm feeling selfish too."

It's as honest as I can be right now. But it's enough to drive the point home. Annie intakes a sharp breath, stiffening in my arms. Her fingers curl around the fabric of my shirt.

She knows I'm going to kiss her if she doesn't walk out that door. Just like I'd planned to kiss her in the pool.

She ran then.

Just like she runs now.

Slowly stepping away, she keeps her gaze leveled with the black-and-white checkered floor. At the end of the day, we're both runners. Like recognizes like. We run to avoid, hide, punish, and sabotage. We'll either run in circles until it kills us, or we'll finally be brave enough to stop.

But not tonight.

Annie inches back toward the door, stopping once to look up at me. "I got you something."

I blink at her, the headache still beating against my temple, warping my vision. The jewels of her dress swirl under the light, glittering and alive.

Hand disappearing into her purse, she sifts around, pulling out a tiny wood-carved keychain. It's shaped like a guitar. I blink until my vision settles.

Annie heaves in a breath and extends her hand, placing the trinket in my palm.

I glance down, and etched across the front is one word: *Hallelujah*.

My hand curls around the keychain, centering me and bludgeoning me at the same time.

A mournful smile curves on her lips. "Happy birthday, Chase."

As she moves farther away, my pulse slams behind my eyes, and the shimmer starts to fracture. The edges of her blur. Her silhouette ripples like a heatwave in the dead of summer.

The lock flicks.

The door creaks open.

A second later, she's gone.

And I don't chase her. Not because I don't want to, but because if I do, I'm not sure I'll be able to let her go again.

So I stay—hand fisted around her gift, head in shambles, and heart scrambling for beats.

Only this time, it's not the running that hurts.

It's the fact that I always let her.

CHAPTER 32
Annalise

"Yes, Mom. I know. Uh-huh." I pace the living room in tight circles with my phone to my ear. Seabass sizzles in a saucepan, the scent of capers and a buttery white wine marinade wafting in from the adjacent kitchen.

"You know we just worry."

My voice dips lower, despite the roar of the range hood and Alex's angry cooking playlist drowning out all sound within a five-mile radius. "You don't need to worry. I've known him forever. This isn't a spur-of-the-moment decision."

Somehow, her sigh overpowers the roar.

I groan. "I can hear your sigh of disapproval."

"It's not disapproval. It's concern. You're only twenty-one years old."

"I'll be twenty-two by the time of the wedding. Does that help?"

"I was thirty-two when I married your father, and I still question that decision."

I roll my neck, then press two fingers to my forehead. "No, you don't. You're head over heels for Dad and always will be."

"Is that our daughter?" Dad's voice pitches in the background. "Get her on a video call."

"Honey, can you call us—"

"On it." I hang up and switch to video chat mode. Two blue-eyed familiar faces light up my screen, sending a deep-rooted tickle to my heart. "Hey."

"Angel," Dad coos, adjusting his cowboy hat.

He looks night-and-day different from the man I grew up with. Gone are the neutral-toned ties, ironed slacks, and freshly shined shoes. In their place, a man who's worked hard through long hours and sacrifice to chase his ultimate dream of living off the land.

Unburdened and free.

To Dad, it's just a cheap cowboy hat he bought at a roadside store. To me, it's evidence. Proof that what you truly desire is always within reach if you put in the work.

"Hi, Daddy." My defenses fizzle out at the sound of his voice. I miss my parents so much. "You look great."

"Yeah? The gray is out in full force." He scratches at his silver-tinged beard and makes a face. "I feel the threads of a midlife crisis unraveling with every new white hair."

"I doubt you'll ever enter the crisis stage as long as you have a working lawn mower," I tease.

Mom nods emphatically, her sandy-gold mane bobbing at her shoulders. "That's true. The obsession hasn't waned."

My father's eyes glaze over as he slips away.

"Dad?"

"Sorry." He blinks back to the screen. "Didn't hear that over the sound of the lawn mower in my head."

I snicker, resuming my unproductive pacing. "Anyway, I hope you guys can be happy for me. This is a big deal."

"That's why we're being the voice of reason, Annalise," Mom says. "It *is* a big deal, and you've hardly stepped out into the world and spread your wings."

"I have a steady job and a condo. Bought, not rented."

"A job at Alex's restaurant, and a condo in Alex's name," Mom reminds me, her tone soft but honest.

My skin prickles like an omen. "We're in this together."

"I certainly hope that's true." She sends me a cautious smile. "Do you have a date planned?"

"Not yet. We're thinking sometime next summer."

"That'll give me time to lose these extra pounds," Dad muses, rubbing a hand over his plump belly. "Twelve, to be precise."

Mom wrinkles her nose, an exact replica of mine. Small and buttonlike. "I've been baking more lately."

"I miss your lemon tarts." I can't prevent the trace of sadness from inhabiting my tone. "Summers haven't been the same without them."

Her eyes gleam as she moves around the room, stepping in front of a window that drenches her in natural light.

Dad pops his head over her shoulder, draping a hulking arm across her chest. "We'll come visit. Anytime. Just say the word."

"You're always so busy," Mom adds with regret. "We don't want to intrude."

"You never intrude."

To be honest, I've low-key dodged their attempts to come visit for nearly a year.

Soon.

Maybe next month.

I'll let you know.

Alex always has something going on, plans popping up whenever they want to fly in.

Tag wasn't wrong about that.

But the truth is, it isn't just Alex. It's me. I'm not embarrassed by the small condo or the job or the routine. What unsettles me is how still I've become inside it all. Like I've been circling the same wounds without ever moving past them.

No risk, no reach, no momentum.

Stuck.

But I'm engaged now.

That's something.

I glance at the ring on my finger, a pear-shaped diamond on a white-gold band. Simple, tasteful. I've never been one for garish things.

Mom plops down on a chocolate-brown loveseat while Dad perches himself on the armrest. She studies me through the screen, curiosity flickering in her navy-swirled eyes. "Montague says you've put a band together. You have a show next month?"

"Oh…yep." While I wasn't keeping the band a secret, per se, I wasn't quite ready to spill the beans. Not because it's not important, but because I'm afraid I'll jinx how important it could become. "It's an outlet for me. It keeps me grounded."

"Your brother is over the moon. Pun intended."

A grin creeps in. "We all mesh well together. The lead singer—Chase—he's unbelievably talented. Gifted in that effortless way. Our harmonies are golden." Lightness infuses my steps as I amble around the room, fluffing pillows and tidying random surfaces. "He builds guitars too. God, they're revolutionary. And you should hear him sing. Tag is good, and I can hold my own, but Chase is next-level. All passion and soul, fused with power and control. The way he can…"

My words trail off.

Either my grin turns goofy or my eyes reflect something I don't intend to give away, because Mom gives me a look—*the* look. "He's important to you."

I stop moving, clear my throat, and curl my toes into the floor. "Yeah," I murmur. "We have a solid connection. He's a good friend."

Mom and Dad share a glance.

Dad's about to pipe in when Alex peers around the corner with a dish towel draped over his shoulder.

"Dinner," he says, eyeing the phone.

"Great. Thank you." Sending him a smile, I turn back to my parents. "I need to go. I'll fill you in on the wedding details soon."

"We love you, angel," Dad says with misty eyes.

Mom waves goodbye. "Talk soon."

"Bye." I click off the call.

Retreating to the eat-in kitchen, I survey the table decorated with colorful platters and serving bowls, all overflowing with vibrant greens, glistening fish, and flaky dinner rolls. My stomach grumbles, both with hunger pangs and a telltale pinch of dread.

I hardly remember how to cook.

In fact, I can't recall the last time I made myself a meal beyond deli sandwiches and bowls of cereal.

As if reading my mind, Alex scans the spread of food with pride. "You've got it made, wifey." He hauls his chair back and plunks down in the seat. "Homemade dinners for life. How many wives can put their feet up at the end of the day, while the husbands take to the kitchen?"

The feeling of dread thickens at the reminder.

It shouldn't though, because he's right.

I'm lucky. Blessed.

Taking a seat across from him, I nod with gratitude as my phone pings beside me on the ivory tablecloth.

I glance down at the text glowing on the screen.

Mom: It's worth mentioning that you looked happier just now than I've seen you look in a very long time. xoxo

My hand trembles as I reach for a pair of tongs and fill my plate with summer salad, the diamond ring twinkling beneath a wagon wheel chandelier.

Anxiety rolls through me like a torrent-tipped wave.

Because I know exactly what she means.

And she's not referring to the engagement.

[Bridge]

~~And if we never find the ending,~~
~~If the melodies run dry,~~
~~Will you still think of me,~~
~~Underneath a midnight sky?~~

No.
Definitely not. Way too sappy.

~~If we never find that secret chord,~~
~~And all the love runs dry,~~
~~Will silence fill the spaces,~~
~~Where music used to lie?~~

Still a nope.

Ugh—I love writing bridges.

Why is this so hard?

A pillar candle flickers from the balcony table, ashy trails of smoke dancing toward the sky. The half-burnt cigarette dangles between my fingers, and I bring it to my lips, taking a lung-filling drag. My gaze pans to the treetops, the glow of the waxing moon seeping through the branches and triggering a soft smile.

I click the end of my pen with my thumb.

Then I make three more attempts to write something decent before desperation takes over.

I text Chase.

Me: Help.

It's not too late, only a quarter past ten. We took the night off from band practice because Zach's daughter had a volleyball game and a subsequent afterparty.

I think we all needed it. A break.

My pulse hitches when his three little bubbles dance to life.

Chase: Let me guess, you're either stuck on a bridge lyric or three seconds away from setting your notebook on fire.

My lips curve up.
The candle flame dances with temptation.

Me: Ha ha. And yes.
Chase: Show me what you've got so far.

I scrunch my nose, deciding the first two lines might work. Send.

Me: "Maybe we were born to drift, lost in spaces we can't name"
Me: That was attempt #8247 and I still can't get the last two lines to stick.

Embers flush orange and crimson as I take another puff from the cigarette and wait.

Chase: Ok, well the song is about a love that was

once strong starting to fade, leaving the person empty and clinging to memory. Lots of metaphors for light/fire burning out.

I suck my lip between my teeth and make a hissing sound.

Me: Correct.

I want to add that it's not personal or based on experience, but let it go.
Not necessary.
My condition for adding Chase's number back into my phone was that all texts would remain strictly business. Also, avoidance makes it kind of hard to communicate with your vocalist.

Chase: So you can bring that back in somehow.
Goodbye = the lost spark.

Tapping the phone against my knee, I give my brain a moment to process.

Me: "Not every goodbye is hollow…?"
Me: One too many syllables, I think.

A swoosh.
Then another.

Chase: Hmm

Chase: How about: "Not every loss is final"

A lightbulb goes off.
I chew on the end of my pen and shoot back the finishing line.

Me: "Some just burn without the flame."

A smile beams as I stare down at the screen.

Chase: You got it.
Me: We finally have a bridge.
Chase: Someone once told me that all the best songs have bridges. 😊

My pulse thrashes in response. Recollection. Memories from eight months ago swim through my mind: Chase, a broken stranger, bleeding out on his couch, and my inherent need to offer a small solace for when he finally breached the other side of it.

Me: The strongest ones don't burn.

I'm zeroed in on the screen, waiting for a follow-up, when a new text message from Kenna flashes, laced with her usual brand of debauchery.

Kenna: Nipple clamps. Yay or nay?

I snort, the introspective moment effectively broken.

Me: For you?
Kenna: No, for my vast succulent collection. Yes for me. I need you to talk me off the ledge or give me a shining endorsement.

Sorry, Kenna.
I've got nothing.

Me: Um...undecided? Never used them.
Kenna: I kind of love how vanilla you are. So cute. So pure.
Me: Shush it. I can be kinky when it counts. And are you getting your freak on by yourself or is there a new guy I don't know about?
Kenna: 😼😼
Me: Kenna! Name.

I switch over to Chase's text thread, checking to see if he replied.
My last message shows Read.
No response.

Kenna: His name is Tyler. I haven't slept with him yet. Just a blow job. But you know I hate giving blow jobs, so that tells you I'm serious.

I chuckle.

Me: I love giving blow jobs. Is that weird?

I give her a few minutes to respond, but nothing comes through.

Leaning back in the chair, I set my phone on my thigh and finish the cigarette in a few more puffs, watching as the billowing branches sweep across the moon like ink dragging over an antique page. The phone dings a reply as I'm crushing out the stub in a midnight-hued ashtray.

Chase: I don't think it's weird. But it's a little weird you're telling me that.

I blink at the corresponding name. Lurch forward in the chair.
Chase…?
Another blink.
Seventy-two more blinks.
And then all the blood drains from my face as I let out a horrified wheeze, my lungs shrinking to sapped little prunes.
Oh my God.
No. Delete. Undo.
Hands violently shaking, I shimmy my thumbs across the keypad, my cheeks the same shade as the red velvet cake I devoured after dinner.

Me: Shit. No. I'm sorry. I meant to send that to Kenna.

Me: Oh god. Please remove your eyes immediately.

His bubbles move.
Disappear.
Move again.
Disappear.
I'm moments away from launching myself over the balcony railing when his text appears.

Chase: ...

What?
No. He can't reply with that. I need photographic evidence that his eyes have been removed from his face or I'm jumping.
I will. I'm going to.
Leaping from my seat, I start frantically pacing the minimal surface area, my fingers carving through my hair so hard my scalp burns. I don't know what to say. He needs to reply with something else. Anything but nothing.

Me: I'm unraveling. It's not pretty. Please say something.

Several seconds pass.

Chase: Sorry. Processing.

I blanch.

Me: What does that mean??

Chase: It means I'm a guy. And my imagination doesn't suck.

Me: Oh my god. Please don't say suck. 🤭🤭

A beat.

Chase: Good night, Annie.

I'm not sure how to respond. So I don't. The damage is done. Eye contact tomorrow will be harrowing at best.

My cheeks burn with the heat of a dozen forest fires in the dead of July as I click off the screen and shove my phone into my pocket, swallowing hard.

Then I blow out the candle.

Sweet dreams, Chase.

CHAPTER 33
Chase

I t's done.

Finally.

The new custom is heavy as hell as I sling the strap over my shoulder and pull it against my chest. It's more showpiece than instrument, but I only plan to use it for one song.

Shaped like a crescent moon with a black burst melting into midnight blue, it looks like it was carved from the night itself. The Luminlay inlays catch the light with an otherworldly glow, like stars waking up under the stage strobes.

My upper body's going to hate me, but she's got presence. All sleek curves and sharp promise. The perfect storm for Annie's "Night Song."

We nailed the outro last week.

[Outro]

I used to chase the sun
A fire bold and bright
Now I watch the embers fade
Waiting for the night

We're one day out from our set at The Soundproof. Five songs, all tightened, polished, and refined. Hours of rehearsals over the past few months. Fingers raw and calloused. Tag's neighbors ready to file noise complaints. But every minute has been worth it.

Toaster sniffs around the sawdust shavings as I prop the instrument on the couch and take a step back, reaching for my phone. Snapping a quick photo, I shoot it off to the group text.

Me: She's ready.

I take a seat and wait for the reactions to pour in.

Rock: LFG!!!!!!
Zach: Whoa. Hella sick.
Tag: 👀👀👀
Tag: 🔥🔥🔥

A sense of pride settles in my chest.

I can't help but think about where I was at the beginning of the year, drowning in debt with a bullet wound in my leg, an empty fridge, and my dog as my only friend. Not long ago, life felt like a pointless, uphill crawl, all sharp corners, wrong turns, and dead ends.

I think about the gas station owner, what I cost him, and how I'm finally getting closer to making it right.

Because now I've got a guitar business that's finally breaking even, a band that feels more like family than an outlet, and tomorrow night, we're opening for Unbidden at one of the most iconic music venues in New York City.

Not bad for a guy who used to pull fifteen-hour shifts carving furniture and hustled random shit online just to afford string packs and instant noodles.

I drag the guitar onto my lap and study the high-gloss polyurethane finish, my fingers skimming over the wire strings.

Another text notification comes through.

Annie: Chase. Wow. It's absolutely stunning.
Annie: I'm crying.

My lips twitch. She probably is.

Me: One more sleep until we hit the stage.

I tap Send.

Rock: Celebrating early, baby!

A picture of a bong pops up on the screen.

Tag: Same bitches

Another picture swooshes: Tag's hand wrapped around a beer bottle.

Zach sends a photo of his daughter holding his bass guitar, the instrument as big as she is.

And then there's Annie.

She sends a picture of the moon.

Annie: One more sleep. One more honey moon. 😊

The energy tonight is absolute electricity, and The Soundproof is alive with it.

Nestled between an unassuming alley and a bustling dive bar, the venue boasts velvet curtains, blackened rafters, and a stage worn by decades of stomped boots and shattered snares. The hallways vibrate with basslines and setlists past as we wait in the green room beneath the stage, a cramped space that smells like old amps and bourbon.

The walls are riddled with signatures and Sharpie-scrawled lyrics from every act that's ever come through. Some legends, some forgotten. I hear the crowd buzzing with anticipation, most here for the headliner, some curious about the no-name band opening for Unbidden.

Luckily we've come prepared.

A worn graphite-gray couch sinks in the middle of the room, half covered in guitar cases and leather jackets, while the hum of the audience filters through the floorboards above, revving my pulse. Tag paces near the minifridge, tapping out beats on his thighs. Zach tunes his bass for the fifth time, and Rock chats with Crowley against the far wall.

"—which is prime for maximum shreditation," my drummer says, his grin goofy and eyes half-lidded. "Are you a shredator?"

Crowley looks perplexed. He folds his arms over a crisp white button-down and sharp checkered tie, the look toned down with the addition of a faded leather vest. He's part businessman, part rock aficionado. "Not sure. Am I?"

Rock eyes his outfit. "You're suppressing the shred. But there's potential."

Shaking my head, I glance at Annie curled in the corner with her notebook, mouthing lyrics like a litany. A smile pulls as I approach, returning my guitar to its stand as the inlays sparkle under the overhead fluorescents. "You're in the zone."

She flicks me a look, face paler than snow. "Is that what on-the-verge-of-puking looks like?"

Now that she mentions it, she does look borderline green.

I crouch down beside her, dropping to my butt. "Nervous?"

"That's a word for it."

"You're going to kill it out there."

"Or die trying. Actually, that's more likely." She gulps. "Probable, even."

My eyes rake down her thigh-length leather dress. Raven black and skintight. A vision pops into my head, but it has nothing to do with her text about loving to give blow jobs.

Nope.

That mental image has been scrubbed from my mind.

On every day that doesn't end in *Y*.

Refocusing, I clear my throat and stretch my legs, our thighs brushing. "My sister used to give me advice whenever I was teetering the line of a nervous breakdown. Back when I played sports, mostly. She would say, 'Always end on a high note.' And that was to say that no matter how many times you inevitably screw up, never let it get to you. Never let it show. Keep going, stay confident, and leave them with the best version of you—the version you want them to remember." I glance over, smirking faintly. "Of course, she said that right before I struck out three times in a row at regionals, but you get the point."

Annie breathes out a laugh, ducking her head. "I like that."

"Something to keep in mind." My head presses back against the scratched, scribbled wall, and I twirl the silver band around my thumb, centering myself.

I'm nervous too. But the rush of adrenaline overpowers the jitters, giving me clarity. This is what I've worked for. This is what Stella always wanted for me.

As Annie tosses her notebook aside, her slinky of black bangle bracelets slides down to the edge of her palm, revealing a gnarly bruise around her wrist.

My stomach twists. I snatch her by the elbow.

She jumps. "Chase, what—"

"What is this?" My touch is gentle but firm, my thumb dusting over the purplish ring glowing on her skin. I lift my gaze, frowning as I stare at her. "Alex?"

Her eyes bulge as she tears her arm away from my grip. "No... no, it's from a bracelet I was wearing the other day. It was on too tight."

She swiftly pulls to a stand, floats away, and approaches Tag near the fridge as he cracks open a beer.

I follow. "Annie."

Ignoring me, she steals Tag's beer and downs half of it. "I need some fuel."

Tag gives me a side-eye before glancing down at his sister. "Fridge is stocked, thank you very much." He snatches it back. "Some vodka in there too."

"I haven't eaten. That won't end well."

"Annie—" I take her by the shoulder and whirl her around to face me. My hand skims down her upper arm with a light squeeze. "Talk to me."

She paints on a smile. "Ready, rock star?"

My jaw tenses, muscles turning to stone.

Fucking Alex.

He did that; he left those bruises. And she still wears his damn ring, ready to spend forever under his thumb, drowning in shadow, smiling through the pain she's convinced herself to bear.

"Yeah," I mutter, having no other choice but to let it go until after the show. "Ready."

Stepping away, I press the heel of my hand to my head.

Pressure starts to thrum behind my left temple.

Fuck.

Not now.

Crowley gives us a five-minute warning, and I use it to lock myself in the en suite bathroom, swallowing a handful of pills in one go. It's just drugstore pain reliever, nothing strong enough. But it's all I have, and I need to get through this set as clearheaded as possible, because once those stage lights hit, there's no turning back.

I lift my eyes to the mirror, cracking my neck, rolling my

shoulders. My reflection blurs for a beat before refocusing, and I blink away the flecks of light skating across my vision. With sheer willpower alone, the headache dulls. It placates into a mild ache, subdued by the adrenaline running marathons through my blood.

I got this.

We fucking got this.

I splash cool water on my face, rake my fingers through my hair, and take a deep breath.

Showtime.

When I reenter the green room, the band is gearing up for our cue.

Crowley pops in and out, inspecting equipment and assessing our spirits. Annie twinkles under the low light with glittery eyeshadow, shimmer-doused skin, and pixie dust in her hair. She glances my way, shoots me a nervous smile. Then she circles a hand around her bruised wrist and drops her head, the smile fading.

I saunter over to her, forcing my concern to take a back seat. My shoulder nudges hers. "Honeymoon phase," I remind her softly.

A tiny grin flickers back to life. "No nerves allowed in the honeymoon phase."

"That's right."

"Always end on a high note," she says, echoing my sentiment from earlier. Squaring her shoulders and standing tall, she exhales a calming breath. "I can do this."

Before I can respond, Crowley points at me. "You're up."

The room stills. No one breathes.

Then something unspoken clicks into place, and we all

converge. Tag cracks his knuckles and slings his guitar across his back while Rock mutters a half-hearted joke that doesn't land, but no one cares because we're already moving.

The hallway narrows, the floor thumping beneath our boots as we follow the pulsing beat of the crowd up the stairs and beyond the curtain. Stage lights spill from the wings, casting our shadows against the concrete wall.

The roar on the other side grows louder, restless, expectant.

My palms sweat around the neck of my guitar.

We reach the side of the stage. Our names aren't lit up anywhere. No banners. No fanfare.

But this moment…*it's ours*.

With a short nod, Crowley steps aside as the stagehand waves us forward.

The lights are bright, electric, nailing us all at once. The crowd erupts, a tidal wave of sound crashing over the stage, and for a second, I just stand there, letting it wash over me. Annie strides out first, now fearless in her silver boots and spine-straight confidence. Tag follows, tossing a wink and an over-the-top bow to the front row.

Zach is next, bass slung low, cool as ever, flashing a grin as he finds his spot. "Breathe. Play clean," he reminds us, like a mantra.

Rock brings up the rear, twirling one drumstick between his fingers as if we're not standing in the middle of the biggest show of our lives. He takes his throne and gives his kit a single tap.

I'm last.

I step into the sea of lights, the weight of my instrument hanging across my chest, my heart pounding like a kick drum in my ears.

The mic waits for me at center stage.

I grip it, glance back at my band, and then scan the room packed wall-to-wall with strangers who have no idea who we are.

Yet.

I bring the mic to my lips. "We're Honey Moons," I announce, voice steadier than I expect. "Thanks for giving the little guys a chance tonight. We've got five songs. Hope at least one sticks with you."

Annie and I share a look, a smile, a tether vibrating with silent strength.

Then I look over at Rock, give him a nod.

He counts us in.

Annie takes her place at the mic stand just left of center, one hand curled around the stem like an anchor. With no guitar to hide behind, she commands the space differently, her eyes scanning the crowd, a white-toothed grin glowing ear to ear.

When the music climbs, she's a storm in slow motion, moving with the rhythm, hips swaying and shoulders dipping. Never over-the-top, just enough to draw eyes in. Her hands tell stories between verses, fingers painting the air when she harmonizes or breathes melodies on her own.

During the instrumental breaks, she drifts closer to each of us, hyping up Rock with a spin, sharing a grin with Zach, throwing Tag a playful eyebrow raise like it's all just a jam session in his stifling garage.

My boots are planted, but everything else moves. The lights sweep across the stage like search beams, and the first row leans in, trying to memorize us. My chest expands with the next breath, and I let it out on the high note. Raw, stretched thin, but dead-on.

My throat's already rough from strain, but I don't hold back. I never do. Every line digs into me before it leaves my mouth, clawing its way out, demanding to be felt.

Annie's voice trails beneath mine, a steady current under the musical downpour. She knows just when to rise and when to fall back, letting me hit the hook hard and heavy, and when she joins me on the choruses, it lands. We're synced tight, fully aligned.

We end the set with "Night Song."

While it works well as a melancholy acoustic, we spiced it up for the show, adding a distortion-heavy riff beneath the chorus and layering in a slow-building drumline that thunders on the final verse. Zach threw in a grungy bass slide that gives it grit, and I rewrote the solo to lean into a psychedelic '60s feel just for Annie. Fuzzed-out and swirling, it's something you might hear echoing through a smoky Laurel Canyon lounge. It aches and haunts but also hits with bared teeth and smudged eyeliner.

As the first note crests, I swap out my performance guitar for the eye candy.

The moment I strum, the guitar sends a signal through a custom MIDI system. Each note manipulates both the soundscape and visuals, the reverb trails bending like heat waves. The frets are embedded with plasma-reactive strips, flaring beneath my fingers, tiny bolts of lightning flickering in blues, purples, and whites.

The crowd reacts.

Roars.

Cell phones glow from the audience as people record, dancing in place, awestruck and hypnotized.

By the time I hit the chorus, it's not just music. It's a full-body experience. Annie's voice soars beside me—*"If I fall, will you still catch me? If I run, will you let go?"*—and when I glance over, she's already looking at me. Our eyes catch, hold, and for a moment it feels like the whole stage angles toward us.

Tag drops to his knees in the breakdown, grinning like a maniac. Zach is steady as ever, anchoring us all with the pulse of his bass.

The song is a storm, alive and breathing.

And we're in the eye of it.

When it's over, there's no string of words, no lyrics, no thought big enough to convey the feeling coursing through me. It's primal, intoxicating, and mind-bending. Fucking euphoric. An energy overtakes me, something I've never experienced before. I glance around at the crowd, my band, my people. We all feel it. This pulsing, living thing.

"We're Honey Moons," I holler into the mic, sweat pouring down my neck and back, lights dazzling me until all I see is bliss. "Good night, New York."

The cheers are volcanic.

Shrieky catcalls and emphatic applause vibrate through me as we retreat from the stage, hands and instruments in the air, everything spinning in a vortex of sound.

As we plow through the green room, I'm at an all-time high.

I don't think.

Just react.

I reach for Annie, scooping her into my arms and lifting her off her feet. She squeals, her face a mask of overjoyed tears as two arms wrap around my neck and her legs shoot off the ground, linking behind my lower back.

I spin her once, twice, in chaotic, dizzying circles, until she's pressed against the wall and our foreheads smash together.

I'm smiling so big, I can't remember what it feels like not to smile.

"Fuck, Annie…" I cup her face with both hands, her legs squeezing me like a vise. "You were incredible. Unbelievable. Fucking *everything*."

She nods frantically, tears streaming down her face in inky smears. "Chase. We did it. Holy shit."

We share a laugh.

A hug.

A moment frozen in time.

We're both slick with sweat. Little beads of moisture run down her neck and disappear into her cleavage.

My gaze dips.

The smile falters.

Our chests are flush together, the swell of her breasts spilling from her dress in pale skin and soft curves, heaving, glistening under the lights.

My lungs are trying to outrun my heart. I'm suddenly starved for her, breathing like air isn't enough, while she's hardly breathing at all.

Slowly, my gaze trails back up to her face.

Two baby-blue eyes pop, huge and searching.

A beast howls inside me, triggered by adrenaline, fueled by the undefinable. Every sense is tingling and alive.

I'm trembling. I'm singing. I'm burning.

I'm hard.

I feel my erection straining against tight jeans, my waist

bracketed between her plush thighs as her dress inches up to her hips, giving me a glimpse of lavender lace. Her breath catches, and I'm already gone, lost in the heat, the hush, the way she looks at me like she's one bad decision away from closing the gap and shoving her tongue down my throat.

I wonder what she'd taste like.

Her mouth, her flesh. Watermelon and salt.

I wonder if she's wet.

My cock jumps, and my hips thrust forward with an involuntary jolt.

I grip her cheeks between my palms, tipping her head back against the wall as my gaze settles on her pink parted lips, and my fingers tangle in long silken hair.

She chokes out a needy sound.

My pulse jackhammers in my ears.

Fuck it—

I lean in.

But the moment shatters when Crowley pokes his head into the room. "You've got a visitor, Annalise. Says he's your fiancé."

Goddammit.

Fuck.

I drop her like a hot potato.

She slides down the wall and scampers away from me, tugging down her dress, fixing her hair, mechanically tucking it behind her ears. The guys look away, pretending they didn't see shit as they gather their gear and head to the fridge.

Crowley sings our praises. Everyone shakes hands, slaps backs, hugs like they all scaled Mount Everest and made it back down without a scratch.

A second later, Alex rushes into the room, eager to mark his territory and steal her away.

Annie freezes, fingers curling into her hands. A lump bobs in the center of her throat as she watches him sweep his gaze around the room.

Their eyes meet. He spots her.

And she runs to him.

I watch the scene unfold on repeat.

Her arms crisscross around his neck, her long, creamy legs circling his waist as he lifts her off the ground and spins her in a circle, pressing her against the wall. Their foreheads fuse together.

She smiles.

He grins.

The only difference is—

He kisses her.

CHAPTER 34
Annalise

I wake up the next morning feeling foggy, out of sorts, and marginally hungover. Considering I only downed half a beer last night, I'm confident the feeling is a post-performance crash.

My brain clicks back on, and the prior evening soars to the surface in ripples of strobe lights, high notes, breakdowns, and a zealous, wide-eyed crowd.

Oh my God.

We did it. And we crushed it.

My heart rate jumps, doing some kind of tango or double reverse spin beneath my ribcage. There's a gnawing ache between my legs. A pressure that wants out. I clamp my thighs together with shame, my thoughts spiraling back to hours ago when Chase had me shoved up against a wall, his mouth an inch away from mine, his massive body pressing into me at every angle.

I felt it—the huge, hard bulge digging into my inner thigh.

Tingles race through me, plummeting south. My legs squeeze tighter. This feeling is both an angry black cloud and a hot day under a smoldering sun. I'm weeping and burning at the same time. My body reacts, and my mind rejects, all while my heart teeter-totters a tightrope, a thread ready to snap. I'm exhausted. Sunk and sapped.

The faucet squeals as Alex leans over the sink in the bathroom, spitting toothpaste into the basin. "Can you *please* stop squeezing the tube from the middle?" he mutters, holding it up from the threshold. "It's not hard. From. The. End."

I blink at him. "I'll…try to remember."

"You've been saying that for years." He slams the cabinet shut. "Also, it's a damn freezer in here."

I glance toward the thermostat, still set to sixty-eight. "I thought you liked it cold."

"Not arctic-tundra cold." He rubs his arms. "Jesus. You're the only person I know who goes to bed and thinks, 'Let's sleep in a meat locker.'"

My face sours as I inch up the mattress and tame my bedhead, reality creeping its way back to the edges of my mind. "Sorry."

Sauntering out of the bathroom, he pulls a hoodie over his head. "Want some eggs?"

"Okay. Sounds good."

"Cool."

He disappears into the kitchen.

With a long sigh, I stare up at the popcorn ceiling as a light breeze shimmies in through the cracked window. It's a beautiful autumn morning after the best night of my entire life, and I have to be at the diner in an hour, shlepping hot plates of food around all day. The notion is equally depressing and soul-crushing.

All I want to do is write. Sing. Perform. And now I've had a taste of it.

All I can think about is heading to Tag's garage and creating more magic. Setting up shows. Reliving it all over again. New cities, new crowds, new opportunities twinkling with the stage lights. My eyes close, and I imagine just that.

For a little while. For a few blissful minutes.

Until Alex hollers from the kitchen, "Want any bacon?"

Another sigh falls out. Back to the grind.

"Sure!" I call back.

Groggy and defeated, I reach for my phone on the nightstand. A dozen text messages light up the face. Mostly from Kenna. Two from Mom. Some from people I haven't talked to in years.

I frown, swiping my thumb across the screen as my vision settles.

My eyes skim the string of texts.

Did you see this?!
Annalise. Wake up.
Look!!!
YOU'RE FAMOUS
Hello, viral! Congrats girl!

I shoot up in bed, throwing off the covers because it's suddenly a sauna in the bedroom. My heartbeat thumps against my ribs. My brain spins. My pulse skitters out of control.

I open the attachments—it's a video.

Of us.
Of Chase.
My song booming through the crowd.
His guitar lighting up the stage.
And 2.3 million views.

CHAPTER 35
Annalise

The week flies by in a whirlwind.

Everything hit a no-turning-back pinnacle when Crowley's text came through midday, hours after I received the first slew of messages, while I was scrubbing ketchup stains off my apron.

> **Crowley:** Hope you're ready. The Soundproof wasn't your peak. It was your beginning.

I've watched that video more times than I can recount, the fifteen-second reel currently sitting at a shocking 7.2 million views. We looked like a band. A real one. Not a garage experiment or a maybe-someday fantasy, but something authentic.

Something people want more of.

Suddenly, everything we joked about, whispered about, wished for, became more than a dream. Now it's a reality. A ticking clock.

At my urging, Kenna's taken on the role of unofficial talent manager, leveraging her social media hustle and an old boyfriend's music-industry hookup to spin our fifteen minutes of fame into big-time stuff. I told her she was being wasted at that diner, that she could do anything, and if she was up for it, I wanted her by my side.

She didn't even hesitate. Even before I insisted on paying her.

Kenna: BESTIE! Labels are sniffing. You guys have a window. If you want a tour, I'll talk to Crowley. We can make it happen. The world is waiting.

My best friend's texts are already spiraling into action-mode as she showcases her managerial knack and puts her go-getter nature to good use.

Interviews with gossip columns, reposts, and reaction videos flood our feeds. Music blogs call it "a cosmic collision of grit and glitter," and someone even dubs Chase "the man who strums stars." My voice gets dissected on social apps and looped into mashups. One viral stitch compares our sound to "if Florence & The Machine and Arctic Monkeys had a love child at a laser show."

I can't stop moving. Rehearsing. Planning. Watching that video over and over, as if it might disappear.

But it doesn't.

It's still there.

We're still here.

Seven days after my ho-hum life shattered into stardust, I race inside Tag's house, drenched in rain and caffeinated to the point of inevitable implosion. The guys and Kenna are huddled down in the basement, talking business.

I hear Crowley's voice on speakerphone as he gives the rundown.

"—East Coast to start. It'll be grueling. Long nights on the road, shows less than twenty-four hours apart. I know you all have jobs and families, but if you're in, I'll make the call."

The now-cold vanilla latte trembles in my hand as I reach the bottom of the steps, my wet hair matted to my face. "Sorry I'm late," I mouth as all five heads turn to look at me.

Chase glances at the phone. "Annalise is here. Give us a minute, and we'll call you back."

"Perfect. Congratulations."

The call disconnects, and Chase stands from the couch. Tag follows as both men slowly approach me, their expressions unreadable.

And then two gigantic smiles beam to life.

"We got it," Chase says.

My brother looks like he's going to cry.

"A tour?" I breathe back.

A tour.

Me, on the road. With Chase. With Tag and Zach and Rock, and even Kenna. With the songs we wrote at 2:00 a.m. in my brother's half-furnished basement, in his overheated garage, and out on the deck beneath the moon, when we didn't even know if anyone would listen.

Tears rush to my eyes. "Oh my God."

"We fuckin' did it, sis." Tag picks me up and spins me around, my coffee dribbling onto my hand and my legs kicking up behind me. "We did it. It's happening."

A sob breaks free, and I don't know if the tears are for him or me.

My big brother.

This was always his dream. His Holy Grail. And now it's coming to life in a Technicolor, fast-motion blur that doesn't feel real. It's like we blinked, and the universe finally blinked back.

Louder, brighter, and wholly on our side.

He sets me down, and I cup a hand around my mouth, trying not to hyperventilate. My eyes catch with Chase's. His are twinkling, glowing, pieces of a storybook future glimmering in the golden flecks. "We need a van," I murmur.

Kenna springs from the loveseat, clipboard in hand. "On it. Irving has one he's willing to sell for the right price."

I blink at her. "Really?"

I'm not sure what's more impressive—how many exes she has with solid connections, or how many still like her enough to do her favors after she dumped them.

"It's a sketchy 2006 Dodge Sprinter, but it's long enough to sleep in, wide enough to haul gear, and ugly enough to never get stolen. He's asking for four thousand so less than a grand between the five of you." She pulls out her phone and shows us pictures of a mammoth vehicle with chipped, once-white paint and a rusted undercarriage. "What do you think?"

Zach leans in with an appreciative nod. "Looks like it'll get the job done."

"Leagues above my Civic," Rock adds, whistling low. "Ugly as sin, but damn if it doesn't look like freedom on wheels."

Kenna flicks her thumbs across the keypad and shoots off a text. "Done deal."

I'm still in a daze. I lick a sticky trail of coffee off my knuckles and veer my attention toward Kenna. "How are you so good at this? You were a waitress a few days ago."

"Yeah. And now I'm lining up a feature in *Rolling Stone Online*—complete with a photoshoot, of course—and negotiating a cut of your merch. Try to keep up." She pinches my arm with an affectionate wink.

Tag gawks at her like he's seeing her for the first time. "Kinda hot. Won't lie."

She wrinkles her nose, then turns to me. "Not to mention, you were also a waitress a few days ago. Now you're a superstar."

"I wouldn't say—"

"Own it, Annalise." She snatches my hand and gives it a shake. "Own it, breathe it, live it. It's the only way."

"You're manifesting for me, aren't you?"

"I always manifest for you. That's what best friends do."

I squeeze her hand with a nod, letting it all journey through me in tendrils of vast potential. "I need you here. Every step of the way."

"Duh. Are you kidding? Why do you think I've been biding my time at your boyfriend's diner for two years? I was waiting for this."

Fiancé, my brain amends.

But I don't bother correcting her.

"You should see my spreadsheets," she continues. "'Project:

Annalise's Big Break and Rise to Fame.' There's color coding, a five-year plan, and contingency options for when you inevitably ditch me for an assistant with better handwriting."

I laugh, the kind that bubbles up from somewhere real. "You're unbelievable."

"And you're stuck with me." She squeezes my hand back before dropping it and straightening her pencil skirt. "Now let's go change our lives with a janky van, a viral video, and way too much talent for one room."

Kenna steps away and grabs Tag by the arm, leading him over to the loveseat where her laptop is open, primed with big, color-coded dreams.

Chase saunters over to me, hands in his pockets. "Got a minute?"

The rest of the guys gather around the loveseat, assessing Kenna's notes. I blink back to him. "Yeah. Of course."

He nods at the staircase, gesturing me to follow. We trek up to the living room where a new guitar is resting on the sofa. It's not a custom but a Gibson acoustic hummingbird with a vintage sunburst.

Catching me eyeing it, Chase sinks down on the couch and holds it up. "Like the new axe?"

"It's gorgeous," I croon, taking a seat beside him. "Must've cost a pretty penny."

"Little bit. Just a few days after the show, all my customs sold for asking price. Figured I should invest in the band with the extra cash."

"Smart. Stocked fridges are overrated."

"I've learned to get by on less." A soft smile carves dimples on his cheeks. "Also, I finally quit the woodworking job last week. Gave Sol my notice."

My head snaps toward him. "Seriously?"

He nods, running his thumb along the strings. "If I'm going to bet on anything, it should be this."

I study him for a beat, his biceps flexing beneath short gray sleeves, and thick veins dilating as he flicks a pick over the strings. "Play something for me," I say.

He shoots me a glance, hunching over the instrument. "Any requests?"

"Whatever you want."

Chase could play "Twinkle, Twinkle Little Star" and I'd be toast. Down bad. Mesmerized through and through.

With a short nod, he shifts beside me, eyes deep in thought. "Do you know 'Trace of You' by Peter Bradley Adams?"

"Doesn't ring a bell."

"It's not widely known. Came up on a suggested playlist a few weeks ago, and I had to learn it. It's simple…but it's the kind of song that stays with you." A steady look. "You know?"

Of course I know; my heart is a playlist. "Yes."

He clears his throat, falters briefly. Almost like the song scares him or intimidates him in some strange way. I brace myself for the lyrics, for the pieces that spoke to him, wondering how they'll speak to me.

Chase swallows and lets out a breath. Then his voice wraps around me in velvet and smoke, softer than usual, but no less alive. His fingers find the chords with practiced finesse, but there's nothing practiced about the way he sings. It's raw and real. Soul deep.

The air stills.

I hear the ache in his voice before I register the words. Grief wrapped in longing. Someone chasing ghosts. It's not a performance.

It's a confession.

And suddenly, I do know the song.

But not from playlists. Not because I've heard it before.

I know it because I know him.

My throat locks with sentiment. A gritty, painful chokehold. Lyrics flow through me, moving like thick molasses, catching in too-tight places.

Don't cry.

Please don't cry.

Stinging pressure builds behind my eyes. I clench my hands in my lap, begging them not to reach for him. The diamond on my finger glints under the lights, reminding me. Scolding me. It's supposed to be a promise, but it feels like a weight.

I cover it with my palm, hiding it away.

The lyrics cleave holes in me. His voice winds through my veins, rewriting my blood.

I love this song.

I hate this song.

Bowing my head, I close my eyes and just wait for it to be over.

And when it is, I want more.

"Here," Chase says, his voice a pitch-perfect note through the murky static. "Try it out."

I force my eyes back open, lashes damp and fluttering. "What?"

"The guitar."

When I finally look at him, he's handing it over to me. A mass of gorgeous, polished wood. Too breakable for my unsteady hands.

I shake my head slightly.

"Have you ever played?"

"Once," I whisper. "A little. Tag tried to teach me, but I wasn't any good. It doesn't come naturally."

"Just takes practice. I can teach you."

He's too close, and he's only getting closer. But the guitar hovers between us, beckoning me to take it. On a deep inhale, I do.

I place it on my lap, fingers curling around the neck. "I don't—"

"Scoot forward."

My body stiffens, pulse jolting. Gulping, I inch toward the edge of the cushion. Chase leans back, just enough to give me space. Just enough to make me aware of how little of it there is.

Then he moves around the couch, behind me.

His denim-clad thigh brushes mine as he gets into position, knees bracketing my hips, chest grazing my spine. The heat from his body sears me, and I feel it all, every breath, every heartbeat, every whisper of his fingers as they reach around to guide mine on the strings.

"Relax," he murmurs near my ear, and I'm pretty sure the word *relax* has never done the opposite so effectively. "Let your hands follow mine."

He adjusts my grip, slow and steady, his calloused fingers grazing my softer ones like they belong there.

Sinking back, I release a breath, a shiver, a prayer.

"Right there," he says.

I feel the words more than I hear them, reverberating through my marrow.

I try to focus; I really do.

But the scent of him, warm and familiar, a hint of smoky cedar and something darker, settles into my lungs, and the room around me blurs like a rain-beaten window. Water echoes off the shingled roof in streams of pitter-patters, pounding in time with my pulse.

Chase hums a chord to demonstrate, then guides my fingers to mimic it.

My strum is clumsy, and I wince. "Sorry."

"Don't be." He smiles against my cheek. "You'll get it."

I won't.

I can't concentrate.

My heart is beating too loud, overpowering every chord.

We try again, and a few more off-key notes breach the air.

"Not bad. Try pressing down a little harder on the *A* string. Like this." His hand wraps around mine, firm fingers guiding my graceless ones.

The contact sends a shock up my arm. My breath catches, nerves curdling in my throat. "I'm really bad at this."

"You're not. You just don't trust yourself yet." His voice drops a little. "Trust me instead."

I nod, barely.

We strum again, better this time. Still not perfect, but enough to take the shape of a melody.

"There it is," he says, voice low and damn near haunting.

I laugh under my breath and risk a glance back. His eyes lock on mine.

Our faces are inches apart. As he swallows, his gaze drops to my lips, then flicks up again, unreadable but charged. The smile is gone. Mine was never there.

I'm fucking petrified.

His hand stills, but he doesn't move away. Just stares at me, breath hot and heavier, focus fixed like he's memorizing the color of my eyes, every swirling, frightened pigment.

A frown creases on his brow. Something creeps across his expression, and his legs tighten around me, caging me in. His hand starts moving up my arm, my shoulder, my neck, landing on my jaw and tilting my face toward him.

A beat.

A lean.

Our lips touch.

Not a kiss, but a graze. The briefest brush of something too big to name. His mouth hovers against mine, tongue poking out to taste my bottom lip.

A tease.

And it detonates inside me.

I suck in a sharp breath, choking down razor blades. I'm frozen. Shaking. Cracking open from the inside.

Panic floods in.

No.

With a sharp gasp, I jump off the couch. The guitar topples off my lap with a dull thud. I don't turn back. Can't look at him.

I just run.

Out of the room, through the kitchen, into the dark, wet night, a trapped scream shredding my throat and tears bursting from my eyes.

The rain falls hard.

But I'm falling harder.

CHAPTER 36
Chase

I should let her go, let her be.

But I can't.

I'm on the move, chasing her out into the rain, still high from the taste of her melon-sweet lips. My blood is roaring, my restraint unstitching into tattered ribbons. If we do this tour, she needs to be mine. No more pretending. No more dancing around the inevitable. I'm so tired of this charade, of being the bigger person.

I bust through the back door, slamming the slider shut. "Annalise."

She's bent over the deck railing like she's going to puke. "I can't. I can't do it."

"Then don't." The rain picks up, dousing me in angry, cold sheets. "You don't need to keep acting like you don't feel this."

Whirling around to face me, she shakes her head, a strand of hair glued across her mouth. "I *do* feel it. Of course I feel it." She swats the piece of hair away, her hands balling at her sides. "Why do you think this is killing me?"

I step forward. "It doesn't have to."

"You don't get it. I'm *engaged*." Her left hand flies up, fingers wiggling back and forth as the pear-shaped diamond reflects off the string lights. "I'm marrying him. I was always meant to marry him."

Jaw tight and body vibrating, I meet her stare. "I see the ring. But I also see this." With another step forward, I wave a hand between us. "And this doesn't lie."

"God, Chase." She grips handfuls of her hair, fisting tight. "You're acting like this is a simple choice of deciding what to make for dinner."

"I'm not saying it's simple, but it *is* a choice. And you're choosing someone who tells you who to be. Not someone who sees you as you are."

Her voice splinters with grief. "That's not fair. You don't understand. Marriage can fix this. It has to. After everything I've put into us, all the years, all the sacrifices…this is the moment it pays off. This is when it gets better."

Regret overrides the ache, and I know my heart is possessing my tongue. But how can it not when she's standing here convincing herself that a ring is salvation? She's not being fair either. She's tying me in knots, then pulling the string, letting me unravel all alone.

I take her by the arm, holding up her wrist. The lingering bruise, now green and fading, is highlighted by the moon.

Her eyes slowly pan to the evidence.

"Did he do this to you?" The question comes out raw, laced with heartbreak. Because I already know the answer. I just need her to say it out loud.

Her mouth parts, but the words get caught. Trapped behind chattering teeth and pride and fear. I watch the shame flicker across her face.

Then she pulls her wrist back like I burned her. "It wasn't… He didn't mean to."

My stomach caves in. "Annalise."

She shakes her head and steps back. "It was just an accident."

"That is not an accident. If someone hurts you, you don't stay. You don't make excuses for them. You walk away." Anguish courses through me, fracturing my thoughts, my waning willpower. "I would never hurt you."

A stuttered breath. "I know."

"This is killing me too," I confess.

Her tears mingle with rainwater.

The downpour intensifies, beating down in savage rivers.

Annie wraps her arms around her body, her tank and leggings soaked through. "It's always been Alex," she whispers, voice hardly penetrating the storm. "He was my first kiss. First dance. He taught me how to ride a bike, how to read, how to braid my goddamn hair." Her lips tremble. "He was there when I broke my arm roller skating. When my parents moved away. When my grandma died. He's in everything. Every memory, every scar. I don't know how to let that go."

I shake my head. "Listen to what you're saying."

"I am listening—"

"You're giving me examples of your past," I say, advancing on her, my boots slapping against puddles as my pulse climbs with every breath. "Tell me about now. Tell me about the person who's supporting your dreams, making music with you, begging you to believe in all that you are. Because you're brilliant, Annie. Absolutely brilliant in every way." I close the space between us until we're nearly chest to chest. "Does he tell you that?"

She goes to speak, but nothing comes out.

I keep going, handing her my heart like it's the only thing I have left. "Does he listen to your songs and *feel* them? Does he stay up all night obsessing over lyrics just because they mean something to you? Does he hear your voice and know, without a shadow of a doubt, that it's the one thing in the world that makes him feel alive?"

"Chase…"

"I know I'm being selfish. I know. And you're right, it's not fair." I steeple my hands as rain breaches my collar, streaming down my back. "But I'm done being the martyr. The bystander. The nice guy. I want you so badly it fucking hurts."

She gapes at me, lashes dappled in raindrops.

The deluge rages on around us, inside us, reflecting in her tortured eyes.

"Don't give me history," I plead, forcing out the final words. "Give me the present. Give me right now."

I don't touch her. Don't reach for her.

Just wait.

I refuse to be the reason she resents this. If she gives in, it has to because she wants to. Needs to. Because there's no other choice.

Lightning flashes, but she doesn't flinch. Thunder booms

overhead, the rain relentless and sharp. Her chest heaves, gaze transfixed on mine.

Then her focus slips. Settles on my mouth.

Her pupils blow wide.

The storm moves through me like a drug, and I know what's coming next.

Annie lunges at me.

Her hands crash into my chest, then fist my shirt like she wants to tear it off. She yanks me down, and her mouth slams into mine with a force that knocks the air out of me.

My tongue dives into her mouth. Tangling, tasting, taking, like I've waited lifetimes for her kiss. Her hands claw up my shoulders, into my hair, gripping hard, dragging me closer as I devour her. I drive her backward until her spine hits the railing.

It's messy. Ferocious. Months of tension snapping like a detonated fuse.

I groan into her mouth, low and guttural, my palm bracketing her neck as I angle her face. Her skin is rain-slick, cold beneath my touch, but her mouth is hell-born fire. Warm and soft and open. Our lips crash and slide, wet from the sky and wetter from us.

She hangs on for dear life, clinging to me like she'll float away with the storm if she lets go. Her fingers rake down my back, nails scratching, her breathy moans rocketing straight to my cock. I grind against her, lifting one of her legs to hook around my hip. She feels me there, hard and ready, pressing between her thighs.

My eyes roll up. I imagine sinking deep inside her as she writhes and yields, sticky with sweat, damp from rain.

Fuck.

I suck her tongue into my mouth, drag her lower lip between my teeth. Her nipples tighten beneath her tank, and I cup her breast, palming hard, my thumb grazing over the pebbled peak.

She shudders, head tipping back, mouth wide open and panting.

Her gasp is dynamite to my blood as she sags in my arms, and I move to her throat, licking, biting, inhaling salt and raindrops. "Leave him, Annie," I rasp, trailing kisses along her jaw. My tongue sweeps against hers, softer now. Coaxing. "Come home with me."

It's all I can think about. Ripping off her wet clothes and burying my face between her legs. Feeling her break, her release coating my tongue.

She gasps again, but this time it's strained, saturated in something heavier than lust.

Pain leaks through.

And I know; I know she's not ready.

Her diamond ring pierces my skin as she grips me tight around the neck.

A cruel reminder. A gleaming wedge between us.

I break the kiss, breath ragged, and lower my hand to her hip. Pressing my forehead to hers, I squeeze my eyes shut.

She shivers in my arms, the fallout imminent.

"Fuck…" I wind my arms around her. Lock her against me like I can shield her from the world. "I'm sorry."

She folds in on herself, burying her face in my chest. Her sob cuts straight through me.

I pushed too hard. Too fast.

Turned her into someone she never wanted to be.

"I'm sorry, Annie," I chant again, again, again, into her hair, into the rain, into every broken space between us. "So fucking sorry."

She rips away from me.

As if touching me was a mistake she can't undo.

Her eyes flare with panic, chest heaving. "What the hell am I doing?" she whispers, more to herself than to me. "What did I just…"

She backs up, hand to her mouth like she's going to be sick. The ring catches the light again, sharp and accusing.

"I can't do this," she chokes out. "I can't be this person."

"Annie—"

"Don't." Her voice cracks in time with thunder. "Please. Please…just don't."

I freeze, fists clenched. The rain pelts my shoulders, but all I feel is the heartbreak in her voice. The horror in her eyes.

She turns, nearly slipping as she bolts for the door, wrenching it open with a slick, shaking hand.

The door slams.

I'm left with nothing but the downpour, the ghost of her kiss still on my lips, and the cold hollow where her body used to be.

I drag a hand through my drenched hair, heart hammering. A growl tears through my throat, but I bite it down.

She's not just running.

She's burning.

And I'm the one who lit the match.

CHAPTER 37
Annalise

"Ready or not, here I come!"

I flick my fingers open, peeking through the crack. Sunlight stings my eyes. I wonder where he could be.

Blinking away the glow, I whip my head in every direction, the playground bustling with children in rompers and moms with strollers and coffee cups.

I pop up from a crouch and step away from the tree. "Where are you, Alex?" I call out, cupping my hands around my mouth. I know he won't answer. That's the whole point.

My jelly sandals crunch against dry grass and wood chips as I poke my head into tunnel slides and peer around fat trees.

Nothing. No Alex.

Five minutes rush by, and all I've done is run in circles. Then my gaze sweeps to the tree line behind the park. The woods.

Surely he wouldn't hide there. Way too spooky.

My heart skips as I think about the witches and warlocks hiding in the woods. Alex told me all about them. They're ugly and mean and eat plump children just for fun.

A shiver rolls through me. But my feet start moving, headed toward the woods.

"Alex!" I yell at the top of my lungs. The wind picks up and the sun dips behind a swirl of gray clouds. "Alex, come on! I'm done playing!"

I trek through the opening of the forest, thicket and branches tangling around my ankles. Leaves smack me in the face. Rocks and pebbles poke my bare toes, making me wince. Minutes roll by. Then a few more. I wrap my arms around my body as fear ripples through me.

A branch snaps in the distance.

I freeze.

A witch!

Terrifying images tunnel through my mind. Bubbling cauldrons and cackling voices. A green face covered in warts and a knobby finger pointing at me.

And the moment I spin around with my hands over my eyes, something tackles me.

"Gotcha!"

I topple backward, landing in a mound of moss and weeds as the air whooshes out of me. My head thunks against the earth, sending a jolt of pain through me.

Then my hands are yanked apart until I'm staring up into two twinkling green eyes.

"You jerkhead!" I smack his shoulder, rubbing the back of my head. "That hurt!"

Alex rolls off me, laughing until he can't breathe. "You should have seen your face."

"You scared me. I thought you were a witch!"

"There's no such thing, Annalise. Monsters aren't real."

"You said they were."

"That's because your nose gets all scrunchy when you're scared." He bops my nose with a dirty finger. "It's kind of cute."

I huff, propping up on my elbow.

"I guess I win," he declares. "You never would have found me."

"You shouldn't hide in the woods. What if a bear ate you?"

"You'd protect me."

"I'm too small. Only nine years old."

"Yeah, but you're brave. And I always feel safe when you're around."

A smile forms, goofy and crooked. "That's true. You're my best friend."

Alex sits up, his knees bent, as he reaches for a stick and draws pictures in the dirt. "Do you think we'll get married one day?"

"Duh. That's what best friends do."

He draws a heart, then adds our initials in the center.

AA + AA.

Annalise Adams and Alex Anderson.

I beam.

"We can have a wedding by the ocean," he says, brushing inky black bangs out of his eyes.

Nodding brightly, I sit up straight and cross my legs. "Right at sunset. With mermaids and dolphins and colorful fish."

"Definitely."

"Monkeys too."

"Monkeys?" He snorts a laugh. "That's stupid. Besides, I don't think they like the ocean."

"We can bring one. As a pet."

Alex draws a monkey in the dirt, but it looks more like a disfigured dog. He looks up at me then, the smile fading. "You'll never leave me, right?"

I frown, confused. "Why would I leave you?"

"I dunno. People leave when they don't love you enough. Sometimes I think my mom and dad might leave."

"They wouldn't leave. They love you."

He nods, but his grip tightens on the stick, carving lines in the dirt like he's trying to dig a hole deep enough to jump into. His voice drops, almost too soft to hear. "Promise you won't ever leave."

A trickling of raindrops break through the clouds. I tip my face to the sky, watching as the treetops shimmy when a sharp breeze rolls through. Rain pelts my cheeks and eyes, and I blink away the droplets, a chill settling in my bones.

Letting out a shaky breath, I reach for Alex's hand and squeeze. "I promise," I whisper.

And I meant it.

God, I meant it.

Silence greets me as I enter the condo.

The same silence from the woods, right before the snap of a branch. Right before Alex tackled me. But this time, there's no laugh at the end. No hands pulling mine apart. No twinkling eyes or promises steeped in childhood innocence.

Just the sound of my heart giving out.

I drop my purse in the entryway and slip out of my wet shoes. My face is streaked with rain and tears, my body shivering with regret.

"Annalise?" Alex's voice seeps from the main bedroom, followed by the sound of footsteps. He pokes his head out from the hallway, his eyes raking over me. "Hey."

I can't find words. Can't smile. Can't move.

Alex knows me well enough to know something is off.

Irreparably wrong.

The condo still lingers with the scent of salmon and veggies after I gulped down dinner, moments before running out the door and into the arms of another man.

The smell congeals in my gut.

Cautiously, he steps forward, meeting me in the center of the living room. His eyes slant with suspicion. "You're soaking wet."

A clipped nod.

"You've been crying."

Another nod.

His nostrils flare. A long pause.

And then: "What did you do?"

The question slices through me. Everything inside me stumbles, my pulse thudding in my ears. The air between us stretches thin, as if the walls themselves are holding their breath.

We stare at each other.

The silence grows heavier, unbearable.

Then the words burst out of me. "I kissed him."

While I planned to confess, I hadn't wanted to like this. This is an ambush. But I can't hold it in, can't go another second with this secret locked inside me, hollowing out my heart.

"I kissed him, Alex."

He blinks like he didn't hear me correctly. But he did. The way the color drains from his face tells me he registered every word.

"I'm so sorry." Nausea wobbles in the pit of my stomach, a boat fighting storm-charged waves. This guilt is no less than a death sentence. "I'm sorry. So sorry. I just…" My voice grows small.

He gapes at me, mouth ajar, eyes dull and lifeless. Then he ducks his head, stares down at the floor.

I step forward, my hands linked together, nails biting into my skin. "Alex…"

"Don't." Hardly a whisper. A broken breath. He swipes a hand over his face and cups his chin. "I can't hear this."

"You have to. Please. I need to get this off my chest before it buries me."

"Buries *you*?" Head snapping up, he glares at me with heat and fire and rage. "You just cheated on me."

I nod because it's true. Because I did. Because I hate myself for it. "I'm sorry. I didn't mean for—"

"Fuck that. Fuck you." He stomps forward until we're inches apart and he's practically spitting in my face. "*Fuck you*, Annalise."

His voice fractures into smithereens.

I cower.

Tears slip down my cheeks, an endless flood. But I have to get the words out. "I know it was wrong," I say, the truth shaking out of me. "I know. I own it. But…I'm not happy. I haven't been for a long time."

His laugh is bitter and sharp. "So that was your fix? Running off to screw another guy?"

"No, it… It was just a kiss."

"Is that supposed to help? Will you sleep better at night knowing it was *just a kiss*?"

My gaze locks onto him. Older. Stronger. Shoulders broader, face harder. But still Alex. Still the boy with the green eyes who used to walk me home and hold my hand like it was a secret. But now those eyes are rimmed red, darker than the sky that day in the woods. "No," I whisper.

"Good." His lips twist into something cruel. "I hope it eats you alive, knowing you betrayed the one person who gave you everything. Who loved you more than life. Who stood by you through every storm, every loss, since we were kids. I carried you, Annalise." A finger jabs at my face. "I fucking carried you."

"And that's exactly where we went wrong!" I shout, voice rupturing, a shot of strength overpowering the guilt. "You carried me. You built this whole life around me. The condo, the job, everything. I have one friend, and you don't even like her. I feel isolated. Lost. God, I haven't even cooked a meal for myself in years!" My face crumples, grief seeping out of me. "And I let you. I let you bleed into every piece of me because I didn't know how to be without you. Because I thought a ring could fix us. Because I thought love meant loyalty, no matter the cost. Even when I couldn't hear my own voice over yours."

Darkness washes over his face. "Right," he rasps. "I forgot. You're famous now. Out with the old, in with the new."

"No. It's not like that." Shaking my head, I reach for him. "I've always wanted that life. Writing, music. And I've tried to be patient. I've tried to hold space for your pain, your anger, for everything you've been through, but somewhere along the way…I started disappearing."

He jerks his arm out of reach.

"I didn't kiss him because I stopped caring about you," I continue, barely holding myself together. "I kissed him because, for just a few minutes, I felt like myself again. Real. Seen."

"That's a bullshit, cowardly excuse," he throws back. "I've never cheated, never even looked at another woman. All. I. See. Is. *You*."

"Do you?"

A heavy silence stretches between us.

Slowly, I lift my arm and show him my wrist. "Did you see this?"

His gaze latches onto the coiled bruise, glowing green and gray.

"Do you even realize you did it?"

Alex swallows.

I watch the fight drain out of him, the fury melting into something else.

Horror. Fear.

He shakes his head. "I didn't do that."

"You did." My voice unravels into threads of sadness. "You did."

"No." He whips around, grabs his hair with both hands. His knees buckle slightly, and he presses against the side of the couch like the floor might give out under him. "I would never hurt you. Not on purpose. I swear to God—"

"But that doesn't make it okay. That doesn't mean I'm not scared sometimes."

He turns slowly, eyes wild and bloodshot. "I'm not a monster."

There's no such thing, Annalise. Monsters aren't real.

But they are.

And they aren't always witches and warlocks with sharp teeth and pointy claws.

Sometimes we create our own.

My jaw trembles. "I can't do this anymore, Alex. I can't be this person."

He stares at me, shell-shocked, stripped bare and hardly breathing. "So that's it? You're just…done?"

"I can't keep living like this. I feel like I'm being torn in two. I'm evolving, and you're—"

"You said we were forever. You promised."

More guilt sears through me. "I know. And I meant it. God, I meant it with everything in me. But forever isn't supposed to feel like a cage. I'm not nine anymore. And neither are you."

His breathing turns shallow, uneven. "What about Thailand?"

He flinches as he says it, the memory now a wound.

I curl my hands, my fingers shaking.

"The lagoons, the monkeys, all that street food you wanted to try." He pulls up from the couch and winds back toward me. "We had a plan. We can still go. Maybe if we got out of here, cleared our heads, we can find our way back to each other. We can fix what's broken."

I press a fist to my mouth, a sob caught in my throat. "A vacation isn't going to change anything. It's an escape, not a fix."

"It is. It will be. I can fix this." His desperation is raw now, his body moving without thought as he reaches me, hands gripping my shoulders. "I'll book that therapy appointment if that's what you want. I'll make the call. Tomorrow morning."

"It's too late," I murmur.

"No. It's not. I can't lose you." His voice cracks, reality setting in. He stumbles forward, hands sliding down my arms until he's clutching at my wrists. Then he sinks to the floor. His knees hit the carpet with a thud, his forehead pressing into my stomach. "Please, Annalise. Please don't do this to me. I can't breathe without you. I don't exist without you."

Tears streak his face, wetting my shirt as he buries himself against me.

My resolve waffles.

Regret, sadness, conviction, and terror, all twisting into something that makes me paralyzed.

I don't know what to feel, what to do.

His arms cinch tight around my waist like a vise. "You're everything. My reason, my anchor. You're all I have. You can't take that away. Don't punish me. Don't leave me."

I try to step back, but he clings harder, his nails digging into the fabric at my hips.

His voice is hoarse, guttural, like I'm tearing him apart. "I'll do anything. I'll give you space, I'll go to therapy every damn day. You want a new life? I'll build it for you. Just don't walk away. Please. I know you still love me."

My arms hang limp at my sides as I tremble in place. "I…I think I have to love myself more."

It's not a lie.

But it hurts like one.

His grip loosens, and after a long pause, he flops back on his heels, staring at me like I'm already gone.

Am I?

What if I'm making a mistake? Alex has been my whole life. My best friend. My first kiss. My almost forever. If I leave now, what does that make me? A coward? A traitor? A girl who wrecked everything over one kiss?

The guilt scrapes at my chest. I want to snatch everything back—the words said, the kiss stolen. Smooth it all over and promise him I'll try harder. I want to fix it.

God, I always want to fix it.

"It's me, isn't it?" He swipes at his face. "You think I'm fucked-up. You think I'm broken."

My gaze drops to my wrist. To the bruise.

He follows my eyes, as if he studies the evidence long enough, he can erase it. Rewrite the damage. Pretend it never happened.

But it did.

I have to remember that.

"I never said you were broken," I reply softly.

Alex pulls to his feet, a single tear cutting down his cheek. "But you're thinking it. You're giving up on me because you think I'm unfixable."

"That's not—"

"Say it, Annalise. Just fucking admit it."

"No, I…I have to go." I press my hands to my chest, where my heart beats like a war drum behind bone. "I-I need space. Time to clear my head, to think. To…"

I take a step back.

I'm not sure what tomorrow holds; all I know is that I need to process this relationship, that kiss, my future.

Chase. Alex. Me.

Everything.

More tears pour out of me.

But before I turn away, I watch his face turn to stone. Eyes turn to sleet.

Words turn to bullets.

Alex sniffs. "You always said I changed after that accident."

I stop in my tracks. My blood freezes.

I blink, watching as a dark mask slips into place.

"I let you think that. Let you believe it. But that's not the truth," he says. "The accident didn't change me—*you* changed me. You broke me, Annalise."

The air in my lungs seizes. For a heartbeat, I believe him. Because that's what I've always done. Shouldered the blame. If I'd been better, calmer, more careful, maybe the accident wouldn't have happened. Maybe he wouldn't be so angry. Maybe he wouldn't lash out.

Maybe we wouldn't be here.

"You were so damn needy," he continues, huffing out a mocking breath. "So clingy. So codependent. It wore me down. Turned me into this."

Guilt rages up like a tidal wave, familiar and suffocating. I see every sacrifice he's made for me, every night he pulled me out of my own darkness, every promise I whispered that I'd never leave. My heart claws at me to stay, to fix this, to prove him wrong by proving myself wrong.

His eyes harden, glassy with venom. "You'll break him too, you know. You'll turn him into someone he hates. And then he'll hate *you* for it. Because that's what you do. That's who you are." A vein throbs in his temple as he twists the dagger deep. "Just give it time."

The words detonate inside me.

They linger.

Ring, hum, tumble around inside my head.

No.

No.

That's not true.

For so long I've let him define me. What I am, what I'm worth, what damage I'm capable of. And I realize now…that was the point.

That's the cage.

He needs me to believe I ruin everything so he doesn't have to face who he's become.

But that's not me. That's not who I am.

As I stare at him, at the man I thought knew me inside and out, I realize he doesn't know me at all. And finally, a different man's voice rings louder.

"You'd be shocked to know how incredibly enough you are, just the way you are."

The pain doesn't vanish. It never will.

But it shifts. Just like that.

My hand quivers as I tug the ring off my finger. The diamond glitters under the light, a promise I thought would bind us back together, when really it chained me tighter. I step forward and press it into his palm, folding his fingers around it.

His mouth parts, a flash of panic in his eyes, but I shake my head. Tears streak hot down my cheeks. "No, Alex," I whisper, steadier now. "I didn't break you."

He winces, eyes flickering with regret.

"You broke yourself."

I stagger back, curl my fingers around the doorknob, and turn it. The sound is small, but it echoes like a crack of thunder.

The door clicks shut behind me.

And for the first time in years, the silence belongs to me.

CHAPTER 38
Annalise

"Van is ready!"

My brother's voice cuts through the fog as I'm curled up in his spare bedroom, the space littered with boxes and clothes strewn over mismatched furniture. Puffing my cheeks with a breath, I toss my notebook aside, the pages scribbled in crossed-out lyrics and smudged ink.

It's been three weeks since that video went viral, and our spur-of-the-moment tour is far from meticulously planned. It's messy, gritty, and ambitious. In two days, we hit the road, geared up to play small venues and college towns along the East Coast. A mix of bars, pop-ups, a beachside acoustic, and an opening slot for a mid-level indie band.

Our socials exploded. Chase went from barely a hundred followers to 500K, and I recently hit the six digits. Comments are begging for tour dates and Spotify links. Our inboxes are filled with praise, requests, and promises. Some legit, some sketchy. Kenna takes over my socials and creates an official band account across all platforms, while Crowley makes connections with industry bigwigs, putting us on the path to success.

We weren't ready. We're still not ready. But that doesn't stop us.

Over ten million views. Thousands of comments and tags.

It's a dream come true…

A dream, shadowed by the fallout of my broken relationship.

I peer down at my empty ring finger, trying not to imagine the look on Alex's face when I placed the diamond in his hand. Or the way he begged for me to stay, to give him one more chance, when I returned to the condo to pack up my things. Or the text messages that followed.

Grinding my teeth together, I thumb through the last string of messages between us.

Alex: Annalise. Please. I'm sorry for the things I said. I was mad. Totally blindsided.
Alex: Hey, call me. I just want to talk.
Alex: I'm willing to forgive you. We both fucked up. Just text me back.
Alex: Why can't you pick up the phone and call me? I deserve that much. You cheated on me. Fuck.
Alex: I'm sorry. I love you.
Alex: I can't do this without you. Please come back to me.

Days later, I finally returned his texts.

Me: It's over.
Me: Go to Thailand. Swim in the lagoons. Feed the monkeys. Eat that weird scorpion-on-a-stick thing you always talked about. Do all the things we said we would.
Me: But not for me. For you.
Me: Please don't contact me again.

He hasn't.
I stare at one of the messages as a knot tightens in my throat.

You cheated on me.

"Annalise!"

My head snaps up. Hauling my legs over the side of the bed, I glance in the mirror, doing a double take. Dear God. My roots are greasy, my skin pastier than week-old mashed potatoes, and my eyes tell stories of sleepless nights and soul-deep guilt.

When I look down, I notice I'm not even wearing pants.

Mortified, I do a one-legged hop into a pair of yesterday's leggings, douse my head in a cloud of dry shampoo, and spritz perfume on every exposed inch of my skin.

Then I race down the stairs and out the front door, painting on a smile. All the guys, plus Kenna, are gathered around the van, now officially christened.

Slapped on the side in high-gloss vinyl is our logo: *Honey Moons*, scrawled in blocky weathered script like it's been scratched onto the side of a bathroom stall at midnight. The double *O*'s are crescent moons, one waxing, one waning, both slivered sharp like fangs.

My smile grows, turning real.

Chase leans back against the rear, one hand in his pocket as he scrolls through his phone. He doesn't look up when I approach, and I don't expect him to. I've been distant over the past two weeks, keeping him at arm's length. Our discussions have been strictly music-related as we focus on the tour, the songs, and the whirlwind journey ahead.

The truth is, I can hardly look at him.

Because, despite everything, Alex's words echo, stubborn and sharp.

You'll break him too.

The bruise on my wrist has faded, but inside I'm still black-and-blue. It doesn't matter that I left. Doesn't matter that I knew I had to, knew it was right. Because another part of me keeps whispering that he wasn't wrong. That I ruined him.

That I'll ruin Chase too.

So needy. So clingy. You turned me into this.

That kiss should've felt like freedom. Instead, it feels like proof. Proof that I'm selfish. Reckless. Unfaithful.

Proof that Alex was right.

Clearing my throat, I turn to glance at my brother, shaking off the misery. "This is incredible."

"Shit yeah, it is," he beams, grin giddy. "Our little marketing guru and merch extraordinaire is well on her way to adding 'graphic designer' to her resume." Tag slings a long arm around Kenna, squishing her against his tall frame.

She scoffs, peeling herself away. But her cheeks flush a little. "I'm a vision girl. I see it. I do it. It wasn't hard."

"What would we do without you?" I stalk over to her, gratitude lacing my tone.

"Well, you're about to find out. I won't be able to swing the tour."

I freeze. "Wait, what? I thought it was a done deal."

"It was...until my sister decided to give birth six weeks early. I'm flying out to Santa Barbara the day you leave to meet my new niece."

Despite my disappointment, I can't be mad about that. She has a life outside of all this, filled with people who need her just as much as I do. Sometimes I forget that...how lucky I am she's chosen to be in my corner at all. "Wow. That's amazing. Congrats to Leila."

"She named her Ribbon. What the hell kind of name is that?" She scowls, horrified. "And what about the nicknames? Ribs? Ribeye? Bonbon? I can't." Sighing, Kenna digs the toe of her sneaker into a divot. "Anyway, I'm sorry I won't be there, but I'm only a text or phone call away. I'll be keeping tabs. And when you really hit the big time, I'll be in the front row, singing every word to every song."

My eyes mist. "I know you will."

As I lean in for a hug, Kenna jerks away, waving a hand in front of her face. "Jesus. You smell like my mother when she was trying to hide her month-long affair with the furnace repair guy."

My nose wrinkles as I sniff myself. *Yikes*. "Sorry. I may have gone a little overboard on the perfume. I'll go hop in the shower."

Stepping away, I survey the van one more time, allowing the

gloom to settle into a warm glow. Two more days, and everything is going to change.

I'm trekking back into the house, nearly halfway out of my shirt, when Chase comes up behind me and clears his throat. I squeak in surprise, shoving my arm back through the sleeve. "Oh, jeez. Hey. I'm shower-bound." I attempt to tame my hair, but it's basically a hunk of solid concrete at this point.

He presses a shoulder against the wall, drinking me in. "Can we talk first?"

My chest tightens, the gloom rushing back to the surface. "Talk? About what?"

A look.

"Everything is fine, Chase. I'm just acclimating. Sorry if I've been distant." I swallow, my heart skipping a beat. "I promise we're good."

"You look like you haven't slept in weeks."

"When do I ever sleep?" I pop a shoulder, chuckling lightly. "I'm used to it. Besides, I told you before, I'm not used to sleeping alone. All part of the acclimation."

"Annie..." He lifts up from the wall, and it looks like he hasn't slept much either. "I don't want there to be a wedge between us on the tour. We should talk about it."

It.

The kiss.

He wants to talk about it. Communicate like healthy, high-functioning humans.

That's fair.

But talking about it makes it real. Gives it fire, life, a heartbeat. And I can't have any more teeth chewing through me.

"Um, yeah. I get it. I'm just not sure what we can really say about it…" I drag my lip between my teeth. "I'm not mad at you."

"I never said you were mad," he says. "But you're hurting. In pain. And I'm a part of that."

"No. This is on me."

"Annie, that's my point. It shouldn't all be on you." Chase takes a slow step toward me, cautious and careful. "I can't change anything. But I'm here. I can help."

Emotion bubbles behind my eyes.

I can't blame him for feeling confused, shunned. I'm finally single. And I'm acting as if I felt nothing when his body pressed into me and his tongue wielded poetry against my lips.

"Chase," I breathe, meeting his gaze. "I just need a little time. To heal. To grieve."

He studies me for a while, his throat rolling. "Right. Okay."

I force my eyes to brighten, to override the blanket of trapped tears. "Thank you for trying to help."

Looking down at the floor, he nods.

"You're going to kill it out there. I feel it." I step toward him, taking his hand in mine. "The man who strums stars."

He gives my palm a squeeze before loosening his grip. As he opens his mouth to reply, he blinks at me several times, then lowers his head with a noticeable wince.

I frown. "Are you okay?"

"Yeah. Yeah, I'm—" He hisses on a sharp exhale, rubbing the side of his head with the heel of his hand.

"Chase…"

"I'm okay. Sorry. Just a headache." Two fingers gently massage his temple as he looks back up, eyes wearier. He shakes it off. "Go shower. I'll be in the van."

"Are you sure—"

He spins away, heading out the front door and disappearing into the autumn sunshine.

CHAPTER 39
Annalise

Thirty-six hours later, the van is jam-packed with five worn-down duffels, a tangled mess of cables and gear, and enough snacks to shame a college frat house.

Kenna triple-checks the merch crates before she heads off to the airport to meet her niece, while Tag tunes his guitar in the passenger seat, his foot propped on the dashboard. Rock is already asleep in the back, curled up like a house cat beside a bass amp.

Toaster is with Solomon for the week—Chase's old boss who pretends he's not obsessed with the dog, even though he hand-feeds him rotisserie chicken and calls him "The Toastinator."

Chase slides into the driver's seat, shooting me a small, unreadable glance in the rearview mirror. It lasts less than a second. Then he turns the key and the engine purrs to life, the gas tank full and prepped for a week of travel.

I climb onto the back bench and wedge myself between an amp and Rock, a bag of Takis in hand and my hoodie acting as a pillow. The smell of coffee and vinyl fills the air.

It's cramped. Chaotic. Magical.

Zach untangles himself from his daughter's hug in the driveway, the last to enter the van as he waves goodbye and hops in, sealing the door shut.

Music blares from the radio.

A crisp fifty-degree breeze sneaks through the open window, filling my lungs.

I pop up from my seat and lean outside as the van rolls forward. "Bye, bestie!"

Kenna slaps a sun hat to her head just before it floats away, shouting at the top of her lungs, "Honey Moons, bitches! That's my best friend!"

She points at me, blows me a kiss, and I try not to sob.

Tag whoops loud, raising a fist in the air. "First stop, Boston, motherfuckers! Let's go melt some faces."

Laughing, I return to my seat, reaching into my backpack and pulling out my battered notebook.

The one that started it all.

I uncap my pen, press it to the page, and write.

TEN SONGS, SIX CITIES, AND A VAN THAT SMELLS LIKE CHEESE FRIES

BOSTON

It's sweaty. Loud. Perfectly imperfect.

The crowd screams before we even strike the first chord, and someone holds up a sign with my lyrics scribbled in pink glitter. I nearly forget how to sing.

Nerves get the better of us, and we mess up the second verse. No one seems to care.

Afterward, we sit on the curb scarfing gas station nachos while reading comments from fans who drove six hours just to see us. My body is still shaking with adrenaline.

Chase holds my hand until the shivers die down.

I let him.

This is real. We're doing this.

PHILADELPHIA

The van breaks down two blocks from the venue. We haul amps through a monsoon, and I lose a boot in a puddle the size of Lake Michigan.

Inside, a guy hands us weed, while a woman in a tie-dye tulip skirt and denim jacket asks if we're "the group that strums stars."

Chase scribbles his name on her chest in black marker.

His first autograph.

Someone cries during our slowest song.

Barefoot and rain-soaked, I cry too.

Later, we all crash in the van. I sleep on a pile of jackets. Rock snores like a tractor.

I don't care.

I'd do it all again in a heartbeat.

NEW YORK CITY

There's a line around the block. The venue smells like beer and dreams.

Strobes dizzy me. The sound is thunder. Chase's plasma guitar illuminates the stage for "Night Song" like a lightning show in the dead of night.

The audience goes ballistic.

When it's over, we huddle in the back alley with overblown hearts, gasping and grinning.

No one speaks.

We don't need to.

Before I retreat to the van to pass out, I glance over at Tag.

He just stands there, staring up at the full honey moon.

A tear glistens on his cheek.

BALTIMORE

We're all exhausted.

My brother slams the side door and storms off mid-argument about who forgot to grab batteries for the mics. Everything feels heavier when you're this tired.

I sit in the front seat, pretending not to cry.

Zach tosses me a box of Sour Patch Kids because, according to his kid, sugar makes everything better.

By soundcheck, we're talking again. Sort of.

That night we play with raw nerves and red eyes. Somehow, the crowd eats it up. Maybe honesty sells.

Someone throws a rose onstage.

Tag slips on it.

We make it look like choreography.

When midnight finds us, we're all cramped inside the van, our gear stacked Tetris-style, chugging water and gorging on cheap pizza. Everyone tells stories, reliving the past few days, laughing until our stomachs ache. When Chase sends me a bright smile, it reminds me that the music isn't the only thing keeping me going.

My brother wraps his arm around me.

We forget about the fight.

RICHMOND

Beach show. Acoustic set.

No stage. Just a circle of strangers on blankets and sand.

I feel weightless.

We play until the sun sets, the tide creeping closer with every chorus.

I sing for the teenage girl in the back row with flamingo-pink hair and winged eyeliner. The girl who DM'd me that our music pulled her out of someplace dark.

When I scan the crowd, I catch someone filming.

The video has a million views before we even pack up.

ATLANTA

It's my birthday. Twenty-two. And it's our biggest show yet.

Sold out. Packed.

Our name flashes on a marquee. A real marquee.

The promoter hugs us like we're old friends.

We play as if we've been doing this forever, but inside, I know it's the last show of the leg. And something's shifting.

We're not the same band we were back in Rutland.

Fame is starting to stick.

So is fear.

Just before midnight, Chase finds me on the lumpy bench seat, the belt buckle digging into my hip and my head pressed against the window like a makeshift pillow. He wraps a coffee-stained quilt around me. Pulls it up to my chin. Brushes a strand of hair out of my eyes.

"Happy birthday, Annie," he whispers.

I turn to thank him.

But he's already gone.

Beside me is a notebook. New. Blank. Bound in soft brown leather with a violet ribbon tucked between the first two pages.

There's a note slipped beneath the cover, folded once.

> For what comes next.
> —C

CHAPTER 40
Annalise

The hotel lobby smells like citrus and money. The kind that gets you rooms with blackout curtains, velvet armchairs, and showers the size of a studio apartment.

Rock spins slowly in place, taking in the upper-class clientele and the giant Christmas tree that nearly reaches the ceiling. "This place has robes."

"And real pillows. Not those travel ones shaped like deflated doughnut failures," Kenna mutters, tugging her suitcase with one hand and filming a slow pan of the crystal chandelier with the other. "No more sleeping on amps."

It doesn't feel real yet. That we belong here. That this isn't some fluke.

It all started a month ago with a call from Crowley.

"You're going to want to sit down for this," he told us as we assembled around the video call while packing up the van to head home from Atlanta. "A booking agent out of New York saw your video at The Soundproof and tracked me down. Said he hasn't seen this much traction off a first tour since The 1975 hit the road."

That agent—Carter Vale, who reps two other chart-topping indie acts—signed us within the week. He's young but sharp, has perfect white-blond hair, and a Rolodex of contacts that stretches from Brooklyn to Berlin.

Carter quickly negotiated guarantees and got our Spotify numbers boosted. Then a few days later, some pop star with forty million followers reposted our clip with the caption, Real music is still alive.

The internet lost its mind. Streams skyrocketed.

Suddenly, we weren't just a garage band with a loyal TikTok following. We were on everyone's radar.

Our agent put together our own headlining tour with real press, real pay, and real hotel rooms. Then, an opener slot for a big-league band on a national tour in Los Angeles, capping it all off.

We even traded in our rusty van for a tour bus. Used, but still a massive upgrade.

It's been a blur. And now we're here, at the start of something life-changing.

I slip my new notebook from my bag as we wait to check in.

Six more shows. Six new cities. All sold out.

I flip to a fresh page and press the pen down.

Tour Life, Take Two: No More Janky Van But Still a Concerning Amount of Cheese Fries

> Hotel is hoteling. Five stars for the lobby alone. I tried to subtly check if the citrus scent is coming from a candle I can actually afford. It is not.
>
> Zach tipped the valet $20 like a celebrity.
>
> Kenna asked if she could take a bath in the minibar. Rock plans to.
>
> Tag keeps saying "we've peaked" every time he sees something new: lobby art, elevators with music, the gold pen at the front desk.
>
> Chase is quiet. All I want to do is hug him. Maybe I will.

I stuff the notebook in my duffel bag as the hotel receptionist checks us into our rooms for the night. They aren't penthouse suites or grand villas, but we feel privileged just to be standing in the lobby of a resort that has a spa giving out complimentary cucumber water.

For weeks we slept curled in the van like dirty laundry. Ate stale pretzels and potato chips for breakfast. Took mid-tour showers at a budget motel off I-95.

Now we have bathrobes and concierge service.

Hardcore fans and loaded merch tables.

We're not rolling in it yet. But for the first time, the money's enough to matter. Enough for Zach to send something home to his daughter, Marie. Enough to buy better gear, better shoes, better coffee. Enough to feel the ground shift under our feet.

Chase asks for an extra key before we retreat to our rooms.

I frown when he hands it to me. "What's this for?"

"You said you have a hard time sleeping alone." His eyes drift to mine as he reaches for the handle on his suitcase. "There's no pressure, but the invitation is there. I can take the pullout."

The edge of the keycard digs into my palm as I close my fingers around it. I can't read him. He sounds so sincere. "Oh… thank you."

He shrugs. "We've all been sleeping together in the van up till now. Figured you might get restless."

I swallow. He's not wrong.

Aside from those two weeks staying with Tag, I haven't slept in a bed alone in years. Even as a teenager, Alex would sneak into my room, or I'd sneak into his. Almost every single night.

Insomnia has been plaguing me, rimming my eyes with dark shadows, dizzying my mind. I hate the sensation of lonely, dark rooms with nobody beside me. No sleepy breaths quieting my racing thoughts. No morning chitchat as the sun peeks through the curtains.

The offer warms me. Because he remembered. Because he cares.

I tap the card against my thigh and bite my lip. "I might take you up on that. But you don't need to take the pullout. We're both adults. A king bed is plenty big enough."

His gaze dips to my mouth for a quick beat, then flicks back up. "I can take the pullout."

Chase stalks ahead in his skintight gunmetal-gray T-shirt and black jeans, his suitcase rolling behind him.

"I'm going to the bar," Kenna chirps, appearing on my right. "Your brother owes me a drink."

I blink at her, my skin newly warm and tingly. "For what?"

"What *doesn't* he owe me a drink for?"

"Valid. You did design a sherpa blanket with his face on it."

"Mm-hmm," she hums. "Granted, the Chase blanket has outsold his by several hundred units."

I saunter toward the elevators, suitcase in hand. "When do I get a blanket with my face on it?"

Kenna grimaces. "Do you really want to go down that road?"

It takes a moment for the subtext to register: my face, fleece, and men who definitely wouldn't be using it for warmth. I scrunch my nose. "Right."

"Are you partaking in our night of Malibu and mayhem?"

"Um…" I turn, watching as Chase settles into the elevator. Our eyes lock the moment before the doors close him in. Clearing my throat, I shake my head, sending Kenna a small smile. "I'll pass. I'm beat. This is probably my one chance to catch up on sleep."

"Heard. Egyptian cotton sheets are hard to compete with." She glances over at the bar, where Tag, Rock, and Zach are already deep into round one. "'Night, girlie. I'll text you in the morning."

"Have fun." I shoot her a wave, then make my way up to the seventh floor.

Chase's room key is heavy in my hand as the floor number dings and the doors peel open. He's only a few rooms down from me. I should probably head to my own, take a long, hot shower, change into pajamas, and inhale enough melatonin to tranquilize a horse.

But…

My pulse revs, my gait slowing as I approach room 721.

I blow out a breath. Second-guess my motives half a dozen times. Step forward, step back.

Five whole minutes later, I'm still standing there, looking pitiful.

"Screw it," I mutter, holding my head high and rapping my knuckles against the frame.

Footsteps shuffle beyond the threshold, and my heart races at double the speed.

The door pulls open.

Chase stands there, sans shirt, a pair of sweatpants slung low on his hips. My treacherous eyes trail over him, landing on the shadowing of dark hair disappearing into his waistband.

Gulping, I glance back up.

His eyes soften at the sight of me. "Didn't expect you so soon."

"Yeah," I murmur. "Same."

"You didn't even drop off your suitcase."

A shrug. "If you're busy, I can—"

"Come in." He takes a step back, widening the door.

The room smells like the lobby, fresh and citrusy. Must be something in the air vents. I stroll inside, my shoulder grazing the front of his chest as my grip tightens on the suitcase handle. The bed is still made, stacked with a plethora of cloud-like pillows, while Chase's suitcase lies sprawled open on the mattress. "Nice digs," I say.

He closes the door. "As Tag would say, we've peaked."

A smile curves. "Feels like we have."

We face each other, charged silence infiltrating the air around us.

Now what?

My brain scrambles for something to say.

I don't know what to do with my hands. Or my face.

Desperation kicks in, and I stick out my tongue, cross my eyes, and cant my head to the side.

Chase blinks like I've been possessed by a five-year-old child.

I maintain the ridiculous expression and extend my right leg until it's horizontal, then stretch it skyward, as vertical as my flexibility will allow. Balance is on my side, and I hold the position.

A beat.

Then, finally—beautifully—he laughs. A genuine burst of amusement.

"Jesus," he says, grinning wide, showcasing a row of perfect white teeth, looking as stunning as I've ever seen him.

Dropping my leg, my face unfurls into a bright smile to match. "There it is."

"What, a smile?" His eyes gleam against the lamplight. "It doesn't take a circus act to get me to smile, Annie."

"I don't know. It felt like extreme measures needed to be taken."

A slight headshake. "You smile, I smile. It's as simple as that."

His words are a shimmer-dusted arrow to my heart.

I tuck my hair behind my ear and glance down at the floor. "Yeah. I guess I haven't been doing that much lately."

Scratching the back of his neck, Chase winds around me and takes a seat at the edge of the bed. "Any contact with Alex?"

My heart stutters. "He texted me in the beginning. A lot. But it's been radio silence since the tour began." I swallow, watching his muscles ripple and flex as he leans back on one hand. "He's in Thailand now."

"Thailand?"

"We were supposed to go together. I figured he'd cancel the trip, but some pictures popped up on Instagram. Bangkok, Chiang Mai. He looked happy."

He hesitates. "Are you?"

I chew on my cheek, then offer a small nod. "Yeah. I'm happy."

Stormy hazel eyes roll over me, toes to top. I'm not convinced he believes me.

But I'm telling the truth. I'm happy. On cloud nine.

Finally, fully alive.

And as soon as I can forgive myself, the peace will come too.

Chase clears his throat. "You can use the bathroom to change. Then we can order food, watch TV. Whatever you want."

"I think I want to pass out if that's cool."

He glances at the time: 10:23 p.m. "It's early for you."

"The travel and performance highs are catching up to me."

"I get it," he says. "Tomorrow's a big day."

Harnessing a soft smile, I unzip my suitcase and rummage around for a pair of pajamas. Out of my periphery, I watch as Chase pulls out his phone, starts to scroll.

I clear my throat. "Everyone's down at the bar. I'll be fine for a few hours if you wanted to join them. There's a lot to celebrate."

His eyes lift through dark, fanning lashes. "I'm good."

"Groupies are probably flocking." I laugh lightly, though the thought clogs my throat with something sharp and ugly. "Could be fun."

"You want me to ditch you for groupies?"

"No," I say quickly. Too quickly. "I mean, you can. If you want. I wouldn't blame you."

He slips his phone into his pocket. "I'm where I want to be."

I curl my hand around a silky pink sleep set. "Have you thought about that?"

"About hooking up with groupies?"

"Yeah," I breathe out, stomach pitching. "Comes with the rock star life. Beautiful women throwing themselves at you."

Chase leans forward, props an elbow on his knee. He rubs a hand over his jaw, watching me, turning a response over in his mind.

He doesn't reply right away, so I keep babbling. "Surely you've considered it. I mean, you're single. Hot. Talented. The way you sing, engage with the crowd…"

"Yeah. It's crossed my mind."

The lump expands in my throat. "You basically have your pick of the litter. You can—"

"I don't have my pick of the litter." He cuts me off, tone gruff. "If I did, things would be a lot different right now."

His truth slips through the cracks. Bruises on the way down.

He gives me a look like it cost him something to admit that.

I pull to a stand. Stare at him, all out of words. My palms sweat around the pajamas.

"Go change. I'll get the pullout ready."

Mouth dry, I watch as he moves to the other side of the room, fumbling with the bed.

Ducking my head, I escape into the bathroom with flushed cheeks and a thumping heart. The door clicks shut behind me, and I press my back to it, exhale hard.

My fingers shake as I change into the pajama set, pale pink with black piping, soft as a sigh. I let the fabric slide over my skin like armor, giving myself time to breathe. Time to not think about Chase on the other side of the door, folding a pullout bed like it's the only thing he can control right now.

When I move toward the counter to wash my face, I go still.

Amber prescription bottles clutter the space around the sink. Four of them, some open, labels peeled. One's knocked over, little white pills spilled like teeth across the marble.

My stomach sinks.

"Chase?" I step out of the bathroom, voice tinged with concern. "What are those pills for?"

He's still shirtless, all corded muscle and blue and black ink, hunched over the unfolded couch as he tucks a fitted sheet over the flimsy mattress.

Faltering, he looks up, over my shoulder, then back at me.

A muscle in his cheek ticks. "Nothing. Just something for my headaches."

"All of them?"

"Hard to perform with a migraine tearing my skull apart." He changes the subject, forcing a smile. "You hungry? I can order room service."

"No, I…" Swallowing, I glance back at the bathroom. "I'm fine."

He nods.

"Are you sure you're okay?" I inch toward him, unease blooming in my gut. "That's a lot of pills."

"It's just pain reliever. Some are preventive. Don't worry about it."

Of course I'm going to worry about it.

I care about him.

He's been suffering, and I had no idea. While he complains about headaches sometimes, I didn't realize it was to the extent of carrying around a travel pharmacy.

But I'm getting the impression he doesn't want to talk about it. So I let it go.

I slide onto the king-size bed. Crawl underneath the covers. Flip off the nightlight beside me.

A few tense minutes roll by as I gaze up at the ceiling.

Chase turns off the remaining lights. "Good night," he says.

"Good night."

The sheets are cool against my skin, crisp in the way only hotel linens are. I curl toward the center, my back to the door, and stare into the dark.

Beside me, I hear the soft rustle of blankets. A squeaking box spring.

I close my eyes, but I already know sleep won't come. Not with everything rattling inside me. Intrusive thoughts. Weeks of insomnia and adrenaline. Loneliness, grief, strobes, and solos. For a moment I forget I'm not curled up on the bench seat of the Sprinter with crooked, twisted limbs, a cramp in my leg, and my brother's hoodie tucked around me.

My mind wanders, recalling the bed I slept in for years. Familiar. Dishware clinks in the far corners of my mind. The scent of fried food lingers in my nose, hot stoves making me sweat.

"I've never cheated, never even looked at another woman."

I slap a hand over my face, willing the ghosts to scatter.

This damn guilt. I can't shake it. Can't let it go.

It's there, assaulting me, every time I close my eyes.

My thoughts spiral, latching onto that moment in the rain. His hands all over me, pressed against my throat, palming my breast. My spine digging into the railing.

Cold water from the sky. Hot, wet kisses. Moans, sighs, gasps.

Another man. Betrayal. Evidence that maybe Alex was right about me.

"I don't know how to carry this, Chase." The sound of my voice is weak and frayed, but loud enough to carry over to him. I hear him shift. See his shadow move as he sits up, a few feet away. "I'm sorry. I…" A little sob falls out. A croak of mourning.

I yank the blankets over my head, burying my face in the dark. Hiding from him. From myself.

I stay like that for a long time, knees tucked to my chest, breath uneven. The ache is everywhere. Between my ribs, behind my eyes, deep in my throat.

That's where he finds me, shriveled up and broken.

The blanket lifts slowly, and the air brushes cool against my skin. My eyes adjust to the faint hotel glow leaking in from the hallway, just enough to catch the outline of his silhouette. Broad shoulders. Tousled hair. Bare skin, chiseled and inked.

I want to see his eyes. Want to know what's in them when he looks at me.

His knee sinks into the mattress. Then the other. He climbs in beside me, his movements cautious, like he's still deciding whether he's allowed to be here. But he must know. Somehow, he knows I need him more than I can say.

"Annie," he says softly.

Just my name. My nickname. The one only he uses, like a secret unfolding between us.

I should have known right then what I was getting myself into.

My chest caves. I curl tighter, my voice crumbling. "I thought…I thought leaving Alex meant choosing me. But what if there's nothing left of me to choose?" It spills out like poison, thick and unforgiving. "What if I already lost myself?"

He just lies there, close but not crowding, the heat of his body warming the air between us. A small shift, and then his hand brushes mine. A solace, an offering.

I take it.

Our fingers link together.

"You didn't lose yourself," he murmurs. "You're still you."

I squeeze my eyes shut. "I don't even know who I am anymore."

"I do. You do too. And I know what it's like to hate yourself for something you can't undo. To relive it on loop. To think maybe the worst version of you is the real one." His thumb traces a gentle path along my knuckles. "But it's not. It's just a version. Just a piece."

A tear slips down my cheek, soaking into the pillow.

"I see the way you carry everything. Always have," he says. "The way you try to protect everyone but yourself. You're not broken, Annie. You're human."

I roll toward him, our faces now inches apart. "I don't know how to fix it."

"It's not about fixing it. It's about learning how to live with everything, the good and the bad. How to love yourself despite the flaws, despite the mistakes. It's about giving yourself grace."

My throat closes. "There's just this awful part of me I can't shake. Like maybe Alex was right," I confess. "What if I hurt you? What if I do ruin people?"

"You don't ruin people," he says with conviction. "You've just carried more than you ever should've had to. And yeah, sometimes that weight makes you stumble. But that's not the same thing as breaking someone."

The words melt into me, gentle and soothing. My grief ebbs, little by little.

Maybe he's right. Maybe it isn't about perfection or destruction, about choosing between saint or monster. Maybe it's about being human, flawed and fumbling, and still being worthy of love anyway. Maybe I don't have to keep punishing myself to prove I'm good.

I let the thought crack something open in me. The tiniest sliver of light.

I shift closer, until there's no space left between us. "I've missed you," I breathe.

I hear his breath waver. A slight hitch.

Then his arm comes around me, gathering me to him like a magnet, an impossible draw. "I've been here," he whispers.

"I know."

I tuck my face against his shoulder, every nerve ending alight. My hand drifts to his chest, fingers splayed across warm muscle. He stiffens. Breathes in hard.

Our legs twine together. My lips whisper against his collarbone.

We stay like that, tangled in silence, for what could be seconds or eternities.

Then he breaks the quiet, exhaling deeply into my hair. "I don't know what's worse," he rasps, voice low and strained. "Wanting you when I couldn't have you, or right now, feeling you wrapped up in my arms, and knowing I still don't."

Something jagged tears through my chest.

Pain, want, need, grief.

"I want you too," I say, voice paper-thin.

"Then I'll wait."

I close my eyes. Let myself sink.

Wrapped in his arms, held so tightly the pieces stop rattling, I finally fall asleep.

Ten hours pass in a blur of breath and dreams. The deepest sleep I've had in months.

When I wake the next morning, the bed is empty. For a moment, panic prickles through me, that old fear of being left behind, of not being good enough, strong enough, brave enough. But then it fades, replaced by something quieter.

I remember his arms around me, steady and sure. His voice cutting through the chaos in my head.

You're not broken, Annie. You don't ruin people.

I start to believe it.

Alex's voice doesn't get to be the loudest anymore. I don't have to keep carrying his definition of me.

It's time to write my own.

I sit up and glance beside me. On the nightstand sits a vanilla latte, still warm. And beside it, a plastic cup, overflowing with maraschino cherries.

The sight pulls a tear from me, but it's different this time.

Not grief. Not guilt.

Something closer to hope.

CHAPTER 41
Chase

The music is the only thing louder than the migraine tunneling through me.

Four different pills. Three shots of whiskey. Two energy drinks. It should have dulled the edges. It didn't.

I'm blitzed out of my head, running on fumes, on noise, on the energy in the crowd as they scream and dance and sing our lyrics like gospel.

The stage shudders beneath my boots, vibrating with bass, electricity, adrenaline—a tonic of progressive rock. Undergarments fly past my mic stand. Someone flashes me. The lights spin like galaxies, but everything in my head narrows. Tightens.

Sweat pours down my back, my hands shaking as I strum. My voice is raw and blistered, but I don't stop. I hold the key. Hit every note.

Submit to the beast.

Annie is fire beside me, owning her verses, hair soaked and sticking to her temples. She throws me a smile mid-chorus, and I give her one back, but it's tight. Forced. My jaw is clenched so hard I'm afraid I'll crack a molar.

Whatever's been living inside me, whatever's crawling through my veins and eating at my brain, it doesn't feel so silent anymore.

It feels loud. Twisted.

And for the first time, I don't want to tame it.

I want to let it burn.

The lights shift, strobe patterns exploding across the stage like gunfire. I stagger for half a second. No one notices.

When the final chord crashes over the room, the crowd goes feral. We hold the moment, arms and instruments raised in sweat-slick hands, grinning like lunatics under the glare of spotlights. Annie blows a kiss into the sea of screaming faces. Rock tosses his drumsticks into the crowd.

I stand there, soaking in the chaos, trying not to hurl. Then I lean forward with a final send-off, growling into the mic, "Thank you, San Francisco!"

The audience erupts.

A woman in the front row reaches for me with both hands, propped up on her friend's shoulders. "I love you, Chase!"

Smirking, I send her a wink, then gaze out at the sweaty, still-moving crowd. "You showed up. We bled for it. See you on the next battlefield."

I toss the mic behind me, letting it crash to the floor as the lights black out.

Backstage is a blur of back-pats and bottled water, our crew buzzing with postshow adrenaline. My hearing's fuzzy. My vision's off. But I plaster on a grin, hair stuck to my face, clothes glued to places I didn't even know about.

Someone suggests a drink.

Someone else is already pouring.

The rooftop bar is carved into the skyline like it owns the night.

Glass panels line the edge, offering a cinematic view of the city below. A gritty, endless sprawl. Amber lights hang from steel beams overhead, casting halos across plush couches and marble tables. The music is low, a steady pulse threading through the clink of highball glasses and the hush of conversations.

Our section is roped off with a velvet cord.

Bottle service.

VIP.

We were schlepped over to the hotel in a limo after a few postshow drinks. I've downed enough whiskey at this point that I hardly hear the howling in my head. My vision is speckled with tiny stars, my blood pumping with aftershocks and adrenaline.

Annie comes into focus beside me, all light and laughter as she splays across the ice-blue velvet couch.

A tight violet dress barely holds in her breasts. Tall black heels cling to her feet, the straps winding up her ankles. Her makeup still looks perfect despite the glaze of sweat on her skin, and her hair is a mess of purple, brown, and blond, still dusted with glitter from her hairspray.

She laughs at something Zach says, smacking him on the knee, and my gaze dips to the contact in a lazy slide.

"Dude, are you stoned?"

I blink a few times, searching for the voice. Tag materializes on my left, hunched forward on the couch with a beer between his hands. "What?" I mutter.

"You look cooked. Did Rock give you the good stuff?"

"No, I..." *Fuck*. I need to snap out of it. "Just whiskey."

"Mm." He brings the nozzle to his lips, taking a sip. "Well, you were fire out there tonight. Best you ever played."

Felt like my brain was trying to eat itself, but hey—rock and roll. "Thanks. You too."

He nods at his sister. "It's getting to you, isn't it?"

I falter, glancing at Annie. Her head tips back in laughter as Zach FaceTimes his daughter, Marie, who's explaining how she shoved a slice of cheese into the DVD player because Elmo was hungry.

Clearing my throat, I pull away. "No. I'm good."

Tag sighs, taking another swig. "She'll come around. It's that soft heart of hers. Doesn't know when to let go and let die. But she sees you. Give her a little more time."

His words eat at me, every syllable drenching me in acid. "Said I'm good." I lean forward and reach for a glass of champagne, swallowing it in one go. "Plenty of fish in the sea."

Around me, those fish blur into a sea of red lips and black dresses—blonds, brunettes, curves, legs, perfume. None of them her. None of them what I want.

But maybe that's what I need.

Simple. Disposable.

A rebound from something I never even had the right to miss.

Tag watches me, his stare a needle threading straight through the bravado. "Don't do it, man."

My jaw tightens.

"Seriously," he says. "Don't. You'll regret it."

"Right." I give a dry laugh. "Better to sit around like a lovesick fool."

"Knock it off with the tragic hero bit. She kissed you because she wanted you. Still does. She just doesn't know how to forgive herself for it."

The burn in my chest isn't the whiskey anymore.

It's her.

Her laugh. Her eyes. The way she looked at me when she thought no one else could see. The way she saw me when I thought I was invisible.

I told her I'd wait.

Just hours ago, she was in my arms and I meant it. Every word.

But I already pushed her too far once. And now she's the one paying for it.

Maybe we both are.

"Listen," Tag says, resting the bottle on his knee. "Don't screw it up now by doing something you'll hate yourself for tomorrow." He nods to where Annie is still laughing, face aglow under the bulb lights. "She's not just any girl. She's my sister. And if you break her heart, I'll break your fucking face."

When I look at him, I can tell he's dead serious.

But then a smile flickers on his mouth. "Cheers."

He clinks my empty champagne glass just before Kenna saunters over from the bathrooms.

"What did I miss? Why aren't we dancing?" She dips underneath the rope, tugging down her thigh-length dress. "Ooh. Champagne."

Tag stands, snagging her by the hand as she reaches for a flute. "Good point. Let's dance."

"Ew." She pulls her arm free. "I'd rather grind on the balding bartender."

He smirks. "He charges extra for emotional damage."

"That reminds me, you owe me for the batch of shirts that say 'Honey Moons Made Me Cry and I Paid for It.'"

Tag squints. "We approved that?"

Kenna sips her bubbly. "Technically, no. But the internet did."

"I swear, you're more trouble than the whole band combined."

A warm body appears on my right, pulling my attention away from the banter. Glittering purple stripes flutter in my periphery as Annie nudges my shoulder with hers.

"Kenna's right. We should dance," she says, a soft smile blooming. "You look miserable."

She looks fucking gorgeous.

I gaze at her, those twinkling blue eyes a shade darker against the night, full lips parting the longer we stare. Dancing with her is out of the question. I'm buzzed on liquor, my willpower dangling by a thread, my blood singing for her. She's already too close. One more inch and I'll haul her over my shoulder, carry her to my room, and strip her bare. She'll be underneath me before she can take her next breath.

"Not a good idea," I murmur.

Annie reaches for a glass of champagne, her eyes glazed over. She's tipsy too. I can tell by the giddy glow on her face.

"Come on. I hate seeing you look sad, especially after the way you played tonight. You deserve to let loose, have some fun." She flashes me her teeth.

I stare at her mouth, throat rolling. Expression strained.

Another shoulder nudge. "I smile, you smile. Remember?"

Sighing, I glance away, down at the shiny concrete beneath my boots.

Her smile fades. "Just one dance," she says. Swallowing the champagne in a few gulps, she springs to her feet, taking me by the hand. "I need an outlet for this adrenaline."

Dammit.

My legs carry me forward before my brain catches up, following her to a corner of the room where bodies already sway in a fog of perfume and pulsing bass.

Annie's arms lift above her head as she starts to move, her hips rolling in slow, lazy circles. She spins to face away from me, grabs my hands, and pulls them around her waist, fitting her body snug against my front.

I exhale sharply, my mouth dropping to the crown of her head, breathing her in. Flowers, watermelon, champagne, and something wild beneath it all.

My palms flatten across her stomach.

She laces our fingers together, lifting my arms overhead with hers, and it's a slow, torturous drag that sends a full-body shudder through me. I lower my face to the curve of her neck, brushing my nose along her damp skin. Without thinking, I nip lightly at her earlobe.

A breathy gasp slips from her lips. She arches into me, pressing her ass against the hard line of my body.

I groan under my breath, clenching my jaw as my hands slide down the length of her arms, then trace her waist, her hips.

Instinct and madness have me tugging her closer, grinding her back into me.

My dick hardens. My blood pounds hot and reckless.

My mind spins with dark thoughts. Every dirty, filthy thing I'd do to her. I imagine her thighs clamped around my face as I tongue-fuck her into oblivion, her breasts heaving beneath my hands, my mouth greedy and ravenous. A million sordid positions flash through my head. Taking her doggie-style, her riding me on the floor, in the shower, against the counter…

Jesus.

This needs to stop.

Untangling myself from her spell, I step away, rake a hand through my hair. When she faces me, there's a rosy flush on her cheeks, confusion in her eyes.

"I'm gonna grab a drink," I say.

"Chase…"

"It's just my head. Need something stronger than champagne."

It is my head. But it's also my heart. She's not ready, and I'm not in the right state of mind to say no when she stumbles into my bed tonight, looking for more than solace.

And yet…I think it's something else too.

Something beyond the ramifications of that stolen rain kiss.

It's fear.

Fear that I'm becoming someone else.

I feel my sanity slipping away with every migraine, with every sharp stab against my temple. Our first time should be sweet, drawn-out, a picturesque fairy tale. She deserves to be cherished.

I'll never forget those text messages she sent me. The way she talked about sex like it was a debt to pay, a duty to endure, something she needed to check out of when a relationship reached a certain point. That gutted me. She needs to know sex is about connection, not obligation.

But right now, the beast inside me is roaring. Hungry and animalistic.

So I need to step away. Put space between us before I do something I regret.

Annie reaches for my hand. "Chase, wait. Tell me what's wrong."

I pull back, the realization stealing my breath. "Sorry…I need to go."

"Chase—"

Spinning around, I charge toward the bar. Order a whiskey. Double. Neat.

I swallow it down, relishing the burn.

Annie ducks her head in my periphery, looking broken, before she trudges back over to the group. I just stand there, the taste of bourbon clinging to my tongue like ash. The music pulses in my skull, but it's muted compared to the pounding in my head.

Like something's clawing to get out.

I brace my palms against the bar, breathing deep, trying to find the version of myself I recognize.

It doesn't come.

Instead, a soft voice curls around me, seeping into the chaos.

"Hey."

I turn.

It takes a beat for recognition to wash over me.

Sunny yellow hair. Tiny frame. Chocolate-brown eyes.

One of the citrus twins.

"Jaclyn, right?"

"You remembered." She beams, sliding closer to the bar, her drink dangling from two fingers. "I didn't expect to find a famous rock star brooding at a rooftop bar. You just set the stage on fire. Thought you'd be basking in it."

I clear my throat and lift two fingers to the bartender, signaling another whiskey. "Keeping tabs on me?"

"Maybe." She flashes a wry smile, tracing the rim of her glass. "I came to your show at The Soundproof but couldn't find you after. Then I saw your video blow up. Impressive."

"Things happened fast. The last few months have been a blur."

"I bet. Congratulations." She twirls her straw through something neon and sweet. "And thanks for the bragging rights. I told all my friends I met you way back when."

I grunt a reply, distracted, as the bartender slides my drink toward me. "You been following the tour?"

"A little. Not in a stalker way, I swear." She holds up her hands, palms forward. "My friend lives in Oakland, so I made the trip out here with my girls. We were in the second row."

I hadn't noticed. "Hope you enjoyed."

"Are you kidding? It was revolutionary. I swear you fixed something in me I didn't even know was broken."

I force a smile, but it feels hollow.

My gaze drifts across the room, pulled like a tide. Annie is back with the group, curled against Kenna, her champagne glass cradled loosely between her fingers.

Her eyes lift, landing on me.

The smile she was barely wearing fades. Her gaze flicks to Jaclyn. Then darts back to me.

Sadness, sharp and devastating, flashes across her face before she tucks it away, turning to Kenna.

I swallow hard, my throat raw.

The part of me that's still good wants to go to her. Wants to rip the floor out from under my own goddamn feet just to get to her.

But another part—the one tightening my fists and drowning me in booze—wonders if she even wants me to.

Jaclyn doesn't miss the exchange. She tips her head, eyes glinting with quiet understanding. "Trouble in paradise?"

I down another sip and roll my shoulder.

I don't answer.

Because it's not paradise.

It's purgatory.

And I'm not sure how long I can stand in it without shattering into something ugly.

Jaclyn leans in, voice low and easy. "Hey, if you're taken, I get it. I won't go there. But if you're not…"

I turn my head toward her. The glass sweats in my hand.

She smiles, slow and inviting, her brown eyes twinkling with implication. "I'm here for two more nights. No strings. Just fun."

CHAPTER 42
Annalise

I can't sleep.

That's not a revelation, but it's more than insomnia, more than adrenaline.

My stomach swirls with anxiety, viscous and toxic.

One moment Chase was at the bar, talking to a blond. When I looked back up, he was gone.

They both were.

He wouldn't do that.

He said he'd wait.

And I was ready. Even during the show tonight, it's all I could think about.

Him.

Finally giving in to this draw, this need. But something about him has been off. His walls are sky-high, his demeanor borderline angry. Surely he could tell I was interested by the way I dragged him out to dance, writhed against him, all tangled limbs and needy breaths.

But he pulled away. Closed himself off from me.

Then he started talking to another woman as I watched from afar, my heart caving in.

I kick off the covers with a growl of frustration. My throat is thick and tight, my pulse pounding with dark tension. Chest heaving, I glance at the nightstand beside me. The cup of half-eaten cherries glows beneath the wall lamp. Beside it, his room key.

It calls to me. Tempting and dangerous.

Rational thought clicks off, and I bound from the bed, sliding into my slippers and grabbing the key. I'm terrified I'm going to walk into an empty room. Because then I'll know.

I'll know he's with her.

Tears bite at my eyes as I race from the room, inhibitions lost to the wind. There's a ringing in my ears, a heavy metal band pounding steel sticks against shrieking snares. His door looms closer. Confirmation hides behind it. Without thinking, I hold the key to the sensor and softly push my way inside. The room is dark. No lights are on.

Oh God...

My chest squeezes. I don't want to know.

I need to know.

I step forward, glancing around, waiting for my eyes to adjust.

Then I hear something. A low moan, coming from the bathroom.

No.

She's here.

Something twisted possesses my feet, carrying me forward. One step. Two steps. I'm prepared to discover sheaves of blond hair whipping around as Chase piledrives her against the bathroom sink. And still, I keep moving. Keep going.

My stomach is sick. My throat stings with bile.

I close my eyes, stopping just outside the open door.

Then, one by one, my eyes open.

I peer into the bathroom, and my breath locks up.

Everything freezes.

Chase is hunched forward, one hand planted against the bathroom wall while the other moves rapidly through the shadows.

I choke.

My gaze dips, landing on dark jeans pooled around his ankles. Boxers caught around his thighs.

I watch, paralyzed, as he strokes himself, every muscle corded and tight. His head tilts back, his Adam's apple bobbing in his throat as a groan slips out.

All the moisture leaves my mouth. Arousal stabs between my thighs.

I can't move, can't breathe, can't look away.

But something spills out of me: a gasp, a croak, a moan.

He stills.

His head flicks up, and our eyes meet through the darkness.

A sheen of sweat glints on his brow line, reflecting off the sliver of moonlight.

Heat scorches my cheeks. Lust and fear and embarrassment.

I should run. Back away. Apologize.

His hand slows but doesn't stop.

My traitorous eyes drift again, watching with confusion and hunger as he fists his cock, his gaze still locked on me. I shouldn't be here. I walked in on something private, personal.

And yet I'm rooted to the floor in my fuzzy bunny slippers.

Swallowing, I flick my gaze back up. Heat and want stare back at me. Darkness simmers in his eyes as he slowly pulls up from the wall and pivots to face me. This is my chance. My turning point. This is where I run, flee, practice my apologies spiels for when morning dawns.

But I don't do that.

I inch forward.

Chase hesitates, then steps out of his crumpled jeans. He pulls his boxers all the way down, stepping out of those too. He's completely bare before me, the scar on his leg slightly aglow, his massive length hanging heavy between his legs, fully hard.

I move another inch. Toward him. An invitation.

And he takes it.

In a flash, he's on me. I'm lifted off the ground, my legs winding around his waist. Our lips crash together. His tongue dives inside, frenzied and alive, teeth clacking against mine, mouths moving and desperate. Need rips through me in firelit waves. I clench my thighs around him, tugging his hair, scratching his neck. He lowers me to the bed, setting me down like I'm something he's dreamed of a thousand times. His mouth breaks from mine only long enough to whisper against my skin, "Been waiting for this. For you."

My breath shudders out as I peel away my tank top, but he slows me, helping me tug it over my head, his fingertips brushing lightly down my arms. Then he's kissing me again, deeper now, need pulsing between us.

When he pushes my shorts down, it's with care, intention. His lips trail lower, heat and attention in every press, until he's between my thighs.

The first sweep of his tongue rips a cry from my chest. My hips jerk, but he anchors me, palms cradling my hips, grounding me while his mouth works me slow, then faster, chasing the sound of my pleasure. He groans into me, the vibration sparking through my veins, his eyes flicking up, locking on mine like he wants me to know I'm the only thing he'll ever worship.

I soak his face with my need, his facial hair chafing my soft skin. He pulls me closer by the hips. Eats me out like a starved man.

I already feel it. Tingles climbing, euphoria blooming. He sucks my clit, sinks his tongue deeper. My body stiffens as I squeeze my breasts, spine bowing off the bed.

All my breath leaves me in a sharp gasp when the sensation hits.

Starlight blankets my vision, my body soaring, aglow, as waves of pleasure sweep through me in a violent, long-lasting shudder.

A high-pitched moan tears from my throat as my mouth hangs open, my ankles linked in a chokehold behind his upper back. Chase doesn't stop. Keeps licking and sucking, feasting on me until the feeling fades and I collapse to the mattress, sapped and stunned.

I don't have time to recover.

He army-crawls over me, hands tangling in my hair. His tongue plunges into my mouth, and I taste myself, the musky, wet desire.

"Fuck, Annie," he rasps, dragging his tongue down my jaw, nipping at my neck. "You're so beautiful when you come."

His hand trails south, two fingers driving back into me, thrusting hard, the slippery sounds of my release filling the air.

I wrap my arms around his neck, still vibrating, tingling head to toe. "Chase…" His pulsing erection digs into my abdomen, spurring another moan. "What were you thinking about?"

The question falls out, impulsive.

He moves lower down my body, finding my breasts. Pushing them together with his hands, he flicks his tongue over each nipple, sucking, devouring. "This. You. Only ever you."

Arousal soars back, drenching me. I hold his face to my chest, writhing beneath him as he draws new swells of pleasure out of me.

He leans back on his knees, eyes storm-dark, chest rising and falling like he's fighting himself. But I don't wait for him to guide me.

My palms slide down his thighs as I shift to a crouch in front of him. His cock hovers near my lips, thick and hard, veins roping beneath flushed skin. His eyelids flutter as his hand wraps around himself, precum slicking his fist. A low moan escapes him, ragged and raw.

"My turn," I coax, curling my fingers over his wrist until he lets go. His eyes flare as I replace his hand with mine. Then my mouth is on him, taking him in deep.

"Christ—" The word clips off, replaced by a tapered moan. He buries his hands in my hair, watching as my mouth glides over him, pulling him deep, sucking and licking. "Holy fuck," he pants out, tightening his hold on my hair. He watches for a minute with hooded eyes before his head tips backward. He guides me in and out, hands palming the back of my head, his parted legs trembling. "Jesus…not gonna last."

My thighs clench in response.

I want him to let go, to spill down my throat. There's power in knowing he's already so close and I'm seconds away from bringing him to ecstasy with only my mouth.

I hum around him, swirling my tongue, tasting his salt.

He dives deeper, hitting the back of my throat. I gag, my eyes watering, but I don't stop. My fingers curl, nails digging. Tears breach the corners of my eyes. Chase watches, dark lust creased across his face. He brushes his thumb across my cheekbone, streaking away a tear.

"That's it." His voice shakes, control slipping away. "That's my girl."

His hand drags through my hair, gripping hard at the crown of my head. He slopes forward, his opposite hand latching onto the headboard for support. I suck him harder, my hand stroking his base as tears stream down my hollowed-out cheeks.

I feel him stiffen, tense. And then his face contorts with pleasure, grip tightening, head craning back as his mouth parts with a feral moan. Ribbons of liquid heat splash across my tongue, hitting the back of my throat. I swallow him down with a needy whimper, drain him dry.

He comes down slow, panting and breathless. His hold on me loosens as he skims shaky fingers through my hair and slides out of my mouth, muscles unlocking and body sagging forward. I fall with him, curling into his side. Skin slick and breathing jagged, I press closer, wrapping my limbs around him.

"Chase," I whisper.

My words stop and end with his name. I don't know what to say, where to go from here.

I lean in and kiss him.

His lips part slowly, tongue coasting over mine with soft, languid strokes.

Then he pulls back with a sharp breath. "That was—"

"Everything," I say, cutting him off. "It was everything." Another kiss, another flick of my tongue against his bottom lip. "I want more."

I want hours, days, months. An infinity of him. My body still sings, begging for it—him inside me, moving, burning, taking all of me.

That was just a taste. A glimpse of everything I crave.

My leg twines between his, my fingers tracing the planes of his chest.

"Do you have a condom?" My index finger draws down his abdomen, trailing the dark, coarse hair.

Swallowing, Chase tucks a piece of my hair behind my ear. "We should wait. I'm, uh…still a little drunk."

My finger stops moving. I blink, studying his face, the glaze of his eyes, the dark shadows. "Oh."

"I should've slowed down. I wanted that to be…" His voice fades out.

"It was."

His eyes close, lashes fluttering, arm lifting to pull me closer. "I haven't felt like myself lately."

My heart clenches. I raise a hand, two fingers brushing his bangs aside then pressing gently to his forehead. "Your head?"

A nod.

"You should see a doctor, Chase."

"I did. Before the first tour," he says. "He told me to wear earplugs and gave me some prescriptions."

A gnawing worry ripples through me, overshadowing the lingering desire. "It hasn't helped?"

"No. Not really. I feel…" Hesitating, he holds me tighter. "Different."

Tears puddle in my eyes.

I think over the past few weeks, the distance between us, the withdrawal. I thought it was me. My ghosts, my guilt, my self-blame. But he's pulled back too. I see it now. I feel it.

He's afraid.

"I'm here, Chase." I press a soft kiss to his lips, pulling his forehead to mine and meeting his eyes through the darkened room. "I'm here."

He doesn't say anything. Doesn't reply.

And part of me wonders…

Maybe that's exactly what he's afraid of.

CHAPTER 43
Annalise

A new day, a new city.

The San Diego sunset douses me in warmth, pouring in through the floor-to-ceiling window of Kenna's hotel room in a spectrum of golds and pinks. My friend is behind me, primping in the full-length mirror, a hair straightener in hand.

She hums one of our songs under her breath, off-key and glorious. "Damn, that's catchy. Wish I could sing it as well as you can."

I stare out the window for another beat, soaking up the colors. Then I turn to her with a smile. "Thank you. For everything."

Grinning, Kenna twists the straightener as a plume of steam fogs the air. "Pretty sure that's my line."

"I just…I can't begin to tell you how grateful I am that you're here."

She flicks off the tool and meets my stare. "I'll always be here. No matter what. Whether you're so rich and famous you're draped across a gold-studded throne with hot, naked men feeding you grapes, or you're living the hermit life, paycheck to paycheck, back to scribbling lyrics on greasy napkins. I'm not going anywhere."

"I know. It goes both ways." I set my phone on a side table. "How are you holding up, by the way? It's been so chaotic lately, so zero to one hundred. I don't want you to get lost in the mix."

"Please." She scoffs, unplugging the straightener and snatching a lip gloss from her makeup bag. "You never have to worry about me. I'm living my best life."

"I know it can get loud. All this noise. If you ever need to stop and take a breath, let me know. We can light some candles and just breathe."

"I appreciate that. But I'm good. Literally the happiest I've ever been."

"Are you keeping in touch with Tyler?"

She puckers her lips, popping the cap back on. "Definitely not."

"I thought it was serious."

"It was. For like a month."

Chuckling, I take a seat at the edge of the bed. "I think my brother likes you."

Her face morphs into disgust. "Gross."

"Why is that gross?"

"I've known Tag since he was a prepubescent middle schooler. God. I can't shake the memories of him running around in cargo shorts, chugging chocolate milk straight out of the gallon, and trying to burp the alphabet."

I laugh, shaking my head. "Still pretty on-brand."

"Yup. I have too much blackmail material." She shudders, then hesitates as she twists to face me. "How are things with Chase?"

My hands curl into the bedcovers. I shove my tongue against my cheek, face heating.

Her eyes flare. "Wow. It finally happened, huh?"

"I mean…something happened."

"Something naked?"

"Yeah."

"Shit," she says, interest piqued. Kenna approaches, takes a seat beside me on the bed. "And?"

Memories wash over me.

The need, the sweat, the moans, the urgency.

The way he hardly looked at me the next morning as we packed our things and hit the road.

It's been almost forty-eight hours since our mouths were all over each other, and it's like it never even happened.

Swallowing, I peer down at the floor. "I don't know. He kind of shut down."

"Fucking men. Seriously." She huffs, standing to grab her vape pen and returning to the bed. She takes a drag and puffs out a thick cloud. "I mean, he has been acting weird lately. Like a fuse ready to blow."

"It's strange," I murmur, brow creasing. "I can tell he's into me. He cares. A lot. But I think he's scared. Like he's going to hurt me somehow. Ruin this before it even gets off the ground."

Kenna sighs, dropping the vape to her lap. "It's complicated, mixing romance and business. Especially in this capacity. You've both been thrown into the spotlight, practically overnight, and you were already walking this thin line. It's easy for things to fall apart."

"I don't want it to. I feel like I'm finally ready to go all in, while he's moving further away."

"Is he still hung up on Alex?" she wonders.

I fold in my lips. "Maybe. But I think it's more than that. He's been getting these headaches…says he feels different. I'm worried."

Empathy splashes across her face. "Migraines are no joke. My mom would get them, and they would incapacitate her for days. Unfortunately, my father didn't have a sympathetic bone in his body and was convinced she was faking it to get out of having sex with him. Probably why she started banging the furnace guy." A huff of disdain. "No wonder I have commitment issues."

I reach over and link our hands together, her golden-tan skin contrasting my porcelain. "I think you turned out all right."

"I have a boatload of childhood trauma, anxiety masked as sarcasm, and a deep distrust of utility workers. But yeah. I guess I'm pretty great."

My temple dips to hers with a smirk, and we sit like that for a while, silent, hands clasped. Then I breathe out a sigh and sit up. "We should probably find the guys and head to the venue."

She pops off the bed. "Ready when you are. Here, take my spare key." She tosses me a keycard. "My room is loaded with merch that I don't want to haul back home. Slap on that salesgirl smile and help me get rid of it."

"On it." I tuck the card into the back pocket of my faux-leather pants, then take a minute to fluff my hair in the mirror and rearrange my sheer, long-sleeved top that's slipped over a lacy camisole. My lips are a bold shade of plum, my hair lightly curled and set, and my eyelashes are a mile long thanks to Kenna's magical mascara.

A smile stretches.

I look good.

Five minutes later, all four guys have been texted, and we're gathering in the lobby, waiting for a limo to take us over to the performance venue.

Chase strolls over to the group wearing black ripped jeans slung low on his hips, a threadbare band tee clinging to his frame, and a leather jacket that looks like it's survived more mosh pits than he has. His silver ring flashes on his thumb as he adjusts the guitar case over his back.

His hand rakes through waves of shaggy brown hair, tousled just enough to look accidental.

He looks like trouble.

The good kind.

The kind you write songs about and never fully recover from.

Stormy hazel eyes flick my way as he saunters over to the group, a pair of scuffed boots thudding against the marble floor with every step. Our gazes hold for several seconds before he gives me a long, drawn-out once-over.

His throat bobs. "You look…"

"Sweaty," I quip, eager to lighten the mood. "I'm already sweating and we haven't even hit the stage."

"I had a different word in mind." His eyes blaze, paralleling the setting sun. "You doing okay?"

I blink. "Why wouldn't I be?"

"We haven't really talked since…" His voice trails off. He rubs his chin.

My stomach pitches with arousal-steeped memories.

Biting my lip, I take a slow step forward, until we're merely a foot apart. "And you haven't really smiled since…" My leg extends, and I grip my ankle with one hand, pulling it vertical, mimicking the charade from his hotel room a few days ago.

Unfortunately, it barely reaches a one-eighty-degree angle, and I teeter sideways, doing a one-footed hop.

Damn leather pants.

At least it gets a smile out of him.

Chase takes me by the shoulders, keeping me steady. His hands are soft, gentle, trailing down my arms as he exhales a deep breath. "I'm feeling a little better."

"Really?" Relief sweeps through me, brightening my smile. "Your headaches?"

He nods.

"Chase…that's great. That's amazing." I inch closer, blanketing myself in his warmth. My heart rate kicks up from our proximity. He smells like sandalwood and sin. Letting out a shaky breath, I press a hand to his chest. "Maybe after the show…we can talk?"

He swallows. "Yeah."

"Limo's here," Tag interrupts.

Rock whistles loudly. "Let's fuckin' go!"

Kenna calls my name while Zach jogs over from the bar, his bass in hand. We all pile into the limo, spirits high and adrenaline soaring. I squish in between Chase and Kenna, while Tag slides in beside my friend.

He hauls an arm around her. "Tonight's the night, baby."

"Oh my God, you're right. Tonight's the night you get stabbed in the face for calling me *baby*." She scoots closer to me, untangling herself from his arm. "Jeez, Tag. A little awareness goes a long way."

My brother is unfazed. "Oh, I'm aware. I'm aware you're secretly obsessed with me, and it's ruining your life."

She hums with disinterest. "I cry into my pillow every night thinking about your man bun."

Tag grins, kicking his boots up onto the opposite seat. "Healthy coping mechanisms, Kenna. Proud of you."

Chase chuckles low beside me, his hand cupping my knee as the limo lurches forward into the sunset. His lips brush my ear when he leans in. "You smell so fucking good."

Tingly heat bursts through me as I press closer to him. "Must be the sweat."

"Must be." His hand drifts up my leg, squeezing my thigh. "I just want to talk tonight…if that's okay. Take things slow. There's a lot I need to say."

I look at him, the city streaking through the window in a stream of headlights and marquees. "Yeah," I whisper. "Me too."

As much as I want to strip him out of his clothes and ride him until dawn, he's right. We should talk. Reconnect. Do this the right way.

Rock lights up a joint, the smell of marijuana wafting through the limousine. "Here's to Honey Moons, motherfuckers. Taking over the world, one shred at a time." He passes it to Zach.

Taking a long drag, Zach blows smoke through his nose. Then he leans back into the seat, the streetlights flashing across his face as he exhales slow and steady. He looks around at all of us. Really looks.

"We're never gonna get this night back," he says, smile crooked. "It's not about the first sellout, or the first time the crowd screamed so loud it drowned out everything else. It's not about whatever happens next—the interviews, the fame, the money, the bullshit—it's just this. Remember it. This night. Right here, right now."

The limo hums with silence for a moment, heavier than before.

Then Tag knocks his beer against Zach's boot with a grin. "Cheers to that, philosopher bass boy."

We all laugh. Too loud, too hard. Because we're terrified and exhilarated and moments away from walking into another show that will catapult us forward.

The joint passes around the limo. Chase takes a drag, painting the space between us with smoky tendrils that look like silver ghosts.

When it's my turn, I choke. Cough until my lungs cave in. Everyone laughs again as Kenna steals it away and tips her head back with a contented sigh.

My brother reaches behind her. Squeezes my shoulder.

We share a look. A teary-eyed smile.

"I love you," I mouth to him.

He ruffles my hair in reply, causing me to squeal in frustration, because that shit took an hour of mirror time to style. I shoo his hand away as the conversation drones on and we relive the long nights in a beat-up van that morphed into high-class hotels, thousands of adoring fans, and music that resonates. That means something.

It's only a ten-minute ride to the venue, but it feels like a lifetime.

It's perfect.

Magic.

Family.

It's a moment I'll remember forever.

CHAPTER 44
Chase

I'm so fucking high.

On the music, the lights, the fans, the strings beneath my fingers. I told Annie I was feeling better. It was a lie. But fuck if I'm going to ruin this just because there's a semi plowing through my brain, day in and day out.

I push it aside. Drown it out with riffs that set the room on fire, raw and desperate and bigger than the pain. The crowd surges with every note, a living, breathing thing that feeds off the energy we're bleeding out under the lights.

I'm a ghost in the static, a fire in the rain
Echoes in the dark still whisper out your name

Rock hammers the drums so hard the floor vibrates. Zach's

bass thrums deep in my chest. Tag's guitar cuts through the air, sharp and clean.

And Annie…

Her voice rises like smoke and silver, spinning through the room, threading through the chaos, anchoring me to the stage when everything else tilts.

I stalk the edge of the platform, dragging the mic stand with me, grinning down at the sea of faces. They reach for us like we're gods. Like we're salvation.

I'm soaked in sweat, half delirious, veins pounding with sound.

And for ninety glorious minutes, nothing hurts.

Not my head.

Not my heart.

Not the fucking war raging inside me.

It's just the music.

After we say good night to the swarms of people and make our way offstage, my phone buzzes in my back pocket. I pull it out, wiping sweat off my forehead.

Carter Vale's name flashes across the screen.

Our agent.

I thumb the green button. "Carter. What's up?"

"Chase." His voice is crackling with excitement, not the usual cool, controlled tone he uses when he's managing five things at once. "You sitting down?"

I glance around backstage at the peeling leather couches, half-downed beers, and haze of sweat and smoke hanging in the air. "Not exactly. We just finished the San Diego set."

"Well, you should probably sit," he says. "That guitar you've been using for 'Night Song.' The custom. The plasma ball one that lights up the entire goddamn stage."

"Yeah?" I wipe my sweaty palm on my jeans.

"There's a company based out of Nashville. Huge. They make high-end custom guitars for collectors, rock legends, hell, even museum installations. They were at the San Fran show two nights ago."

I blink, my eyes catching with Annie's across the room. "Okay…?"

"They want it." There's a sharp laugh in his voice, like even he can't believe it. "Not just a one-off either. They want to buy the rights to the design. Reproduce it. Limited run, special line, your name attached."

The room slants for a second. I hear the guys laughing in the corner, cracking beers, unwinding. But for me, everything zeros in on this moment.

"Jesus," I manage to croak out. "How much are we talking?"

Carter chuckles, low and thrilled. "They're starting the conversation at half a million. But I think I can negotiate."

My hand tightens around the phone.

Half a million.

For a guitar I designed in my dark, shitty living room, half done and desperate, with my dog at my feet. For something I built out of insomnia and heartbreak and whatever stubborn pieces of me that refused to quit.

"Are you serious?" I rasp.

"Dead serious. I'm working on that number, but I'll send over the details tonight. Check your email in a few hours."

"Yeah. Okay. Yeah." I'm in a daze, still blinking through the weight of it. "Thanks."

"Congratulations, Chase. Hope you're ready."

I hang up, staring at the phone like he might call right back and tell me it was just a joke.

Holy shit.

My temples pound, my heart galloping between my ribs.

Annie watches me from the other side of the room, a towel draped over her shoulders, her lips parted like she's about to ask if I'm okay.

I clear my throat, clinging to whatever breath I can conjure. "Hey…guys."

Conversation falls away, and everyone turns to look at me.

"That was Carter." Hesitating, I squeeze my eyes shut for half a beat to keep the room from spinning in and out of focus. "My guitar. A company wants it."

Annie steps forward, setting down her bottled water. "What do you mean?"

"I mean they want to buy the design. Manufacture it. Sell it."

Tag pushes off the wall, eyebrows lifting. "For real?"

I nod, still feeling like I'm dreaming. "Yeah. Carter said…half a million to start."

For a second, no one moves. No one breathes. Four pairs of wide eyes stare in my direction, all of them blurring. I swallow hard. Wait for the phone to ring, for Carter to laugh and say, "Gotcha." No one believes me. I don't believe me.

But then Annie lets out a shriek that cuts through the silence like a blade.

Kenna does the same.

Tag, Zach, and Rock leap off the ground, whooping and hollering at the top of their lungs as beer sloshes from spouts and fists punch the air and lights streak across my vision.

I don't even see her coming.

A black leather blur flies at me, arms and legs winding around my body as tears drench my neck and hair whips around me in a vibrant curtain. I teeter backward before catching my balance, spinning Annie in a circle, and pressing her up against the wall.

She grips my face, teeth glowing white, lipstick smeared. "Oh my God. Oh my *God*."

"Holy fuck. This isn't real. It can't be real."

"It's real, Chase. It's so real."

My forehead falls to hers.

I cling to her. Hold her.

And this time, I kiss her.

I crash my mouth to hers. Hot, wet, voracious. My hand plants against the wall, the other holding her up by the thigh. Our tongues twist, aching, starving, and I don't care who's watching, don't care about my head, or the show, or even the goddamn guitar.

My blood is singing. The beast is howling.

I need her. Have to have her.

I don't want to talk.

I pull away, drawing in a breath, watching as her lashes flutter with want. Then I drop her to the floor and take her by the hand, dragging her away. "Come on."

The guys call out to me. Want details. Want to know everything.

I hardly hear them.

The only thing pounding louder than my head is the sound of my boots scuffing the concrete as I haul her through the back hallway.

Past the green room.

Past the vending machines and flickering fluorescent lights.

I find a door marked "Storage" and yank it open. It's nothing but a dark, narrow closet stacked with amps and road cases, reeking of dust and rubber.

I shove us inside and kick the door shut, flipping the lock with a click.

Before she can say a word, my mouth finds hers again, rougher this time. Annie gasps into the kiss, grabbing at my shirt, fisting the fabric like she's afraid I'll disappear.

I lift her, not gently, not slowly, planting her on top of an empty amp case. Her legs part instinctively, wrapping around my hips, yanking me closer.

She tastes like citrus beer and salt, and when I grind against her, she moans into my mouth, the sound ripping the last shred of restraint out of me.

This isn't careful.

This isn't sweet.

This is everything we've been fighting for and against, slamming together at full force in a forgotten corner of a building we just conquered.

And God help me—

I never want it to end.

A string hits me in the side of the face, and I reach for it, tugging hard. The single bulb brightens, illuminating the space in a dull yellow light. I need to see her. Every inch of her.

Annie's cheeks are flushed pink, her eyes glazed over. "Chase—"

I dive back in. Tug her head back by the hair, tearing down the side of her throat with lips and teeth. She mewls. Moans. My fingers shake, working the buttons of her pants, yanking down the zipper as she shimmies out of them, trying to kick them free. I rip off a heel and pull the fabric off until her legs part wide, the leather hanging by an ankle.

A slip of lacy black underwear comes into view.

I tug it aside and launch forward, plunging my tongue inside her, longing to taste her again. She collapses back on her elbows with a gasp-like scream, squeezing my hair by the roots. I link her legs around my neck, driving deeper, letting her soak my face as my dick throbs against tight denim, hard and painful.

"Chase, Chase, Chase…" She pants my name like her favorite song. "Oh God…"

I suck her clit. Swirl my tongue. Growl and groan, clasping her hips in a death grip as I eat her out like a savage.

"Need you inside me," she pleads.

My eyes roll up, imagining sinking inside her velvet heat. A groan leaves me, and I pull to a stand, roughly unlatching my belt. Annie's fingers tremble as she bends forward, undoing the button, sliding the zipper down.

Before my jeans tumble to my feet, I reach into my back pocket and pull out a condom.

Her breath hitches when she spots it.

We're doing this.

Hard, dirty, fast. In a fucking storage closet.

I wait for her to stop me. To tap the brakes, ask for something better. A bed. A hotel room. Even the goddamn tour bus. But she doesn't. Heat flickers in her eyes as she drags my jeans down my legs, yanks off my boxers, and takes my dick in her hand.

My jaw falls open on a pornographic moan.

I'm pulsing in her hand, hard as steel, a thrust away from blowing my load. The last time her mouth was on me, I hardly lasted two minutes, so fucking pent up it took all my willpower just to make it that long.

I bring the condom wrapper to my mouth and tear it open with my teeth. Annie kicks off her other heel, pulls her pants all the way off, then removes her underwear and tosses it to the floor. She leans back and props her feet up on the amp, spreading her knees apart.

Her pussy glistens under the low light.

My vision blurs. Mind spins out of control.

Fuck.

I propel forward, the tip of my dick sliding up her inner thigh and teasing her wetness. She chews her lip, head tipped back and hair spilling all around her. My hand raises, curling behind her head, tangling in the damp strands, and dragging her face to mine. Our noses touch. Foreheads meet. I grind against her, growling against her lips, "You want this?"

She wraps her arms around me. "Yes. Please."

I grip her by the waist and yank her forward. Slip inside an inch. Then another. Our eyes are locked. I watch her face, the way her lips quiver, pupils dilate, brows bend inward as she waits for me to fill her.

I don't make her wait long.

With a hard jerk of my hips, I thrust inside all the way. Her moan rockets through me, blending with mine. My forehead rolls against hers as I glance down between us, watching as her tightness swallows my cock, my face pinched with euphoric agony. She clings to me, my shirt, my neck, my hair, my face. Her hands are everywhere, her body adjusting to my size, her breaths falling out in gasping, shallow bursts.

I pull out, then drive back in. Harder.

Again. Faster.

Fuck.

Fuck.

My fingers twist in her hair, fist locking, as I rail into her, over and over. The amp thunks against the wall. I drag my hand down her body and up her camisole, palming her breast, my other hand squeezing her thigh, holding her to me. She grabs me by the face, crashes our mouths together. Our kisses are clumsy, wet, dancing to a rhythm we can't keep up with.

I fill her mouth with my tongue, angling as deeply as I can go, while my hips jerk back and forth, in and out, gaining momentum with every hard thrust.

She bites down on my tongue, reaches behind me to grab my ass, nails carving into bare skin as my muscles clench in response.

"Chase…"

"Fuck, Annie." I gather her closer, breaking the kiss to bury my face in the curve of her neck. My hands grip her by the ass, lifting her off the amp as I pick up the pace, graceless, inelegant, fueled by lust and affection and pain and…

"Fuck, I love you."

The confession pours out of me.

She stiffens. Clings tighter, arms flying around my neck as she lets out a cracked moan.

My face is pressed against her neck, mouth trailing kisses across her skin. "I love you so fucking much."

She grinds against me, legs curling around my waist like a vise.

I lower her back to the amp. Bend forward, my hands planted on the surface, arms caging her in. I find her eyes. Her wet, wide eyes.

My hips pump faster. More, more, more. She's soaking me. The amp keeps thumping against the wall, the slippery sound of her desire bringing me to the edge.

Her head falls back. Mouth opens wide.

As her face contorts with pleasure and her splintered moan rattles my bones, I let myself go. I come hard, sinking my face to the arc of her neck, biting her shoulder as my release takes flight.

For a blissful moment, the pain is gone, overpowered by the orgasm ripping through me in volatile, lightning-kissed waves.

Hot streams pulse through my dick, filling the condom as I jerk and shudder, wrapping her in my arms and squeezing her tight.

We come down slow.

Heady, ragged breaths. Slick skin. Damp hair. The string from the lightbulb flicks against my cheek, pulling me back to reality. Lifting up, I stroke a hand through Annie's hair, then trail it down her face until I'm holding her jaw in a tender grip. "Hey."

She swallows hard, blinks toward me. Her hand lifts, fingers trembling as she touches my chest, right over my heart. "Did you mean it?" she whispers.

The air between us hums. The sting of bleach and dust. The ache of everything we just did, hanging like a noose around my neck.

I go still.

Because I did mean it.

Every wrecked, blurted word.

But not like this.

I just confessed my love while fucking her on an amp in a dirty storage closet.

Christ.

Exhaling sharply, I back away and remove the condom, tossing it into a tiny plastic garbage bin.

I glance back at her, guilt journeying through me.

She deserves a real love story. Fireworks, roses, popping champagne.

Not that.

"Annie…" My voice scrapes raw.

Her gaze searches mine as she presses her legs together, vulnerable and waiting, and something in me fractures all over again.

"I…" I trail off, shaking my head.

Stepping forward, I reach out, my hand curling behind her neck, tightening at the nape.

I open my mouth—

But nothing good comes out.

I drop my gaze, let out a rough breath, and say, "We should get back."

Her body stiffens immediately.

I feel it. The way she peels herself away from me, slowly, like touching me burns.

"Right," she breathes out, voice pinched and pained.

By the time I gather my jeans and hook them around my hips, she's already pulling on her pants in frantic, jerky movements. Straightening her blouse. Taming her hair.

Stalking toward the door.

I move to follow. "Annie, wait."

"It's fine," she says, hardly holding it together. "I'm fine."

"I didn't mean—"

She yanks the door open without looking at me.

And then she's gone, disappearing into bright hallway lights.

I sag in place. My face falls into my hands as I collapse against the amp, and the headache rushes back, louder than ever.

Shit.

I fucked up.

Again.

But that's not how I wanted it. Not how it should have happened.

I lost control.

The notion eats through me like rust.

Cupping my jaw, I stare at the string dangling from the lone bulb above, the room vibrating with her absence, her scent still clinging to every inch of me.

With a snarl, I yank the cord.

Darkness swallows me whole.

I guess that's the thing about love stories.

The best ones hurt.

CHAPTER 45
Annalise

Hours later, I'm pacing my hotel room, a throb between my legs, an ache between my ribs. It's almost midnight. Everyone shot straight to the bar when we got back, except for me and Chase. He tried to pull me aside to talk, to explain, his eyes wrecked and bloodshot, tone desperate.

But I ran.

Told him I was too tired to talk tonight.

I drag my hands through my hair, still wearing my performance clothes. His scent clings to the leather and lace, and I'm not ready to let that go yet.

"I love you so fucking much."

I can't unhear those words. Can't erase the rawness in his voice as the confession spilled out mid-thrust and he clutched me so hard I couldn't tell if he was breaking me apart or fusing me back together. Either way, I'm changed. Reshaped in every way.

And then he shut down again. Rejected my yearning for confirmation, my need to know if those words were real or just a side effect of lust and adrenaline.

I need Kenna.

She'll know what to say, how to navigate this pinwheel of broken thoughts.

Only problem is I left my phone in her room before the show.

I blow out a breath.

My eyes swing to the three keycards tossed onto the nightstand, all identified by a single letter drawn in Sharpie.

The *C* card calls to me, glowing and alive.

Courage. Clarification. Comfort.

Catastrophe.

Launching forward, I grab the one with a *K*.

Kenna's room is two floors below mine, and the elevator ride is long and torturous. I chew on my thumbnail. Tap my foot. Stare at the glowing numbers until the one I'm looking for lights up and the doors pull apart.

My heart dashes along with my feet as I prepare myself for a night of ugly crying over the cheap Moscato we picked up at a local convenience store this afternoon.

Her door approaches, and I lift the card, hovering it over the sensor until I hear the click.

I rush inside. "Ken—"

Then I freeze. Slap a hand over my mouth.

My eyes bulge out of my head.

There, on the bed, is my best friend riding my brother like a female buckaroo at her last rodeo as she bounces so hard I'm half expecting a judge to pop out and hold up a scorecard.

The headboard smacks the wall.

Tag moans, latching onto her hips.

My brain turns to goo. My eyes melt out of their sockets.

This was the absolute worst day to have twenty-twenty vision.

As I'm backing away, I stumble over a pair of jeans and topple against a piece of furniture. Kenna stops moving, whips her head around. Tag launches into a sitting position.

I blanch.

She scrambles.

He throws something at me and shouts, "Annalise! Get the fuck out!"

I glance down as the item lands on my shoulder.

A pair of boxers.

Not helpful. Not at all.

"S-sorry!" I stammer, flicking Tag's boxers away like they're a biohazard.

"Don't you knock?" Tag blares. "Goddamn!"

No. I don't knock. This is the second time I've forgotten how to knock and walked into a porno. My cheeks are on fire as I continue backing away while mentally dialing my therapist. That's when I remember—I left my phone in here.

Shit.

"One…one sec!" I hightail it over to the opposite side of the room.

"What the hell? Jesus, just go!" Tag howls, yanking the covers up over his body while Kenna is nothing but a blanket-born lump molded into the bedspread.

"Need my phone!" Holding a hand to the side of my face to block the evidence, I snatch my phone off the table, then sprint back toward the exit, tripping twice.

Tag's curse sees me out the door as I slam it shut behind me. Finally. Freedom.

I'm in a horror-drenched daze as I zombie back to my room, hardly remembering the elevator ride up. That was unexpected. Tag and Kenna. Kenna and Tag.

She was completely disgusted by the idea just a few hours ago. Now she's—

I halt in place when I spot a familiar figure sitting in front of my room, his back against the door. Chase looks up as I stall a few feet away, my air escaping in a stunned breath.

Swallowing, I pin my lip between my teeth, taking in his sagged shoulders, chalky face, and mess of hair in full disarray.

The last few minutes dissipate, different memories replacing the psychiatry-inducing comedy sketch I just walked out of.

"Chase," I whisper.

Slowly, defeatedly, he stands. "Hey."

"What are you doing here?"

One shoulder pops up. "It's midnight."

My throat stings. I step closer, lessening the gap between us, reliving the storage closet moment on repeat with every inch toward him. "We don't have to talk tonight. I know things are kind of…raw."

His hands twitch at his sides like he's desperate to reach for me. "That's why we need to talk. I can't wake up tomorrow morning without you beside me. Not after that."

"I just—"

"Please," he says.

My walls dissolve, so easily, so effortless. All it takes is a look in his eyes or a crack in his voice to strip me bare, and my self-preservation falls by the wayside. I nod. "Yeah. Okay," I breathe out. "Come in."

We shuffle into my room, the door clicking shut behind us. Not a second later, I'm in his arms. Smashed against his chest, his hands in my hair, his body warm and hard and safe.

"I'm sorry." He kisses the top of my head, lips lingering as he inhales my scent. "So sorry."

Cautiously, I wrap my arms around his middle and press my cheek to his swiftly beating heart. "You don't need to apologize."

"I do. You deserved more. Better than that," he says, his breath tickling my baby hairs. "We deserved better."

I shake my head against him. "I don't need shooting stars and serenades, Chase. I just need you. You taught me not to shut down when things get messy…now I need you to do the same." I lift my head and stare up at him through glazed eyes. "I don't care if our first time was on a dirty amp or a bed of roses. That doesn't matter. What matters is what comes after. Every moment that follows."

He wavers, his face in creases. Then he untangles himself from my arms. "I just…I don't want to be like him."

I frown. "What do you mean?"

"Alex," he says, gritting out the name. "I can't be like him. If I hurt you, it's over. I'm done. I'll never fucking forgive myself."

My pulse revs, unease coursing through my veins. "Why would you think that?"

"Because something's fucking wrong." He jabs a finger to his temple. "With me. With my goddamn head. I'm losing control. I don't recognize myself anymore. There's this *thing* inside of me, like a fucking parasite. It's loud. It's dangerous. It's breaking me the fuck apart."

I gape at him, wide-eyed, my heart fracturing. "Chase, no…" Reaching for him, I take his hand, linking our fingers together. "They're just migraines. The music, the noise—it's making it worse. But you're okay. You are. When we get home, you can see your doctor again, get stronger meds. You can—"

"I meant every word I said." He stares down at the floor, jaw tight, his palm squeezing mine. "I meant it, Annie. I love you. I shouldn't have said it like that, in the heat of the moment, but God help me, I've never meant anything more."

A gasp falls out of me.

Tendrils of beautiful disbelief.

My eyes water as I take a step toward him. I wait for him to look at me before whispering, "I love you too."

His eyes shimmer with incredulity.

God, his eyes—the true source of his power. And it's not in the glints of gold or the unique amber swirl. It's deeper. He looks at me in a way that makes it so easy to fall in love.

I was helpless the moment our gazes locked in that rearview mirror.

"I love you," I repeat, breathless, soaked in relief like a weight's been lifted. I take his hand again. "You've always seen me, from day one. When no one else listened, you heard me. When I doubted myself, you fought for me. You carried my dreams when they were too heavy for me to hold. You were there, even when

I gave my heart to someone else. You stayed. And you believed in me anyway."

His breath shudders. His fingers tighten around mine like he's afraid if he lets go, the moment will evaporate.

Tears spill down my cheeks as I press closer. "You were my safe place before I even realized I needed one. You always have been." I take his face between my hands, lower his forehead to mine. "That's the man you are. Don't question that. Don't ever doubt that."

Exhaling a long breath, his lashes flutter, his arms circling around me. "I'm a fucking mess," he rasps, burying his face in the curve of my neck. "But I love you. It's the only thing I'm sure of."

His mouth brushes my throat, a trembling exhale skating over my skin.

He hugs me tight.

Careful. Adoring.

No frantic hands, no desperate grabbing. Just him, holding me like I'm something breakable.

I braid my fingers through his hair and tilt my head back, inviting him closer. A soft sound escapes when his lips find mine, a slow, aching pull that makes my knees buckle.

He lifts me up and carries me to the bed, crawling over me, his body a shield.

This time, it's not about lust.

It's about everything we can still have and everything we're scared to lose.

His mouth drags up my neck, open and hungry, but his hands stay clenched at my waist like he's fighting himself. Holding back with barely-there restraint.

I slide my hands up his chest, feeling the hammering pulse beneath his wall of muscle, and pull him down to me.

A broken sound of surrender rumbles out of him as his mouth crashes into mine.

His body presses me into the mattress, solid and sure, his touch fierce but aching. His fingers sink into my hair, pushing it back, memorizing every thread.

I tug at his shirt, yanking it over his head, his muscles tight like a bowstring about to snap. My clothes follow, fabric tossed beside the bed in a cloud of black.

Gasping against his lips, I scrape my nails down his bare back, spurring him on. His hips grind between my legs, all that tension coiled tight and spilling over. Yet even in the urgency, there's something devastatingly careful in the way he handles me, like he's terrified of breaking the one thing he's desperate to keep.

When he rolls on a condom and pushes inside me, it's with a ragged groan against my lips, his hands framing my face, forcing my eyes to stay on his.

"Stay with me," he grits out.

I cradle his face between my palms, pulling him closer until there's no space left between us. "I'm not going anywhere."

His mouth moves down my jaw, over my collarbone, teeth nipping a path. He thrusts into me, hard and deep, a full-body claim that punches the air from my lungs.

His free hand palms my hip, then my waist, tracing every curve, learning me by touch alone—rough, reverent, *his*.

Our bodies find a beautiful rhythm, every thrust a silent vow he doesn't know how to speak aloud.

He drives into me again, and again, grinding deep, dragging broken sounds from my lips that only make him hold me tighter.

"Annie," he breathes out, a prayer and a curse all at once. His forehead drops to mine, sweat-laced skin sliding together.

"I'm with you."

The friction builds, every grind of his hips unraveling me. My back arches off the bed, my fingers clawing at his shoulders, trying to pull him closer, needing more, needing everything.

Pressure coils in my core, sharp and hot, the pleasure blurring into something bigger. Something I can't contain. His name rips from my throat as I fall apart beneath him, my body clenching and shuddering, taking him with me.

A cry breaks loose from my chest, and he catches it with his mouth, swallowing the sound, kissing me, absorbing every shattered piece.

When he comes, it's not quiet. It's a guttural, broken roar ripped from his throat, as if loving me and leaving me are the same violent thing.

I hold him through it, our bodies locked, our hearts pounding together.

And when he finally collapses on top of me, dropping his cheek to my chest, I thread my fingers through his hair and part my lips with the one thing I know will reach him.

Music.

"I Only Want To Be With You."

CHAPTER 46
Annalise

Our last show in Los Angeles has been the best one yet.

Maybe it was the wall-to-wall fans, the killer set capped off with a roaring encore, the $725,000 paycheck looming from Chase's guitar deal, or the fact that everyone is getting laid.

Either way, morale is through the roof.

Backstage after the show, locked in the tiny en suite bathroom off the green room, Chase drives into me, my skirt bunched up around my waist, my underwear pooled around one stiletto, and my right leg lifted toward the ceiling, ankle gripped tightly in his white-knuckled fist. I'm pressed against the door, the frantic, frequent thuds a clear indicator of what we're doing to anyone within earshot.

My eyes flutter shut.

He tilts my face up by the chin. "Hey."

"I'm with you."

Chase groans against my mouth, his jeans caught around his lower legs. "We should go somewhere else. A bed. Somewhere softer—"

"No. Keep going." I dig my nails into his bare ass and shiver when he moans. The punch-drunk smile on my face grows wings as sweat pours down my neck and he sucks my tongue into his mouth.

Then my smile turns to dust when he changes the angle slightly, stabbing a spot that unravels me instantly. Before I know what hits me, an orgasm tears through my body like a lightning storm. He feels my scream before it leaves my mouth, and his hand flies up to smother it. I bite down, the heady shriek dying against his palm.

Three more punishing thrusts, and he tenses, stills, and releases, shuddering violently, his face tipping back with pleasure through a tapered moan.

Pure bliss.

Blinking lazily in the aftermath, my smile returns. "Mmm."

Chase takes a second to recover before lowering my leg to the floor. "Jesus…"

"I didn't realize I was so flexible."

He presses a kiss to my hairline, then disposes of the condom and drags his jeans up his legs. "Really?" he says, latching his belt buckle. "You gave me a full-on demonstration. Twice."

"Okay. That's valid." I step into my underwear and slide the lace up my thighs, readjusting my skirt into place. "I guess I never realized it would come in handy so soon."

Chewing on his cheek, he studies me through half-lidded

eyes, as if making sure I'm okay. His hair is a chaotic mess, and his neck is glowing with red marks from my fingernails.

We've been insatiable.

After every show, I'm hauling him into a bathroom, a storage closet, any shadowed corner we can find. And when we're back in the hotel, doors locked and time on our side, he slows down. Touches me like I'm fragile glass, even when I'm begging him to unleash.

He zips his jeans and steps closer, his thumb brushing soft over my cheekbone. "You sure you're good?"

I bite my lip, leaning into his touch. "If I wasn't good, would I be dragging you into broom closets every night?"

The heaviness leaves his eyes as he smacks me on the butt. "We should get back out there. Limo will be here any minute."

We shuffle out of the bathroom with flushed cheeks and just-been-fucked hair. Unfortunately, my brother is the first person to spot us.

Tag sniffs, tossing us each a beer. "Shit. There you are. I had no idea where you two went or what you were doing."

My face flames as I catch the can. "We were arguing."

"I love arguing."

Chase shoots me a wink before being summoned by Rock, who is dying to know Chase's thoughts on whether drinking enough Monster Energy can make you immune to brainwashing.

I traipse over to the couch for my purse, avoiding all eye contact with Tag, and find Kenna deep in conversation with Zach about the cosmic energy of a corpse flower.

A perfect distraction.

"Oh! Annalise. I was just telling Zach how you guys should start a side project called Corpse Flower."

Zach scrolls through Spotify. "Already taken."

"Seriously? A metal band, probably. Typical." She turns to me. "Those flowers actually represent growth and new beginnings. It's a beautiful thing."

"I'll keep that in mind." I sip my beer. "Are you ready for the drive home tomorrow?"

She perks up. "You mean a three-thousand-mile cross-country drive in a tour bus that smells like feet with your brother drooling in my cleavage? Absolutely. No way am I bailing on you guys for a first-class red-eye home."

Tag scowls, storming past her toward the minifridge. "Safer that way. Can't have you falling in love with me."

"Please. I've had a better experience with airline neck pillows."

"Neck pillows don't give you tacos and orgasms at three a.m."

My gaze ping-pongs back and forth. I'm expecting a witty comeback from Kenna, but she goes silent, sinking deeper into the sofa.

I have no idea what's going on with those two. Nobody said a word about the awkward run-in in San Diego after I accidentally walked in on my worst nightmare. I still haven't found bleach strong enough to scrub away the images that haunt my eyeballs.

To my surprise, Kenna has been uncharacteristically vague.

And I'd rather gargle glass and chase it with a beehive than press my brother for details.

After another ten minutes of decompressing, we're all piled into the limo, headed back to the hotel to enjoy our final sleep on the tour. Come sunrise, we'll be homebound, waiting to see what happens next.

As I march into the hotel lobby, Chase gives my hand a squeeze. "I'm gonna hit the shower. You have your key?"

I pull it out of my pocket and shimmy it around. "I'll meet you up there."

He sends me a panty-melting smile, and I watch as he saunters toward the elevators, a cupid's bow lodged inside my heart.

I'm mid-sigh when Tag rams his elbow into my ribs. "Ow!"

"Love to see it."

"Me in pain?" I glare at him, rubbing away the sting.

His face softens, his head canting to the side. "You in love."

I blink at him through a swallow. Then a smile blooms, warm and tender. "Thanks. Me too."

He shoves a hand into his pocket. "I have a surprise for you. Hope you and Chase already got your plans out of the way for the evening."

Heat scorches my cheeks, and the glare returns. "Please never speak of that again."

"Gladly."

"What's the surprise?"

Unable to tamp down the grin, Tag takes a large step left, disappearing from my sightline. "See for yourself."

Frowning, I glance around the lobby, looking, searching… until my gaze lands on the unexpected.

I gasp.

Tears wash over my eyes.

Not a moment later, I'm running across the emerald marble

floor, my hair whipping around my face, my heart nearly bursting through my chest.

"Daddy!" A sob escapes as I launch myself into my father's open arms.

"Angel," he says, squeezing me tight. "God, I've missed your hugs."

With wet cheeks, I pull away and fall against my mother, burying my face in her shoulder. "Mom. Oh my God."

She strokes my back, shaking with her own tears. "Oh, honey. We're so proud of you. Both of you."

In my periphery, Dad pulls Tag into a bruising man-hug, slapping his back with his eyes squeezed shut. It's beautiful. It's wonderous. It's everything and more.

As I wipe away the tears, Tag hauls an arm around my shoulders and pulls me against him. "Surprise, sis."

"I cannot believe you're wearing those T-shirts." I'm grinning like a fool as I scoop a tortilla chip into a stone bowl of guacamole. "You look absolutely ridiculous, and I am so here for it."

Mom boasts a colorful mural of Tag's face.

Dad wears one of Kenna's sneak-attack shirts that reads, "Honey Moons Made Me Cry and I Paid for It."

My brother cringes. "Kenna's fired."

"Kenna has single-handedly paid off the rest of your credit card debt."

"She's rehired."

My mother scarfs a steak taco, sour cream dribbling out the side. "We've watched every single show. They're all on the YouTube station."

Dad's cowboy hat dips forward, nearly falling off his head. "Our town has been in a tizzy over you guys after your mother broke down into tears at a board meeting," he says, dabbing his face with a napkin. "Now there are posters taped to light posts. Flashing marquees and signage that say, 'Congrats Honey Moons.' We've heard Rutland is even bigger. Even brighter."

My heart skips, imagining my hometown basking in the excitement along with us. "This feels so surreal. One minute Tag is playing at coffee shops while I'm collecting napkins with half-assed lyrics between waiting tables, and the next minute we're here. Playing in front of thousands of people who know every word to every song."

"You're making a big impact," Mom says. "It's more than music. People recognize that."

"That's all Annalise." Tag shoots me a warm smile. "Her lyrics are golden. They hit."

"It's all of us," I counter. "You guys bring the words to life in ways I never imagined."

Mom sighs dreamily. "You're all so talented. And Chase is quite the presence onstage. What a voice. Where on earth did you find him?"

My brother and I share a glance, speaking at the same time.

"He accidentally kidnapped me."

"Lucky karaoke break."

Our parents frown, eyes narrowing as they flit between us.

I laugh awkwardly. "Right. He gave me a ride home one night, and we got completely lost. Ended up in some hole-in-the-wall bar on karaoke night."

"Best wrong turn he ever took," Tag says, an earnest look sent my way.

"You have a lot of chemistry onstage." Mom eyes me. She's definitely fishing. "Are you still in contact with Alex?"

"Oh…no," I murmur, dragging a chip through the half-eaten guac. "But I think he's doing better. We both are."

"For the best," Dad adds. "I never thought he was the one. Something was a little off about him."

"And it was well before the accident." My mother leans forward on her elbows, two gold earrings feathering against her cheeks. "I know you blamed it on that. On yourself. But it was always there. The anger. The control."

I swallow, fiddling with the sleeve of my dress.

For years I carried the guilt like a second skin, as if leaving him was a betrayal. Instead, by staying, I was only betraying myself, settling for less than what I deserved.

I remember Tag standing in his kitchen, voice rough with frustration: *"He didn't change. You just stopped pretending it didn't scare you."*

I wasn't ready to hear it then; I needed the story where I was the fixer.

Now I'm seeing it for what it was.

More importantly, I'm finally living what it wasn't.

Thankfully, Tag veers the conversation in a different direction, filling our parents in on tour life, after parties, and Chase's guitar deal. I zone out for a few minutes, thumbing through my phone. Through Instagram. My eyes scan Alex's latest photo, a panoramic view of the ocean. Empty beach. Setting sun. His feet buried in the sand.

The caption reads, Healing isn't always loud. Sometimes it's sitting still.

Compassion trickles through me.

I'm happy for him. Maybe he's finally finding his peace.

I give the photo a "like" and tuck my phone away.

An hour slips by, and we say good night to our parents, planning to meet for an early breakfast before hitting the road. With Christmas around the corner, we promise another visit soon. I wrap each of them in a long hug, eyes misting as I watch them head in the opposite direction.

I turn to follow Tag as he walks me back to my room. "That was amazing," I tell him, folding my arms across my chest. "Thank you for arranging that. I needed it. A piece of home."

"Figured the surprise was worth it." Hands in his pockets, he bumps me with his shoulder as we stroll down a long hallway. "How are you holding up? Finally sleeping?"

"Yeah." I nod brightly. "Things are good. Really good."

"You look better. Got some of your color back." He pinches my cheek.

Grinning, I smack his hand away. "I have a lot to be thankful for," I say, my heart full. I glance sideways, catching the smile that's barely left his face since our first video blew up. "I'm so proud of you, Tag. Watching your dreams come true is the best part."

"It's *our* dream. A team effort."

"I know. But I just keep flashing back to you sitting on your couch that night, years ago, looking so defeated, wondering how much longer you could keep doing this. The struggle, the grind, the uphill climb with no end in sight."

Tag goes quiet beside me. His jaw shifts, like he's trying to decide whether to speak or let it pass. "I remember," he says finally, voice low. "I was close to walking away for good. Didn't even tell you that part."

"You didn't have to. I saw it."

The silence stretches between us. Not uncomfortable, just full. Full of all the things we survived.

"You were the one who kept saying it would happen," he murmurs, looking at me, his eyes glassy. "When I didn't believe it anymore, you still did. You always did."

I blink against the sudden sting. "Because I knew you weren't done yet."

He nods, smiling softly.

We approach my hotel room, pausing just outside the door.

Tag turns to me. "I'm glad you found your voice again," he says, the words steeped in emotion. "You kept writing. Singing. Pushed yourself when it would've been easier to hide. And now look at you…out here chasing the things that always mattered, building something real."

I open my mouth, but nothing comes out. There's too much lodged in my chest. Gratitude. Relief. That dizzying mix of finally finding my way.

"I'm proud of you too, Annalise," he finishes. "You've been brave as hell."

With watery eyes, I lean in and hug him, clutching hard, drinking in the scent of safety and home. "I love you."

"Love you too, sis. Get some sleep."

I pull back, swiping a tear away. "You too. We have a long drive ahead."

"I got some shit to help me wind down. I'll be out like a light."

"What shit?"

"Just some Xanax."

My nose wrinkles. "Okay. Text me when you're up and we can meet up with Mom and Dad."

Nodding, Tag steps back and sends me a lazy two-finger salute. "Good night."

"'Night."

I watch Tag disappear down the hall, then slip into the hotel room, finding Chase already passed out in the bed.

A smile tugs. He's sprawled diagonally across the mattress, fully clothed, boots and all, one arm thrown over his face and the other draped across his chest like he passed out mid-thought.

His chest rises in steady rhythm, lips parted slightly, hair tousled from the show. Or maybe from my lust-driven hands. There's a fading mark along his jaw where I kissed him too hard in the bathroom.

I move quietly, slipping off his boots, unbuttoning his shirt halfway so he can breathe easier. He barely stirs.

After changing quickly, I slide into bed, careful not to jostle him. But as soon as I settle, his arm finds me like muscle memory, pulling me against his hard frame.

He exhales deeply—warm breath fanning across my shoulder—and tucks me in closer.

And just like that, I exhale too.

Letting the day go. Letting him hold me.

Letting it last.

My phone pings beside me on the nightstand, jarring me from sleep.

Half conscious and bleary-eyed, I reach over and search for my cell, the room still dark. The sun still down. My eyes are slits, the bright screen barely coming into focus.

But I see it. Read it.

Read it again.

A message sent to the group chat.

Kenna: HELP- room 312

It takes a second for the words to register.

Kenna.

Help.

Help.

I shoot up in bed, wide awake, heart thumping. Blinking repeatedly, I shove at Chase's arm, dragging him from sleep. "Chase. Chase, wake up."

"Mmm…" He stirs, rubbing a hand over his face.

Not a moment later, there's a pounding at the door.

My eyes fly open. Pulse spikes.

"Annalise! Annalise, wake the fuck up!"

It's Kenna.

Oh my God.

Chase sits up, tousling his hair. "What the…"

I shoot out of bed, my bare feet slapping the tiles as I race to the door and whip it open.

Kenna stands there, bouncing in place, half dressed, her hair wild and mascara smudged. "Annalise. God, come on. Hurry." She grips me by the wrist and hauls me from the room. "It's your brother. He—"

"*What?*" A cry spills out of me as I catapult forward.

She's tight on my heels, sobbing through the words. "He won't wake up. I can't wake him. I don't know if he's breathing. I called the police. I just don't…I don't—"

"Shit, shit, shit." My lungs rattle. My limbs are putty. I tear across the hallway, burst through the stairwell, and leap down several sets of stairs.

Chase calls out. "Annie!"

"It's Tag!" I scream back, tears streaking in rivers down my cheeks. "Oh God. Oh God…"

Kenna pulls ahead, hands trembling as she fumbles with the room key, wearing nothing but a baggy band T-shirt. "He took something. I don't—I don't know what it was…" The key slips from her hand. Slips again. "Dammit!"

I pound on the door. "Tag!"

Nothing.

I want to fall apart. Die.

Chase cuts between us, ripping the key away and shoving the door open the moment it unlocks. He runs in first, shirt half-open, feet bare. "Christ," he says, beelining toward Tag who's sprawled out on the bed, motionless.

He's on him in seconds. He grips his shoulders, shaking him hard.

No response. No groan. Just deadweight.

My knees buckle. I catch myself on the doorframe, my body frozen, mouth open but silent. The walls tilt. The world narrows.

Kenna hovers behind me with the door open, sobbing, her hands tangled in her hair. "He was breathing a minute ago. I-I tried to wake him. He took a pill to help him sleep—"

"Pills?" Chase tilts Tag's head back, checks his mouth, his neck, his wrist. "Shit, no pulse," he mutters. Then louder. "No fucking pulse."

"No…no, no, *no*." My voice finally comes, but it's a whisper. Broken. Barely mine.

Chase launches into action. He climbs onto the bed, hands braced over Tag's chest, and starts compressions. "Call them again," he orders. "Tell them to fucking hurry."

Kenna's already redialing, crying into the phone, while Chase counts under his breath, sweat starting to bead at his temple. His arms pump hard, fast, desperate.

One. Two. Three. Four.

"Come on. Come on, man. Stay with me," he grits out.

I'm paralyzed. Sick.

My brother. My brother is dying. My brother is *gone*.

A sudden crash behind us.

Zach.

"What the hell—?"

"OD," Chase says without looking up. "He's not breathing."

Zach pales. "Shit." He spins. "I've got Narcan. Two rooms down."

He takes off running.

Chase keeps going, rhythm brutal, unrelenting. My ears ring with the thud of his hands hitting Tag's chest. A sound I'll never forget.

Moments later, Zach busts back in, fumbling through his

backpack. "Hold him," he barks, ripping the cap off the nasal spray. "Lift his head."

Chase obeys. Zach presses the nozzle into Tag's nostril and delivers the dose.

"C'mon," Zach mutters. "You're all good, buddy. Come on. You're good."

Time crawls.

The room spins.

I hold my breath until I'm blue.

Then Tag jerks violently, coughing, a wheezy gasp forcing its way into his lungs. His whole body seizes, a violent inhale crashing through him like he's clawing his way out of death.

He chokes, eyes flying open, unseeing.

Limbs twitching.

Muscles locking, then loosening in jerky waves.

"Shit, there it is," Chase breathes, exhaling hard as he backs off and presses forward on his knees. "Fuck, man."

Tag's eyes flutter. His lips tremble. He tries to sit up, but his body doesn't cooperate.

"Tag!" I sob, rushing toward him and collapsing beside the bed, squeezing his hand. "God, Tag. I'm here. I'm here."

Sirens wail in the distance.

Kenna cries out, landing beside me.

Chase releases a ragged breath, barely holding it together, while Zach slumps against the wall and stares up at the ceiling.

Tag is alive.

He's *alive*.

But the fear—that hollow, bottomless kind—has already made a home in me.

CHAPTER 47
Chase

It's wild how fast everything can change.

One minute, we're watching Tag fight for his life on a hotel bed. The next, we're signing big-money contracts, packing out venues we used to dream about, and answering calls from managers who wouldn't have given us a second glance when we were nothing but a garage band.

The West Coast run turned into a sprint we couldn't slow down. Interview requests, sponsorships, festival invitations, photoshoots. Every day, something new lands in our laps, and the stakes get bigger.

Gear cases slam shut around us, the heavy thud echoing off the warehouse walls. Dust floats in the pale light filtering through cracked windows.

"Somebody kill me now," Kenna groans, dropping onto a

battered leather couch that probably came with the building. "I'm too pretty to die stacking amps."

I kneel by the pedalboards, coiling cables I can barely see straight. The pressure in my head is drilling deep, making the room swim if I move too fast.

"You good?" Tag claps me on the back as he passes with an armful of mic stands.

"Yep." I shoot him a nod, swiping the sleeve of my hoodie across my sweat-glazed forehead. "Just beat."

We're back in LA for two days, rehearsing for a surprise pop-up show that our agent thinks will "keep the hype train rolling" and hopefully land us a label deal. After barreling up and down the coast, living out of buses, hotels, and gas stations, we're already planning the next lap.

Bigger venues. Bigger crowds. Bigger expectations.

And if Carter has his way, we'll be locked in a studio by February, cranking out an indie album at record speed. He even floated a European tour for spring, dangling sold-out venues in front of us like a prize we weren't allowed to blink at.

For the first time, it isn't about fighting to survive.

It's about keeping up.

Tag eyes me with a trace of suspicion, as if he's not buying what I'm selling.

But who the hell am I to complain about a headache when he literally came back from the dead two weeks ago?

The Narcan saved his life. Thank fuck for Zach, who'd packed it without fanfare or explanation. It wasn't until after the paramedics left that he finally told us why.

His old bandmate back in Castleton had been using, trying to take the edge off late-night gigs and early-morning shifts.

Zach found him slumped over in a rehearsal space, gray and barely breathing.

He didn't have Narcan then.

Turns out the Xanax Tag took wasn't just Xanax. The single pill, bought off a random groupie to help him sleep, was laced with fentanyl.

Enough to kill him.

Almost did.

Setting aside the mic stands, Tag pulls off his beanie and saunters toward me. "You're a terrible fuckin' liar," he says.

My eyes narrow. "Pot, meet kettle."

"You think I'm not good?" He huffs a derisive laugh. "I'm fantastic. Better than ever."

"Mm."

"Death has a way of making you feel invincible." He flashes a grin that doesn't quite reach his eyes. "Like you've already burned through your worst day, so what's left to be afraid of?"

Wish I could say the same.

Death feels decidedly different for me.

It's gripping a bathroom sink somewhere backstage, head pounding, vision tilting sideways, wondering how much longer I can ride this without crashing. It's heaving my guts out in a gas station toilet, clinging to the porcelain like it's my only salvation.

It's losing myself in my girl, the animal taking over as I try so goddamn hard to cherish her while her pretty face goes in and out of focus.

My muscles tighten. I study him—his messy hair, faded band tee, the edge in his smile that wasn't there before. "Is that why you've been acting like a rock star cliché lately?" I probe.

Tag shrugs. Sniffs. "Might be. Or maybe I'm just finally living like I've got nothing to prove."

"Bullshit," I say, softer now. "You're still trying to outrun that night."

He doesn't respond right away. Just tugs the beanie back on and looks past me. "Yeah," he mutters. "Guess you don't walk away from something like that without a few ghosts in your closet."

Then he turns, heading back to the sea of gear like he didn't just admit something he'll never say again.

My shoulders loosen. Relief floods in because he's here. Breathing. Moving. Cursing under his breath about tangled cords.

But the image of him lying on that hotel bed, lips blue, still haunts me. Or the sound of Annie crying herself hoarse outside the hospital room, curled in the fetal position across my lap. Or the sight of Zach's trembling hands when the EMT finally nodded and said Tag was going to be okay.

Tag jokes now, but I know he's still carrying it. We all are.

And it scares the hell out of me. Because if death can slip that quietly into his pocket, it could just as easily find its way into mine.

Into any of ours.

"There's my rock star."

I pivot, watching as Annie skips toward me, a mod-dress vision in smoky eyeshadow. There's a cigarette between her fingers, the embers stark against the dusk. "Hey," I say.

She's smoking again. It seemed like she'd ditched the habit somewhere between breaking up with Alex and our East Coast tour. But ever since Tag's brush with death, she's been lighting up like it's the only way to keep from unraveling.

She doesn't talk about that night, but I see it in the way her hands shake when she thinks no one is watching, her gaze full of shadows, or in how she drags each inhale like it's tethered to something heavier than nicotine.

"It's been a long day," she murmurs as she steps into my space. Her free hand finds the hem of my shirt, tugging me closer.

"Long week." I press a kiss to her temple. She smells like smoke and hotel shampoo and something distinctly her.

Annie leans in, cigarette dangling from her fingers. "Want to grab a bite to eat?"

I nod, glancing around the jam-packed room.

The label booked us a warehouse rehearsal space on the east side. Concrete floors, busted couches, a fridge that sounds like it's trying to self-eliminate. Perfect for a last-minute pop-up show that's somehow already sold out.

"Come on." She stomps out her cigarette and takes me by the hand.

The sun is setting over Los Angeles like a crackling fire hearth. Low and golden, casting everything in a haze of heat and exhaust. Out here on the east side, it's all warehouses and taco trucks, graffiti-tagged alleys, and that constant hum of something just barely holding itself together.

We don't make it ten steps before a trio of girls spot us from across the parking lot. One lets out a squeal that cuts through the noise like feedback off a mic.

"Oh my God, that's them!"

They descend fast—smiles wide, phones out, already filming as if documenting history.

"Chase Rhodes! Can we get a picture? Please? My sister will die."

Someone shoves a napkin and a Sharpie at me.

Annie steps back as the women swarm.

"We'll be at your show tomorrow. We have killer seats." The blond smacks her gum. "Will you guys play 'New Moon Rising'?"

"Yeah, it's on the setlist." I pop the cap between my teeth and scribble my name on a Starbucks napkin. "Thanks for coming to the show. You local?"

"Denver," they all say at once.

Annie hangs to the side, head bowed. I wave her over. "Annalise."

She smiles nervously. "They're here for you. I'm—"

"Are you shitting me?" a brunette perks up, the purple streaks in her hair all too familiar. "You're my idol. I'm low-key obsessed with you."

"Hardly low-key," the blond adds.

"She's right. High-key as hell. I need a selfie stat." Her grin is leagues above giddy. "Please?"

With a look of enchanted surprise, Annie steps over to the group and reaches for the marker, smile widening. "Um, thank you. So much. That means everything to me."

"Are you two dating?" the third girl wonders.

I palm Annie by the neck and give a loving squeeze. "Yeah, she's my girl."

They all swoon.

We pose for selfies, sign a few more autographs, and the girls take off, squealing under their breath as they dart back across the street. When I turn to Annie, she's close to tears.

"You okay?" My fingers trace the bow of her back in a featherlight slide. "You're the one who looks starstruck."

"I'm…" She swallows. "I wasn't expecting that. I mean, I'm used to signing autographs after the shows, but it's usually you and the guys with the hardcore fans."

"Nah. That's in your head. They go wild over you."

She peers up at me, all light and sunny skies. Then she snatches my hand, links our fingers, and hauls me toward a nearby diner boasting happy hour specials.

We stroll in and take a seat in a two-person booth. Annie scans the menu, her tongue poking between her lips. "I want everything."

"So order everything." I lean back with a half smile, drumming my fingers on the table.

"Right." She snickers.

"I'm serious. I can afford it now."

Her lashes flutter as she blinks down at the selections. "I'll just get a burger and fries."

I stare at her, wondering what she's thinking. My mind races with glimpses of the future, a tangle of unknowns. Are we going to move in together when we settle back home? Buy a house? What's the next step?

The ink on my guitar deal hadn't even dried before they started calling it a "revolution." A game-changer. Custom orders stacked up like firewood, and every day since has felt like stomping through puddles of gasoline, waiting for the blaze to overtake me.

I have close to seven figures in my bank account, and that should feel like winning.

But it's terrifying.

I've never laid roots or built any real life for myself. It's been day to day, no brakes, wondering if the ground beneath my feet would hold another second.

Now I have a girlfriend. The most precious piece of me. Life going forward is more than just me, my dog, and a far-off dream.

It's here. It's happening.

And I have no fucking clue what to do.

Annie pulls out her phone and starts scrolling. "Did you see that picture I tagged you in?"

I whiz back to the present. "What picture?"

"Instagram."

I hardly do social media.

My follower count is just shy of a mil, and my inbox is flooded with unread messages. Kenna combs through every now and then, posting strategically timed band-related photos with emoji-ridden captions, just to keep my presence alive. To keep the fans hungry. According to her, aesthetic matters.

Shaking my head, I grab my phone and open the app. A smile lifts when I see the most recent picture glowing on her profile grid: the two of us sitting on a curb outside some no-name diner at midnight, a half-empty bag of fast food between us and a busted neon sign flickering overhead. Her head's tipped back in laughter, eyeliner smudged, while I'm looking at her like she's the only thing that's ever made sense.

The caption reads: Conquered LA. Busted a lung. Signed so

many autographs I forgot how to spell my name. And this is still the best part of my night.

My heart does something ridiculous. Skips like a scratched vinyl, then drops to a rhythm I feel in my throat. I find her eyes across the table. "I fucking love you."

Those blue eyes gloss over with a swell of tears. She chews her lip, sets her phone down. "I love you too. So much."

Her nose scrunches with affection.

Then she reaches for a fry the moment they're set in front of her, and I just watch. The way she licks the salt from her skin. The way she tucks her hair behind her ear like she doesn't know I'd sell my soul to keep her this close.

She's mine. She chose me.

So why am I still holding my phone like it might bite?

On a whim, I glance back down at the app and type his name before I can stop myself.

Alex Anderson.

The guy who had her for years before I ever even knew her name.

The newest post loads. He's sitting on a sandy beach, the ocean sprawled out before him, the sunrise kissing the water just right.

The caption is vague. Some bullshit about healing.

But there it is: liked by theannaliseadams.

A shot of insecurity trickles through me.

I lock my phone and flip it over, pressing my palm to the screen, hoping that'll smother the flicker in my chest.

Across the table, Annie is laughing at something Rock texted to the group chat.

I try to let it go. Try to remind myself that it's just a like. Just a photo. Just a guy she doesn't love anymore.

But my mouth is faster than my sense. "You still talk to him?"

Her laugh fades as she looks up. "What?"

"Alex," I say, tone neutral. "Do you still keep in touch?"

She blinks, like I've caught her mid-step. "No. Why?"

"Just noticed you liked his latest post."

She frowns, chewing the inside of her cheek. "Oh. Yeah. I was trying to be supportive."

That should be enough. It *is* enough. Still, my voice dips with vulnerability. "So you're still following him?"

Her frown deepens with confusion. "I guess," she says quietly. "He was such a big part of my life for so long. And it felt kind of mean to dig the knife in deeper after everything, you know?"

I nod, every muscle cinched tight, doing my best to act like it doesn't matter. Like it didn't just throw a wrench in the peace I've been clawing toward all week.

She leans across the table, brow furrowed. "Chase, look at me," she murmurs. "It's nothing. It doesn't matter. I love *you*."

I believe her. But belief doesn't quiet the ghosts. And it won't stop the pounding in my skull that comes every time the stage lights fade.

So I make the same silent promise I've been making night after night: keep the pain hidden. Keep her safe when the darkness takes over.

Because I'd rather wreck myself in silence than risk her seeing me as someone she can't trust to love her right.

When she turns back to her fries, I unlock my phone again, scrolling to distract myself and quiet the noise.

That's when I see it.

Not on Annie's feed. Not even from someone I follow. Just a headline buried beneath a few swipes of the explore page:

Local Vermont Gas Station Vandalized Following Viral Shooting Story

I click it before I can stop myself.

The article is short. Just a paragraph about broken windows and spray-painted walls. No one hurt. Just damage. A message from the public, blaming the man who pulled the trigger on me.

I stare at the screen, nausea curling slow in my gut.

Because that wasn't supposed to happen.

The truth got out, and the world did what it always does—picked a villain and lit a match. But the man behind that counter wasn't evil. Just scared. A cornered animal. A father trying to protect what little he had left.

And now he's paying for it.

I lock my phone and slide it into my pocket, pushing aside the sting buzzing in my chest.

I need to make it right with them.

The check comes, and we leave most of the food behind, too caught up in each other to care. Outside, the night's backdrop settles around us. Our steps fall in rhythm, the shuffle of boots on pavement and the hum of passing cars filling the comfortable silence.

The air's cooled. The kind of LA night that tries to pretend it has seasons. A breeze tugs at the hem of her jacket as she slows near the curb.

Then she tugs my sleeve, pulling me off course. "Come on."

"Where are we going?"

Taking my hand, she drags me over to a worn wooden bench tucked beneath a crooked streetlamp, a little ways from the restaurant. It overlooks a hill, half obscured by trees, the city glowing in patches beneath us. The moon is round and bright, the sky dusted with stars.

We sit.

"The moon is full tonight," she whispers, pressing her temple to my shoulder.

I spare it a quick glance. "Yeah."

My eyes close as I wrap an arm around her and let myself sink. The noise falls away. The fresh air fills my lungs, mingling with a trace of her. Warm, soft, feminine.

Mine.

God, the way I lived for these moments. Songwriting with her beneath a honey moon. Pouring our souls into lyrics and strings. Letting the night hold us when the world felt too loud.

Back when it was just us, a guitar, and whatever pain we hadn't put into words yet.

I press a kiss to her hair, the weight of her against me grounding something that's been slipping for days. "You remember that night in Philly?" I murmur. "You were barefoot and drenched, crouched under that willow tree after the show, scribbling lyrics before they slipped away. The paper was soaked through, ink bleeding all over your hands. You said the universe was trying to drown your muse."

She chuckles. "It was."

"You still got a song out of it."
"My favorite one yet."

New moon rising
Shadows on the run
I feel the world restart beneath a different sun

Smiling softly, I fix my eyes on the horizon. "Not the last though."

I hold her tighter, letting the moonlight stretch over us. If there's a quiet left in this life, I'll find it here. In her, in the dark, in the music we haven't written yet.

"We're going to make it, right?"

Her question steals a breath. Frowning, I slowly turn, glancing down at her as her eyes peer up at me, wide and glassy. "The band?"

She smiles at me, but it doesn't quite reach her eyes.

She doesn't reply.

"Yeah." I pull her closer, hold her harder. "Yeah, Annie. Of course we're gonna make it."

Swallowing, she returns her head to my shoulder and grips my palm, squeezing tight.

I rub two fingers over my temple, grinding against the pressure, willing it to back off.

Just one more show.

One more set until we're home.

One more promise I pray I can keep.

CHAPTER 48
Annalise

ONE BAND, FIVE PASSPORTS, AND ZERO PLAN (BECAUSE KENNA BROKE HER FOOT & WE ARE LOST AF): EUROPE, PLEASE BE GENTLE

PARIS

It's March. Paris is damp, chilly, and gray.

The venue is a converted cathedral, and the acoustics turn our opening chords into something that sounds like witchcraft.

Tag snaps a guitar string mid-song but keeps playing anyway. When the crowd cheers, he grins through it, feeding on the noise.

Backstage, Chase is quieter than usual. He cracks open a Coke, sneaks a pill past his lips, and brushes a hand over his temple like it's just a passing headache. When I catch his eye, he throws me a faint smile that doesn't quite stick.

After the show, we ride scooters through the rain to a café that serves breakfast at midnight. I lean in, kiss powdered sugar off his mouth.

This time, his smile sticks.

And I let myself believe it.

LONDON

We shoot a live interview with a music magazine.

The cameras roll. We're mic'd up and swarmed with handlers.

We laugh, we joke, we play our parts.

When the lights cut, Chase pulls me out a side door, into a hallway lined with unused amps and coiled cords.

He tickles me until I can't breathe.

I leap into his arms, wrap my legs around his waist as he pins me to the wall, and we disappear into the soundproof shadows of the industry that made us.

Back in the green room, I fix my hair, still glowing.

Chase avoids the mirror.

BERLIN

They chant our name before the lights go up.

Zach takes his shirt off mid-set. Rock crowd-surfs.

My brother disappears for twenty minutes before the encore. I find him sitting alone in the green room, staring at a wall like he wants to climb through it.

When I take a seat beside him, he wraps an arm around me. I press my head against his shoulder, hugging him harder than ever before.

I think that's all he needed. Because when he storms back onto the stage, he's fire.

Larger than life.

At the hotel, Chase pulls the curtains closed, shutting out the city lights until the room is hushed and dim. He tugs me into bed beside him, his thumb drifting along my arm in gentle strokes. He loosens, sinking against me like he can finally rest.

I press closer, letting my heartbeat answer his.

BARCELONA

We play an open-air festival in a courtyard that smells like sangria and clove smoke.

It's the biggest crowd yet, thousands of bodies moving in time with every beat.

Chase busts out a guitar solo so good the whole place roars.

When it's over, he retreats into silence, his throat raw, eyes rimmed red. He pulls me against him on the walk to the limo, pressing a lingering kiss to my temple.

I melt into it, but the longer he holds on, the more I wonder if he's steadying me or himself.

Kenna sends me a text at 3:00 a.m. because she's six hours behind. I tell her I miss her.

She knows.

———

ROME

We soundcheck in an abandoned opera house with gold ceilings and crumbling frescoes.

Rock takes my lipstick and writes something in Latin on the dressing room mirror. We laugh, but none of us ask what it means.

The show is a dream, every note clean, every voice in the crowd screaming like they know our souls.

Afterward, Chase slips away, saying he needs air.

Back at the hotel, I stay awake longer than I should, replaying the music in my head and holding on to the part of the night that felt like magic.

When the mattress finally dips under a new weight, Chase slides in beside me. He sets a paper cup on the nightstand, cherries piled inside, and pulls me close like he never left.

———

AMSTERDAM

Our last show.

We sell out a warehouse with no heat and questionable wiring.

It's chaos. Glorious, messy, wild.

Chase forgets the second verse to "Our Last First Goodbye." I cover for him. He smiles wide.

After, the high carries us into the back lot where fans cluster by the exit gates. Flashbulbs. Screaming. A dozen hands reach out, everyone shouting our names like we owe them pieces of ourselves.

I feel one grip my wrist. Tight. Too tight.

A guy in a denim vest pulls me toward him, asking for a kiss. I yank back, heart spiking.

Chase is there.

Fast. Loud. Shoving the guy back with a snarl I've never heard before.

Security rushes in. Cameras flash. Fans scream for selfies as Chase hurls himself between us, a wall made of fire.

In the hotel room, Chase paces, jaw locked like he's still in the fight. I sit on the edge of the bed, trembling in the aftermath.

When he finally calms, his eyes soften, and he cups my cheek in a warm hand. He asks if I'm okay.

I nod.

But for the first time, I see it clearly:

I'm not sure if he is.

We stay one more night in Amsterdam, wandering the canals, hand in hand beneath a silver sky that couldn't decide if it wanted to rain. Bicycles zip past in every direction, street performers play violins under stone archways, and we share a paper cone of fries drenched in mayo, laughing when half of it falls into the canal.

The city is all charm and crooked beauty. Leaning houses, narrow bridges, tulips bursting from windowsills like confetti.

The hotel room feels like another world.

Minimalist, too clean, and still. The kind of place that tries to look expensive but feels empty. The curtains are drawn, and everything feels muffled, the room holding its breath with us.

Chase is spread out on the bed just after midnight, bare chested, an arm draped over his eyes. I brush my teeth and pop a mint to replace the taste of Marlboro, then pad back into the room, feeding a comb through my hair. "Do you want to talk about last night?"

His arm moves away from his face, but he doesn't answer right away. When he finally sits up against the headboard, I catch the faint scrapes across his knuckles from that single punch he landed before security dragged him off.

I step closer, setting the brush aside. "Chase—"

"We don't need to talk about it." His tone is even, almost light, like he can flick it off as easily as lint.

Sighing, I climb onto the bed beside him. My knee presses into the mattress, and his gaze flits down, lingering for just a beat before sliding back up to me. A tired smile softens his mouth. "You're so beautiful."

The compliment warms me, but it doesn't erase the image of him outside that venue with fire in his eyes. "I've never seen you so angry," I admit quietly.

He glances away. "He grabbed you, Annie. He could have hurt you."

"He was just a drunk fan."

"I don't want anyone to hurt you."

"Chase…" Inching closer, I place a hand against his chest, absorbing the beats of his heart. "I don't want you to hurt either. Are you okay?"

His gaze wheels over to me, eyes darkening for a second before another smile tugs, brighter than the last. "Of course."

"Are you sure?"

"Yes." He takes my wrist, presses my hand into his chest, harder, deeper. "I'm more than okay. You don't have to worry about me. I promise."

His heart thumps, galloping and alive.

I collapse against him in a desperate sprawl, burying my face in the curve of his neck. "I need you," I say, clinging to his shoulders as I crawl into his lap, straddling him.

His hands trail down my body. When I shift, he surges forward, taking my mouth in a breath-stealing kiss. My tongue meets his on instinct. Wild, hungry, frantic. He squeezes harder, his hips jerking up off the bed.

I grind down, palms braced against his neck, our bodies moving with urgency. Our mouths clash, all teeth and tongues and beautiful ache. He pulls my shirt over my head, and as our lips break apart, he follows the arch of my body, diving to my breasts, licking, tasting, devouring.

A second later, my underwear hits the floor, and I'm ripping his belt open, yanking his jeans halfway down his thighs. I take a moment to trace the jagged scar roped around his thigh, then climb back on and sink down onto him in one hard, quick motion.

Bare. No condom.

I don't care.

I'm on the pill.

He groans, sharp and guttural, propping himself on his elbows, lips parted, eyes wild as he watches me take his cock, nothing between us. "Annie—"

"Need to feel all of you," I gasp, moving fast, frenzied, trying to outrun the worry in my chest.

He sits up all the way and pulls me into him, wrapping an arm around my back, our foreheads pressed tight. His thumb skims my jaw, firm enough to guide me back to his stare when my eyes start to slip shut. His voice is low and rough, but tender beneath the strain. A gentle urgency. "Stay with me."

The words thrum through me, grounding me. I clutch his shoulders, lock onto his gaze, my body syncing to his rhythm.

"Jesus," he chokes out, guiding my hips. "That's it. Stay with me, Annie. You feel so good."

I clench around him, taking every inch, watching his head fall back, throat exposed, body shaking. My hands cradle his face, dragging his gaze back to mine, our lips barely brushing. "I love you."

"I love you."

"So much."

"So fucking much."

An orgasm crashes seconds later, rocketing through me. Embers and tinder and firelight. Everything. All I need.

Him.

Just him.

He hooks my hips with both hands and rams into me two more times before letting go, growling his release against my throat and clutching me tight.

I feel it all. Pulsing, tingling, tangible, alive. Here.

He's here. I'm here.

We're okay.

We lie there in the quiet, skin against skin, hearts still beating too fast. I listen to the sound of his breath start to even out, feel his body slacken beneath mine, the adrenaline finally letting go.

Eventually, I slip out of bed, careful not to wake him. I find the hotel's notepad and tear a page from the top, the paper flimsy and lined with gold.

The pen shakes, but the words come easy. Small and strange and true.

I fold it once and leave it on his nightstand.

Right beside the glass of water and the pills he never took.

You glow with the night
And I still trace your shadow
Beneath the same moon

CHAPTER 49
Chase

I feel good tonight. Better than I have in weeks.

Since starting on a new prescription, the pressure in my head has eased into a dull, manageable ache. It's wild how much a little relief can shift your whole perspective on everything, from the day ahead, to the future you stopped letting yourself believe in.

It's been a week since we toured Europe, and we're back in Rutland for a spring break festival across town.

Home base.

Cops are everywhere, trying to keep the peace and the crowd in check, but the vibe is electric. People are camped out in lawn chairs and sprawled on colorful blankets, waving foamboard signs and homemade posters while they wait for us to take the stage.

We all gather in the pop-up tent that's roped off and swarming with security. Familiar faces bleed through the chaos: Annie and

Tag's parents waving from behind the barricades, my old boss Solomon nodding like he always knew this would happen.

Zach's daughter, Marie, is here, clinging to her mother's side, wide-eyed and smiling, while a couple of his old bandmates hover nearby, proud and a little out of place.

Rock's newest girlfriend—some LA metal chick with ink from neck to ankle and piercings I can't count—dances like the set's already started, her black hair whipping in time with nothing but the energy in the air. Even Declan and Lillian, the wedding couple we played for before everything took off, showed up and are grinning ear to ear.

It's loud. Wild. Unruly.

But for the first time in a long while, I can hear the magic through the madness.

I don't have to fake it today.

Kenna limps over on a pair of crutches, after breaking her foot two days before we set off on our European tour. "I'm barely recovered from Tag dropping an amp on my foot, and now he expects me to run merch like it's the Olympics."

Tag winces. "You said you'd catch it."

"I said I'd help. Not that I wanted to die under it."

We all laugh.

Kenna shoots Tag the smallest smile, one she thinks we don't see. Then she blows out a breath and trudges over to the merch table strewn with T-shirts, mugs, keychains, and a giant banner with a QR code that lets fans pre-order our debut album releasing in August.

Annie pops up from the chair, giving Kenna her seat. She flicks her half-smoked cigarette, smashing it into a pile of weeds with her shoe. "Why does playing a few miles from home feel like our biggest show yet?" she wonders, floating around, organizing until everything's just right.

"Because of the stakes. Literally everyone you've ever met is in that crowd." Kenna collapses into the chair and discards her crutches. "No pressure."

"Oof."

"You'll kill it as always. I'm dying to hear the new song you whipped up."

"It was a joint effort," Annie says softly, her eyes lifting to me across the tent. "Chase and I wrote most of it overseas between shows."

I send her a smile that grows into a white-toothed grin.

Real. Genuine.

She blinks at me. Processes the moment like it stole her breath.

Then she smiles back, beaming, glowing, and full of love.

Kenna whistles, glancing between us. "Jeez. Get a room."

Annie's eyes stay locked on mine. "We've had rooms in multiple countries. Some with ocean views."

They snicker.

I'm pulled from the moment when Tag sidles up beside me, slapping me on the back. "You look better."

Pivoting toward him, I shove my hands in my pockets. "I'm on some new meds for my migraines. Finally doing the trick."

"Sweet. Love that for you." He nods at his sister across the way, eyes going reflective. "Pretty sure you had Sis half convinced it was just jet lag. But I knew better."

I frown a little. "Yeah?"

Tag shrugs, but it's slower, less of his usual swagger. "I've worn that face. The one that says, 'I'm fine, don't look too close.' You only pull it out when the ground's falling out from under you." He gives a small laugh. "Trust me, I had the deluxe version."

I nod softly, the air heavier between us.

Then his grin reappears, just like that. He nudges me with his shoulder. "But hey, yours came with better hair and a prettier guitar. So, points to you."

"Baby steps," I murmur.

He claps me on the back again, this time hard enough to jolt my spine. "Well, try not to die onstage. I've got fifty bucks riding on you nailing that high note in 'Monowi.'"

"Jesus." I shake my head and breathe out a laugh. But before he spins away, I clear my throat. "Hey…how are you? Really?"

Tag glances at me, jaw ticking. His eyes flicker before he slaps on a smile. "Living the dream."

"Yeah?" I study him, searching for the crack. The lie.

But a softness comes over him, loosening his shoulders as he exhales through his nose. His gaze drifts over to Kenna, just for a beat. For a fleeting second. "Yeah, man," he says. "Yeah. I'm doing better. Think I'm finally good."

We share a look, something steeped in history.

Resentment, regret, the kind of shit you only work through by bleeding on the same stage night after night. There was a time he wanted to knock my teeth in.

Now we're rhythm and lead. Battle-scarred and still in tune.

He nods once, turning to go. But not without tossing a glance over his shoulder. "You screw up the bridge, I'm stealing your solo."

I smirk. "You steal my solo, I'm cutting your reverb mid-set."

He grins, flips me off, then disappears into the noise.

And somehow, that's the closest we've ever come to saying *we're* good.

Someone calls five minutes to stage.

I grab my guitar, sling the strap over my shoulder, and take one last look around.

My family. My girl. My second chance.

A small keychain swings from my belt loop. A wooden guitar, etched with a single word: *Hallelujah*.

The birthday gift Annie gave to me eight months ago.

I unclip it, let it rest in my palm. My thumb traces the worn edges, the flaking paint, the grooves carved by time and touch. It centers me. Anchors me.

A lifeline, small and mighty.

I give it a quick kiss, then reattach it to my belt.

The lights are waiting, but I already feel like I'm home.

As we take the stage, I glance around at the screaming, moving audience. The electric guitar is a welcome weight in my hands, the energy more therapy than drug.

I inhale a long breath.

The kind that fills your chest all the way.

The kind that actually sticks.

I glance at Annie standing beside me, her hands curled around the microphone like it's a secondary lover. She looks calm, but I know better. I can see the pulse in her neck, the way her shoulders rise just a little too high with each breath.

Still, there's fire in her eyes. Stage fire.

Our gazes lock for half a second, long enough to say, *"We're here. We made it. Let's go."*

Tag strums a few warm-up chords behind us. Rock flips a

drumstick. Kenna gives us a wave from the side of the stage, foot in a boot but smiling anyway.

I squeeze the neck of my guitar. Annie mouths the first line of the set under her breath, our newest song, written in crinkled notebooks and on hotel napkins as we bounced across Europe.

It's called "No Maps."

The lights dim.

The crowd roars.

And together, we step into the noise.

See the world and sing along
Shake hands with kings and vagabonds
Walk the roads where empires fell
Hear the stories books don't tell

The lights hit, and it feels like stepping into the sun, the crowd below us a living thing.

Every chord hums through my bones, and for a moment, I forget.

Forget the pain, the pills, the quiet way Annie looks at me when she thinks I'm not watching.

Up here, it's just sound and skin and sweat.

The buzz of the amp. The beat of the kick drum in my chest.

My fingers fly. My voice holds.

Sip the wine of stolen thrones
Trace the cracks in ancient stones

The lights streak across my vision, but I keep my eyes open.

Every note I play hits like a muscle memory I don't remember learning. The crowd is howling back at us, louder than the amp behind me.

But all I can focus on is the sweat trickling down my spine and the slight twitch in my left hand.

It's starting again. Barely there.

But I feel it.

That shift. That edge.

The one that tells me something's coming.

So we run
With blistered feet and borrowed time
Chasing stars we'll never find
No maps, no prayers
Just broken chords and midnight stares

I glance at Annie. She's fire and control. A goddess in denim and violet light.

Her voice hits that note in the third line, and the audience goes still, feeling it in their bones.

I strum through the chorus, blinking hard as my vision blurs for a second too long.

My fingers go numb for half a beat.

I bite down on the inside of my cheek, hard enough to taste blood.

Stay. Focus. Breathe.

Bleed with wars
And love gone wrong

A pressure blooms behind my left temple. Deep, sharp, alive.

It claws its way into my skull, twisting tighter with every cheer from the crowd.

My knees wobble. I fake a step back, mask it as part of the rhythm.

Annie looks at me. I miss the cue.

The chord slips under my fingers, wrong, jagged.

She knows.

She always knows.

And just as the next line echoes out across the crowd, the migraine punches through.

White-hot and splitting.

I blink once.

Then everything starts to tilt.

Art is living
We are the song

My vision cuts out. Static and black noise. I can't fucking see.

Sound warps.

My eyes roll up.

Next thing I know, I'm plummeting face-first off the stage.

CHAPTER 50
Chase

She's lying in bed beside me, pressing a warm compress to my forehead. Her touch is butterfly-soft, voice melted velvet.

"I'm here," she whispers.

I close my eyes, focusing on the brush of her knuckles across my cheek.

Complex migraine with vasovagal syncope.

That was my official diagnosis after a brief post-fall hospital visit. My vitals were good, blood pressure stable. By the time I got there, I was lucid, oriented, and answering all of their how-many-fingers-am-I-holding-up questions.

I played it cool. Cracked a few jokes. Blamed it on stress, too much whiskey, and a brutal tour schedule. I let them run their tests—everything but a scan.

Because if they find something, it stops being a maybe.

And if it's real, if there's something in my head waiting to take everything from me…

Then it's over.

Her.

The music.

All of it.

And I'm not ready for that.

No one pushed for imaging once I was talking. No slurred speech, no long-lasting effects. Just a jaded rock star who took a nosedive into a sea of people.

Annie wanted more. I could see it in the way her eyes searched mine, like she was waiting for a punchline I never delivered.

But I shut it down.

Said I was fine.

Said it wasn't that bad.

Said what I had to.

Now I'm here, two days later, lying in the dark beside her, the room still humming like the stage never emptied. She presses the compress to my head again, gentler this time, her fingers brushing my temple as she curls up beside me.

"A new listing came through," I say, reaching for her hand. Our fingers intertwine. "Three bedrooms. Two bathrooms. There's a screened-in sunroom off the kitchen, perfect for late-night writing. A big patio too. For when the moon is full."

A little croak escapes her. "That sounds perfect."

We've been scrolling the real estate apps for weeks, looking for a place to call our own after my contract on this rental is up at the end of June. In the meantime, she's moved in with me while we navigate our upcoming tour schedules.

Toaster jumps up on the bed, plodding over my legs until he's nestled on the opposite side of me. My free hand lands in his thick mane of fur, fingers skimming and scratching.

"My brave little Toaster…"

Annie rolls my ring between her thumb and finger, head resting on my shoulder. "I think we should cancel the Vegas show. Until we figure out what's going on with you."

I tense. "That's not necessary."

"Chase—"

"That was a one-off. I had too much whiskey, my meds wore off, and I lost my footing."

"I never saw you drinking."

My jaw clenches. I hate lying to her, but I don't want her to worry. To think I'm going to hold us back. Her career is resting on my shoulders. Tag's too. Rock, Zach, even Kenna. We're in our prime, gaining momentum every day, and the only thing that'll kill me faster than my head is the notion that I might be the reason it all falls apart.

I refuse to be the one to smother their dreams.

Removing the compress from my forehead, I toss it onto a pillow. "We'll do Vegas," I tell her. "It's our last scheduled show."

Her breath catches. "Chase, please reconsider—"

"One more. Then we break. House hunt. Breathe. Reconnect." I pull her across my chest as Toaster paws at my side, nosing my ribs. "After that, I'll handle it. The band can pause for a while, and I'll be back on my feet soon. I'll be okay."

"What if it's something…worse?" Her breathing all but stops.

It's not.

It *can't* be.

"They're just migraines," I tell her with as much conviction as I can muster. "My family has a history of them. I can manage this. One day at a time."

"Promise me you'll get a scan after Vegas." She burrows her face in my neck, begging, needing me to swear. "Please, Chase."

"Yeah," I whisper, kissing her hair. My eyes close as I breathe her in, memorize her soft skin, and stamp her scent into my bones. "I promise."

Vegas is a dream. Another much-needed reprieve.

But the last time I had a reprieve, I plunged off a goddamn stage and faceplanted into a swarming mass of people.

At first they thought it was part of the show—rock star takes a dive, crowd goes wild.

Meanwhile, I was sprawled on the ground and twice as pathetic, choking on static and sweat, praying no one saw the panic in my eyes.

Or worse, that I couldn't see theirs, not until my vision sparked back to life.

But sure. Let's roll the dice in Vegas.

What could possibly go wrong?

So far, nothing. Not for the hour-plus set where I pour everything out, let my soul bleed across the stage, feel the reverb like red-hot shockwaves licking down my spine, and duet with Annie as if we're invincible.

The crowd's electric. My girl's glowing.

The guys are shredding like their lives depend on it, while

I'm praying I make it to the last note before the lights go out again.

I do.

I finish the set, alive and whole, dancing on thunder as the crowd roars.

And somewhere in the back of my mind, I hear my sister's voice:

Always end on a high note.

My throat burns.

This feels like a high.

But I'll lie down and die before I let it be the end.

After we decompress backstage, swapping bottled water for beer, we sign autographs and mingle with fans in the courtyard before heading back to the hotel.

One more night away from home. Then reality will set in, and I'll be forced to tackle the brain-eating monster in my head.

Because I promised her.

I swore it.

The air is thick with heat and leftover adrenaline, voices hissing in my ears. I keep moving, smiling, nodding, gripping Sharpies tighter than I should. Annie stays close.

Then the crowd shifts.

And everything stops.

They're just...*there*.

I blink, squint, keep blinking, wondering if my vision is fucking with me again.

But no.

I see them.

My parents.

Fredrick and Donna Rhodes.

Not much older than I remember. Not younger either. They look exactly the same, like time's dared to skip over them but slammed into me at full force. Mom is in a slate-gray blouse and pearls, clutching her purse like a shield. My father's hands are tucked behind his back as he stares at the son he hasn't seen in years.

My vision tunnels.

The noise drops out. All I can hear is a funnel cloud in my ears and the hollow hum of memory slamming into my ribs.

I grip a wrought iron fence just to stay upright.

I should move. Say something. Anything.

But I can't.

Because suddenly I'm standing in a black suit that didn't fit, watching them bury my sister. I'm packing a bag in silence while my mother cries in the next room and my father tells me to "be strong."

I'm hearing Stella's voice, raspy and begging.

"Please don't make me go. Please. I feel sick. My head is killing me…"

And I'm seeing them wave her off anyway, chasing medals instead of mercy.

My throat closes.

I can't breathe.

Annie's hand finds my arm.

I didn't even know I was shaking until she grips tighter.

"Chase," she says, low, steady. "What's wrong? Your head?"

I blink. Once. Twice.

They don't move. Just stand there, like they have any right to be here.

I look away before they can approach. Before I collapse under the weight of everything I never said.

Because if I don't, I'll drown in it.

Just like she did.

"Um…" I turn to Annie, straightening from the fence. "No. Sorry, my head's fine."

"You're trembling."

"Just the postshow high. It'll wear off."

She doesn't believe me. I don't blame her.

I steal another glance over Annie's shoulder. They're still there, rooted to the pavement, blurring into the white lights like ghosts here to haunt me when I'm already long past plagued.

My mother's hands twist around the strap of her purse. My father shifts his weight, wanting to come closer but unsure if he can.

The pressure builds behind my eyes. Heat and grief and all the things I've refused to say out loud for years. I could walk away; I've done it before. I could grab Annie's hand, disappear into the hotel, and pretend this night was nothing more than a killer show.

But then I hear her voice again.

Always end on a high note.

And maybe that doesn't mean what I thought it did. Maybe it's not about applause. Maybe it's about finally finishing the song.

My pulse skips. "I'll be right back," I murmur.

Annie frowns. "Chase?"

"I just…I need to handle something."

She starts to follow, but I shake my head. "Stay." I force a small smile. "Don't worry. I'm okay."

I don't know what I'll say. I don't know if I'll yell or fall apart. But my legs move anyway. Because silence didn't save her.

And it sure as hell won't save me.

I cross the courtyard in slow, uneven strides. Every step feels like walking into a fire I swore I'd never touch again.

My dad straightens as I approach. Mom's eyes brim with hope, nerves, maybe guilt.

I stop a few feet away. Not close enough to hug, but not far enough to run.

None of us says anything at first, the silence wrought with a coal mine of fossils and decay.

Then my mom's voice cracks through it. "You were incredible up there."

Dad clears his throat. "You've done well for yourself, son. We're…so proud."

Words elude me. My jaw aches from holding it shut.

I stare at them for a long while, unblinking. And I realize they do look older now. Tired. Smaller than I remember. Threads of silver vein their tawny brown hair, while flecks of gray reflect in their once-golden eyes.

"What are you doing here?" I manage.

"We weren't sure if we should come," my mother says, her voice shaky. "But when we saw the tour date…Vegas was close. Only a few hours."

"We thought maybe it was time," Dad adds quietly.

Time.

Like the clock mattered once she drowned.

I scrub a hand over my face, shake my head. "Fuck. I can't do this."

"Chase…" Mom's hand finds my arm, curling around my bicep. "We don't blame you anymore. We want to move forward. Find our way back to each other."

"Blame me?" My brows arch, voice pitching with audacity. "Yeah. I don't blame me either."

That's not entirely true.

But it's easier to lie. To pretend I was a helpless bystander when I could have dragged Stella to my car and taken her to a hospital instead of a goddamn swim meet.

"We were angry," she says, wiping at a tear, her eyes hazel and haunted. "Broken. Furious you turned your back on us after everything…" She pauses, regroups. "You just disappeared, Chase. No goodbye. No explanation. You even took the dog."

Guilt slices through me, bitter and damning.

I shove it down, twist it into something uglier. Something I can control.

"You made her go," I breathe out, the pain still fresh, still buried deep. "She was sick and begged to stay home. And you made her go anyway."

"You say it like we knew," Dad snaps, voice tight with emotion. "Like we actively signed her death warrant that day. Like we looked her in the eye and said, 'Go die in that pool.'"

I swallow, closing my eyes, forcing back the black cloud of missteps and warning signs that went unread. "She didn't even know if she wanted it anymore. Swimming. She told me. But you never listened. You just wanted a shining success story."

"We never dreamed it would *kill* her," Mom chokes. She takes a breath, tries to pull herself together. "I know this isn't the place. But we didn't know how else to reach you. We tried—we tried so hard—but you changed your number. You vanished, drove off to God knows where. And we were left with nothing but two empty rooms."

Dad's face crumples. "We lost both of our children that day. And we've been trying to find at least one ever since."

My heart clenches as the ache behind my eyes spikes.

I blink hard, trying to clear the haze, but the courtyard lights are too bright, the crowd too loud, everything pressing in from all sides.

My breath shortens.

Not here. Not now.

I press my fingers to my temple, jaw clenched, trying to ride it out without giving anything away.

But Mom notices. "Chase?" Her voice is soft again, braided with concern. "Are you okay?"

I nod too quickly. "Fine. Just…the noise. It's nothing."

She steps closer, instinctively reaching for me like she used to when I was a kid with the flu. "Are you getting migraines?"

Her question lands like a dart.

My parents share a glance.

Before I can respond, Dad clears his throat. "There's something else," he says.

The shift in his tone pulls me up short. My headache throbs harder.

I look between them. "What?"

"Let's go somewhere. Grab a cup of coffee," Mom says. Then she takes my hand, grazing her thumb against my knuckles. "There's something you should know."

CHAPTER 51
Chase

I wander up to our hotel room hours later, sucker punched and in a daze. Annie's follow-up text remains unanswered, and I know she's tucked inside this room, wide awake and worried sick.

Me: My parents are here. I'll see you back at the hotel.
Annie: Do you need me? Can I meet them?

I never responded.
Even now, I don't know what to say.
All I want to do is touch her. Hold her. Sink inside her and beg for her goodness and light to vanquish my demons.
My hand shakes as I swipe the keycard over the sensor.
The soft whir of a lock. The door creaking open.

I trudge inside, watching as Annie leaps out of bed with her heart in her eyes, her gaze glimmering blue and lovesick.

"Chase." She drinks me in. Assesses every inch of my sadness. "I was worried."

I'm sure I look pale, chalky, and half dead, the black shadows saturating the warmth in my eyes.

I need her.

I need her.

She pads toward me, knowing something is wrong. "Tell me what happened. Talk to me."

My jaw shifts. Throat rolls.

Her stare gleams with anxiety and dread, taking my silence as an omen.

"Chase, please—"

I grab her. Before she can take another breath, I'm hoisting her into the air and tossing her on the bed. The mattress bounces, her air locks up. A second later, I'm crawling on top of her, my mouth devouring hers so fiercely, I nearly crack a tooth. My tongue plunges inside, my body smothering her softness in hard muscle and heat and trapped emotion.

When I pull away, nearly gasping, I pin her wrists above her head and rasp against those watermelon lips, "I need you."

I watch the way her pulse throbs in the delicate arc of her throat, causing the little mole below her ear to shudder and dance.

She nods quickly, brows pinched together. "Take me."

A growl rumbles in my chest.

Something howls in the far corners of my mind.

Fear.

Need.

Devastation.

My grip is bruising, punishing.

I release her wrists, flipping her onto her stomach in one fast, rough motion. I tear off her pajama shorts. Rip open my belt. Pull her underwear off with my teeth as my boxers drop to my ankles. With a savage tug, I yank her forward, splitting her thighs apart and thrusting into her from behind. She cries out, gripping the bedcovers, her face smashed into the lump of sheets.

I rut into her, hands gripping her hips with the force of a dozen men.

Again. Again.

I feel possessed. Broken. Desperate.

She claws at the bed, her voice muffled, meeting me thrust for thrust. My hand cuffs the nape of her neck as I lean forward, hitting deeper, my pace nearing violence as our bodies slap together and she soaks my cock.

Warm. Good. Sweet.

My girl.

My everything.

"Annie, Annie, Annie…" I chant her name, reminding myself she's still here, that I'm still here, that we're still here.

She writhes beneath me, her hand reaching behind me to grip my neck. "Oh God…Chase. More. Don't stop."

I fist her hair, angling her head to the side so I can devour her throat, inhaling the taste of salty sweat and lingering perfume. My teeth clamp around the soft flesh, my tongue swirling the edges of that tiny mole.

Then I zone out.

Blackened vision and wayward thoughts.

The room falls away, her whimpers fading into white noise.

I'm grunting, thrusting, disintegrating.

I'm gone. I'm nowhere.

She's still beneath me, warm and gasping, but something breaks loose in my head. My sight darkens at the edges, a tunnel with no end. My thoughts scatter like ash.

And I move without meaning.

Like something in me is trying to burn itself out.

I don't hear her anymore. Can't find her.

My hips pump hard and brutal as I pin her wrists to the bed again, needing leverage, an anchor, something to tether me to reality.

To her. To us. To me.

Her pussy strangles me. My hand is still tied up her long hair, clutching hard, my face buried in her neck as my other hand grips her thigh and my cock pummels her slick heat.

My mind is gone. But when she breaks apart beneath me, sobbing her release into the mattress, my body reacts, and I splinter into pieces.

I come so hard, the room spins.

Bending. Tilting.

Pleasure rockets through me, eclipsing the agony, slaughtering the demons in my head with swords and bullets. My legs shake, body buckles, my head thrown back with a roar.

I fill her. My cum spills out, trickling down her milky-white thighs as I shudder through the aftermath, collapsing on top of her with a fractured moan.

I'm breathing hard. She's breathing harder.

I realize I'm crushing her, so I pull up slowly, slide out, and just stand there.

Staring. Vision glazed, flickering with white lights.

I wait for my brain to click back on. Wait for the room to stop spinning.

Weakly, she pushes up from the bed and turns to look at me as I haul my pants up my legs and flick the zipper. I scrub a hand down my sweat-slick face. Try to get a handle on my oxygen. My thoughts. The present moment.

And I see it.

That's when reality comes crashing back like a sledgehammer.

I bite down on my tongue so hard, I'm close to chewing it right off.

I won't look at her. I can't.

I do.

Every muscle goes stiff like a goat playing dead.

Her hair is in disarray, mauled by my hands. Mascara is smudged under her eyes.

There's a bite mark on her neck, bruises already blooming on her hips and thighs, red handprints all over her body.

She looks wrecked. Destroyed.

By me.

Holy shit.

I did that.

I blacked out, went somewhere else, and became the one person I swore I'd never become—

Him.

CHAPTER 52
Annalise

I don't know why he's looking at me like this.

All I know is that I'm staring into the eyes of a man who looks like he's battling the five stages of grief all in one blink.

I scoot forward, reaching for my shorts and dragging them up my legs. I'm shaking, confused, wondering what to say to wipe that glaze from his eyes.

He staggers backward before I can speak. "What…" His voice cracks, fades. Small and broken. "What have I done?"

I stare at him, speechless.

That was good. Amazing, even. I like it when it's all teeth and scratches, hard thrusts and throat-scraping moans. I don't want him to hold back with me.

"I don't mind it rough. That was—"

"No." He's still shaking his head, still moving away from me. "That wasn't *rough*, Annalise. That was fucking unacceptable."

"Chase, no…"

His face contorts with grief. "Look at what I did to you."

Locking my jaw, I glance down at the red marks on my skin as the sting on my neck pulses from his teeth. My eyes lift to his. "It's nothing I haven't done to you." I crawl off the bed and move toward him, gesturing at his face. "You still have a scratch mark from the last time we—"

"This is different."

"How is it different?"

"Because I'm becoming the person I tried to save you from, goddammit!" He grips his hair with both hands, mouth hanging open with disbelief. With pure agony. "Jesus…I'm so sorry."

The bomb comes out of nowhere, exploding at my feet. Ice laces my blood as I leap off the bed. "No…" He can't think that. Can't believe it. "No. You're not him. Not at all. Why would you say that?"

He collapses against the wall, hands covering his face like he's hiding from his sins. "Don't fucking do that."

"Do what?" I demand, voice pitching with dread.

"Make excuses for the person who hurt you. I hated it then, and I hate it now."

"You didn't hurt me!" Tears leak from my eyes in rivers. "That was consensual sex between two people who love each other."

"Is that what you told yourself with him?"

A dagger twists in my gut. Horror and shock. "I don't care if you were rough with me. I liked it. I wanted it. You don't scare me."

"I scare me," he says.

No.

God, no, he can't do this. Not now. Not after everything.

He wants me to find the parallels. He wants me to hate him.

And I don't understand.

"What happened tonight?" I whisper. "With your parents?"

His jaw tightens. "Doesn't matter."

"It does matter. Something happened. Something hurt you."

"I hurt me. I hurt you, so I hurt me." He stabs a finger at his chest. "I was barely there, zoned out, mind blank. I don't know where I fucking went, but it wasn't anywhere good."

The words rattle through me.

Because I remember.

I remember the way he always holds my face, so steady, so careful, whispering *"Stay with me, Annie. Look at me."*

How he keeps me anchored, how he makes sure I'm there with him in every kiss, every touch, every shiver.

Even when it's quick and urgent, it's always intentional.

But tonight, something slipped. Not out of cruelty.

Out of pain. Out of a storm I can't see.

And that's the part that terrifies him.

He sinks to the floor, spine hitting the wall with a thud, legs splayed like the weight of it all finally caved him in.

I approach him with a chest full of lead, falling to my knees between his legs. I don't touch him. Don't reach. Not yet. "Chase…"

His head drops into his hands. "I can't do this."

"Yes, you can. Whatever this is, we can work through it—"

"You don't get it." His voice is hoarse, shredded. "I looked at you, and for a second…I didn't see you. I didn't see me. I just acted. On nothing. On instinct. And it wasn't loving. It wasn't careful. It was…" He trails off, eyes haunted. "It was fucking wrong. It was the opposite of everything I've tried to be for you."

"Stop," I say firmly, crawling toward him, heart hammering. "That's not what it was. You're human. You're fighting something I can't begin to understand. But it's going to be okay. When we get home, we'll figure out what's been going on, get you checked out—"

"It's too late." He looks at me, broken, jaded, and furious with himself. "You deserve the world, Annie. Music and freedom and kindness and peace. You deserve so much more than what that was. What these last few months have been. I can't keep doing this. It's fucking killing me. And I refuse to become someone you have to justify."

"Chase, please." My heart hollows out as I reach for him, taking his hand, squeezing tight. "I told you. You're not him."

A beat.

A long, tormented beat.

"Yeah," he finally says, untangling his hand from mine. "There is one difference."

I swallow hard, not wanting to hear the answer. But I still ask. "What's that?"

His head lifts slowly, his throat bobbing with sorrow. With dissolution.

We lock eyes.

He doesn't say it. But I see it.

I hear the unspoken words sweeping through me like a burial hymn.

My heart careens to a dead stop inside my chest. "No…" I whisper, eyes puddling with pain. "No. Don't you leave me. Don't you dare walk away."

A tear slips from the corner of his eye.

Inches its way down his cheek.

I can't find my breath. My heartbeats. My thoughts.

The only word dancing through my mind is *why*.

Why is fate so cruel? So negligent?

The notion that obstacles only come to those equipped to tackle them is a sham, and clinging to hope with no promise of survival is a brutal, drawn-out demise.

Nothing is fair.

Everything is hard.

And if I don't get through to him, we're going to sink before we ever have the chance to truly soar.

"Listen to me, Chase. Please, listen." I take his hand again, both hands, gripping tight and shaking sense back into him. "I love you. I love you so much. And I know you love me. Not every moment is easy or gentle or kind. Love is full of hardships, of mistakes and regrets and misspoken words. It's fragile—the most fragile thing in this world. But fragile things are a gift because we *protect* them. We hold them tighter. We fight like hell to keep them whole."

Another tear slips loose. But he shakes his head, lets out a long, hard breath. "You're not seeing this for what it is. For who I am, for what I'm becoming. You're acting like we're written in the stars, but—"

"Dammit, Chase," I cry out, stomach in knots, my dreams

dancing in the wind, a gust away from unraveling. "We're not written in the stars. We *are* the stars."

His eyes glisten, jaw clenched. Fresh tears fall like rain, softening the creases on his face, the deep lines of grief and long-fought struggle.

I press his hand to my chest. "This—*us*—it's worth protecting. Even on the days when we feel like we're coming undone."

A shudder runs through him. His fingers curl around mine, tentative but firm, like he's afraid they'll burn.

"I'm not asking you to be perfect," I whisper. "I'm just asking you to stay. To fight. With me. For me. This is worth it. This is so worth it."

His eyes close, our hands locked together, his heart beating faster. And for a long, aching moment, neither of us says a word.

We just hold on.

Like fragile things.

I press my forehead to his. "We can do this. We were meant to do this."

His breath stutters. One shaky inhale, then another. And when his eyes finally open, they're glassy, but clearer somehow. He's resurfacing.

He doesn't speak. But his grip tightens a little as he leans in.

And then, carefully, like he's scared I might break or scream or run—

He kisses me.

Soft. Barely there.

But it says everything.

That he's still here. That he wants to be.

When he pulls back, his forehead rests against mine again, and we just breathe. New life, new purpose, new dreams.

And maybe tomorrow will be hard. Maybe the next day will be worse.

But right now, in this fragile, trembling moment…

I believe in us.

This isn't the end.

It's not over.

This will never be over.

Sunlight pours in from the hotel window.

My lashes flutter, eyes chafed and burning. Lids swollen. It takes a moment for reality to kick in, for my brain to rehash memories from the night before.

Chase.

A sad smile creeps across my lips as I dig my face into the pillow and sigh. My mouth is dry, limbs heavy. But I feel lighter somehow, because we made it through the worst of the storm.

I reach for him instinctively.

But my hand lands on a pile of cool sheets.

I blink fully awake, head snapping to the side.

The bed beside me is empty. Cold.

Panic lurches in my chest as I sit up too fast, the room spinning. "Chase?"

Silence.

Maybe he went for a walk. Coffee. Air.

My heart kicks harder as I glance around the room.

No hoodie on the chair. No boots by the door. No phone charger.

No sign of him anywhere.

A chill races down my spine.

I stumble out of bed, pulse spiking, yanking open the bathroom door.

Empty.

No toiletries, no used towel. No Chase.

A thousand possibilities spiral through my head, each one worse than the last. My breath comes too fast, too shallow.

He wouldn't leave. He wouldn't. Not after last night.

Not after he held me. Not after his arms wrapped around me slow and careful, like I was breakable, but so was he. His breath was shaky against my neck, but steadying with every beat. His fingers threaded through mine beneath the sheets, and he pulled my hand to his chest as if he was afraid he'd stop breathing without it there.

I remember the way his thumb brushed over my knuckles, grounding himself to reality. To me.

I remember his heartbeat slowing.

His lips ghosting against my forehead.

"I love you," he whispered. "I love you so much, Annie."

And I believed him.

I let myself fall asleep wrapped in that lie.

Warm, hopeful, safe.

And now he's gone.

Anxiety spikes, the world narrowing around me.

I look toward the door again. Across the room. Every corner, every nook.

Then I see it.

A folded piece of paper on the nightstand.

My name is scrawled across it in the messy, slanted way he signs autographs when he's tired.

No.

No, no, no.

I move, racing to the nightstand, my hands shaking as I reach for the note.

Hope bleeding out. Gut screaming.

And the moment my fingers brush the page, I know.

This is a goodbye.

My eyes skim the letters, the curves, the dotted I's.

Three lines. That's all he left me.

> Annie,
>
> I'll forever wonder if you were my best friend or the girl I was supposed to marry.
> Either way, you're the love of my life.
> Never stop chasing your midnights.
>
> —C

Beside the note is his silver ring.

I scream.

Sob.

Break into infinite pieces.

The paper slips from my fingers as my knees hit the floor.

And just like that—

All the music dies.

Night Song

I used to chase the sun
A fire bold and bright
Now I'm standing in the ashes of a hollow,
wasted fight
Every promise turned to smoke
A matchstick in the sky
A dying light, a smothered flame
Our pieces drifting by

But you, you never faded
Even when the world turned cold
A candle out of reach
A spark I couldn't hold

Do you hear the echoes?
Do they haunt you in the night?
All the words we left unspoken
Longing for the light
If I fall, will you still catch me?
If I run, will you let go?
I've been lost inside this winter
Tracing footsteps in the snow

We used to dance in time with thunder
Never feared the lightning strike

But now the storm's gone silent
Lost its will to fight
And so we dance on broken glass
To notes we left unsung
A song that never started
Ashes on my tongue

Maybe we were born to drift
Lost in spaces we can't name
Not every loss is final
Some just burn without the flame

I used to chase the sun
A fire bold and bright
Now I watch the embers fade
Waiting for the night

CHAPTER 53
Annalise

**SIX MONTHS, ONE MISSING PIECE, AND
NO MAP: CHASE, PLEASE COME HOME**

MAY

It starts with silence.

No phone call. No note beyond the one he left behind.

His house is packed up, empty, and abandoned. Toaster is gone too.

Tag says to give him space. Kenna says to give him hell.

As if I have a choice in either of those things.

The media starts circling like vultures, asking if Chase is in rehab or jail.

No. Maybe. We don't know.
I move in with my brother.
One suitcase. One broken heart.
One of Chase's old hoodies he left on the tour bus.
And a journal full of half-songs, still clinging to a trace of him.

JUNE

I spend a lonely Saturday night at Sand Bar, sipping on rum.

Alex walks in with a girl on his arm.

He ditches her halfway through the night and slides onto the stool beside me, all casual charm and old ghosts.

He tells me about Thailand. Blue beaches, quiet nights.

The scorpion on a stick was overrated.

He says he's doing better. Healing.

Part of me is happy for him. Part of me envies the peace he found.

"You look like you're waiting for someone to come back," he says.

I don't correct him.

Around midnight, I pull out my phone and unfollow Alex on all my socials.

Then I order another drink.

No cherries. Just ice.

JULY

Chase's social media goes dark. Kenna doesn't know what to do, so she does nothing.

No sightings. No rumors. No clues.

We try to rehearse without him.

Tag takes over lead and flubs the intro to "Haloed." Rock throws his sticks at the wall.

Nobody says what we're all thinking: it doesn't sound right without him.

At the end of the month, we play a show in upstate New York.

It's a mess. No unity, no direction, no heart.

The crowd looks smaller.

I sing our old songs with a lump in my throat and my eyes on the wings of the stage, hoping he'll walk out with his guitar slung over his shoulder like none of this ever happened.

And then he'll kiss me.

AUGUST

We cancel three shows. Then five.

Finally, Carter releases a statement: "creative hiatus." Any chance of securing a label deal is officially off the table.

The fans are kind but confused. They want answers.

So do I.

I finally get my driver's license.

It takes me three tries and a deep breath that feels like swallowing glass, but sixteen-year-old me would be proud.

Back then, it was raining.

I remember the sound of the wipers. Alex screaming at me from the passenger's seat, telling me I was doing it all wrong.

The hiss of metal. The silence after. The guilt.

But today I pass.

Parallel park without crying.

Thank the instructor without shaking.

I walk out of the DMV with a temporary license clutched in my hand, my photo slightly crooked, eyes too wide.

Still, it's mine.

Proof that I can move forward.

SEPTEMBER

The band stops practicing.

No more check-ins. No more late-night theories.

Everyone's waiting. Holding their breath.

September is when the money shows up. Deposits are wired to every member of the band.

No note. No sender name.

But we know.

The house is quiet.

I sleep on the couch in the basement because I swear I still smell him in the timeworn cushions.

I dream of his voice.

But loving him is no different than dreaming: I open my eyes, and I wake up.

Fall is coming.

I feel it in my chest.

Like change. Like death.

I try to write a new song, but all I get are scribbles and tear stains.

The only lyric that sticks is "you promised."

OCTOBER

The leaves turn golden. I don't.

My brother puts pumpkins on the front porch and lights cinnamon candles.

He's trying.

I pretend I don't see the concern in his eyes when I skip dinner three nights in a row. When I stare too long at the TV without registering a word.

I write half a song. Just pieces. Four chords and a broken chorus I can't sing out loud.

Sometimes I think I hear Toaster scratching at the door.

Sometimes I think I hear Chase call my name.

But it's just the house settling. Just memory playing tricks on me.

Halloween comes, and my costume is no different than the last few months.

I sit on the porch with a bowl of candy and wait for ghosts.

None of them look like him.

> *Take me back to*
> *Midnight skies*
> *Fireflies*
> *Whiskey eyes*
> *And honey moons disguised*
> *As beautiful lies*

Earthworms have five hearts.

I learned that in fourth grade, sitting cross-legged in the grass while my teacher held one up with gloved hands and a plastic magnifier.

"Five hearts," she said. "So even when they're torn in half, sometimes they still twitch."

That stuck with me.

Not the hearts—

The twitch.

The way something can be broken and still pretend to live.

That's what I've been doing since Chase left.

Not living. Not healing.

Just twitching.

Like a severed thing that doesn't know it's already dead.

I wonder how many hearts he tore through.

All five?

Or did one stay untouched, quiet, waiting, buried beneath the wreckage of the others?

Because I swear, I still feel something beating in my chest sometimes. When I hear his voice singing our songs. When I catch the scent of his cologne in my dirty laundry bin. When I wear his silver ring around my neck.

When I look at a goddamn toaster.

He didn't just leave.

He eradicated himself. Scribbled an inky line through our story.

Like our love was a cancer he had to cut out.

And still, I twitch.

I breathe.

I lie to everyone who says I look better now.

I'm not. Not even close.

And the worst part is, if he came back tomorrow…

All five hearts would beat again.

CHAPTER 54
Annalise

Thanksgiving comes and goes. Down comes the fall foliage, and up goes the twinkling holiday lights. It all looks the same.

Gray, dull, and hopeless.

It's been two years since I met Chase Rhodes in my brother's beaten-down, slushy-stained red sedan. He was fighting for his life then.

Now I'm fighting for mine.

I curl up on the couch with a fleece blanket as Kenna floats around my brother's living room, lighting candles that smell like sugar cookies and peppermint pie. She hums Christmas songs under her breath, and I crack a smile when a note goes wildly off-key.

She shoots me a wink. "I knew my terrible singing would come in handy one day."

"Mm," I mutter, snuggling deeper into my blanket burrito of despair. "There is always a trace of joy to be found in tragedy."

"You want to know the real tragedy here?"

"Not really."

"You haven't changed out of those ridiculous pajamas for a week. I swear, every time I see you, I'm forced to look at that off-putting pattern of hamsters reading romance novels."

"You're lucky I didn't order the onesie version."

She tucks the lighter in her pocket, a smile blooming. "Yeah, well, I think we both know it's time for you to get off the couch, start writing again, and put the band back together. Chase was a big piece of it, but he wasn't everything. You have too much talent to go to waste."

My heart plummets at the mention of his name.

Maybe all five.

I pull the blanket up to my chin and set my jaw. "Morale is a bit low, in case you haven't noticed."

"Of course I've noticed. Jesus, Annalise, this destroyed us all. But it's not the end. It's not over. And if you keep living like it is, you'll never start *living* again."

I swallow. "I don't think I'm ready for your unsolicited wisdom yet."

"I don't care. I love you too much to watch you become a shadow of everything you are. It hurts me. It hurts Tag. It hurts your limitless potential." Blowing out a breath, she strolls over to me in an oversize sage sweater and earthy brown leggings. "I'm pissed at Chase. I'm so mad at him for breaking your heart. But you know what? I respect him too. It took guts to walk away for the greater good. Because he would rather leave than treat you any less than you deserve."

A bitter sting presses behind my eyes.

The kind that comes too fast, too sudden.

I tear off the blanket, shooting to my feet. "No. We're not having this conversation again."

"I just don't want to see history repeat itself. I've watched you lose yourself before. With Alex. You gave and gave, until there was nothing left."

"Don't, Kenna. I love you, but don't. This is not the same." I shake my head, hard and fast. "I've done a lot of soul-searching these past few months. And I finally see it for what it was. With Alex, I was surviving. Every day was about making it through, not about being happy. I convinced myself that was love, but it wasn't. Love doesn't drain you until you're empty. Love gives back. Love makes you more."

I drag in a ragged breath, pressing a hand to my chest. "And Chase…he was always the one reminding me I was enough. Every time I broke, he was there to catch me. Every time I slipped into the dark, he pulled me back into the light. Even when we stumbled, I never questioned it. He never made me feel like I owed him anything."

Kenna watches me, her eyes wide and glassy, lips quivering.

"That's the difference," I say, voice cracking. "Alex hollowed me out until there was nothing left but fear. Chase filled me back in. Piece by piece, note by note, until I could finally see myself again. And I won't confuse survival with love ever again. I won't confuse fear with devotion. Chase isn't Alex. Not then, not now, not ever."

My voice cuts off, leaving us in a chasm of silence.

Kenna swallows hard, her lashes wet as she blinks at me, taking it all in.

Tag wanders down the stairs from his bedroom, scratching the back of his head. He glances between us, taking in the scene, the dynamic, the tension in the air.

I fold my arms and look away.

"Hey," he says tightly.

Kenna sits up, reaches for her purse. "I'm gonna go."

"You can stay." Tag moves into the living room in a white T-shirt and sweatpants. "I'm about to make steaks."

"Nah. I'm in my vegan era for at least the next month." Kenna pops up from the couch, her hands disappearing inside the sleeves of her sweater.

I'm a stone block in the middle of the room, quivering with feeling. Pain, grief, anger, uncertainty. I keep my eyes trained on the floor as Kenna approaches with caution.

"Annalise," she whispers. "Hey. Look at me."

My eyes lift. Shimmering with all that feeling.

She pulls me into a firm hug. "I love you. So much. And I hear you, okay? I know they're not the same. I saw the differences too. I'm only trying to help you heal."

I soften in her arms, nodding against her shoulder as I hug her back. "I know."

"I'm sorry I upset you."

"I know."

She strokes my unwashed hair. "Let's go Christmas shopping tomorrow. I'll buy you some new stones. Candles. And then I'll feed you tacos until you pass out with a smile on your face."

My laugh is sob-drenched as I squeeze her tighter. "Sounds perfect."

Pulling back, she leaves me with a flash of teeth. "I'll text you around lunch."

"Okay."

And then she's gone, her eyes meeting with Tag's before she walks out the door, something unspoken passing between them.

I swipe at my face, fix my hair. Then I clear my throat. "I'll get the steaks ready."

Tag follows me into the kitchen. "I got it. Go rest."

"I've been resting for months. I need to stay busy."

"Do you even know how to cook them?"

"Dubious." My chest tightens. "But it's never too late to learn. Accomplishing a perfectly cooked, medium-rare steak was on my bucket list for twenty-three."

"Annalise."

Ignoring him, I rummage through the fridge, pulling out random items.

Steaks, Worcestershire sauce, mustard, raspberry jam.

Tag peers over my shoulder. "Are you planning on cooking, or committing a hate crime against fallen cows?"

I slam the fridge shut and sniff. "It's called creativity."

"It's called let me handle it. I'll call you when it's done."

"Said I got it."

I reach for the steaks and slam them on the counter. Then I peel them out, one by one, snatch a mallet, and start hammering on the beef until it tenderizes.

Until my heart tenderizes.

Until I can't see through the tears, and the juices and blood start to blur into the horror movie that my life has become.

Tag's hand flies out, snagging my wrist. "Sis…"

"No!" I shout, shoving him away. "Let me do this. I need to do this."

"Annalise—"

"Go ahead," I snap. "Tell me I'm losing it. Tell me I need to stay calm and to grow up."

"No." He exhales sharply. "I would never say that to you."

I whip around, mallet still gripped in my hand. "Maybe you should. Maybe I need to hear it."

"What you need is to put the murder weapon down and let me cook you a steak."

"What I need is *him*. I need Chase, Tag. Nothing feels right without him. I can't do this. I can't…" I toss the mallet on the counter and drag my hair back by the roots. "I hate this. Everyone is back to normal, as if we weren't international superstars months ago. Kenna is lighting candles and humming Christmas songs. Rock is touring France, sipping wine with his girlfriend. Zach is off skiing with his daughter, and you're living your best life like Chase walking out on us was a temporary blip. Like we'll all be backstage together soon, holding hands and singing fucking kumbaya."

He scoffs, eyes narrowing. "You think you're the only one who lost him? You think it didn't hurt me too?"

"You didn't even like him half the time."

"Bullshit." He scrubs a hand through his hair. "I did like him. You know I did."

"Your stakes weren't even close to mine. You shared guitar solos with him. I shared everything. My heart. My body. My goddamn *soul*."

"I know," he says, softer now. "And I hate that he left. But maybe it was the right call. Maybe it was what you needed, even if you can't see that yet."

"I know what's best for me. And it wasn't that."

"You think he's happy out there? All alone in that cabin, knowing you're—"

He stops short.

Bites down on his tongue.

A thick swallow snakes up his throat as his eyes dip to the floor, like he can scoop those words back up.

I blink, stunned.

Trembling and barely breathing.

I gape at him. "What cabin?"

Tag's face goes white. "Nothing. Forget it."

"What cabin?"

Shaking his head, he swivels away and charges into the living room.

"Tag! Don't walk away from me." I follow, breaking into a run, tripping over my feet. "What do you know? Has he contacted you? Do you know where he is?"

"Let it go, Annalise."

"Absolutely not. You can't—"

"It was just a hunch." He whirls around. "You need to leave it."

My eyes are huge, borderline crazed. "Never," I breathe out.

I stare at him, my world dissolving like paper-mâché.

I feel ambushed, bowled over, and thunderstruck.

But I know. I see it all over his guilty face.

Betrayal.

"You know where he is," I whisper brokenly. "You've known this whole time."

Tag looks like he's been gut-punched. He doesn't deny it. Doesn't even try.

"How long?" I croak.

He rubs the back of his neck, exhaling sharp. "Dammit…"

"How. Long." Each work stabs like a dagger.

"Six months."

Something in me detonates. "What?"

My brother swipes both hands down his face, trying to erase the shame in his eyes. "Fuck," he curses. "I'm sorry. You were never supposed to find out. I was trying to protect you."

I blink a billion times.

My eyebrows swing up like they're trying to escape what I just heard.

Oh my God.

Oh my God.

This isn't happening.

First Chase. Now Tag.

Two completely different betrayals. Two cracks in the same fault line.

One left me. The other stood beside me and said nothing.

Is that all I am? Someone people walk away from and lie to in the name of *protection*?

Because I don't feel protected.

I feel stripped. Exposed. Like every person I've ever trusted has been holding a secret behind their teeth, just waiting to let it rot.

"How dare you," I rasp, tears pooling in my eyes. "How dare you stand by and watch me suffer, all while you had the remedy in your back fucking pocket."

His eyes flare. He looks shattered. Taking me by the shoulders, he bends to eye level. "I never wanted this."

I wriggle out of his grip. "Don't touch me."

"Christ, Annalise, I didn't plan any of this. A guitar showed up at my door—one of his builds. No note." He swallows hard. "So I traced it."

The air leaves me. "How?"

"There was a return label. Rural post office, no name. I got curious." He lets out a bitter breath. "I dug into it, dropped the band name once or twice. One thing led to another."

"You found him?"

"Yeah," he murmurs. "I found him."

For once in my life, I can hardly string together a handful of words. "Is that where you really went back in June when you said you were visiting your college buddy in Boston?"

A rueful nod.

"So you lied."

"Because he begged me not to tell you," Tag says, stepping forward. "He said if you knew where he was, you'd come after him. And he didn't trust himself not to let you."

My stomach pitches. "That doesn't make sense. I don't—"

"He was scared. He told me everything that happened that night…minus a few details I made him leave out." Sighing, he rakes a hand through his hair and stares over my shoulder. "He said he hurt you. Said he was afraid he was becoming—"

"Yeah, I got that speech too," I cut in, grief spilling down my cheeks. "He fed me the same noble, self-sacrificing story. But you know what no one did? No one asked me. Not once. Not what I wanted. Not what I could handle. You both made choices *for* me like I'm some delicate flower who needs shade and watering, when all I needed was to be heard. To have a voice in my own story."

Emotion glimmers in my brother's eyes as he stares at me, pleading for forgiveness with just a look. "He didn't want to leave you," he says. "God, he looked broken. But he was convinced staying would hurt you more, and I believed him. I believed him because I couldn't watch you go through that again. I believed him because if someone has the balls to walk away from the love of their life, they're either a coward or they're trying to save her." He pauses, reaching for me again. "And Chase isn't a coward."

"I don't need saving anymore," I counter, pulling back. "I just need him. I've needed him for *eight months*."

Tag's eyes meet mine. Glassy. Torn. "I know."

"I can't believe you kept this from me."

"I thought I was doing the right thing," he says. "That you'd move on, start living again."

I shake my head, blindsided, reeling in the aftermath of another catastrophic blow.

My jaw tightens as I clench my teeth, gaze lifting.

Something softer punches through the steely haze.

"Is he…okay?" I croak.

Tag blinks at me, then looks away. "Subjective."

"It's a straightforward question."

"I don't know, Annalise." He throws his arms up. "He looked

like hell, okay? But he loves you. Misses you. So…I don't know how to answer that."

I square my shoulders and take a step forward. "Give me the address."

Silence. He doesn't move.

"Tag."

A long pause. A longer sigh.

Then, reluctantly—

"Top dresser drawer."

CHAPTER 55
Annalise

I roll up to the gas station with an address in my pocket and a lump in my throat.

The building looks different: fresh paint, new signage, a gleaming red Coke machine out front where the old one used to buzz and leak. The cracked pavement's been repaved, the flickering overhead lights replaced. It's almost unrecognizable.

Except for the memory etched in my bones.

This is where Chase bled.

Where the world tilted and time split in two.

Where our story began.

Killing the engine, I sit for a minute, staring at the storefront like it might open its mouth and confess something. My reflection catches in the glass, and I hardly recognize the face staring back at me.

Someone weathered. Someone tired. Someone missing.

I hop out and walk inside, planning to stock up on road trip snacks as I make the fourteen-hour drive to Sevierville, Tennessee.

That's where he's living now.

A cabin in the woods. A life of isolation and self-loathing.

I pulled up the property on Google Maps, studying the street view as if it held answers. The road was narrow and crumbled, hemmed in by thick trees that swallow light. No neighbors. No traffic. Just a gravel drive that disappeared behind a slope of overgrown pine and shadow.

A place designed to be left alone. To fade.

And still…I'm going.

Because no matter how far he runs, I refuse to let him hide forever.

The welcome bell chimes, sounding brighter somehow. An older man hangs behind the counter, flipping through a magazine, glancing up with a nod in my direction.

"Filling up?" he asks.

I clear my throat. "Just looking around."

"Take your time."

Stocked shelves glimmer with overpriced snacks, packs of gum, and rows of energy drinks promising a jolt of life I can't remember. The air smells like stale coffee and motor oil, a combination that's almost soothing in its simplicity.

I peer over at the man as I scour the aisle that's brimming with colorful candy and chips.

I recognize him.

The man who shot Chase.

He was all over the news. Twice. Once for the attack, and

again when the gas station was ransacked by furious fans once they learned about Chase's history with this place.

I remember the press conference from two years ago.

The store clerk in front of a wall of cameras, choking on his apology. Said he panicked. Said he'd been robbed multiple times in the same month. Said he thought Chase was reaching for something more than a can of dog food in his hoodie pocket.

He wept in front of reporters, talking about his daughter, about how she was in medical school and how he was working double shifts to help with the loans.

Said he couldn't afford to lose the station. Couldn't afford to lose everything.

Chase never pressed charges.

And while the D.A. tried to build a case anyway—reckless endangerment, excessive force—with no victim testimony and a city quick to rally behind its own, it didn't stick.

The man kept his job. Took a leave. Came back quieter and older.

Now he's behind the counter, wiping his hands on a towel, his soft eyes smiling at me as I grab a bag of trail mix, a bottle of water, and begin to check out.

"Will this be all today?" He rings up my items, reaching for a plastic bag.

"Yes. Thank you."

A woman strolls in from the back room.

Black hair, warm skin, sleek heels that *clickety-clack* against the linoleum. She moves like someone who doesn't belong behind a counter. Just a visitor.

His daughter.

She eyes me briefly, offering a smile, then starts restocking a tray of scratch-offs.

Nodding my thanks, I take my receipt and head toward the exit. I make it halfway before I pause, something gripping me.

A pull.

A memory.

A need.

I turn back around, heart thudding.

"Do you…" Hesitating, I take a step closer. "Do you recognize me? From the band Honey Moons?"

The man's eyes narrow slightly.

The woman straightens behind the scratch-off display.

"Honey Moons," the clerk echoes. "Yes. That's the one he was in."

The air shifts. Not hostile but wary.

He doesn't need to be named.

"I'm not here to cause trouble," I say quickly. "I just…" I glance around the store, this cleaned-up version of a place that still carries blood in its corners. "I just wanted to stop by since I remember what happened and I—"

"Whole town knew. Then the internet knew. Then they lit us up." The man adjusts his eyeglasses, gaze unreadable. "You know how many windows were smashed once word got out? How many death threats we got?"

The woman's arms fold. "It got ugly after everything made the social media rounds. People threw bricks. Spray-painted awful things on the windows. Branded my father a monster."

"I know," I say softly. "I'm sorry."

She exhales, tapping her burgundy nails on the counter. "But he came back, you know. This past spring."

My pulse kicks up. "Chase?"

Spring.

The same season he disappeared, leaving nothing but a scribbled note, an "I love you" fading from his lips, and a broken heart full of loss in his wake.

"Yes. He handed me a check," the man says. "Didn't ask for anything. Just said he wanted to make it right. For the station. For my daughter. For what it cost us."

"He asked about my medical schooling," she adds, her voice softening. "Said he hoped I made it all the way through."

My eyes sting. "He…never told me."

The woman studies me for a beat, her brown eyes tender. "He didn't say much. Just that he'd made mistakes. That this was one he could at least try to make right, and that he wished he'd come by sooner."

I blink fast, throat thick. "That sounds like him." Then I look at her, absorbing the quiet warmth behind her words. "I'm Annalise."

She offers her hand across the counter. "Parvati."

"Thank you. For telling me."

She gives a small nod.

As I turn to leave, Parvati calls out one more time. "Hey… if you see him, tell him we appreciate the money. It saved us." She looks down as she unzips a backpack with a hospital badge clipped to the strap. "And let him know I'm still going. Two years into my residency. Neurology."

Her fingers brush the tag: *Resident, Parvati Singh—Rutland Regional Medical Center.*

"Yeah," I murmur, fingers curling around the plastic bag, my chest full. "I will."

Then I push open the door and step into the frost and sunlight, heart pounding, mind racing, the past pressing closer with every mile I put between me and that station.

I drive.

Toward the cabin.

Toward Chase.

Toward the love song we never finished.

It's smaller than it looked in the pictures: tin roof, log siding, a tiny porch made of wind-beaten wood planks.

A painted brown door and a single square window make up the face, the home devoured by billowing, mature trees.

I choke on my own heart, and it tastes like grief and fear.

Eight months.

Eight months he's been here, living and hiding.

Away from me. Away from everything.

All because he was scared of what he was becoming.

But I know the truth.

He was becoming my rock, my light, my savior.

My favorite song. The honey moon in my midnight sky.

As I sit in the driver's seat, clutching the wheel, I stare at the house like I might be able to see through the logs and catch a glimpse of the man who abandoned me.

Anger stabs at my chest. Remorse. Red-hot pokers of buried pain.

I need answers. I need clarity. I need him.

With a deep breath, I switch off the ignition and pocket my key fob. The house seems to move farther away with every step I take. Everything blurs. The trees, the rust-colored logs, my thoughts. I don't know how he'll react. I don't know how *I'll* react.

My mind takes me back to August when I sat behind the wheel for the first time in years. My palms were slick. My heart thundered so loud I could barely hear the instructor.

I remember the tunnel of motion, the trembling, the ache in my jaw from clenching it so hard.

I thought I might crash again. Lose control. Fall apart the way I did the first time.

But I didn't.

I took a breath, gripped tighter, and kept going.

This feels the same.

Like stepping into the wreckage before the impact and trusting that this time, maybe the wheels won't spin out.

I climb the steps slowly, my pulse badgering at my throat.

One knock. That's all it takes, until suddenly I'm sixteen again, barreling toward something I don't know how to stop.

I wait on his front stoop, hands tangled in my fuzzy sweater, makeup half melted from the car's heat vents. The air is warmer here. Softer. A fifty-degree breeze brushes against my skin like a memory I'm not ready for.

Then I hear it—

The rapid *click-click* of nails against wood.

Toaster.

Tears blanket my eyes, distorting the door in front of me as I shift my weight from foot to foot, every second stretching like a lifetime.

Breathe, Annalise.

Just breathe.

Footsteps follow.

Heavier. Familiar.

I wait for it.

The twist of a knob, the creak of a door.

And when it happens, I'm not ready. I'm not ready to face him.

My stomach coils with anxiety and fear and hope and love.

So many vivid memories. So much history.

The door cracks open a sliver, and there he is—

Chase.

Blinking into the hazy sunlight. Squinting as he registers me.

Another blink. A beat.

And then recognition settles in, mirrored in his eyes, raw and unguarded.

He pulls the door open wider, standing before me in a white T-shirt and dark-wash jeans—feet bare, dog at his side, wearing a dumbstruck expression.

He looks the same. He looks different.

A dream dressed as devastation.

Chase swallows hard. "Annie."

My body vibrates as I stand on his stoop, slack-jawed and sunk, unable to look away. We stare at each other for a long time. Saying nothing. Saying everything.

A spectrum of mixed emotions rockets through me.

How dare you.

I miss you.
Why did you leave me?
Can I come in?
You look different.
You look perfect.
I love you.

Chase's lips part to speak, but nothing comes out. Just a strangled sound, bleeding with all the same things I'm feeling.

Then he looks down at the wooden porch like he still wants to hide.

My hands curl at my sides. "Surprise," I whisper.

He blinks again, clearing his vision, before his chin slowly lifts. "Annie, I—"

I cut him off by pushing through the door. "So, this is it, huh? Where you went? What you abandoned me for?"

My gaze sweeps the small, cluttered living room. The cabin can't be more than a thousand square feet, yet every inch feels heavy with the life he's been building without me.

The couch is pushed awkwardly to the side, cushions worn and slouched. There's a workbench wedged against the front window, bathed in natural light, littered with clamps, chisels, strips of rosewood and maple. Half-finished guitar bodies lean against the wall like sleeping ghosts, and a soldering iron rests beside a coiled cord.

A cracked coffee mug holds picks and nails. Sketches are pinned to the wall with thumbtacks that showcase blueprints, wiring diagrams, and fretboard designs. It smells like varnish and pine.

This isn't a living room.

It's a refuge. A workshop.

A war zone.

"It's nice," I murmur, panning back to him. "Cozy. I'm happy for you."

His hand grips the doorframe, every muscle stretched tight, every vein dilating. With his back facing me, he stares out at the silent street.

Toaster races over, winding around my ankles, his soft fur a small antidote to this wound of sadness hellbent on taking me down.

I crouch to pet him. The only sweetness buried in the rubble.

"I'm sorry," Chase says, barely a breath, hardly loud enough to hear.

His words only fuel my fire.

I lift to a stand, heart beating like a conga. "That's not good enough. It will never be good enough."

"I know." Exhaling a long breath, he finally pivots, wedges his shoulder against the frame. "You weren't supposed to find me."

"I'm well aware," I bite out.

"I didn't want you to see me like this."

"Like what? A coward?" I can't let go of this anger. I'm choking on it. Suffocating. "Too bad. Tag told me where you were. And if you thought for a second I wouldn't burn the whole world down looking for you, then you don't know me at all."

His jaw tightens as he stares at me from across the room.

I chomp down on my lip, holding back the emotional dam. "I have to say, it kills me you wouldn't do the same."

Breathing heavily, he closes his eyes as the door thunks shut. "You don't understand."

"Of course I don't. I don't understand any of this. How you could vanish into the night without a goodbye. How you could leave us all stranded in Vegas with no answers, no explanation. How you could leave *me*. I thought we were…" My words get clogged.

He takes a slow step forward. "We were everything you thought we were."

"Liar."

"No." Another step. "We were. We are. Nothing has changed for me—not the way I feel about you, the way your songs and your voice have followed me around for eight torturous months like a ghost I can't shake. I hear you in every awful fucking silence. I feel you in every sunset I don't deserve. In every moon, every midnight. There's only you."

"Bullshit!" Tears burst from my eyes, hot and wild, as I slash a hand through the air, cutting his words in half. "Bullshit, Chase. If you loved me, you would have stayed. Fought. But all you gave me were empty promises and this broken fucking heart that feels too heavy to carry around most days. You abandoned me. Betrayed me. Even now, you wish you never saw me again. That I never found you. I see it in your eyes."

He visibly flinches, as if I reached across the room and slapped him. "I never wished that," he murmurs. "I want to see you more than anything in this world."

"Prove it."

His eyes burn, locked on mine, but there's something fractured behind them, something unspoken. He opens his mouth like he's going to say more, then clamps it shut.

"You talk about ghosts?" I continue, fighting through the

misery. "I *became* one. And now you want to stand here and tell me you still love me like that makes this okay?"

His face crumples as he takes another step forward. "I wanted to tell you. Every goddamn day, I wanted to call. To explain. But I couldn't find the words that wouldn't break you."

"So break me," I demand. "Tear me apart. Rip out my heart and stomp on it, because at least then I wouldn't be walking around with this hollow, useless thing rotting in my chest where our story—our *future*—used to be."

"Annie…" He moves toward me, gait intensifying.

But then he stumbles.

Not on something small. Not on a loose shoe or some stray cord.

A whole-ass coffee table right in his path.

His shin slams into it hard, and he grunts, catching himself on the wall.

Something cold licks down my spine.

He doesn't curse. Doesn't laugh it off. Doesn't even look at the table like it betrayed him.

He just…freezes.

I study him, brows bending. "What's wrong?"

My gaze zips around the room again, taking in the half-completed guitars, covered in a thin layer of dust. Enough for me to know he hasn't touched them in weeks. Maybe longer. The workbench is messy but undisturbed. No fresh sawdust. No wood glue scent. Even the soldering iron is cold.

That's when it clicks.

He hasn't been working.

Not even on the one thing that's always saved him when his world fell apart.

Chase wipes a hand down his face, cups his jaw. "You need to go."

"Absolutely not." My eyes widen as I peer back at him, head shaking with disbelief. "I drove fourteen hours to get here. I'm not leaving until you talk to me. Until you explain yourself."

"It's better if you go. Live your life." Pain streaks through his voice, splintering the edges. "Pretend you never met me."

Agony breaches my bones. Digs a hole in my chest.

"You don't mean that," I breathe out, finally unlocking long enough to move forward. My eyes drink him in, his twitching muscles, his hand braced on the wall like it's the only thing keeping him standing. He's pale, brittle, and breaking. And I don't know how to slip through his cracks. "Chase, please. I'm right here, begging for you to talk to me, to *see* me—"

"That's the goddamn problem," he snaps, shoving off the wall, his hand tearing through his hair like he could rip the pain out by the roots.

I still, my breath hitching.

His eyes meet mine.

Frantic, haunted.

"That's the problem, Annie," he says. "I can't."

CHAPTER 56
Chase

SIX MONTHS EARLIER—JUNE

"This is lovely, Chase. I think it suits you."

My mother floats around the old cabin, assessing every cobwebbed corner. It's far from lovely. It's a goddamn prison cell, dressed up in pine, hardwood, and a picturesque background of canopied trees and roaming black bears.

After spending twenty-four hours packing up my rental house, I shoved my clothes into boxes, gathered my guitar-building tools, collected my dog, and drove across the country to Arizona to stay with my parents for the next four weeks.

I knew it was bad then—my failing vision.

Halfway into the drive, I missed a crucial exit and didn't realize it until I was nearly an hour off course. Signs blurred. Headlights smeared into streaks. I kept the window cracked to feel the wind shift when I drifted too close to the edge of the road.

Now I'm here. In this goddamn pinewood cage my parents call a "healing retreat."

My mother smooths a dish towel over the counter like that'll fix something. "It has everything you need. Running water, peace, good light…"

Good light.

Christ.

I force a nod, even as the sunlight through the window scorches my eyes. Everything's too bright or too dim lately. There's no in-between. No clarity.

I sink onto the edge of the stiff couch, my dog curling loyally at my feet like he's afraid I'll vanish if he blinks.

"Do you want me to unpack your tools?" she asks, too cheerfully. "Might be nice to build something again."

My eyes close.

I can't even thread a needle without squinting for five minutes. I've sliced my finger twice in the last week trying to sharpen a chisel.

But it's all I have. My only outlet. My saving grace.

"Yeah," I mumble. "Sure."

She hums under her breath. "I wish you found a place closer to home. We hate that you're so far away."

Home.

My home isn't there.

My home isn't here.

My home is wrapped up in paper-white skin, vivid purple streaks, an angelic voice, and watermelon lips.

Annie.

My girl. My love. My real home.

But not all homes are permanent.

And not all love stories end with a happily ever after.

My father shuffles in through the side door with a bear horn in his hand and a baseball cap pulled low over shaggy, almost-gray hair. "Got the grass mowed," he says, sweat dripping down his face. "Place looks less like a hermit's bunker and more like a rock star's hideout now. You should hire a weekly landscaper, considering you're sitting on a good amount of savings and barely anything else to spend it on."

I grunt a reply.

While I prefer living under my means—having lived that way out of necessity for too many years—I make a mental note to contact companies. Who knows when my vision will be gone for good. Although running a lawn mower over my foot sounds less painful than my current reality.

Mom winds toward me, clearing a path. Then she takes a seat beside me on the couch as Toaster sniffs her arm and gives her a lick. "Honey, we want to make sure you're okay before we head home," she says, worry tingeing her tone. "You haven't been alone in over a month. It scares us that you're out here by yourself with hardly any cell service, let alone friends close by."

"I'll manage. I've done it before."

She swallows, tucking a glossy piece of hair behind her ear. "This is different."

"What, because I'm handicapped now?"

Her eyes flick to mine, sharp with the kind of pain that comes from knowing too much. "No. Because you're shutting down. Again."

I look away.

For years after Stella died, I blamed them for everything.

Her downfall. Her death. My pain.

The way they couldn't even say her name out loud, like grief might crack the walls if we let it breathe.

So I cut them out.

I ran.

I told myself they'd failed her, because it was easier than admitting I'd failed too. That I'd refused to face it. That I let my regret fester into resentment and wore it like armor.

It wasn't until the MRI tech made a soft noise behind the glass and I saw my mother's face crumple beside me that I realized how wrong I'd been.

They hadn't stopped loving me.

I'd just stopped letting them.

So when they offered to help—to let me stay with them, to cook, to sit with me in waiting rooms that smelled like bleach and dying hope—I let them.

Because maybe I wasn't the only one who needed a second chance.

My mother sighs, brushing a speck of dust off her jeans. "We went with you to every appointment. We sat through every scan, Chase. I heard the surgeon say it. I know what you're facing. And I know you think pushing people away makes it easier."

"It does," I mutter.

"It doesn't," Dad cuts in, leaning against a wall, his arms folded. "It just makes it quieter. More lonely."

I clench my jaw, something hot and sour building in my throat. I don't want to do this. Not now, not when everything inside me is already hanging by a thread.

"I'm not ready," I admit, barely audible.

"I know." Mom slides her hand over mine. "But when the time comes and you finally decide you don't want to go through this alone, please let that girl of yours know. She deserves more than silence."

I don't respond. Just stare straight ahead.

Because I'm not sure I deserve her anymore.

And I'm even less sure I ever did.

My father stands near the window, staring out at the swaying tree branches that dance to a silent song. When he finally speaks, it's quiet, matter-of-fact. "Thing about mistakes," he says, still not looking at me, "you don't always realize you're making one until it's already done. Until the damage is sitting in the room with you."

My heart clenches.

Throat closes.

Palms start to sweat.

All the best mistakes have names.

Example number one: Billy Fritz.

He was the bully I beat the crap out of in eighth grade after he shoved Stella off the monkey bars and she broke her arm.

An immediate suspension followed, then a grounding that bled into summer, keeping me isolated in my bedroom with nothing but brainless cartoons and my guitar.

Stella tiptoed into my room one afternoon with a cast on her arm and a cherry Popsicle in her good hand. "If I ever get married someday, I hope my future husband is as brave as you."

Just like that, it was all worth it.

Example number two: My Sentra.

I was eighteen, driving up to the Colorado mountains with bald tires, a half tank of gas, and my buddy riding shotgun, swearing we were headed into the greatest weekend of our lives.

The car didn't make it.

We ended up stuck at a roadside diner all night, drinking burnt coffee, playing cards with a waitress named Midge, and betting on which trucker would fall asleep mid-story.

Best breakdown I ever had.

Example number three: Key West.

I had just left home, burned through most of my cash, and thought saltwater might fix what failures couldn't.

I slept in my car, busked on street corners, and ate enough gas station sandwiches to question my will to live.

But the sunsets were biblical.

And for a little while, that felt like enough.

That leads me to my favorite mistake: Annalise Adams.

The one that didn't wreck me all at once.

She did it slow. Quiet. With every look, every laugh, every song, every time she saw straight through the version of me I let the world believe.

And by the time I realized it, I didn't want to be fixed.

I just wanted to be hers.

But then the headaches started. The changes. The fear. The world blurred, the music faded, and terror became a permanent fixture behind my ribs.

So I did the one thing I swore I'd never do.

I ran again.

I left her.

Told myself it was mercy. That disappearing was kinder than dragging her through the dark with me. I thought it would be easier for her to hate me than to watch me fall apart.

I figured if I left her angry, it'd hurt less in the long run.

I was trying to protect her, trying to spare myself the sound of her breaking.

But I've heard it anyway. Every day since.

Now, only time will tell if this mistake will end the same way as all the others.

Or if the lights finally go out for good.

CHAPTER 57
Chase

PRESENT DAY

It takes a moment for my words to settle in. To click into place.

And then I hear the air leave her in a noticeable *whoosh*.

"Chase," she rasps, a hand lifting to her mouth. "Chase, no."

She launches herself at me, taking me in her arms. Two soft hands cradle my face, forcing our eyes to meet.

Her touch. Her scent.

God, how I've missed it.

"You can see me," she says, desperation bleeding through. "I'm here. I'm right here."

My watery gaze finds hers as my head shakes, breath sawing out in agony-drenched gasps. "Shapes," I murmur. "Lights. The streaks in your hair." I drag trembling fingers through her hair. "But not enough."

She's close to hyperventilating. She can't find any air.

"I couldn't put you through this. I was changing—physically, mentally. I couldn't do that to you. Love isn't always about staying. It's about knowing when to walk, when the cost of staying might be worse than the loss of leaving."

The pain. The pain is excruciating.

But it's not my head this time. It's having her in my arms while not having her at all. She's still so far away. A beautiful mirage I can't grasp.

Annie clutches my cheeks tighter. "You don't get to rewrite love like that. You don't get to make it noble and erase me from the ending."

Tears slip from my lashes, catching in the stubble on my jaw. "I didn't want you to see me like this. Weak. Angry. Falling apart every time another piece of the world goes dark."

"You think I wanted the version of you that only shows up when things are easy? No way. That's not how it works. I want you, Chase. Even broken. Even terrified. Even sick."

I suck in a breath, then untangle myself from her arms. "Please, Annie. Just go. You have to."

"No."

"You're strong. And you still have music—"

"*You're* the music!" she shrieks. "You. Only you. All the music died the day you left me. My heart is with you, Chase."

Devastation rips through me like a fault line finally splitting open.

Surging forward, I grip her cheeks between my hands and press my forehead to hers. "Then your heart is with a dead man."

The words are jagged and low, spilling through clenched teeth like they're rotting on my tongue.

Because it's true.

Because I am.

Because it's over.

The secrets. The hiding. The harrowing truth.

"What?" She gasps. Her hands fall from my face. "Don't say that. Don't you *dare* say that."

I just stare at her. Haunted. Hollow.

As honest as I've ever been.

"You're not dying," she whispers, more to herself than to me. "You're not *dying*."

I stay silent.

Don't correct her.

And that's when I feel the shift.

The fear deepening, turning into something raw and paralyzing.

"Chase," she says again, louder now, stumbling back a step. "Don't do this. Don't just stand there and look at me like that. Tell me it's not true."

My eyes flutter closed. I exhale like the words are knives in my chest.

"It's a tumor," I finally say. "Glioma. Along the optic chiasm."

And for the first time, I'm grateful I can't see her clearly.

Because I don't think I could survive the look in her eyes.

The black storms swirling in crystal-blue seas.

She chokes on a sob.

"It's low-grade on paper, but aggressive as hell," I continue. "The kind that usually shows up in kids, not grown men. And when it *does* show up in adults—especially along the optic pathway—it hits harder, faster. It's not always fatal, but this one's pressing on all the wrong nerves in all the wrong places. If it spreads deeper, I'm done." Tears pool in my eyes and spill over, unchecked. My knees threaten to give out, but I stay standing, if only to prove I still can. "The vision loss is permanent. I don't see people anymore, Annie. Just shapes. Movement. You're a silhouette in front of a dying sun. The streaks in your hair are the only thing I recognize. The rest is…gone. Your beautiful face. Your eyes. The way you looked at me like I was worth saving, worth loving. It's torture. It's worse than death."

My legs give out.

I collapse in the middle of the room, elbows on my knees and head in my hands.

Annie buckles in front of me, clutching my face. "Listen to me," she begs, choking on tears. "Listen. Please. There's still time. You can see a doctor, you can—"

"I *have*," I say, sharper. "I sat in a white room with one of the top neurosurgeons in the country. He looked me in the eye and told me to get my affairs in order. That if the vision loss is all I get, I should be grateful."

She croaks.

Speechless. Wordless. Stewing in disbelief and denial.

"Even though it's technically low-grade, it's in the worst possible place. They can't get near it without cutting through things that control basic functions—speech, memory, movement. One wrong move and I'm not just blind. I'm gone."

"No…" She shakes her head, squeezing me tighter, trying to evict the trespasser in my head with nothing but love and hope and futile words. "No. That's not…there are second opinions. Treatments. Trials. We can fly anywhere. I'll make the calls."

My forehead drops to hers. "I'm scared," I admit, just a whisper. "I can't play. Can't build. Can't drive. I miss steps. I hate the dark. And sometimes…sometimes I wonder if it would've been easier if I'd never met you. At least you wouldn't have to carry around this burden of falling in love with a dying man."

She pulls me to her, wraps me up in warmth and begging, until my face falls against her shoulder. "You don't get to lie down and wait to die, Chase. Not when I'm right here, telling you to fight. Not when there's still hope."

"I don't want that. I can't carry the weight of someone else's hope. I'm barely surviving my own reality, and I refuse to let you be tied to a walking death sentence."

She grabs my face. "You idiot," she breathes. "You beautiful, broken idiot. I'm not tying myself to a man. I'm loving him."

The breath stutters out of me, sharp and broken.

I close my eyes.

My forehead slides against her as I cradle the back of her head. "My sister," I say, chest heavy. "She didn't just drown."

Annie pauses, then pulls back. "What do you mean?"

"It's what we believed," I say. "What everyone believed, even though she was a strong swimmer. We thought she was just dehydrated. Sick. Tired. That it was a tragic accident." I pause, swallowing hard. "But after I left town, my cousin started getting brutal headaches. He got checked out, and they caught it. Same tumor, low-grade, in his optic pathway. His is treatable due to the tumor's location. He's still alive."

Annie doesn't speak, doesn't move.

"My parents had Stella's autopsy reexamined. Brought in someone new. And this time..." My throat tightens. "They found it. A tiny mass. High-grade glioma, buried deep. It was missed the first time, but it was there. And it wasn't benign. Likely caused a stroke or an aneurysm."

Her voice is barely audible. "So...she didn't drown?"

"She did," I murmur. "Her lungs were full of water. She was still alive when she went under, but she couldn't swim. Couldn't scream for help. She probably seized or lost consciousness, and no one saw it happen. So the cause looked obvious. No one thought to look closer."

Annie sinks back on her heels, wiping at her face as the full weight of it lands. "When did you find out?"

I exhale, the memory bitter in my mouth. "That last night in Vegas. My parents told me after the show."

I've tried to forget everything about that night.

The way I tore into her.

The way I used my sorrow like a weapon.

Looking back, I see it now—the edginess, the way I'd go from managing to miserable without warning. I thought it was just the pain.

But it was the tumor. Pressing in the wrong place, disrupting hormone levels, scrambling signals that were never meant to get crossed. I wasn't just angry; I was chemically off-balance.

And I tried so hard to hide it from her.

Then I scared myself enough to walk, believing that a volatile, dying man had no place in Annie's life.

But she's still holding me. Still hanging on to whatever pieces I have left.

Gently, she reaches for my hand, her fingers threading through mine like a lifeline. "You should've told me. Because I wouldn't have run. I would have stayed. I still want to stay."

My heart squeezes. "I don't know how to let you."

"Start here. Start right now. Because I'm not going anywhere. I will never leave you." Her voice collapses on the words. "And maybe there's still hope. We can fight this. You and me. Just tell me what to do."

For once, I don't have an answer.

Only this unbearable ache in my chest that says I can't let her go.

Not now. Not ever.

My voice breaks as I look at her, drinking in her blurry borders, beautiful shape, and purple stripes. "Just…hold me."

She doesn't hesitate. Annie pulls me in like she's been waiting to do it since the day I left.

Arms around my shoulders. Fingers in my hair. Her cheek against mine.

I fold into her. Every jagged edge. Every broken part.

We end up on the bed, curled together in the dark. The room is filled with the sound of her breathing, steady and strong, anchoring me to something real.

Toaster finds us moments later, weaving into our two-person cocoon.

My family.

A life I want more than anything.

Then, as the minutes stretch and the light drains from the room, Annie begins to sing.

Holy doves and marble arches.

Kings and thrones and beauty and moonlight.

Secret chords.

"Hallelujah."

Her voice trembles through the verses, cracking on the lines that cut too deep. More breath than melody. More prayer than song.

By the time she reaches the chorus, my tears spill freely.

I grieve.

Everything I've lost.

Everything I'll never live to see.

She holds me through it, arms wrapped around me like she's trying to hold the world together.

She cries too.

And somewhere between the weeping and the war, her voice becomes the only thing that doesn't hurt.

CHAPTER 58
Annalise

By the second night, I finally charge my phone and text my brother back.

Tag: Are you good? Did you make it?
Tag: You better be alive.
Tag: I swear to god, if you're dead and didn't tell me...
Tag: Sis. Answer me. Proof of life or I'm driving over there myself.
Tag: In the car. Bringing Kenna. Last chance before we show up with flashlights, a trunk full of houseplants, and whatever the hell she's been manifesting this week.

I glance at the time stamp on the last message and my anxiety loosens when I see it was sent less than an hour ago. He was either bluffing or he didn't make it far.

Me: Sorry. I'm here. I'm alive. You don't need to come.
Me: It's bad, Tag. I'll tell you everything soon. But he needs me, so I might stay for a few weeks until we figure out a long-term plan.
Me: PS: I'm still mad at you.

His bubbles dance to life.

Tag: Jesus. Don't ever ghost me again when you're nearly 1000 miles away and only got your driver's license two minutes ago.
Tag: Also, define bad...

Something in my throat sticks.

I peer over at the man beside me, fast asleep with an arm draped over his eyes.

Then I send a quick response and discard my phone.

Me: He's sick. Tumor. Vision loss. Talk more soon.

The cell pings beside me, but I let it be for now.

Moonlight blankets the room in a faint pearly glow, highlighting chalky skin and a mop of overgrown light-brown hair. He's still muscled and toned, relying on weight training and exercise to pass the time. In the corner of the bedroom, I spot a small rack of free weights, a yoga mat rolled tight, and a half-empty container of pre-workout powder tucked beside a scuffed kettlebell.

Chase moves when Toaster jumps on the bed and splays his paws over his thigh. One knee lifts, his arm falling away from his face as he stretches, stirring back to life.

I crawl toward him, brushing thick bangs from his eyes. "Hey," I whisper.

He blinks a few times. Tries to find my face.

I can't tell how much he sees, but it's enough to have him pulling me into his arms and sprawling me across his chest as he exhales a long breath of relief.

Warmth. Heaven. Home.

Snuggling deeper, I bury my nose against his neck and hold him tight.

"Hey," he says back.

I shiver when he inhales my scent, his chest heaving underneath me. "It's after ten. You fell asleep early."

"Mm." He extends both legs, one winding between mine. "How bored were you?"

A smile flickers. "Not bored. I went through your kitchen trying to find something to cook. It was bleak."

"That's a word for it."

"Have you been living off pantry staples for months?" I poke my head up, finding his eyes. "How are you getting groceries?"

He drags his fingers through my tangle of hair. "I stocked up when I got here. My parents drive in once a month with premade meals and frozen casseroles."

"What was the next step going to be? Your long-term plan?" I wonder, tracing designs on his chest. "You can't live like this forever. Alone. It's not safe."

"I don't know," he says. "I wasn't expecting my vision to go this fast. Figured I'd be set for a while."

"God, Chase…" I exhale deeply, pressing my temple to his collarbone. "Will you consider coming home with me? Letting me take care of you?"

I swallow, waiting, terrified of what he'll say.

He stiffens. Goes silent for several beats. "I don't want to be a burden, Annie."

My cheeks heat. I prop myself up, staring down at him, wishing he could see the pleading in my eyes. "Stop saying that. I love you. I will literally do anything for you. Whatever it takes."

His muscles draw tight as he holds back all the things he wants to say.

No.

I don't want that for you.

You deserve to live a carefree life.

Before he second-guesses himself and spews words I refuse to hear, I roll off him and bring the covers up to his chin. "Go back to sleep," I whisper. "I'll be here when you wake up."

He twists toward me, reaching for my face until he finds the lock of pale hair striped across my jaw. He tucks it behind my ear. "Promise?"

Leaning in, I kiss him on the cheek. "Maybe."

A smile crests, lingering on his lips as he dozes back off.

He knows it's a yes.

I spend the next afternoon in town, stocking up on clothes, groceries, and basic necessities, the volume on my phone turned all the way up in case Chase texts or calls.

An hour of my day is spent at a rustic boutique in Sevierville. It's narrow and creaky-floored, nestled between a fudge store and a shop that exclusively sells black bear souvenirs. Inside, it smells like cedarwood and lavender. Wind chimes dangle from the ceiling, catching stray drafts, and every wall is lined with racks of clothes in every shade imaginable.

The owner, a woman with fire-red hair and a rhinestone jacket, helps me pick out the loudest outfits in the store: bright oranges, sunflower yellows, rich teals, and bold floral prints.

"I'm trying to be easier to see," I tell her with a half smile as I hold up a fuchsia sundress patterned in giant hibiscus flowers.

She grins. "Then you're right on track, sweetheart."

I leave with two shopping bags full of clothes I never would've picked six months ago.

But this isn't about me anymore. It's about making sure Chase can still see me in whatever fragments of the world are still left.

Around 3:00 p.m. I burst through the front door, out of breath, colorful fabrics and random fruits spilling out of bags as I double over in the living room. "There was…a bear…"

Chase blinks at me from the couch, setting his guitar aside. "I get a lot of those."

"Well, I was holding a bag of peaches and wearing chartreuse. I figured I had a fifty-fifty shot of being mistaken for a snack or a threat."

He tilts his head. "What did it do?"

I drag in a breath. "Made eye contact. Judged me. Wandered off. Honestly, it handled things better than I did."

One corner of his mouth twitches, but he holds it back.

"I also may have left an entire reusable bag of groceries in the driveway," I add, toeing off my shoes. "So if we're low on rice, blame the dubious and terrifying Tennessee wildlife."

Now he smirks. "I knew you were a closet runner."

"I'm not. But adrenaline plus platform sandals will surprise you." I finally drop the bags, peeling off my jacket and kicking a pineapple upright. "Also, we're having stir-fry. Unless the bear comes back for the bok choy."

He chuckles under his breath.

And just like that, for the first time in eight joyless months, I hear it.

That sound.

The one I was afraid I'd never hear again.

Chase, laughing.

It steals my breath. Whatever breath the bear didn't take.

I try to shake off the tendrils of emotion, the awestruck glee. Try to play it cool. Clearing my throat, I pull out blouses and dresses, all vivid, all multicolored, all for him. "On the bright side, I'm now the proud owner of twelve outfits that can be seen from space." I move toward him, harnessing a smile as I hold them up, draping them across my frame. "What do you think? This one has…cacti wearing sunglasses on it…" I squint at the print. "Okay, that's distinctive. Definitely a vibe. Kenna will be impressed."

I cringe at my rambling.

Wrinkling my nose, I lift my gaze to Chase as he stares at me. He looks glassy-eyed. A little stunned.

My heart twists. "Everything okay?"

"Yeah, I..." He swallows, scooting closer to the edge as he studies the ridiculous shirt, blinking repeatedly. "You bought those for me?"

I fold in my lips, nodding slowly. "I mean, they're for me. Unless you're really bored and want to have a dress-off à la Cameron and Christina in *The Sweetest Thing*."

Still rambling.

I don't know what's wrong with me.

Chase's smile flickers back to life, his shoulders slackening.

I chew my lip, stepping toward him. "You said you could see the purple in my hair. So I just thought maybe you could see—"

The moment I'm close enough, he reaches for me, pulling me forward by my belt loop until I'm caged between his denim-clad thighs. A gasp falls out. My hands brace against his shoulders, fingers curling into heat and muscle.

I melt when he grazes his fingertips up the backs of my thighs, his forehead dropping to my abdomen, warm breath seeping through the thin fabric of my blouse. Sagging, I sink into him, trailing my hands up his neck until they land in waves of silken hair.

My eyelids flutter at the contact. Intimate. Habitual.

Eight lonely months filter through my mind of tearstained pillows, empty beds, and stiff couches. Absence. Something vital severed at the quick.

But now he's here, in my arms, breathing and warm, his cheek pressed to my stomach as his hands tighten around my thighs, bringing me closer.

Tingles light me up from toes to top. A need that never died.

I lick my lips, mouth dryer than a decade-old tumbleweed, and a question slips out, unprecedented. "Have you been with anyone else?"

He falters, stilling at the question. Then his face lifts, brows bent like he must not have heard me correctly. "What?"

Embarrassment trickles through me, laced with stupidity. "Sorry…I don't know why I asked that."

"No," he says quickly. "God. No. Only you."

Tears puddle in my eyes. "Okay."

"Annie…" Chase drags his hands up my legs, my butt, the small of my back. "It's only been you. For years. There's no one else. It's you in every thought, every quiet moment, every dream that isn't dark and terrifying. Just you. Don't ever question that."

My breath hitches. "Me too."

He pulls me closer until I'm half leaning over him, and his mouth trails up, hovering just below the space between my breasts. My grip on his hair tightens, and I can't help but wonder what comes next.

We haven't kissed yet.

We've held, and we've touched, and we've curled into U-shapes, tangling together until we don't know where the other one begins. But we haven't kissed.

And now it's all I can think about. His lips on mine. His tongue inside me, anywhere, everywhere. My breathing is soft but erratic, and so is his. I feel it whispering uncertainty and desire against me. I raise my leg and press my knee to the cushion, on my way to straddling him.

But then he stiffens.

Peering down, I watch his eyes close tight as he fights against something. "Chase…"

He inches back, hands slowly falling from my waist. "Bok choy, huh?"

I frown, disappointment creeping in. "Yeah. And steak stir-fry."

"Did you learn how to cook?"

Sweeping hair off my face, I step backward, adding space between us. "Not really. But I learned how to batter a steak into pulp. Surprisingly effective coping mechanism."

He nods, scrubbing a hand down his face.

And that's that.

The disappointment follows me into the bedroom while I tuck my clothes into drawers and hang my dresses in the small closet. A bright red pair of lingerie lingers in my hands as I brush my thumb over the satiny fabric, then hide it away.

An hour later, the kitchen is a mess: vegetable peels everywhere, a cutting board stained with soy sauce, and a skillet spitting oil like even it can't stomach my inadequacy. I've used every pan I could find and googled "how to cook" at least three times, convinced everything is either raw, overcooked, or plotting revenge.

The steak is half seared and half suffering, but I've cut it thin and tossed it in something resembling sauce. There's garlic, ginger, soy, sesame oil, and the evident panic of someone trying not to poison the person she loves.

I plate it with shaky hands, set two mismatched bowls on the table, and step back like I've just disarmed a bomb. "Bon appétit," I murmur, wringing my hands together as I watch Chase squint down at the plate of mayhem.

"Smells good," he says.

"You lie."

"No." A grin twitches. "It's really good, Annie. Thank you."

I allow myself to relax, exhaling a breath as I take a seat beside him at the hand-carved table in the eat-in kitchen. "I guess you can't go wrong if there's garlic."

He drags his fork across the plate, scooping up soggy vegetables half drowning in mystery sauce. Despite the poor execution, I can't help but feel proud.

Years of my life were lost to codependency, to submission masquerading as love, to letting someone twist devotion into control. I shrank myself to fit inside a version of a life that was never mine until there was no space left for who I really was.

My dreams deflated. My confidence dimmed. My spirit wilted.

I see that now.

Sometimes it only takes one person to make you realize everything you've been giving up in the name of someone else's idea of happiness.

And I would still choose this every time. Every day. In every lifetime.

Chase.

No matter how flawed, broken, or lost, he'll forever be the truth that unraveled all the lies I used to live by.

After we finish eating, I stand and collect our empty bowls, the quiet between us full of things unsaid. He stares in my direction for a moment as I float around the tiny kitchen in a neon-orange dress and tries to memorize whatever glimpses he can.

Then I return to the table and take him by the hand. "Come

on," I say, tipping my head toward the door. "Let's sit out on the deck."

Moments later, we're perched in two side-by-side rocking chairs, hands interlocked, our eyes on the inky horizon speckled with stars.

It's peaceful. Familiar. It takes me back to all those nights we sat in my brother's backyard, a notebook in my lap and a guitar strapped around his torso. A connection bloomed. Fate intervened. And a love story unfurled, just a seedling at the time.

Now we're here, not so different than we were then. Not entirely.

He still plays like the world might end mid-chord, I still write like I'm trying to stitch myself back together, and somehow we still fit, both of us made of broken parts that only make sense when they're touching.

I glance over at him, lit by moonlight and memory. "Did you know Leonard Cohen spent five years writing 'Hallelujah'?" I say, breaking the silence. "He wrote something like eighty verses. Sat in a hotel room in nothing but his underwear, banging his head on the floor because he couldn't get it right."

Chase stares at the twinkling sky like he's trying not to fall apart. "I didn't know that."

"I didn't get it before," I continue. "Why someone would keep going like that. Keep pushing when it's all pain and silence and dead ends. But now I do." My hand squeezes his. "Because that's what you've been doing, Chase. Every day. Fighting to rewrite a story you think already has an ending. Trying to make peace with something that was never fair to begin with."

He leans closer, rocking back and forth. Forward and back.

I swallow hard, tears stinging. "Maybe it's not about finding that secret chord or perfect verse," I finish, twining our fingers together. "Maybe it's about finding the courage to keep singing anyway."

Chase lets out a shaky breath, jaw tight, eyes still locked on the night canvas.

The silence stretches between us. Heavy with the weight of everything we've survived to get here.

I rest my head against his shoulder, emotion trapped behind my eyes, my throat, my ribs. My gaze follows his, locking on the sea of stars. "What do you see right now?"

He's quiet for a long time. So long I almost think he won't answer.

Then, finally, brokenly, he says, "I just see…pieces."

And it guts me, how much pain lives in those four words. How much tragedy.

How much beauty too.

Because pieces are still pieces.

And if they're still here, still shining…

Then so is he.

I squeeze his hand and whisper back, "That's okay. We can make something out of pieces."

His shoulders dip as he exhales, those words giving him room to breathe again.

We stay there in silence, the stars scattered above us like a shattered map.

Not whole. Not fixed.

But still burning.

CHAPTER 59
Annalise

There's a question at the forefront of my mind the next morning as I change into a knee-length sunflower dress and comb a brush through my shower-damp hair. It's been sitting there for a few days, poking, festering, too petty to say aloud.

But as Chase wanders into the bedroom in a pair of sweatpants, his chest bare, I swallow my pride and blurt it out. "How come you sent all the guys a custom guitar?"

What I really meant to ask was, *"Why didn't you send anything to me?"*

I watch him stall behind me in the mirror, mid-bend as he reaches for a stray T-shirt.

"What?" he says.

"Tag told me you sent him a guitar. That's how he found you." Swallowing, I go back to brushing my hair, distracting myself from the lump in my throat. "He said Rock and Zach got one too. They just never thought to trace the return address."

Faltering, he scoops up the shirt and flings it over his shoulder, pivoting to face me. "I planned to send you one."

I blink into the mirror, then set the brush aside. Swiveling around, I lean back against the edge of the dresser. "You did?"

"I, um…" He scratches his head. "I never got to finish it."

A curious frown bends. "Oh."

"I was taking my time with it. It was more…involved," he says softly. "Then my vision went to shit and I couldn't focus. Couldn't see anything clearly."

My eyes water. "Sorry. I didn't mean to assume—"

"Don't apologize, Annie. I should have sent it anyway. I never wanted to leave you with nothing."

An ache spreads across my chest because I know what *leave you* implies. More than walking away. More than a tepid goodbye.

Something permanent.

I push off the dresser and take a step toward him. "Can I see it?"

Hesitation grips him for a heavy beat. Then he nods. "Yeah. It's in the shed."

He tosses the shirt aside and leads me out the back door, past the brittle patch of wild grass and down the uneven stone path toward the shed. Morning sunlight filters through the trees, dappling his shoulders in gold.

My pulse thunders with every step, unsure of what I'm about to see.

When Chase swings open the shed door, I'm hit with the scent of cedar shavings and dust, the kind that clings to forgotten projects. Everything is neat but worn, tools lining the wall, paint cans stacked like a timeline of lost plans. He crosses to a workbench, not needing clear vision to know where to go, and kneels near the corner of the shed.

He lifts the sticker-covered case that's marked with memories from all the places we've toured before popping the latches and flipping it open.

Inside sits a guitar unlike anything I've ever seen.

The instrument is deep, dusky purple, somewhere between bruised violet and midnight blue. The finish gleams across most of the body, except where the carvings begin. There, the wood is raw. Unsealed. Not quite completed.

And then my breath catches. The world tilts.

Because etched into the body are...lyrics.

My lyrics.

Curving in and out like constellations, each line carved with intention. No pattern, no order. Just raw feeling.

My words. My heart.

"I don't need light if your voice is the spark."

"Even the moon envies how you pull the tide in me."

"I'd become the night if it meant reaching you."

Tiny silver stars are inlaid around the sound hole. Along the neck, the fret markers shimmer with mother-of-pearl crescents, a different phase at each one. At the twelfth fret, a single full moon gleams like liquid honey.

"I wanted it to feel like you," he says quietly behind me. "Like your voice after dark. Calm. Haunting. A little magic."

My fingers hover just above the strings, too stunned to touch. "You built this for me?" I whisper.

He nods, swallowing. "I started building it after you left your notebook on the bus. Thought maybe if I couldn't find the right words…yours would be enough." He shrugs like it's nothing. Like it didn't just undo me completely. "Didn't get to finish the carvings or the final coat. There was a lot more I wanted to add. But, yeah. It's yours. Always was."

I study it, and this time, I see it for what it is.

A love letter I never expected to receive.

My throat tightens, eyes burning. I stare down at the guitar, overwhelmed.

Then I set it gently back in the case, close the lid, and launch myself at him.

Chase stumbles a step before catching me, wrapping those strong arms around my waist, his chin tucking over my shoulder as he leans back against the workbench for support.

"You didn't leave me with nothing," I murmur through the tears. "You never left at all."

He squeezes me tighter. "Annie…"

"No. You never left. Never." My breathing kicks up, pulse doubling in speed. "You can't leave me. You—you can't…" The tender emotion shifts into something uglier as panic overtakes me. "No, no… Chase, you can't ever leave—"

"Whoa, hey." He takes my chin between his thumb and finger and tilts my head up. "It's okay. Shh, don't cry…"

Everything hits at once, a comet to my core. I'm shaking, breaking in half, my heart splitting down the middle.

There. Here. Him. Me. The past. The future.

A future I was just getting a glimpse of before he left, now I can't see it without him.

I don't want it without him.

Agony rockets through me as I tremble hopelessly in his arms. Everything becomes too real. Too doomed. Too over.

A strangled sob escapes. "Please don't leave me, Chase. Please stay. Please be okay."

Absolute devastation glitters in his caramel-colored eyes. Because he can't calm my fears. He can't erase my sorrow. He can hardly see me. All he can do is hold me.

But it's not enough.

I need more.

Crying my heart out, I take his face between my hands and pull his mouth to mine. Our lips crash together, tongues colliding. Safe, warm, alive.

Still here. Still mine.

I moan and weep and beg, taking everything I can before it's gone.

Tears track down his cheeks, mingling with my own. We're both wet, soaked with pain and need. My hands grab at anything tangible—his hair, cheeks, neck, shoulders, chest—then sweep down his body until I'm fumbling with his waistband.

He croaks out a sound, clamping a big palm around my wrist. "Annie, wait."

"No, please, God, I need you," I sob. "I need this."

His forehead falls to mine, head angling back and forth as he locks up and pulls back. "Annalise."

My voice cracks, and I stumble away from him. I shake my head, dragging my hands through my hair until I'm squeezing it by the roots.

Then I bolt from the shed.

"Annie," he calls out.

I hear him following me, somewhere between my skipping pulse and thudding heart. When I glance back, I see him misjudge the doorway, his shoulder clipping the frame hard enough to make him stagger. He blinks, nearly losing his footing in the grass before he pushes on.

The sight guts me.

Rubble and prickly grass gouge my bare feet, and I slip and slide as I run for the door, part of me hoping the bear jumps out and devours me whole. Swallows all this pain in one gulp.

I tear into the house, hardly breathing, barely standing.

A moment later, Chase reaches for me, pulling me to him, his breath ragged like he's sprinted through hell. "Please don't run," he says, one hand curled around my waist, the other braiding through my hair. "Please. We can't both run."

He holds me like he's terrified I'll slip through his fingers again. But it's he who's slipping through mine.

"I'm sorry," I whimper. "I'm sorry. I just thought—"

"You have no idea how much I want you."

His breath shudders against my hair as I tip my face up to his, grief running wild down my cheeks. "Then let me in. Let me love you," I plead. "While there's still time."

Eyes squeezed shut, he clenches his jaw so tight it looks like it hurts. "I'm scared," he rasps. "I'm scared of me. Of how I touched you that night. How far gone I was. I was angry, and lost, and I didn't care about anything as long as I still had you."

"I wanted it," I whisper. "Every second of it."

He looks at me, and I see all of it: the fear, the guilt, the grief that's been sitting behind every word he's spoken since I came back. A quiet kind of torment.

I move closer, slow and deliberate. When I lean in, his hands twitch upward, almost like he might catch me, but they falter, dropping back to his thighs.

Still, I press my lips to his. Soft, patient. Begging him to believe me.

He exhales, forehead falling to mine, lips unmoving. "I don't want to hurt you."

"You won't." My voice cracks, but my hand is steady when I cup his cheek. "That's the difference, Chase. That's why you'll never be him. Because you care too much. Because the thought of hurting me rips you apart."

His eyes close tight.

"You don't need me to absolve you," I finish, my thumbs brushing over his skin. "You need to forgive yourself."

The dam breaks.

He melts into me like he's drowning, and I'm the first breath he's taken in years. His hands slide into my hair, down my back, anchoring me with a desperation that's both tender and hungry. The kiss deepens, tasting of every sleepless night, every unsent message, every regret we've been trying to strip away.

His erection strains against cotton pants, growing full and heavy between us.

We stumble backward, collapsing onto the couch without breaking apart. Our limbs tangle as he pulls me into his lap, as if he never wants me anywhere else. His hands roam my thighs, hips, waist, rediscovering places he thought he'd never be allowed to touch again.

I straddle him, and he stills, breath lodging.

Our mouths meet again.

No frenzy. No fury. Just longing, unraveling in reverent touches and shaky breaths. He peels my dress down inch by inch, a gift he's afraid to open too fast. His hands drift across my skin, relearning every curve, every scar—lyrics he forgot how to sing.

The momentum builds.

I yank the dress off and toss it aside, pressing myself to him until my breasts hover at his mouth. He groans, cupping them in both hands before rolling a nipple with his tongue. My body arches, bows, and I tip my head back, grinding into his lap, chasing friction. A shudder racks through him as I hold his face to my chest, moaning his name like a wanton prayer.

His mouth stays latched as his hands trail lower, sliding under the band of my underwear. He lifts his hips, and I reach down, tugging at his sweatpants until his cock springs free.

Thick, flushed, already leaking.

My breath hitches.

I wrap my fingers around him and begin to stroke. Chase lets out a broken sound and falls back against the couch, head sloped, lips parted, chest rising fast. His hands grip my hips, the only thing tethering him to this earth.

I shimmy out of my underwear and climb back into his lap, his cock teasing the slick heat between my thighs. But before I can sink down, he lifts me, strong hands bracketing my ass, and hauls me up to his mouth.

His tongue slides between my legs.

My entire body shatters.

I cry out, clinging to him, bucking against his mouth as he devours me with that same bruising mix of hunger and worship. His hands pin me open, guiding my movements, coaxing out every fractured moan, every tremble, every gasp of his name like a song he already knows by heart.

I grind against his face, shameless and wild, until an orgasm blindsides me, hitting hard, sudden and ferocious.

I'm still quivering when he lowers me back to his lap, his lips slick with me, eyes feral and glassy like he's witnessed something holy.

"Come here," he breathes, voice wrecked.

I reach for him, hands threading through his hair, pulling him into a kiss that's all teeth and tongue, messy and consuming. His cock presses hot against me, nudging where I'm already aching, already soaked. I shift my hips, guiding him to my entrance, and we both freeze.

His hands tighten at my waist. "Are you sure?"

"I've never been more sure of anything," I murmur, touching my forehead to his.

He exhales, releasing a breath he's been holding since the day he left.

And then he pushes inside.

I sink onto him, into him, the melancholy melting away.

We gasp in unison, our bodies going still as he stretches me open, careful and slow, his hands shaking where they hold me. My nails dig into his shoulders as I cling, grounding myself in the heat, the fullness, the overwhelming relief of him being inside me again. Of this not being a memory or a misstep, but a moment.

A picture-perfect piece.

His lips graze my temple, my cheek, my mouth as he bottoms out, and we stay there—connected, frozen—just breathing each other in.

Then we move together. A slow, desperate rhythm. No rush, no need to prove anything. Just the soft slap of skin, the quiet pants and moans, the sharp edges of grief worn smooth by love.

I ride him with everything I have. Every wound, every want, every shadow of the girl who waited for him to come home.

His hands guide my hips, his lips brush my throat, and when my body starts to shake again, he presses a hand to my chest, right over my heart.

"I've got you," he whispers. "I love you."

When my climax peaks, I take him with me. His moan splinters against my mouth as he releases deep inside me, clutching so tightly, afraid the world will tear us apart for good.

But it doesn't. Not yet.

It's just us.

Shuddering. Spent. Entwined.

And for a second frozen in time, nothing's broken. Nothing's lost.

We're exactly where we belong.

Late-afternoon sunlight spills across the bedspread as I lie beneath him, naked, writhing, glazed with sweat and bliss. We've been insatiable. Minutes shifted into hours, and when we finally made it to the bedroom, we never left, the time lost to kisses, sex, cuddling, catnaps, and more sex. I've savored every moment, begging for each one to span infinite measures and lifetimes.

I can't lose him; I can't think about losing him.

So I've lost myself instead. In his body, his words, his love.

It's all I can do.

Collapsing backward on the bed, I exhale deeply, folding a heavy arm over my eyes. Chase army-crawls up the mattress, kissing my nose.

A drowsy smile blooms as I push damp hair off my forehead, the wispy blond strands stuck to my temples. "Mmm…I missed this."

"I missed you," he says, pressing another kiss to my lips. "So much."

I twine my arms around his neck and pull him down until his cheek presses to the swell of my breasts. We're both hot, sticky, and exhausted. Raw emotion continues to battle inside me, shifting from laughter to terror to heart-wrenching sadness with every blink, every beat. One minute I'm smiling so big my jaw aches. Then I'm coming, screaming his name as pleasure surges through me. Then I'm crying. Sobbing. Envisioning an ending without him in it.

But for now I'm content because he's still here.

As fatigue steals me away and my eyelids grow heavy, I hear something at the front of the house. A door opening, then clapping shut. Toaster's nails click against hardwood.

Footsteps.

Voices.

A symphony of voices.

I startle, jolting into a sitting position as Chase rolls off me and searches for his clothes. "Your parents?" I wonder, swinging my legs over the side of the bed, taking the blankets with me.

He shakes his head, ruffles his hair. "They aren't due for another two weeks."

Scrambling, I shoot off the mattress and dive into the closet, yanking a dress off a hanger and shoving my head and limbs through the holes. Then I race over to Chase's dresser and toss him a T-shirt and a pair of jeans.

The voices grow louder.

And then, "Yo, you have guests."

Oh my God.

It's Tag.

"No welcome confetti or live orchestra? No charcuterie board? So disappointing."

Kenna.

My eyes pop. Using my fingers as a comb, I fix my hair then straighten my dress, doing an awkward dance-hop into fresh underwear. The moment Chase has his jeans hooked around his hips, I grab him by the hand and charge out of the bedroom and into the living room.

Tears. Immediate tears.

"Oh my God?" I cup a hand around my mouth, lost for words. "You actually came?"

My brother and my best friend stand beside the coffee table with smiles on their faces.

"Surprise," Kenna says, her arms full of houseplants.

Before I can get another word in, the door bursts open again.

Rock and Zach saunter through the threshold, Rock carrying a small amp and Zach with his bass guitar slung over his shoulder.

Suddenly, I feel like I'm Kevin McAllister in *Home Alone*, watching his family arrive home on Christmas morning.

Except this is louder.

Messier. Realer.

Kenna starts crying, which of course sets me off again, and then she's shoving a potted plant into my arms like it's a newborn and she's the proud aunt.

"I told you I'll always be here. You can't get rid of me," she says, brushing a tear off my cheek and squeezing my wrist with her free hand. "I meant it."

Tag steps forward next, pulling me into a hug so tight my ribs protest. "God, sis, you look like a person again," he mutters into my hair. "Was worried you'd gone full swamp witch out here."

"I was moments away from braiding bones into my hair," I say into his shoulder, laughing through the tears, my lingering resentment falling by the wayside.

Rock and Zach stroll over like they never left our orbit, like it hasn't been eight months since our band dismembered and we scattered across the country, licking our wounds in silence.

Zach sets his bass down by the window and gives me a quiet, knowing smile. Rock cracks a joke about how he half expected to find us building bunkers and stockpiling canned beans, convinced Chase had gone full-off-grid prophet.

Then my brother slowly walks up to Chase.

He says nothing. Just stares him down.

Chase stiffens, shoulders squared, sensing his presence.

Tag eyes him for another second, then drops his guitar with a *thud* and grabs him in a fierce hug. "I should punch you," he says into Chase's shoulder. "But I'd probably break my hand, and we've got shit to play."

Chase exhales a breath, and it sounds like something inside him finally lets go. "Shit," he says hoarsely. He pinches the bridge of his nose, tamping down the rush of emotion. "I wasn't expecting this."

"That's the point of surprises." With a clap on the back, Tag pulls away and flops down on the couch. "You vanish for eight months, Annalise sends me a text that nearly gave me a stroke, and next thing I know we're in a rental van with a busted aux cord and Kenna screaming at Siri somewhere outside Scranton."

Kenna lifts a hand. "She told me to turn left into a *lake*, Tag."

"Still better than when you rerouted us through an Amish parade."

Zach mutters, "They waved, at least."

"I stand by my route." She sniffs, then pivots to face me. "The journey was low-key traumatic if I'm being honest, thanks to your insufferable brother narrating the entire trip like we were on a true crime podcast."

Tag scoffs. "Sorry for trying to bring context to our emotional road trip. I think the listeners appreciated it."

Zach nods solemnly. "Season one was stronger. The pacing dipped around Harrisburg."

A sob-like laugh spills out of me as I swipe tears off my face. "Trauma's very on-brand for us."

Kenna sends me a wink, her expression soft.

"So this is where you've been hiding, huh?" Rock cuts in, surveying the space. "I was this close to assuming you'd joined a doomsday cult, bro. Figured we'd find you with a beard down to your balls and a manifesto about government satellites in the well water."

Chase chuckles, shaking his head, still looking blindsided.

Grinning, Rock points to the ceiling. "I swear I saw a drone circling the driveway. Probably the feds tracking your Spotify plays."

"Could've been the bear," Zach deadpans.

I gasp. "You saw the bear?"

"That thing looked like it pays property taxes."

More laughter fills the room, cracked and wet and beautiful. It echoes through the walls of this little house like music. Like forgiveness. Like home.

Chase slips his hand into mine and squeezes.

When I look at him, I see the man I fell in love with. Still worn, still healing, but not alone.

Not anymore.

Because they're here. We're all here.

And whatever comes next—surgery, recovery, more tears—we won't be facing it in silence.

We'll face it together.

As friends.

As a band.

As a family.

CHAPTER 60
Chase

Colors and shapes blur together as I haul an acoustic onto my lap and let muscle memory take over. Tag sits beside me, strumming familiar chords, humming melodies under his breath.

It feels like nothing's changed—which is a goddamn lie.

Everything's changed.

My body, my brain, the way the world slips in and out of focus like it's deciding whether I deserve to see it. But this moment still lives in the bubble of who we used to be.

Luckily, my headaches have become manageable after finally getting on a new prescription called Dexamethasone. The pressure's eased, the sharp edges dulled. The relief is real.

But so is the countdown.

Tag doesn't say anything about the tremor in my hand, or the way I pause too long between transitions, waiting for my eyes to catch up. He just plays. Syncs with me like he always has.

We land on a chord progression we haven't touched in over a year, and suddenly he's grinning, shaking his head. "Jesus," he mutters. "This takes me back."

I smile. "To that rooftop in Baltimore?"

"Shit, yes. That was the night those girls tried to climb the fire escape to get onstage."

"They made it halfway."

"One of them threw her bra and it landed on my tuner pedal."

"You didn't even flinch."

"I'm adaptable," he says, mock defensive. "I was like a war hero. Middle of a solo, blitzed out of my mind, ducking under flying lace."

We laugh, and it's the first time in a while that my body doesn't feel like a battlefield. No scans. No shadows eating at the corners of my sight.

Just music. Nostalgia.

"I didn't think it would happen that fast," I say quietly. "The sold-out venues, the fame, the fans. I thought we'd have years of opening for shitty cover bands before anyone cared."

"Yeah, well, some people spend a lifetime chasing it. We caught lightning in a bottle overnight. That kind of thing makes you family whether you planned on it or not."

"I'm glad it was you." I clear the catch of emotion in my throat. "I'm glad it's still you."

Tag doesn't shift toward me when he answers, still focused on the guitar. "I'm not going anywhere, man. You get sick, we show up. That's just the rule now."

My windpipe tightens, but we keep playing.

Me, blurry and scared.

Him, solid as ever.

I blink hard, fingers drifting across the strings. "Thanks for coming."

Tag nods. "Of course."

"I mean it. We've only known each other, what, two years? And half that time you hated me. You didn't have to show up."

He exhales through his nose. "Listen, we've slept in vans together, showered at roach-infested motels, played dive bars and pretended it was Madison Square Garden." A pause. "You watched me almost die."

"But you didn't."

His lips twitch. "I puked on your feet in Richmond."

I groan. "You insisted that barbecue was safe."

"My point is," he says, levity lacing his tone as he finally twists to face me, "I don't need a decade to give a damn. I don't need a pretty beginning either. You're my frontman. The love of my sister's life. That means you're one of mine. And I don't let mine go through hell alone."

My chest squeezes with sentiment. "Yeah," I say, voice barely holding. "Goes both ways."

"I know we've only done a couple laps around the sun together, but seriously. Bandmate, friend, future best man—whatever you need, I've got you. We all do."

That hits harder than I expect.

The best man part.

I press my tongue against my cheek, nodding once, hard. "I don't know what comes next," I admit. "I'm scared shitless."

"Good," he says. "Means you're still here."

The silence that follows is full, heavy in a way that says everything else we've been too proud or too broken to admit.

Then come the footsteps.

Annie moves into the room slowly, not wanting to interrupt. Her hair's pulled back in a high ponytail, and I track the trail of multicolored silk bobbing as she approaches.

She settles beside me without a word, her presence folding into the space like she never left my side. Her hand slides to the back of my neck, the gesture light and familiar, and I lean into it instinctively.

Tag taps the front of his guitar. "You always said things happen for a reason, sis," he says, voice softening. "That even the messy shit lines up somehow."

She lets out a wry breath. "That doesn't sound like me at all."

"Right." He snorts. "You know, I used to think it was just something people said to make sense of the madness. But then I think about how we met this asshole under the most messed up, wrong-place-wrong-time circumstances…and here we are."

She inches closer to me. Doesn't argue.

"If you really believe everything happens for a reason, then I guess this all started with that gas station clerk," Tag adds.

Annie's thumb pauses its tender strokes.

He continues. "I mean, a little less trigger finger and none of this happens. No band. No tour. No Chase-and-Annalise."

"Yeah," Annie says after a beat, her tone low. "At least they dropped the charges. The family seems to be doing well."

"Still wild." He nudges me, waves a hand in the air. "One second you're pilfering dog food, and the next you're stealing a car with a bullet in your leg and my sister in the back seat."

My face sours. "She wasn't supposed to be back there."

I feel Annie shift beside me. Not away, but inward. Her fingers falter slightly at the base of my neck, just for a beat, and resume their rhythm like nothing happened.

Then she murmurs, almost to herself, "Yes I was."

The guys pick up pizzas in town, and we play music on my living room floor, beers in hand, laughter on our lips, and old memories coming alive between chords and ancient stories. For a while, it's easy to forget why they're here. Easy to pretend everything's normal and that I'm not walking around with a clock ticking inside my head.

Annie stays close, head tipped against my shoulder, hand brushing mine more often than it used to. I feel her eyes on me, lingering. Watching.

And I'd give fucking *anything* to see them. To go back in time and memorize them better. The icy blue, the shimmery flecks, the glaze of love.

Later, when the others have crashed in a row of sleeping bags in the second bedroom, and Rock is snoring like someone left a chainsaw running in the hall, Annie nudges me with her knee and gestures toward the back door.

"Come on," she whispers. "Air."

We slip outside, the wood cool under our bare feet, the night thick with crickets and the distant rustle of trees. The stars are brighter out here.

Or maybe I'm just trying harder to see them.

But we don't make it far, stopped short when a soft noise breaches the air.

Not from her. Not from me.

A breathless laugh—hushed, close, and then cut off. Footsteps shuffle just out of my clear range of vision, near the far end of the deck, behind one of the support beams.

I squint into the blur, but it's useless. What I can pick up is movement: shapes pressed together, a hand slipping around a waist, someone murmuring something low and half laughed. A pause. Then the unmistakable sound of a kiss, slow and familiar.

I turn slightly toward Annie. "Is that…?"

She cups a hand around her mouth, smothering a giggle, then tugs me backward into the house, granting privacy. "Kenna and Tag."

Frowning, I scratch my head. I'd wondered, based on context clues. "That's actually a thing?"

"It's a semi-thing. A weird thing. But…I think it's a good thing." She quietly closes the door, taking my hand again, reminding me she's close. "I walked in on them after one of our West Coast shows. It was horrifying. Truly traumatizing."

"Shit. I didn't know you walked in on them."

"They both refused to talk about it. I think Kenna was ashamed." She sighs, pulling me over to the couch. "Looks like she got over that."

My gaze shifts to the back door on instinct, only catching the sway of leafy branches through the glass. "Good for them." I settle on the couch, absorbing the heat of her body pressing against me. "How do you feel about it?"

"I love it," she says, braiding our fingers together. "Can you imagine them ending up together? Getting married? And then if you and I…"

Her voice trails off, tripped up with emotion.

I turn toward her but don't press. I feel the way her grip tightens, how her thumb stops moving over mine. She doesn't need to finish the sentence. I already know the ending she was afraid to say out loud.

Get married.

Have a future.

Had more time.

The silence that follows is different now. Sadder.

Laughter from earlier still echoes faintly in my mind, muffled and strained, but it doesn't quite reach. Not anymore.

I lean back into the couch and stare at the ceiling, a cedar blur above me. I focus on her hand in mine. Something I can feel.

"I hate not knowing," I admit, my voice quiet. "I hate waiting around to see how much worse it gets. Every day feels like someone's flipping a coin I don't get to see land."

Annie doesn't say anything at first, just shifts closer, her head resting on my shoulder. "It's not going to get worse tonight," she says softly. "That's all we need to worry about right now."

She tries to sound hopeful, but I can sense the way the words stick in her throat like they don't quite fit, too neat for what she's really thinking.

She stays there for another minute before pulling back, sitting up straighter. Her fingers slip from mine. "I, um…I need to go out of town for a few days."

I blink, caught off guard. "What?"

"Tomorrow. I'll leave early and head back right away. I already talked to Kenna and the guys. They'll stay with you and make sure you're okay."

I study her face, but it's impossible to get a read. I can't make out her expression, just the way she tucks her hair behind her ear, the violet stripes streaked from roots to tips, and the neon-yellow pattern on her sundress. "Where are you going?"

She hesitates for several seconds. "There's just something I need to take care of. A meeting. It's probably nothing."

"Annie."

"I wouldn't go if it wasn't important."

I huff a perplexed sound, fused with disbelief and worry. "That's not an answer."

She exhales, the way she does when she's trying to keep herself from unraveling. "It's not something I want to explain yet. Because it might not lead anywhere. And if it doesn't…I don't want you building hope on something that turns out to be a dead end."

That lands sharp.

I want to argue, want to demand more. But I know her. I know that tone. She's not shutting me out—she's protecting me. The same way I tried to protect her when I left.

So I swallow my frustration and nod, even though everything in me tightens. "You'll tell me if it matters?"

"The second it does."

Emotion bubbles behind my eyes, cracking my voice. "And you'll come back?"

"Chase…" She grips my hand again, holds tight. "Of course I'll come back."

Annie leans in and presses a kiss to my cheek, lingering there, trying to memorize the shape of me.

I believe her.

I know she's with me until the end, whenever that might be.

But the fear is already rising, thick and choking. Not because I don't trust her, but because I've lived the before and after of losing someone, and I know how fast everything can turn.

Sometimes by death. Sometimes by choice.

"I'll come back," she says again, firmer this time. "I promise. I love you."

She's right in front of me, her face foggy but close. Her love undeniable.

So I don't tell her how scared I am.

I just nod.

And hold on tighter.

CHAPTER 61
Annalise

I'm too tired to drive straight through.

One lonely, anxious night is spent at a hotel in the eastern panhandle of West Virginia, which ends up being a pointless pit stop, because I don't sleep. Not for a second. I toss and turn, spinning different scenarios over in my mind, missing his arms around me, and praying something horrible doesn't happen during the few days that I'm away.

At 4:00 a.m. I say *screw it*, crawl out of the stiff, cold bed, check out early, and hit the road again. I'm grateful for the twenty-four-hour drive-through that grants me a few hours of caffeinated focus as the sun slowly crests into daybreak, saturating the dark-blue sky in a wash of tangerine and gold. The window is cracked open, spitting icy winter air into the car, and paired with my Bluetooth set at peak volume, I manage not to fall asleep during the seven-plus hour drive into my hometown.

It's after eleven when I pull into the parking lot with nerves in my throat and a tentative miracle zipping around my chest.

Before I head inside, I check my phone, responding to a handful of missed texts.

> **Chase:** Text me as soon as you can. Hope you're okay.
> **Kenna:** All is well here. Tag made Michelin-star-level omelets. Did you know he could cook? Damn. Anyway, thinking of you. Check in soon. 🖤

Tag sends me a picture of his omelet.

It does look phenomenal.

Smiling, I shoot back a few love-laced responses and pocket my phone, then jog inside the gas station. The welcome chime greets me, soothing my anxiety for half a second.

Behind the counter is a familiar face—not the one I'm looking for, exactly, but it's a start. A piece to the puzzle.

"Hello," he says. "Are you…" His voice trails off when he looks up from his magazine showcasing old vintage cars. A frown furls. "Oh. It's you."

"Yeah." I clear my throat, folding my arms over my puffer coat. "It's me."

"Filling up?" he wonders guardedly.

"No, I…I was actually looking for your daughter. Parvati. Is she working today?"

A curious headshake. "No. She does assist occasionally in her free time, but today she has a double shift at the hospital."

My face falls. "Oh. I see."

"Can I pass along a message for her?" He's already reaching for a notepad and a pen.

"Well, I'd really like to speak with her. In person." I bite my lip, my stomach pitching. "Do you think that's possible? Does she take a lunch break or anything?"

He studies me for a beat, clearly confused. "Yes. Most days she eats lunch at a diner a few miles from here. Charlie Barker's. Are you familiar?"

I blink, eyes widening. "I am. I used to work there."

"I can send her a text message. Perhaps she can meet you." He glances at his gold watch. "She goes on break in an hour."

"That would be great. Please let her know I'll meet her there. It's important." A mix of adrenaline and unease churns in my gut. "Thank you so much."

"Annalise, right?" He presses forward on the counter.

"That's right."

"Is everything okay?"

No. Maybe.

God, I hope.

My lips tremble as I inhale a breath. "That's what I'm trying to find out. I'm hoping she can help me with something. Something big."

He squints at me, trying to untangle my vague response. "Are you—"

"Do you believe everything happens for a reason?" I blurt.

He pauses, the question catching him off guard. The pen stills in his hand. "Sometimes," he says slowly. "Other times, I think we just find the reason afterward. When we need one."

I nod, the air swelling in the back of my throat. "I think I need one now."

He watches me closely, his curiosity softening into something quieter. Almost like recognition. "I'll text her now," he says. "I'll let her know to expect you."

"Thank you."

I turn to go, but he stops me with a quiet, "Annalise?"

I look back.

"If this has anything to do with what happened that night…" His eyes turn glossy through his wire-framed glasses.

"This isn't about blame. I promise."

"Then what is it about?"

I hesitate because there's no clean way to say it. No way to wrap the depth of it into one neat sentence. "I'm trying to save someone," I say, my voice teetering a whisper. "And I think she might be the person who can help me do it."

Something flickers in his eyes, but he doesn't press for more. "Good luck," he replies gently, pulling out his phone.

I step outside, the cold biting through my coat, adrenaline still spinning in my stomach. The sun's barely climbed above the trees, and it already feels like the most important day of my life.

I don't know what I'll say when I see her.

But I know who I'm doing it for.

And I know I'm not leaving without trying.

I try to make myself invisible as I slink back in the plush red booth, a freight train of old memories cannoning through me. I know he's here. Working in the kitchen, sweating over hot stoves, barking at the staff as they try to keep up with never-ending lunch orders.

Tapping a fork against the tabletop, I glance around the diner, hardly recognizing any of the waitresses. "It's The Same Old Song" by Four Tops jingles from the jukebox, one of my favorites. I'd play it every time I needed a pick-me-up, and Kenna would join me for a few silly dance moves, our laughter contagious as patrons watched and bopped along.

A half hour rolls by, and I order a coffee and a small plate of cottage cheese and peaches, barely touching my meal, too nervous, too buzzing, too terrified.

Swallowing, I shift my gaze to the double doors that lead into the kitchen.

I should probably say hello. If he spots me sitting out here for over an hour, coiled tight with nerves, he's going to think I'm here to see him. To talk. To heal old wounds.

That's the last thing I want.

Slowly, I rise from the booth. The fork clinks against the edge of the plate as I shuffle off the seat, shed my coat, and swipe my sweaty palms down my jeans.

This is just a quick hello—a courtesy, nothing more.

But when I round the counter and catch sight of the kitchen through the small square window carved into the swinging door, I stop cold.

There he is.

Alex.

Exactly as I remember him.

Red-faced. Jaw clenched. Shouting orders with that same

sharp tone that always made me wince and wilt. He slams a pan onto the stovetop hard enough to make the shelf above it rattle. One of the younger cooks flinches. Another avoids eye contact altogether, head ducked as he preps a plate in silence.

I wait, watching.

Just to see.

Just to make sure I'm not projecting the worst onto him. That maybe he's changed.

But no.

It's all still there—that volatile, bottled-up rage that never had anywhere to go except outward. The cursing. The scowl. The anger he wears like armor and spreads like wildfire.

And suddenly I'm twenty-one again, back in that stifling condo, holding my breath while he stormed around the kitchen, pissed at the world and everyone in it.

I back away from the door before he has a chance to look up. My legs move on instinct, carrying me back to my booth. The coffee's gone cold. The peaches look like they've melted into syrup. I leave a twenty-dollar bill on the table and disappear out the main entrance.

My hand circles my opposite wrist, massaging, rubbing away the memory of viselike grips and painful bruises.

I realize now that some people grow. Evolve. Shed their damage and learn how to be better, live kinder, and love softer.

Others stay exactly who they are.

And right now, I'm too focused on saving someone who *wants* to be saved than to waste a single second on someone who never did.

Twenty minutes later, I'm pacing outside the restaurant when a figure approaches on my left. I pivot around, catching sight of baby-blue hospital scrubs peeking through a billowing trench coat, and shiny black hair pulled up into a severe bun.

Two dark-brown eyes pan the entrance, doing a double take when they spot me gripping my cell phone so hard it might crack in my fist.

Parvati falters briefly, blinking with a trace of uncertainty. "Annalise," she says, stopping just short of the doorway. "My father said you wanted to see me."

Nerves tighten every muscle in my body. "I did. Thank you. I wasn't sure if you'd... I didn't know if you'd even come."

"Do you want to talk out here?"

"Yes. Please," I say quickly, glancing back at the glass doors. "Out here's better."

She tugs her coat tighter, but she doesn't complain. Her badge is still clipped to her waistband, and there's a faint shadow of exhaustion under her eyes from sick patients and long hospital hours. But she looks calm. In control.

I don't feel either of those things.

"I know this is strange," I begin, pocketing my phone. "And I don't want to take up too much of your time. I came here because..." I trail off, swallowing the raw truth behind what I'm about to say. "Because I didn't know where else to go."

Her inky brows pull together, but she stays silent, waiting for more.

"It's about Chase," I tell her.

Cautious recognition flashes in her eyes. "I see."

"He, um...he has a tumor." Emotion swells, and the words fall out cracked, shards of broken glass spilling from my lips.

"A low-grade glioma. It's centered near the optic chiasm. They said it's rare in adults, aggressive in the worst way. He's losing his vision fast. They've already ruled out surgery."

Parvati straightens. "I'm so sorry to hear that."

"The doctors told him it's wrapped around his optic nerve," I go on. "So tight, they can't even attempt removal without risking…well, everything. They said it's twisted in all the wiring near the chiasm. That one wrong move would kill him."

Her expression pinches with focus. Medical mode. "Yes," she says quietly. "That area's a minefield. A low-grade diagnosis doesn't mean it behaves gently, especially when the location is that unforgiving."

"I've been trying not to lose hope," I admit, voice strained. "But I also can't just sit back and do nothing. I love him. He's everything to me. So I came here, hoping, praying that you might be able to help him. That you can do something. Anything."

She sighs, her eyes never leaving mine. "Annalise, I don't have the kind of experience to take on something like that. I'm still early in my residency. Neuro is incredibly delicate, and that part of the brain is practically sacred ground."

"I understand," I whisper. "This was kind of a shot in the dark, and I just…I believe everything happens for a reason, you know? That it's all connected somehow. Even the bad, terrible things that feel unexplainable at the time." My breathing picks up with edging panic. "And that day at the gas station…it set everything in motion. Him and me, the band, you and your family. Now this. And maybe that sounds ridiculous to you, but I had to ask. I had to try."

For a second, Parvati doesn't speak. She studies me like I'm a textbook of overlapping systems, trying to trace the origin of whatever force brought me to her.

Then she says, carefully, "When it's that close to the chiasm, surgical margins become a nightmare. It's not just about removing the tumor—it's about preserving everything else it touches."

I nod, swallowing hard, my hope fading like a dwindling candle flame. "I know."

"But there are emerging techniques," she adds, her gaze turning contemplative. "Neuro-oncology consults. Combined protocols that use intraoperative MRI, mapping, even awake craniotomies to preserve function. It's high risk. But it's not impossible…" She trails off, drumming her fingers against her thigh. "The right hands can change outcomes. It's smart to get a second opinion."

The sting behind my eyes swells, biting and burning.

But hope flares, the candle dancing back to life.

"I can't promise anything," she continues. "But I do have mentors. People who specialize in these things. Skull base surgeons, neurosurgeons at major hospitals. They've seen things I haven't even studied yet. I could reach out. See if anyone is willing to look at his case."

My breath catches on a choked sob. "Really?"

Parvati watches me for a beat, then reaches into her coat pocket for a napkin and a pen. She presses the napkin to her knee and scribbles down her contact information. "Have him send me everything," she says. "Scans. Bloodwork. Doctor's notes. I'll get it in front of someone."

"Thank you," I whisper, the weight of it hitting me all at once. "Parvati, thank you so much."

The glimmer in her eyes is soft but real. "I should warn you, his vision loss will be permanent. That sort of thing is irreversible. I don't want you to cling to hope that one day he might—"

"I know. I get it." I fold the napkin carefully, like it's something precious. "This isn't about fixing what's already broken. It's about holding on to what's left."

Parvati nods once. "Good."

"Chase has already lost so much. But he's still him. Still here. And if there's any chance of keeping him that way, I have to take it." I glance down, running my thumb over her handwriting. "He made me realize that we don't have to fix everything. Sometimes just showing up when it's hard is the most defiant thing we can do. Loving someone when it's messy. That's what matters. That's what counts."

She pauses before reaching over and laying a steady hand on my arm. "Then we'll fight for what's left," she says, a watery smile blooming. "And I do believe things happen for a reason. My mother lost her hearing when I was nine. Sudden nerve trauma. One day she was fine, and the next…" Parvati blinks toward a tall tree like she can still envision it happening in high-definition. "We thought it would ruin her. She was a musician—violin, mostly."

I hold still, listening.

"She didn't get better," she continues. "No miracle. But she adapted. Learned to read vibrations through the floor. She started composing again using visual sound waves and retrained her hands for piano. Her world got smaller, but somehow fuller too." She looks back at me, and there's something fierce behind the glassiness in her eyes. "That's when I decided I wanted to go into medicine. Not to undo the damage, but to help people find a way forward inside it. That's what you're doing, Annalise. So I'll help you. I'll do what I can."

My whole body vibrates as I register her words and allow them to sink in, to reach the parts of me that have been clenched tight, braced for more loss.

Pressure burns the backs of my eyes as I look at her, not as the daughter of the man who pulled that trigger, but as a woman shaped by her own heartbreak, who chose not to be buried in it. "I don't know how to thank you," I manage.

Parvati smiles, squeezes my hand. "We don't always get to change the story," she says quietly. "But sometimes we can change the ending."

I look out across the parking lot, everything blurring.

For the first time in a long while, I feel like there's a thread I can follow. Something real to hold on to. Something that might actually lead us out of the dark.

And I promise myself, that whatever comes next, I'll carry this hope, and I'll carry Chase, the same way I've always carried music.

Heart first.

Close to my chest.

Even when no one else can hear it.

CHAPTER 62
Chase

The crunch of rubber against gravel pulls me from a moody guitar riff and sends my heart into overdrive.

Annie.

Pulse revving, I toss the instrument aside and launch to my feet, a cacophony of voices seeping in from the back deck as my friends scarf down burgers and beer, twilight turning the sky a blurry coppery hue. It's been days since I felt her cocooned against me, her heat and joy and love the only antidote to this constant state of disrepair.

Toaster follows me to the front of the house, leaping and prancing, his tail thumping my leg as I dart out the door. The silhouette of her black sedan comes vaguely into focus, squashing the remnants of my fear. Fear that she wouldn't come back. That she'd have a change of heart once she left this nightmarish bubble of inevitable tragedy and realized how free and burdenless she could be out on her own.

I hear a car door clap shut, followed by footsteps kicking up rocks and pebbles.

And then her voice, hoarse and sweet and beautiful.

"Chase!"

I zigzag down the walkway, nearly tripping over divots and weed patches. Her outline inches into my periphery, my favorite shape. Then the colors register. Her hair, her hot-pink sweater, even the flush on her cheeks.

The moment she's within reach, I grab her, folding her in my arms until she's off her feet, legs swinging up behind her. I whirl her around in a clumsy circle. She clings to me, face buried against my neck, hair tickling my jaw. Emotion squeezes my throat as relief balloons my heart.

"You're here," I murmur.

She nods frantically against my shoulder. "Of course I'm here."

When I set her back down, I keep her close, hands bracketing her hips, lips dusting over her mound of sweet-smelling hair. The scent of watermelon and flower gardens wafts around me, mingling with nature and crisp air and last night's rain.

"Are you okay?" she breathes, holding my face in two hands. "Let me look at you."

My eyelids flutter as the pads of her fingertips trail my jawline. "I'm okay."

"I'm sorry I was gone so long. I had to…" Her voice trembles as she skims a thumb over my bottom lip. "Chase, I met with someone. Parvati."

The name ripples through my chest with a pang of familiarity.

I go still, scanning through memory.

Parvati.

The gas station clerk's daughter?

"I-I told her everything," Annie continues, her voice gaining strength. "She remembered you, of course. I explained what was going on. The tumor, the prognosis, the vision loss…"

My jaw shifts, a frown bending.

"She's still in her residency, but she has connections. Mentors. Surgeons who've worked on tumors like yours. She said it's risky, but not impossible. Not entirely."

I don't realize I've taken a step back until I feel her hands drop from my face.

"Chase," she says carefully.

I shake my head, the fear creeping in before I can stop it. "Annie…"

"I know what that doctor told you. I know how final it sounded. But this wasn't the same conversation. This isn't just more bad news dressed up in different words."

"My parents searched for answers too. Something better. Something more hopeful. And every time it felt like they were handing me a rope and pulling me back up, but then it always ended in the same place. I just fell harder."

"No…no, listen to me, this isn't the same." She reaches for me again, linking our hands together. "I have a good feeling. This could work. This could—"

"I'm tired," I whisper brokenly. "Not of living. Just of hoping when it's already so dark I can barely see anything left."

"Then let me be the light." Her words crumble around the edges. "I'm not asking you to believe in some grand cure. I just need you to hang on. To try. To let *me* try. Even if it's only more time, it's still something. Whatever keeps you here longer. Whatever it takes. It's worth it, Chase. This life you've built—that *we've* built—it's so worth it."

A single tear slips down my cheek.

But for the first time in months, the terror doesn't feel so paralyzing.

It just feels…human.

Annie pulls back and shoves a hand inside her pocket until something is pressed to my chest.

A paper square. A napkin.

"It's not lyrics or haikus. But it's still music. Poetry. Words filled with hope." Her voice buckles with emotion. "And maybe that's what we've been doing all along. Writing songs out of broken things. Spinning sadness into meaning."

I stare down at the napkin, the handwriting skewed and blurred. Letters, numbers, maybe an email address. Maybe a map to something better.

More time, more moments.

I hold it in both hands like it might disintegrate if I blink wrong, just like I did with all her other napkin notes, wrinkled and inked with magic.

"She said to send the scans," Annie whispers. "All of them. She'll get them in front of someone who knows what to do."

My throat burns. My legs feel unsteady even though I haven't taken a step.

"Chase," she says gently, stepping closer, pulling my forehead down to hers. "Please let this be something. Let this be ours to fight."

I nod once. Then again, harder, faster, because if I speak, I'll lose it completely. "I'm terrified," I finally manage.

"So am I," she says. "But scared people still move forward. One step. That's all I'm asking."

I slide the napkin into my pocket and cup the back of her neck, tucking her against my chest. The smell of her shampoo, the warmth of her body, the steady beat of her heart…

It's everything that's still mine to hold.

She brushes a kiss to my lips. "Remember what I said to you that night at the café? About cards?"

I nod again, those early days flickering through my mind: Annie with spring flowers in her crown of braids, vanilla lattes, curious glances, and acoustics that sounded like a fresh start.

Fleeting moments. Fragile beginnings. Building blocks.

More tears spill down my cheeks. "Everyone has cards."

A choppy exhale escapes her, and it sounds like relief and love and exhaustion all wrapped in one breath. "Even the worst hands can still be played."

The thread between us pulls taut again—not as a rescue rope, but as a lifeline.

And not for climbing out. But for climbing through.

Toaster circles my ankles, paws at my legs.

Annie begs me with just a touch. A kiss. A silent plea.

Keep going. Keep fighting.

So I do the only thing I know how to do.

I reach for the strings and start writing the next verse.

"This world is full of conflicts and things that cannot be reconciled. But there are moments when we can reconcile and embrace the whole mess, and that's what I mean by 'Hallelujah.'"

—Leonard Cohen

CHAPTER 63
Chase

The ceiling is white.
 Too white.
Too quiet.
Except for the steady *beep-beep-beep* of the monitor beside me, measuring something I'm supposed to trust.

Hands move around me like shadow. Gloved, fast, impersonal. A nurse asks me to confirm my name, birthdate, what side the tumor's on. For the fifth time.

I answer on autopilot. My mouth is dry, my arms strapped loosely at my sides. An IV is taped into my hand, the blood pressure cuff tightening with a hiss.

The smell of antiseptic and latex curls under my nose.
This is real.
This is happening.

They said *no* before. Every doctor. Every chart. Too deep, too dangerous, too tangled.

But Annie found someone who said *maybe*.

And that was enough.

A heart monitor chirps louder as my breathing quickens.

The anesthesiologist leans in. Calm. Rehearsed. "You'll feel a little sting. Then nothing."

I nod, barely.

Because what the hell do you say when your brain is about to be poked and gouged?

One of the nurses adjusts a warm blanket over my legs.

A mask lowers over my face. "Oxygen," someone says. "Just relax."

I can't see faces. Everything's gone soft at the edges.

A hand brushes mine.

But it's not Annie. She's gone. Forced to stay behind.

Her voice was solemn, thick with emotion as she said her goodbyes in the pre-op holding area. "Come back to me, Chase. I'll be here when you wake up."

Tears. So many tears.

I froze.

I wanted to say something. That I'll come back. That we'll write more music together beneath the honey moon. That we'll kiss and dance and live.

That I'm going to marry her one day.

She'll wear my ring, and I'll sing her songs, and we'll build something that doesn't feel like an ending.

Now I'm floating somewhere between the warmth of Annie's goodbye and the cold fluorescent lights above me.

Plastic. Rubber. Oxygen.

My eyes sting. Maybe I'm crying. Maybe I'm dying.

I try to picture her.

Annie in her pink sweater, hair swinging in front of her face, hands cradled in mine.

But the lights blur. The voices fade. The borders of the room distort and shift as the beeping grows distant.

And then—

Water.

The splash of it. Chlorine thick in the air. Light refracted on the bottom of a pool. Bare feet on concrete.

My name echoing faintly through summer heat.

Stella?

I'm not in the hospital anymore.

I'm somewhere else. Somewhere I haven't dared to return to in years.

And she's here.

The water is warm. It laps at my ankles as I stand at the edge of the pool, sunlight flickering across the surface like broken stars. Somewhere, cicadas hum. A song plays.

Our favorite song.

The sun pulses, gentle and golden and strange.

"Chase."

Her voice floats toward me, familiar and distant, like it's being pulled through time.

I turn, and she's there.

My sister.

Older than I remember, not a girl anymore. Hair tucked

behind her ears, freckles faded, towel slung over one shoulder, and skin glowing like summer never ended.

I try to speak, but nothing comes out. Only air.

She kneels by the water, dipping her hand into it. Ripples bloom around her fingers. "I've missed you," she says softly.

My throat doesn't work right. My voice isn't mine. "I'm dreaming. You're not—"

"I know."

My feet are rooted to the concrete. If I step in, I'll shatter. I'll drown. "I tried to save you."

She doesn't respond right away, just trails her fingers through the water until gentle ripples reach toward me but never touch.

Tears burn behind my eyes. "I didn't get to you in time."

"No," she says. "But you tried. And I want you to try again. This time, for you."

I stare at her. She's wearing the teal swimsuit she cried about the summer Mom bought it too small.

Stella sits at the edge of the pool, knees pulled up, one arm hugging her legs.

I can't move. Can't speak.

"They didn't take it all," she says, not looking at me. "That wasn't the point."

I shake my head. "Take what?"

"The weight," she whispers, tapping her temple. "The ugly thing. The part wrapped too tightly around you."

She lifts her eyes to mine, and they're not sad.

They're steady. Kind.

I miss them so much. Those eyes.

The way she'd look at me like I was her greatest protector.

"We couldn't touch the center. It's still there. But we carved out space. Enough to stay. Enough to keep the music going."

I feel like I'm splitting open.

And then my vision blurs. Fogs. Slips away.

No.

I was only allowed a glimpse.

"My eyes… Stella, I can't—"

Her hand reaches out, brushes just beneath mine in the water. "It's okay," she says softly. "That part's gone. But you don't need eyes to see. Not really."

I squint hard, but I can't see her anymore. She's a mirage.

All I can make out is the water glowing around her as she stands, the pool casting reflections that dance across her skin like candlelight.

A warm hand presses over my eyes. "You won't get this back," she whispers. "But you'll get other things. Things that matter more. If you let yourself stay."

"What happens next?" I rasp, melting beneath her touch.

The shape of her head tilts like it used to when I'd ask her questions. "You'll find out. Bit by bit. There'll be scans. Time. Careful watching. But the story's not over, Chase."

She steps back, water dripping from her fingers, each drop catching a shimmer of that fading, dream-spun sun. It's all I can make out.

"Live loud," she says. "Louder than the loss. Louder than the fear. Loud enough for both of us."

The cicadas quiet.

The light bends. Dims.

"And when it hurts…" she finishes, voice fading into ash. "Sing anyway. Even if it's off-key. Even if all you've got left is the broken hallelujah."

I reach for her.

But the ripples swallow her first.

Stella slips into the light, into memory, into silence.

Gone.

All that remains is the echo.

Fractured. Holy.

And then…

I come to.

Noise returns. Monitors beep. Faces blur overhead.

A hand squeezes mine.

I blink into the light, catching pale skin and purple stripes.

A sob punches the air.

Warm tears hit my knuckles, and relief crashes over me like surf.

I swallow hard, choked and shaking.

I'm here. She's here.

It's not over.

And the only thing dancing through my mind is:

Halle-fucking-lujah.

CHAPTER 64
Chase

SIX MONTHS LATER

"You're on in fifteen!"

Carter's voice slices through the noise of The Soundproof like a bolt cutter. He paces around, headset probably crooked as he wrangles cables or people or both. I can't see him clearly, just a smear of motion and energy in the corner of my periphery.

But I feel everything else.

The buzz of amps in standby. The soft thud of boots crossing the room. The vibration of laughter. Zach cracks his knuckles as Kenna argues with someone over whether glitter is allowed onstage.

Either way, she's using it.

Annie hums a melody under her breath, half distracted as she braids her hair or rewires her in-ear pack. I can't tell anymore unless I ask.

And I don't always ask.

Because sometimes not knowing keeps me from mourning the fact that I can't see it.

I'm seated on the edge of the couch in the green room, fingers working across the frets of my guitar out of habit, not thought. Muscle memory keeps me grounded. The strap's a little frayed at the end, soft from years of sweat and calluses, and my thumb rubs the edge like it's braille.

Something I can still read.

"Chase," Annie says quietly, close now. Her hand finds my shoulder and squeezes gently. "Come on. Everyone is here to see you."

She leans in a little, and I catch the faint trace of peppermint on her breath. No more smoke, no sharp spice of nicotine clinging to her skin. She gave it up months ago. Said she finally wanted to breathe easier again.

I rise with her, slow and steady.

We step into the corridor, and the sound deepens—low conversation, echoing heels, the shifting of bodies.

I don't see faces.

But I feel their presence.

We wind through the hallway and out into the edge of the crowd where friends, family, and fans mingle.

Someone says "miracle."

Someone else says "inspiring."

Someone claps me on the back while another calls my name. It's a blur of voices, warmth, and scent.

I feel Annie beside me, a breath away, guiding me without pushing, always a heartbeat ahead. "Your parents are over there," she says near my ear. "Even Parvati and her father showed up."

I pause, heart tightening as their names sink in. The crowd fades for a second, voices dulling, space stretching wide like the venue itself is holding its breath.

I didn't expect them to come.

"Chase." Parvati's voice is steady, and there's a softness in it tonight. Something less clinical, more earned.

Annie touches my elbow, angling me toward her.

I extend a hand. She takes it.

"I couldn't miss this," Parvati says. "Look at you. Back on your feet, looking like a genuine rock star."

A half smile quirks as I recall Annie smothering my hair in gel and muttering something about "controlled chaos" while pinning back a rogue curl. She straightened my collar multiple times and dressed me up in three different leather jackets, debating which one offered equal parts comfort and aesthetic.

Not because she didn't trust me to do it, but because touching me calmed her down.

Helping is her love language.

"I was going for half-feral prom king," Annie chirps, linking her arm through mine. "I think I nailed it."

"Certainly." Parvati chuckles, squeezes my hand with both of hers. "I'm proud of you. You're quite the success story."

I nod through the ache in my throat. "Thank you. For everything."

My mind reverses back in time, recalling those foggy days post-surgery.

They didn't take it all. That was never on the table.

Parvati explained it slowly, almost afraid the words might break something in me if they landed too fast.

First came the targeted radiation, fractionated over weeks, to shrink the tumor and relieve the pressure before they ever dared go in. Then came the surgery. Endoscopic, trans nasal, through the skull base.

They mapped every inch with real-time neural monitoring, lighting up my brain like a constellation, because even a fraction off course meant more than losing what little vision I had left.

It meant losing everything.

They called it a debulking. Took what they could from around the chiasm without disturbing the structures that kept me breathing, speaking, remembering who I was. Left the rest in place like a landmine defused but not removed.

She said it was delicate, but they got what they needed. The pressure's gone, the swelling's down, and the tumor hasn't grown.

For now, I'm safe.

I don't know what that's supposed to feel like yet. I'll need regular MRIs for the rest of my life, every six months. Maybe sooner if something shifts. We're not out of the woods.

We're just not running out of time.

And somehow, against every warning, every impossible scan, every too-careful voice telling me not to hope, I get to keep the story.

The music still plays.

"No need to thank me," Parvati replies, voice kind. "You're my success story too. I'll always be able to say I had a hand in saving *the* Chase Rhodes. The man who created the guitar that lights up like it belongs in a sci-fi movie."

I breathe out a laugh, ducking my head.

"My mother saw your guitar line at a music therapy convention," she adds, voice pitching with amusement. "The one that looks like it makes lightning. She took pictures and said, 'Isn't that the man you helped save?' I didn't even have to look. I just said, 'Yeah. That's him.'"

My smile pulls wider, the lump thickening in my throat. "It was just supposed to be a gimmick. Something to catch the eye while we were playing empty bars."

"Well, it caught more than that," she muses.

She's right; it's everywhere now. Our sound might've catapulted us forward, but that design—that glowing Frankenstein of wood and wire—that's what turned heads first.

They put my name on the line when it went national. Rhodes Series. Custom run. Full production. I still get emails from teenagers learning their first chord on something I dreamed up on a folding table with duct tape, a drill, and a defiant dream.

"I never imagined it would outlive my vision," I admit, wincing slightly.

"But it didn't outlive you. That's what's important." She makes a humming sound. "You lit up the world, Chase. Even before it went dark."

She lets go of my hand.

Then another voice cuts in. Masculine, gruff, familiar. "Just promise me if they make a glow-in-the-dark surgical scalpel, you'll name it after my daughter."

A warm hand takes mine, grip strong and solid. "Mr. Singh," I murmur. "Thank you for being here. Means a lot."

"You've done a lot for us. For our store, our family. We will let bygones be bygones."

I shake his hand, holding for several beats, not saying anything. I wonder what he sees when he looks at me now: a mistake, a thief, a stain on his memory.

But I don't press. Don't ask for more. Because something tells me he sees everything I'm feeling.

Forgiveness. Humanity. Grace.

At the end of the day, we're all just broken strings, still part of the same song.

We say our goodbyes, and their footsteps are swallowed by the hum of the crowd. The moment lingers, unfinished in the best way.

Not a beat later, two arms wrap around me, and I'm pulled into the scent of something familiar and old as memory. Lavender, dryer sheets, and whatever intangible thing turns a house into a home.

"Oh, honey. You look amazing." My mother's voice cracks as she squeezes me tighter than I expect, like she's been holding this in for six months.

Or maybe since Stella.

I hug her back, pressing my face against her shoulder, letting the moment seep. Her breath is shaky, full of something too big for words.

"You doing okay?" I manage.

She nods against me. "I am now."

Dad steps in beside us, clearing his throat. He doesn't do hugs, not usually, but today he rests a hand on the back of my neck and keeps it there. A solid, anchoring touch.

His thumb brushes the edge of my collar as he leans in close. "She'd be proud of you, son."

I swallow hard, blinking back the sting. "Yeah. I think she would be."

"She'll be watching you tonight." Mom releases me with a final squeeze, stepping back to dab her eyes, just a whir of motion. "Sing a song for her."

"They're all for her," I say, distorted images flashing through my mind of sun-dappled water, ripples, and teal. "Every single one."

Annie makes small talk for a minute before taking me by the hand. "Five minutes," she whispers.

I nod, saying goodbye to my parents. The crowd is starting to swell, and the din of it builds, bone-deep. Electric.

We retreat into the wings.

I hear Kenna pull Tag into a hug. Rock whoops at the top of his lungs. Zach smacks me on the shoulder while Carter calls out something into his headset, and Crowley offers a staticky reply. Annie helps me shoulder my guitar, her fingers skimming down my arm, tethering me.

"You okay?" she asks softly.

My throat tightens. "We'll find out."

She doesn't flinch. Just cups my face between both hands and leans in until her forehead touches mine. "But you're ready," she whispers.

"Yeah. I'm ready."

I'm ready.

Even with the darkness still lingering around the edges.

Even with the music feeling different now. Less clean, more raw.

I grip my guitar, find the pick where I always keep it, and roll it between my fingers like a coin I can't afford to lose. The keychain Annie gifted me is clipped to my belt loop, and I give it a squeeze before heading onto the stage, the band following, vibrating with newfound energy.

Then the house lights dim.

The crowd erupts.

Crowley nudges my shoulder and murmurs, "You're on, my friend."

Annie presses her lips to my cheek, then reaches up, fixes the fall of my hair. "Let's go burn it down," she says.

I do.

Not because I can see the path in front of me.

But because I know the sound of coming home.

We finish the set with a final song. A cover.

A juiced-up, fast-paced version of "I Only Want To Be With You."

The crowd is losing it. I can feel the stomp of boots through the stage floor, the growl of roars in my ribs. My fingers blur across the strings, and the neck of the guitar hums in my grip like it's alive, answering every heartbeat with its own.

By now I've memorized the space. The distance between me and the mic stand. The tilt of the wedge monitor by my feet. I can see the lights flashing overhead, feel the warmth of them on my face, sweat tracking down the back of my neck.

Tag howls something to my left, pure chaos and joy, his guitar squealing under a final distorted riff. I feel the thud of his boots through my soles.

I grin.

Show-off.

He shoulder-checks me on the way to the front of the stage, light and deliberate, a gesture that we made it. That we're still us. I chuckle under my breath and toss a quick chord back his way like a musical middle finger.

Then Annie's voice cuts through.

She's not just singing the lyrics. She's throwing them. Hurling them into the crowd like a lifeline wrapped in fire. When I join her on the last chorus, our voices braid together, worn and fierce and ours. The way they always were. The way they were always meant to be.

As the final note rings out and the crowd erupts, I take a step back, steadying myself in the feel of the stage under my feet.

Crowley kills the house lights behind us. The temperature drops, the air thick with adrenaline and the echo of a thousand lives pressed into one room.

I find Annie's hand before she finds mine.

She's shaking, laughing. Her fingers intertwine with mine, and then she's there, bowing beside me, a vision of neon-orange and purple-streaked hair.

Tag's final chord fades into smoke and heartbeat and noise, and for a moment, I just stand there, soaking it all in.

The crowd's still screaming, still riding the high of the set, and I should be walking offstage, grabbing water, maybe an oxygen tank. But I don't move.

Instead, I reach for the mic again.

"Thank you, New York," I croon, breathless, voice rough with nerves and a telltale high. "Before we go, there's one more thing I need to say."

The crowd begins to hush, a slow ripple of curiosity cutting through the cheers.

I feel Annie shift beside me, her hand still in mine. She squeezes, just once, probably thinking I'm going to thank the fans. Give a heartfelt speech.

She doesn't know I'm about to tip her world sideways.

I take a breath. "This next part wasn't on the setlist."

A small tide of laughter rolls across the front rows. I turn slightly toward Annie, angling my body just enough to feel her there. I can't see her face clearly, but I know her. Inside and out.

I know the slope of her head, the wrinkle of her nose, the tremble in her breath when she's caught off guard.

"Annalise," I say into the mic, swallowing hard. "Annie."

She laughs softly under her breath, nervous and warm. "Chase…"

"I used to picture this." I inch toward her, trying to smile around the thunder in my chest. "Not the stage, not the crowd, not the lights. Just you. Always you."

My heart pounds as my skin sweats.

The crowd starts to murmur.

"We've played midnight sets in bars that smelled like spilled whiskey and magic. We've snuck around hotels like teenagers, hiding something everyone already knew. We've cried in parking lots, collapsed backstage from the weight of it all, and spent days in a rundown van that smelled like cheese fries."

Laughter flickers from the audience.

Annie chokes back a joyful whimper.

"We've survived international tours, secrets, pain, and a diagnosis that nearly took everything from me. But we've held on anyway. And we're still making music. Still choosing each other."

I release her hand just long enough to reach into the inner pocket of my jacket. My fingers close around the ring box I've carried for weeks, waiting for this.

I drop to one knee.

Annie gasps.

"I've been a lot of things in this life," I say, voice raw. "Broken. Bleeding. Lonely, lost, healing, determined, and scared out of my damn mind. But I've never been sure of anything the way I'm sure of this. Of you. Of us."

I lift the box and open it.

The ring gleams—delicate, silver, and shaped like a crescent moon wrapping gently around a tiny cluster of diamonds, stardust caught mid-fall.

It feels like her.

"Annalise Adams," I say, tasting her name like it's the only thing that matters. "I fell halfway in love with you beneath a honey moon, and the other half came just as easy."

A tiny sob breaks free.

She doesn't move. Hardly breathes. But I feel every bit of her, anchored in the moment.

"I've spent years trying to make sense of this life. And somehow, you were always the quiet answer waiting in all of it. I don't need perfect, Annie. I just need you. The girl who held my hand through the dark and sang me back to life." I hold up the ring, my pulse tearing through me. "Will you marry me?"

For a second, she doesn't say anything. Just stares at me through tears I can't see but feel pouring from her like light.

Then she laughs, wrecked and radiant.

She sinks to her knees in front of me, grabbing my face in both hands and kissing me hard, fast, full of every lyric we never wrote down.

When she finally pulls back, her voice breaks on one word. "Maybe."

I hear the smile in her voice, feel the love wrapped around all her perfect pieces, and I swear her eyes are twinkling with every star, every moon.

Grinning wide, I pull her closer.

Dip her.

And cover her mouth with mine.

"Sounds like a yes."

EPILOGUE
Annalise

FOUR SEASONS, A SECOND CHANCE, AND NO MORE RUNNING

🍂 FALL

The shows feel different now. Louder in the right ways. Softer in the ones that matter.

A label picked us up. We're back on tour.

Not a hundred cities in a hundred days, not chasing numbers or fame, but choosing our stops like we choose each other. With purpose. With breath.

Rock starts journaling.

Kenna's suspicious. I'm proud. Zach is just shocked he found a pen.

We opened our fall leg in Asheville. The crowd knew every word to our new single. Chase couldn't see them, but he could hear the love. He stood next to me onstage and said afterward, "That was the clearest I've ever seen."

I wrote that down. I don't want to forget it.

❄ WINTER

Chase had another scan in December. Stable. Two syllables that meant everything.

We celebrated with grilled cheese and champagne. Not fancy. Just us.

He's still healing. Still adjusting. There are days he disappears into his music and days he just disappears, needing quiet, needing less. I don't take it personally. I get it. And when he reappears, he's softer. Calmer. Like whatever storm he went into left him lighter somehow, even if it still rains now and then.

We don't talk about fear the way we used to. Not as a monster in the corner, but as something we've learned to live beside. Something that reminds us to hold each other tighter.

Some days, we make music.

Some days, we make space.

Both feel like love.

Tag started a nonprofit in January. A support fund for survivors of opioid overdoses and their families. He doesn't talk about what happened to him. Not directly. But I see it in the way he shows up for the ones who haven't figured out how to stand back up yet.

He named it "Second Verse."

I cried when he told me. He pretended not to notice.

🌼 SPRING

Kenna accidentally proposed to Tag.

We were packing up after a show, and she was ranting about his socks ending up in her makeup bag. Then, out of nowhere: "Maybe we should just get married if you're gonna keep living in my damn suitcase."

Silence.

Panic.

Then she bolted.

Tag didn't follow her right away. He just looked down at the place she'd been standing, grinned, and said, "Guess I need a ring now."

Three days later, he pulled her out onto an empty venue balcony after soundcheck, dropped to one knee with a ring he definitely didn't buy in a hurry, and asked her for real.

She said yes.

They've been fighting over who proposed first ever since.

Mom and Dad visited last week. They're lighter than I remember them. Less worried about all the wrong things. Mom cried when she saw Chase's guitar line in the store near our venue. Dad asked for a T-shirt with the band name in glitter. Kenna was so proud.

Chase paid me a compliment that made me blush, and Dad

said, "He's got limited vision, and he still sees you better than the last one ever did."

I've never believed in spring more than I do right now.

❀ SUMMER

I walked barefoot down an aisle made of wildflowers while my band members played something that sounded like moonlight. Tag stood beside Chase, unusually quiet, his jaw clenched like he was holding back every feeling he didn't know how to say. Kenna reached over and slipped her hand into his.

The sun came out just as I said "I do."

Chase smiled wide.

"I love your smile," I whispered.

He pulled me close and whispered back, "You smile, I smile. It's as simple as that."

There was no spotlight. No stage. Just our people. Our sound. Our love, stripped down and honest and real. The kind of music you don't need to rehearse. The kind you feel in your bones.

Later, when the cake was half eaten and my dress was grass-stained at the hem, Chase picked up an old acoustic and played something slow. Something just for me. I sat and watched him in the flicker of the lanterns, and for a moment, I saw what the world sees when they call him the man who strums stars.

Just before we packed up for the night, I spotted an earthworm on the edge of the path, glistening from the brief evening rainfall.

Five hearts.
Still surviving. Still moving forward.
Summer ends on the perfect high note.

It's a full moon tonight.

A floating ball of honey.

We lie in the grass behind the white Cape Cod—our brand-new house in the heart of Rutland—with Toaster sprawled between us like a little furnace in a fur coat. Chase has one hand laced in mine, the other resting on his chest, fingers tapping out a rhythm he hasn't written yet. He hums under his breath, trying to lure the melody closer.

Half Motown, half stardust. All him.

The deck behind us is partially finished, splintered wood stacked like building blocks for a life still unfolding. But the view is already perfect. Wide and soundless in a way we didn't know we needed. He said he wanted a place to hear the sky while he worked. Said the silence here sounds like possibility. So different from the roar of stages and city lights.

There's a candle burning back inside the kitchen window. The same one I lit months ago, whispering something into the wax that sounded like *thank you*.

I used to dream about escaping, about a vacation somewhere warm and far away, where nothing hurt and everything stood still.

I don't need that anymore.

Not when I have this.

I turn my head toward Chase, fingering his silver ring dangling around my neck. "What do you see?"

His eyes are aimed at the sky. He's quiet; he's always quiet when it matters. Then he smiles, slow and certain, the way he does when he's not just answering, but telling the truth.

"Pieces," he says.

It's the same answer he gave me back in that cabin when everything felt like it was falling apart. Back when the world cracked open and asked if we still wanted to stay.

But this time, it doesn't sound broken.

Because I know exactly what he means.

Pieces of a fractured sky.

Pieces of a beautiful life.

Pieces of the night still holding us together.

THE END

Playlist

"I Only Want to Be With You"—Lauren O'Connell
"Loneliness"—Bear's Den
"Dead Eye"—Middle Class Rut
"It's The Same Old Song"—Four Tops
"Metropolis"—Wintersleep
"While My Guitar Gently Weeps"—The Beatles
"The Killing Moon"—Lauren O'Connell
"Two Coins"—City and Colour
"Looking Too Closely"—Fink
"Fade Into You"—Mazzy Star
"She Says"—Howie Day
"Always Two"—The Silent Comedy
"exile"—Taylor Swift, Bon Iver
"Don't Let Go"—Deepfield
"Black Magic"—The Amazons
"Bare"—WILDES
"Trace of You"—Peter Bradley Adams
"I Believe in a Thing Called Love"—The Darkness
"Over My Head (Cable Car)"—The Fray

PIECES OF THE NIGHT

"If You Could Only See"—Tonic
"Zzyzx Rd."—Stone Sour
"Whatever I Fear"—Toad The Wet Sprocket
"Nutshell"—Alice In Chains
"Black Cloud"—POSTDATA
"Will You Love Me Tomorrow"—Lauren Spencer Smith
"Indigo"—Sam Barber, Avery Anna
"Imperfect"—Stone Sour
"Comin' Home"—City and Colour
"Unsteady"—X Ambassadors
"Pieces"—Andrew Belle
"Hallelujah"—Jeff Buckley

WANT MORE JENNIFER HARTMANN?

**READ ON FOR A SNEAK PEEK
AT *OLDER*,
A FORBIDDEN AGE-GAP ROMANCE.**

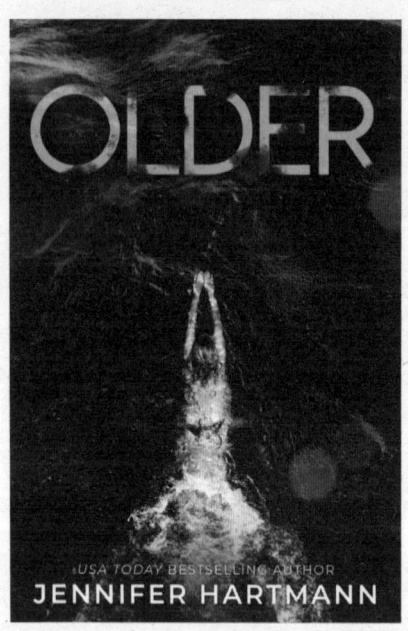

Prologue
HALLEY

I GRIPPED THE EDGE OF THE MOTTLED MATTRESS AS A LEATHER BELT WHIPPED across my bare back.

My punishment was ten lashes and an early bedtime with no supper.

My crime?

Love.

I loved more than I should have. I loved all things, big and small. Today I'd loved a biscuit-colored bunny with an injured leg that had scampered across our driveway. I had loved it enough to carry it into our one-car garage and tend to the wound with a purple Band-Aid I'd snuck from the hall closet while Mom was sound asleep with an empty bottle of gin clutched to her chest.

Father had come home from work thirty minutes early and caught me wallowing in that love, holding the trembling bunny in my arms and humming my favorite song to calm its quivering. Blood had oozed all over the garage floor, the same shade of red as his angry face when he'd discovered the mess.

"In the house. Right now." Violet veins had popped in his neck, meaty fists clenching at his sides. "Meet me in the den."

I'd obeyed.

And now my body jerked with each flog.

Father made me count out loud as the ruddy-brown belt slashed down on me and painted fiery lines across my skin. Tears burned behind my eyes, but I refused to let them fall. He hated emotion. Hated weakness. Crying only made him more furious.

Mom slept through the whole thing.

Not that it mattered—she wouldn't have stopped it anyway. My mother turned her back on me whenever my back was beaten to every shade of blue.

Maybe it was out of fear. Maybe it was out of unlove.

Father didn't love me; Mom didn't love me enough.

I guess that was why I loved too much. I had a lot of loveless holes to fill.

When the punishment was complete, I lowered my dirt-stained T-shirt and tipped my chin as Father relaced his belt through the belt holes of his worn jeans. "I'm sorry, Father. I'll go clean up the mess now." My feet itched to rush past him toward the garage, but I waited for permission.

Father eyed me, his icy gaze sliding down my bony frame as I folded in my lips to keep them from quivering. "You'll go straight to bed, that's what you'll do."

"But it's only four o'clock. It's too bright and sunny to fall asleep, and—"

"You want to lose supper tomorrow, too?" He thwacked me upside the head with a flat palm. "Do as you're told, you smart-mouthed brat."

"Yes, Father." I slunk past him with defeat as my cotton shirt scratched at the nasty welts blooming on my spine.

"You know what? Think I changed my mind," Father said before I slipped out of the den. "I'll bring a hot plate of supper to your door."

My stomach grumbled with anticipation.

Was he lying?

Father was never kind to me.

Maybe he saw how upset I was. How petrified and sad. There had to be a spark of humanity buried inside his jet-black heart.

Pivoting around, I felt a flicker of hope jump between my ribs as I stared at him with wide eyes. Father smirked and latched the belt buckle into place. "I'll leave a nice helping of rabbit outside your room in a few hours. My treat."

It took a minute for his words to sink in.

And when they did, they sunk me.

My bottom lip wobbled as dread pitched in my stomach, overriding the hunger pains. All I wanted to do was throw up. "I'm not hungry."

"You'll eat what I give you and you'll be grateful. Now go to your room."

I spun on my heel with lightning speed, just so he didn't see the waterfall of tears erupt as I choked back a sob.

But he stopped me one more time.

"Oh, and Halley? Don't you go sneaking into the garage to save that pesty rodent. You'll fail. And you'll suffer the consequences for disobeying me."

The back of my neck pricked with icicles. "Yes, Father," I choked out.

"Wouldn't matter, anyway. You've never been good at doing hard things."

He was right, I decided, as I holed up in my bedroom that afternoon and slid beneath the starchy covers, tucking myself into a ball as my body shivered in the aftermath of my beating.

I was a late walker, a late talker, a late learner in so many chapters of my life.

I was never able to earn my father's affection, no matter how desperate I was, how needy and fraught.

I couldn't put my fractured family back together.

I couldn't even save that little bunny.

Father was right…

I wasn't good at doing hard things.

Acknowledgments

To my husband, Jake: Thank you for dreaming up a plasma ball guitar when you were a teenager and for letting me borrow that vision for this book. You're so much cooler than me. Thank you for humoring my "does this sound like a real band?" questions and for making sure my fictional musicians don't embarrass themselves.

And thank you, above all, for being my muse and my music.

From the day we first met at a local metal-band show, to today—when we get caught dancing in the kitchen to songs that mortify our children—our love story will forever be my favorite setlist. Loud, unforgettable, and always on repeat.

Huge thanks to Chelley St Clair for tackling the massive development edits with me, for keeping my spirits high with laughter and GIFs, and for reminding me that the extra effort is always worth it in the end. I can't imagine this journey without you.

Thank you to my amazing team, always working behind the scenes to make my words shine a little brighter. And to my incredible readers—thank you for giving my stories a home, for sharing them with friends, and for keeping the inspiration flowing.

You are the encore I never stop chasing.

About the Author

Jennifer Hartmann resides in northern Illinois with her own personal romance hero and three children. When she is not writing angsty love stories, she is likely pondering all the ways she can break your heart and piece it back together again. She enjoys sunsets (because mornings are hard), bike riding, traveling, bingeing *Buffy the Vampire Slayer* reruns, and that time of day when coffee gets replaced by wine. She loves tacos. She also really, really wants to pet your dog. XOXO.

Website: jenniferhartmannauthor.com
Instagram: @author.jenniferhartmann
Facebook: @jenhartmannauthor
Reader Group: facebook.com/groups/145154332790534
Twitter: @authorjhartmann
TikTok: @jenniferhartmannauthor